HELL'S

DOCTOR

LEE F. JORDAN

Black Rose Writing | Texas

ISBN: 978-1-61296-018-0
PUBLISHED BY BLACK ROSE WRITING
www.blackrosewriting.com

Printed in the United States of America
Suggested Retail Price (SRP) $20.95

Hell's Doctor is printed in Chapparal Pro

*As a planet-friendly publisher, Black Rose Writing does its best to eliminate unnecessary waste to reduce paper usage and energy costs, while never compromising the reading experience. As a result, the final word count vs. page count may not meet common expectations.

Many people were involved in the development of this novel, which I sincerely appreciate. Cat S. Ginn skillfully and magically brought the artwork to life. Landon J.P. Ginn was the creative force behind the cover design, development, and spine artwork. And Mark Primeau added valuable ideas and criticism that always brought me back to Earth. I would also like to thank my family for their continued support of my writing.

I could not exist without them.

Hell's Doctor

"There are only three kinds of pain: physical, such as cutting through the bone marrow of a prisoner's leg with a dull hacksaw; emotional, such as torturing a prisoner's family slowly; or psychological, which destroys the hope of the mind."

- Hell's Doctor edict

PROLOGUE

Sixty seconds.

That was how long David Masters figured he had to live. The doctor in attendance, the one who quickly located the vein in his left arm and then stabbed the IV inside, started the process over a minute ago. Judging from how long these things usually took, David figured sixty seconds might be on the hopeful side.

His arms, legs, and torso were strapped down by leather to a gurney. He was lying on his back in the death chamber, awaiting the state's sentence to be carried out. The sentence that he earned. The doctor was only doing his job.

He let his eyes move to his immediate right so he could see the viewing window. The withdrawn curtains revealed twelve sets of eyes staring with malice and contempt at him. He knew selected family members of his victims wanted to watch. Some others were probably journalists looking for a headline. The only thing he knew for certain was that no one from his family was out there. He had forbidden that.

He wanted to die alone.

Fifty seconds.

Fear set in, and David trembled. The hard trembling that encased his entire body in fear so much that he couldn't physically control the emotions sweeping through his veins. Couldn't stop his nerves from jerking and moving of their own accord. His stomach jumped like it was on a trampoline in a schoolyard, and his toes curled downward as if they had a mind of their own. He could feel them curl ever farther around themselves until he was sure they were digging into the soles of his feet. His leg muscles tensed and his jawbone locked itself down.

He twisted and pulled a little against the leather holding him down. He wanted to be brave. He wanted to take it like a man. But David Masters knew he was a coward. He had always been a coward, and even his body knew it.

Forty seconds.

Muscle paralysis was supposed to kick in, he knew that at least. He'd read the pamphlet the state provided prior to his execution date. The one that stressed the *humanity* of the whole procedure. Three steps. Three steps and he'd be dead. Simple, clinical steps. Like placing his foot on the brakes, starting the car, and putting it into gear. And away he went. He didn't have to do anything but provide the vessel. And the vein, of course.

Sodium thiopental was the appetizer that caused him to lose consciousness. Pancuronium would be the light snack and cause muscles paralysis. And then potassium chloride was the ten pound steak and lobster main course. The one that stopped his heart and caused cardiac arrest.

But maybe the muscle paralysis drug wasn't working. Maybe the damn doctor, who the state appointed for this kind of chicken-shit execution and who probably got a big, fat bonus if he could make him suffer a little more, screwed up the cocktail. Gave him a little less than was required and his muscles could still move. Were still alive with their own protest of his impending death.

David convulsed internally. He let out a loud sob against the humanity of it all. He was scared shitless of dying. As he laid there, he decided he would no longer go quietly. Fuck the state. Fuck this doctor. And most importantly, fuck this execution thing. He was too young to die. Regardless of what the state said.

Thirty seconds.

"Why are his eyes still open?" whispered a perplexed warden.

David let out a loud, long scream and struggled mightily against the binds that held him down. He whipped his head up and cursed at the viewers behind the drawn-back curtain and glass window. The viewers reacted like gut-shot prey as their eyes widened and several of them recoiled. The rest edged closer to the window. Moving in for the kill. They wanted to see him suffer.

"What's wrong? What the hell is going on? Christ fix him! Shut him up for Christ's sake!" The warden screamed at the physician giving David the drugs. "Make him stop!" He could already hear the six o'clock news reporting this fuck-up. It might cost him his job. Not to mention the fact he was about to make a run at the state senate. It was all going into the toilet because this guy wasn't dying quietly. Hadn't read the pamphlet, obviously. "Close those curtains. Now!" He pointed to a guard who was frantically trying to do just that.

"How the hell should I know? He shouldn't be moving. Hell, he shouldn't even be awake," the doctor answered. Sweat beaded up on his brow. This was supposed to be an easy five grand. A down payment on a Porsche. Nothing more.

David collapsed against the gurney as the potassium chloride kicked in and his heart fluttered. His eyes closed and the warm sensation coursing through his veins spread quickly to his outer limbs and across his body like an ocean wave cresting just prior to the shoreline. It was almost a floating feeling, like he'd become weightless at some point. His body no longer had a heavy, gravity-induced feeling as his heart stopped beating. The pain wasn't so bad after all.

Twenty seconds.

The warmth turned cold, and David had the strangest sensation. It wasn't even that he could actually *feel* it; but he knew something happened that was causing his last seconds to be uncomfortable. The fleeting image of a train speeding towards a tunnel filled his conscious. He could see the gap in the mountain ahead and the train was moving toward it with unbridled aggression. The train trembled and shook as it sped onward. The gurney felt every turn and shake on the tracks, like an earthquake was moving up the metal legs.

Something was terribly wrong.

He shouldn't be aware. He shouldn't have any feeling or sensation, but yet he did. He should've been dead and not able to imagine anything. How could he think at all? How could he know any of this? Or none of this?

What the fuck was going on here?

Ten seconds.

With a violent jerk, David felt the gurney give way to an explosion from underneath him. He tried to struggle awake to whatever state of consciousness he could muster. Without moving his head, David could see the floor beneath him had lit up and multi-colored laser beams were being thrown around like it was Mardi Gras.

The floor was no longer the sterile black and white tile of the death chamber but was instead a bed of sand and the sand was moving. It was twisting and turning simutaneously, and little wisps appeared to make small tornados that would lose their shape as soon as they formed. The sand seemed to be *alive*.

The violence of the first explosion stopped, and the gurney started sinking. The sand was rushing faster and faster into the center of itself like a whirlpool. David didn't know how he knew he was going into the sand, but he knew it as surely as he knew he wasn't dead.

As he watched from above and descended into the sand from below, an opening appeared on the right side of the sand bed. A small hole, about the size of a coffee cup, opened inside the swirling, pulling sand, and an arm popped out. And then directly underneath the arm, an eye opened and stared at him without blinking.

He stared in terror as another hole on the other side of the sand bed opened and another arm began lifting towards him. Then a corresponding eye opened under that one. Openings were popping out of the sand in several places and David watched in horror as more and more arms came out of the holes and each one brought its own staring eye with no color. Looking at him and holding his gaze.

The arms had spikes for fingers and sensationally long, painted black nails at the end of each one. He felt the arms positioning themselves and the spikes digging into and around his body as they engulfed his chest and legs in an enormous bear hug. The vise-like grip exerted a pressure on his chest that caused him to hear several of his rib bones break smartly in two. A hundred little puncture holes squirted blood across his chest from the finger spikes.

The arms pulled downward with abandon and David felt the sand swirl and close in and around, first the back of his head and then on and around him as he was completely enveloped. The sand entered his eyes, ears, nose, and mouth.

He saw all the eyes blink rapidly.

One second.

And when David Masters left this earth, he screamed.

CHAPTER ONE

When Mack Teacher looked up from his desk, it immediately reminded him of two things. First, he had an appointment with someone named "Randy"; and second, if the girl that walked through his front door was "Randy", her parents hadn't been very imaginative.

"Hello," was all she said as she took her hat off, sat down in the chair in front of his desk, and crossed her legs. Her hat was a black and tan leather beret that partially covered her face and eyes from Mack as she walked through the door, but now she took it off and he could get a good look at her.

"Hello," Mack replied as he automatically sized her up. She was small, maybe five feet and one or two inches tall. Young, by his standards. Maybe late twenties. Brown, layered hair parted on the sides that she flipped over constantly to see him with both blue eyes instead of just one; high cheekbones and an angular face that rounded off at the chin; slim build with narrow hips; and medium-sized breasts with a tight fitting shirt that was almost see through. She wasn't trying to hide some of her assets from prying eyes, but she seemed to let the world know they were there. He was going to have to try hard to keep his eyes from drifting downward as she talked. This was business, not pleasure.

He stood up and offered his hand to her. She pulled her legs up under her like a cat curling up on a sofa. Looking at the proffered hand, and then back up to meet his eyes, she reached out and took hold of it. Her grip was light and her wrists were lacking strength, Mack noticed.

"My name is Randi," she told him when he sat back down.

Mack leaned back in his chair and closed the desk drawer he had opened. "I'm Mack Teacher. They call me Teacher."

She nodded like it was a simple fact that everyone knew. "I know."

"Do you have a last name? Or is there a reason you don't want me to know it?" Mack didn't like to assume anything about his clients. It was a dangerous habit to get into. Especially here.

"Owen," was all she said.

He wasn't any good at small talk. The kinds of things that came naturally to other men never came easily to Mack. He couldn't even walk into a bar and sit down next to a good looking woman and strike up a conversation. If it hadn't been for Melody approaching him in the library in college, he probably would have remained unmarried for his entire life.

"Did your parents want a male child pretty badly or were you a surprise after they decided on a name already?" Mack asked.

"Don't know exactly. You'd have to ask my mother that question. I never really knew who my father was, anyway. He split early," she replied with a quick glance at him through the one eye that wasn't covered by her hair. She just as quickly looked down at the floor. "Not much for decorations, are you?"

"What makes you ask that kind of question?"

"I just thought you might have a bigger office and a secretary or something. That's all," she said almost disappointedly. She glanced around at his Spartan office. No pictures on the walls of friends or family; not much on his desk other than a phone and a cup holder for pens; some old books on a table next to the side of her chair that she didn't bother to read the titles of because she didn't care; no one else waiting in a nonexistent waiting room. Even drab white painted walls with obvious dirt smudges. Mack made no apologies for it to anyone.

"I'm sorry if it's a little unimpressive at first glance. Decorating was not one of my strong points," he smiled at her. "They have a tendency not to give you much to work with around here. I make do all right. Sorry."

She moved her head from a perpetual tilt so that her hair fell away from her eyes again and Mack could see that she had softened somewhat at his smile. She took a moment to glance back down at her feet and move some imaginary lint away.

"It's okay. I just thought there'd be more."

Mack leaned back in his chair. It wasn't a good idea to prompt clients too much. Most people that walked into his office would either blurt out their problem, or warm up to it and then tell him. She seemed like the "warm up" kind.

She looked him square in the eyes as she said, "I need you to find something for me."

"Okay." He let her talk at her own pace and bring it out as she wanted it to come out.

"I can't really go into any kind of detail," she said simply.

Mack had been in this business for over twenty years. When he graduated college with a degree in criminal science and a new wife on his arm, the FBI seemed like the best fit for him. He spoke both Spanish and French, had traveled all over the world while working summers on cruise ships, and didn't want to be tied down to one location in any city. The FBI came calling at a recruiting seminar and he jumped at the chance.

But that hadn't exactly been the lifestyle Melody wanted and Mack never seemed to get the kinds of cases he wanted to work on, so after the Bureau moved them three times in three years, Melody said enough and Mack left the bureau and opened up a small investigative agency in Dallas. Then they moved to California to be closer to her family. The pay was lousy, and the hours were long, but they were mostly happy. It was a struggle sometimes with what little money he brought in, but it usually wasn't all that dangerous. That made her happy.

During the time at his own agency, Mack learned he had a unique talent for finding things. He was a good listener and had a sharp eye for details. That combination, along with an uncanny knack for solving puzzles that came from good genes, proved effective on more than one occasion. He could still see his dad sitting in front of their fireplace during the warm summer nights, smoking a cheap cigar and working on a crossword or logic puzzle he brought home from work. His dad could solve them all. Mack picked the talent up from him and never regretted it.

But he never expected this to happen. Never expected to end up here doing this kind of work. Sometimes life's decisions work out completely different than expected.

"In my experience, most people who are looking for something usually have some help to give me to get me started," Mack said as he looked at her. "A name and a description of the object would be a good place to start. What is it?"

"I'm not really supposed to tell you that much."

"Why not?" He already didn't like the sound of this.

"Well, Mr. Teacher, my mother will be coming here in just a minute to tell you the rest. She told me not to say anymore then I already have."

Mack didn't say anything for a very long while. He and Randi sat quietly across from each other and just stared.

His palms turned clammy and the hair on the back of his neck stood up. This was not good at all.

CHAPTER TWO

It might have been the décor or it might have been the lighting. It could've even been the furniture in the place that spoiled his mood today, but all that Victor Stevens knew for certain was that he was in a foul mood. And nothing anyone could say or do would improve it. He angrily pushed past a group of nurses in the hall with no kind of acknowledgement of his own lack of courtesy, and then flung the door to the room open until it hit the backstop and made a very loud and distinct "thud." Victor didn't care who or what heard him and he didn't care that he was probably disturbing the relative peace and tranquility that otherwise occupied this level.

He just didn't care.

Walking past the admissions desk and grabbing the set of files on the end of the tabletop, Victor pushed open the two swinging doors and then turned right. He heard the person standing at the desk grunt at him, but he'd be damned if he would respond. Not today.

With a quick glance back to see if anyone was following him or even observing him from the mostly deserted hallway, Victor stopped in his tracks and then abruptly whirled around and stepped into an adjacent janitor's closet.

He was alone in the darkness and tried to collect his thoughts for the coming surgery. The scrutiny he was going to be under today was intense. Sure, the others had occasionally taken an interest in him a long time ago, but to actually have some of them present beside him today and observe his every move was something entirely new. And he didn't like it.

He knew his work was satisfactory, but not exemplary, and with a new fish coming into the tank every other day, Victor knew they could shit-can him at a moment's notice. No forewarning. No phone call. No pat on the back or gold pen. Just some drone of a guy shoving him out of the way like an old ham and cheese sandwich and the next guy stepping up to the table.

They once told him how wonderful he was and how his ideas were going to change the entire structure of this place, from the bottom all the way to the top. All he had to do was keep his head in the game and reap the rewards. It seemed pretty simple.

When Victor graduated from Oxford College with a shiny new medical degree and nothing but bright lights ahead, he knew he was destined for greatness. But then that thing happened and then another couple of things conspired against him and suddenly he was no longer rising in the medical field. He was sinking. And fast. He often felt like an incredibly heavy anchor was tied around his neck and kept dragging him down. Some days, he felt lower than whale shit at the bottom of the ocean.

Today was one of those days.

Reaching into his jacket pocket, Victor withdrew a tiny yellow packet. Glancing up nervously at the door, Victor made sure it was locked from the inside, even though he wasn't sure the locks around this place worked. More than likely, it deliberately set them not to lock. Victor opened the packet and let the aroma of the little blue-green dust fill up his senses. He breathed deeply long enough to enjoy the sensation, and then quickly opened his mouth and raised his tongue to put the dust directly under and onto his gums.

The rush surged, and he threw his head backwards as the drugs hit his system almost instantly. Victor sagged to his knees and reached out to the slimy walls of the closet to steady himself. The drugs acted as both a morphine and an amphetamine and sent all of his senses into a rage at once. His heart beat stronger and the needles under his skin announced their presence. The drug was wonderful. Good and good for you, he always said.

It hadn't always been the case that he needed a little pick up before a major surgery, but lately it was the only way to get through some of this stuff. Nothing that he saw or did bothered him. In fact, it never did, but the monotony of it all bothered him. The high took care of that.

Victor stood up straighter and adjusted his jacket, smoothing out a couple of wrinkles here and there to make it look better. Impressions were so important to these people. You had to look the part and not just act the part to succeed.

He ran a hand through his shoulder length black hair and then wiped his mouth. He hated it when he drooled, but it was an adverse reaction to the drug. The way he felt, it was well worth it.

Strengthening himself, Victor reached for the door and just before his hand touched the knob, he hesitated. Blinking his eyes, he shook his head back and forth momentarily and tried to clear the sudden thoughts that jumped into his brain. Failure was not something he could contemplate. If he didn't do a good job, they would move him to another level.

Fuck that.

He had to insure he was on his best game today. They would be watching. They were always watching, but today was going to be worse. Like some kind of lab rat under a fluorescent light with a large microscope. Open for all the world to see. Naked and drooling.

Victor shook his head and then opened the door and walked back into the hallway before anyone could notice he was missing. Looking both left and right, he straightened his jacket again and headed to the operating room.

Victor pulled his mask tightly across his face and then turned around so that the nurse could tie it securely behind his head. He never really understood all the protocol that went with this job. Like the mask, for example. Like he was really preventing germs from spreading. He just couldn't buy into that theory.

Walking through the two swinging doors, Victor recognized two orderlies that he worked with before. They were standing off to the side, almost at attention, which was itself unusual. Par for the course.

On Victor's immediate left were two more people hiding behind surgical masks. He knew immediately that he didn't know either of these two, but he also sensed they weren't here to bust his balls. They seemed a bit out of sorts and slightly nervous. Medical students.

On another day, when Victor knew the brass wouldn't be here watching, he would have enjoyed their attention and the almost idol-like worship he got from newbies like these two. Today, they were just a further pain in the ass. He had to teach and impress at the same time. Thankfully, his quick kick earlier was still working or he couldn't handle it.

Walking up to the group gathered at the table, he nodded. The problem with training any of these students was that they arrived with such a limited amount of ability anyway, and little or no formal training, that Victor couldn't really work with them. But then when you added in the imagination that was required to keep your place at the table here, he knew that most couldn't hack it. Literally or figuratively. It truly took a special deviant to keep this position. And even though both guys would someday soon try to get his job, he wouldn't let that happen. He didn't get here to give it away.

He stopped and looked up before even acknowledging that a patient had been prepped and readied at the table before him. Three sets of eyes were staring intently at his every move from behind a dark glass overhead in the observation room. He didn't know who it was, but he knew they wanted him to fail. After a certain amount of time, the brass always wanted change. Corporate downsizing or some such bullshit.

That wasn't going to happen either.

Victor fiddled with his fingernails as the orderlies slid the patient underneath him and onto the table. The face of a large man with dark blue eyes looked up at him. The eyes were swollen and there was blood dripping out of his nose. It looked to Victor like he'd taken a beating before arriving on the operating table.

He motioned to the nurse to his right, and she handed him the clipboard attached to the patient. He scanned it for the information he needed and then handed it back.

"Mr. Byron Michaels. Welcome to our little party. You are at the entrance to the City and I will be the one to guide you from here on out," Victor said as he leaned over the table.

Byron's eyes were half open, and he was semi-conscious. When Byron was just a rookie on the Los Angeles Police Force many years ago, one vet taught him the power of controlling his reactions with his mind. Control was always a better response than panic. He inhaled slowly and attempted to control his breathing. Must've been wounded on the job, he thought. Hopefully, not too badly. He felt little pain at the moment, which was good.

Licking his lips, Byron took a moment to assess his situation and wished for a drink. An ice cold beer would've been the first choice, but anything wet would suffice. He felt parched and sand paper replaced his tongue. They'd worked him over pretty good, and through the fog and haze, his mind was rapidly coming into focus.

Byron looked up and saw aisles of meat hanging from the ceiling in perfect order. Slabs processed and prepared, still dripping from fresh cuts and slapping their contents onto the surrounding ground. He lifted his head off the rough pillow that held it and looked down at his bindings. The knots were secure, and he couldn't reach them. Splattered over his white shirt were several drops of fresh blood from the carcasses overhead. Butcher shop leftovers.

Meat slabs in an operating room?

And three pairs of eyes behind a dark screen in the ceiling.

"Do you like the view, Mr. Michaels? We try to decorate to our patient's comfort. It's all about you, of course." Victor motioned to the hanging slabs of beef.

Byron blinked his eyes and, though both were swollen, he could focus just enough to make out that one of the slabs didn't look like a cow. Byron gasped as he realized it was a *body* hanging over his head. And worse of all, it was twitching.

"The chart says you've been assigned to us, Mr. Michaels. We'll do our best to make sure that you're comfortable," said a nurse standing to the left of the Doctor. She said it like she was talking to a disinterested waiter while ordering Chinese food off a menu. She was short, a little less than five feet, Byron guessed, and had deep brown eyes with a small white spot on the cornea of the left one. The rest of her face was covered by a surgical mask, like she just came from the operating room. Her eyebrows were missing and two scars remained. Liked they'd been peeled off.

He needed to practice his control right now. "Aren't you supposed to give me some kind of anesthesia?" he asked. He was frantically trying to think of a way out of here. He needed time. He flexed his shoulders to test the restraints.

He decided on another tactic. Survival. Stall. "Do you mind answering a couple of minor questions?" Byron asked. His lips had gone to a purplish color and his left eye was closing from the swelling. The blood had dried to a thick, snot-like sediment under his nose. He couldn't even remember getting beat-up. His memory seemed to fade in and out.

Victor stopped and looked at Byron. They were always the same. Unsure where they were and about to hear the worst thing they could imagine.

Victor truly relished this part of the surgery. He grinned slightly and focused his full attention on his patient.

"You can ask anything you wish, Mr. Michaels. I will be happy to answer if I can. What's on your mind?"

"Well, I've sort of figured out I'm not in Kansas anymore, Dorothy. But I'm not really sure where the fuck I am, and I think that would be a good place to start." Byron looked up as best as he could through swollen eyes.

"You are correct. You're not in Kansas anymore. This is the City."

"What City?"

Victor cocked his head to the side. "That's the name we call it. You would know it by any of another host of names."

The sarcasm returned to Byron. Something he could not control. "Okay. I'll let you play this out for a little longer, but then I really have to get going. I've got an appointment coming up with my hairdresser. This girl is so hard to get in to see."

The two of them stared at each other for a moment while neither spoke. Byron was tied down to a pallet looking up and Victor was leaning over him looking down; their faces were only two feet apart. Victor came a little closer, so he had only to whisper, and Byron could hear every word. This was what kept him going.

Victor reached up and pulled the mask clear of his face so the words were not muffled in the least bit. "Mr. Michaels. You have died and are in Hell."

CHAPTER THREE

Mack hadn't said anything since Randi told him her mother was coming for a brief visit. With an unconscious movement of his right hand, he softly rubbed the third finger of his left hand under the desk. The place where his wedding ring used to rest. He never removed it. Bad luck. But then they took that too, of course.

Randi reached up and quietly slid her hair completely away from her face so that she could look directly into his eyes. She never grew tired of watching the reaction of people to the news of her mother's arrival. Her mother had that kind of effect.

"Why? Does that bother you, Mr. Teacher?" she asked innocently. "Is there something about my mother that bothers you?"

Mack felt like he just walked into a maximum security prison and they assigned him a cell with someone named "Bubba", who was six foot eight and three hundred pounds. You knew you were going to get fucked; you just didn't know *when* it would happen.

Mack wiped his hands off on his faded pants and then reached into his desk and got out a small handkerchief. With a smooth motion, he brought the kerchief up and over his face, wiping away all the sweat that suddenly occurred there. "It's just that I'm not used to having anyone famous here. No one like that has ever visited my office. Are you sure that I'm the right man for this job?" He hoped reverently that she said "no" and left his office as quickly as she had appeared.

With another wave of her hand, Randi dismissed the question. It was beneath her. She was used to this.

"No, Mr. Teacher. I don't make mistakes where my mother is concerned."

Mack nodded and wished immediately that he had gotten into another profession. Any other profession. With the practiced control that aided him so well whenever he faced a difficult situation, Mack controlled his emotions. He started by first closing his eyes and slowing his breathing.

Somewhere along the line after college and during a short stint with some surveillance unit, Mack had plenty of time to practice the art of control. If he could just get his breathing to slow down long enough, then he could manage how fast his heart pounded. The rest would fall into place.

After what seemed like a long moment, he reopened his eyes. When he could no longer control the outcome, it was best to be in complete control of himself. His breathing returned to normal, and he felt his heart beating slower. He had no idea if this was real or imagined, but it helped to calm him down considerably.

He tried to act busy for a moment and opened the top drawer on his desk, where he kept a small piece of a mirror. He always liked to take a quick look at himself. It wasn't driven by any sort of vanity, but he still liked to look confident, even at times like this. Although short at five feet ten inches, with a normal build that included a paunch around his middle from too many donuts, he looked unkempt and distressed even now.

The eyes were still blue. The hair was still a dirty blond that used to get whiter in the summer and darker in the winter. The nose was a little too large for his type of round face, and normally there was a smile on that face. Mack always had an amiable smile. Suit and tie, never quite fitting right. Especially today. Nothing distinguishing at all to separate him from the others.

He cleared his throat. "If Annicka wishes to come here, then she is certainly welcome. I can no longer control her actions than I can control the wind." His focus had returned. He would deal with whatever was coming as best as he could.

Randi shook her head in agreement. "No. No one can truly control her."

Mack knew whom she meant by "no one." Someone he hoped never to be in the same room with during this eternity. He sat back in his chair and let his head fall slightly.

Another day in Hell.

As if on command, the walls seemed to shimmer momentarily and like there was an open door where his closed door rested, Annicka glided into the room with Mack and Randi.

Annicka didn't just enter the room; she slithered into it as if something was slipped under the door like a wave of cockroaches all running in unison. At one moment she hadn't been there and then, like a weight being laid delicately upon his throat until he couldn't breathe, Mack felt her enter the room. Entering all of his senses through the very pores in his skin.

Mack immediately stood up from behind his desk and looked directly at the floor. He would not, could not, look at her until it was offered to him.

Annicka sensed his fear. It was a symptom she enjoyed.

She glanced down at her still sitting daughter and nodded approvingly, as Randi looked up. They hadn't verbally communicated in any manner, but still some understanding passed between them. Mack didn't know any of this as he still stood with his head bowed.

He could feel her presence in the room like a blast furnace had been opened. It was as if the room became smaller without any construction crews chopping or sawing anything. Where once he thought his office large enough to handle three people comfortably, now he thought it was too small even for just one. A tight fitting coffin. And the dirt was being laid on top of the coffin while he squirmed inside. As he stood there, he trembled slightly and waited for her to speak first. It would be a punishable offense to address her.

"Teacher." It was a simple statement of recognition. No introduction necessary, or intended. "You may look at me."

He nodded and raised his eyes to look at her. He had heard many stories throughout his years here. So many things were rumored. Tales of debauchery, treachery, trickery, and every other nasty word that ended with an e-r-y seemed to go on daily in the City of Hell. He always figured most of them were true.

She was levitating slightly, just sort of hovering above the ground. The bottom of her gown rested about two inches above the floor. And the gown, indeed the complete image of her, was swaying. Billowing. Not moving physically as far as he could tell, but still moving. Kind of like one of those wave machines they had back in the seventies that rocked back and forth and the plasma inside jostled up and down, never coming to rest. Annicka was changing.

No, not changing as he thought about it, but *shifting*. Her image was hard to pin down to anything exact because the features were shifting without stopping. At one moment she had black eyes, then they were green. Her hair was flowing out behind her from some imaginary gale force wind that Mack couldn't feel. The hair was a river of dark red with occasional black strands and even an ending or two in blond. Striking. If he'd been looking at her after twelve martinis, he might have thought he'd see something like this, but not now. Not stone cold sober.

She seemed to have a distinct face, but he couldn't tell through the shifting. The features were in the correct position on her face, but they were moving all at once, just enough for him to not concentrate on anything else about her. The face was angular and round like Randi's, and the skin was very pale. Almost chalk. They were definitely related. Mack averted his eyes from her face and looked down. He'd seen enough of the image to last a long time in his nightmares.

But he couldn't tear his eyes away from her gown. It was transfixing as it moved in that wind that Mack couldn't feel, but she obviously could. Flowing back and forth, the gown was red and white. It was shapely to her hips but then wide at the bottom as it hovered above the floor. Like something worn to a state dinner at the White House or possibly an 1880s ball.

The gown looked like it was made from red and white satin and covered in blood stains. The bottom was tattered and the blood must've come from many tortures that didn't go well for the victim. The white went dirty years ago and came encrusted with snot and mucus many centuries old. The sleeves were full length and covered her arms to her hands.

Her hands were another matter altogether. Mack could see that her left hand looked like a curled up claw, perhaps from a previous accident. Where her right hand should have been was some kind of green seaweed. It moved in constant motion and whipped back and forth in her sleeve. He could make out some kind of suction cups on the ends of what he thought should've been her fingers.

On her shoulder sat a frozen cat. But this wasn't like any cat in a pet store. He even knew the cat's name was "Feral" and, for all intents and purposes, it appeared to be dead. It didn't move, not even to blink its eyes. The eyes appeared to be fixated on him whenever he looked at the cat. The fur was molten black and smeared down by some kid of axle grease. The claws were at least an inch long and very thick and at the moment were firmly planted into the shoulder of Annicka. If the cat didn't hiss every couple of minutes, he would've known for sure it was dead.

Annicka's mouth opened slightly, and a stench filled his nostrils as the putrid smell of burning corpses wafted across the room towards him. The cat hissed once more as he lowered his eyes to the floor.

"I demand you to look upon me," Annicka said.

Mack looked back up and decided he could not anger her in any way. It wouldn't be good for him.

"My daughter Randi has come to you with a request. You will grant it."

He could only nod and hope she left soon.

"You are to find an item for us, Mr. Teacher."

He couldn't help it. The words escaped his mouth before he could stop them. "You don't know where it is in the City?" As soon as he said it, he knew it was a mistake. Her abilities as a Lower were so far over anything he could imagine that he wondered why she couldn't just seep into some other room and pick the thing up.

Annicka's shimmering glow took on a dark aura instantly. She would not be provoked here, but rather would display.

"I do not answer to you. You are but a puny higher being that serves me, Mr. Teacher. To be crushed at my amusement. You have an ability I require at present. You have solved many puzzles. This task will prove to be one of them. Why I do not know where it is cannot concern you. You will locate it and guide me to it or I will deal with your failure personally."

The shimmering waves of heat around her began shifting rapidly and Mack could hear a tiny, but clear laughter coming from underneath her dress. He did not know who was in there with her. Her features became harder to discern when she was angry. He didn't want to see her get angrier.

"The Lowest likes to foster competition on occasion between his council members. As his will is always immortal law, we must abide with limited abilities during these times. That is all the information you need. Randi will accompany you on the journey. She has some strengths that may prove to be useful to you when the time comes to extract information from patrons here in the City."

He had to ask. "My knowledge is not extensive, Miss." He would not use her name. To do so could draw her wrath if she didn't like the way he pronounced it. Any inflection or change in his tone could prove dangerous. "I will do anything you or your daughter request." He looked at Randi and then looked away from Annicka again.

Annicka's green eyes flashed to black. Slowly, deliberately, completely ignoring his statements, she raised one hand and motioned. He clutched his chest, winced in a surprised look of pain, and then fell to the floor.

"You will not question me again. This is your punishment." Annicka waved her hand ever so slightly towards him in a downward motion and he curled up into a fetal position, knowing what was coming. He'd seen this before. She was simply reminding him.

The lights dimmed in Mack's mind as he laid on the floor of his office and then he was instantly transported back to that time. The time of his death.

The sun broke through the clouds early that morning, pushing aside a cool fog that rolled in the previous night from the ocean to the shores of San Francisco. This time of year, the early spring, it wasn't unusual at all to have a foggy morning and have the bay bridge traffic almost come to a standstill. The local weather men could have easily predicted such a morning, and in fact said the same was to be expected for the entire week. Just another foggy morning in San Francisco. There were many of them.

The temperature was a comfortable fifty-nine degrees, and Mack Teacher stood at the window admiring the majesty of it all. Even though he couldn't see through the dense fog, living here for the past several years ensured him that the fog would burn off by mid-morning and then a cloudless day of perfection would take over. It would be a deep, blue sky that stretched as far as the eye could see and the sun would take the chill off of his shoulders as he ran along the track near the water. A perfect life. The morning, the birds, the coming summer. It was too much to behold.

He would miss all of it.

Yesterday, he buried his beloved Melody in a cemetery close to the ocean. While he couldn't afford a high dollar grave site because of the meager wages from the detective agency he owned, he'd been able to borrow some funds from one of his friends. That and the insurance money had paid enough to pick out a spot Melody would have liked. For the rest of time Melody would be able to see and smell the ocean she loved.

It was one of those things no one really ever talked about. Oh, sure, Mack had gotten an occasional brochure in the mail and had subsequently turned it over twice before throwing it out with the morning's garbage. Once, he even remembered setting his morning coffee cup down on top of one of those damn brochures. Sign up now, before it's too late. Decide where to lay your loved ones to rest now before they're gone. One less thing to worry about when that time came.

And it came. Oh shit, it came all right. Long before it was expected. Hell, when you're Melody's age, you have all the time in the world. This wasn't supposed to happen. It happened to other people. Not them. They were golden. Kids and a bigger house in the future someday. They dreamed of it and spoke in hushed tones on their last vacation. Lying together on the beach, Melody even came up with a couple of names for the children.

Stupid now. Stupid to dream for the future and plan when you really weren't guaranteed that it would come. There was no one to take this defective package back to and get a refund.

Cancer was the most merciless killer Mack had ever known. It ate Melody away in four months from the day she was diagnosed to where she was less than eighty pounds and a mere shell of the wonderful person she had been. In front of his very eyes, the woman he planned to grow old with was shriveled and looked to be about seventy when she was really only forty-two.

He hated cancer. It was a devil with a body and an evil agenda. It didn't care. Had no mercy and no remorse. It owned them and he couldn't stop it.

Melody died a quick but painful death stretched out over the four months. She knew it was coming, and the one thing he could not get his mind over was the way she never complained. Not once. Not one time. Not why was it her? Not the pain and the drugs and the radiation were too painful to bear. Nothing like that. She was stronger than he ever imagined himself to be.

And as he held her hand at their bedside in the home she loved and helped him create, Melody slipped away and Mack's hatred grew to an inferno. It wasn't a home without her. It was only a house.

He hated hospitals. He hated doctors and the horseshit they called hospice. He hated nurses and caring looks from friends. He hated knowing smiles and plate lunches left for him by neighbors that were glad it wasn't them. He hated it all.

Mack turned from the bay window and walked to the center of the living room floor. Carefully, he moved Melody's favorite chair to one side to give him a comfortable space. He turned to his left and walked over to the table in the dining room and, grabbing a small chair, he dragged it back to the middle of the living room.

He stopped one time as he passed the full-length mirror in the hallway that he hung for her. She liked to look nice when she went out. Mack never cared one way or the other how he looked, but standing there this morning, he didn't like what he saw looking back at him.

He snapped out of his reverie and turned from the mirror. Nothing left to do but the obvious. He removed his watch and took his billfold out of his pocket. He then climbed up onto the chair and, throwing a rope over a beam on the ceiling of the house, Mack looped a noose around his neck. He took one more good look at Melody's picture on the bureau, then kicked the chair out from underneath himself.

Annicka watched as Mack lay curled up on the floor of his office. He was sobbing slightly, and she was smiling. Her eyes turned back to their green color.

"Arise, Mr. Teacher."

He did as best he could and struggled to compose himself. His own private hell was to relive his hanging repeatedly. The pain was intense, the memory torture, and the imagery so real he could feel the rope burn into his neck every time the sight was forced upon him. Lately, because the City found him to be useful, the vision hadn't been used against him so often.

Annicka knew which strings to pull. But as the council member, that was her job. To torture the patrons in the worst way imaginable. To tailor each of their private hells to conform to their darkest fears.

She was an expert at it.

"I remember when I first watched you relive your own hanging, Mr. Teacher. It seems as if that is still appropriate to keep you in your place. "

Mack nodded as he regained his strength. The memory was so *real*. He was there again. And again. And again.

"Suicides are sometimes the most fun," Annicka said to Randi. "They are also the most pathetic. If you had been a little stronger, Mr. Teacher, like your poor dead wife, Melody, you wouldn't be here with us in the City."

He looked up at Annicka as she mentioned the name of his wife. He knew that none of his secrets or fears were his anymore. They hadn't been for some time. Nor would they ever be again.

"You will find something called 'The Black Rose' for me, Mr. Teacher. It is a special rose that harbors a secret. The name neither matters to me nor influences my quest. I must possess this rose. If you find it quickly, I will release you of some of the more vivid memories you have. If you fail, I will reduce your status here to one of the higher levels. Randi has some information that will prove useful to you."

Annicka shook her powerful head of hair. "I will send someone to assist you in your journey, for it will not be easy. It will be painful, Mr. Teacher, I am sure of that."

With that, the light behind Annicka seemed to be pulled away from her, back through an imaginary door that Mack had never seen, and like water into a funnel, Annicka seeped away from his office.

Mack slumped back down into his chair. He could not win this one. Annicka had left him her personal spy as his sidekick, and if he failed, she would extract an even greater vengeance. His eyes suddenly clouded as he realized something that, until this moment, he hadn't thought about.

He was supposed to fail. In the City of Hell, no one ever succeeded at anything.

CHAPTER FOUR

Byron blinked his unswollen eye as best he could and then licked his lips. He couldn't have possibly anticipated that answer. How could this be true? It just couldn't.

He felt a sudden rush of blood from his head down to his toes and then, without warning, Byron opened his mouth and his stomach clutched and he vomited up a month's worth of greasy hamburgers all over the surgical gown of Victor Stevens. He simply could not stop his stomach as it lurched violently and emptied itself straight up into the air. Most of the food particles and whatever else he ingested in the last twenty-four hours found their way into the face of the Doctor, but the rest held to the laws of gravity and came splashing back down onto Byron's face and into his open mouth.

"Jesus Fucking Christ!" Victor screamed at the top of his lungs. He hadn't had a squirter in a long time, and the fucking nimrod orderlies were supposed to empty the asshole's stomach before they ever got to him. This was exactly why it was a requirement, so when he told the pain babies they were in Hell, he didn't get this kind of shit all over his face.

Victor realized that the three pairs of eyes looking down on him from the ceiling viewing room would chuckle at his problem. He had to stay in control. If he lost it now, they would descend on him like buzzards on road kill in the Arizona desert.

He calmed himself instantly and then turned to the orderlies standing directly behind him. With a vast amount of vomit, puss, old corn, bits of a cheese taco, and something green hanging from his mustache and face, Victor reached out to the closest of the orderlies and grabbed him by the neck. He pulled the man up close enough to smell his breath.

Reaching behind his back, Victor grabbed the first instrument on the operating table that his hand could reach and then slowly brought it up to where the orderly could see what he was holding. It was forbidden for the orderly to resist or fight back with a lower being. Anything other than total subservience from a higher being towards a lower being would be punishable by a thousand years of unimaginable torture.

Even Hell had rules.

Brain stopped vomiting and lay sobbing on the pallet as his mind tried to grasp what had happened to him. He hadn't been a religious man during his life. Never really gone to church except when he was a child with his mother. Never really stopped to question his own worth, or that of anyone else for that matter. Never taken the time to think about what would happen when he moved on from his time on Earth. Raised Catholic, but far from devout. Apparently, he should have listened more in Sunday School. Maybe some of that information would've been useful.

It had to have been what happened that night on their farm. The night he freed his mother and his sisters from his father. It had to have been that.

Maybe nothing could help him now.

"You're in for a rare treat, Mr. Michaels," Victor said as he raised what looked like a very sharp scalpel up to the face of the orderly. "Normally, the pain babies we get here don't really appreciate the amount of pain they're going to feel. But because this higher being disrespected me, he must be dealt with before I can give you the proper attention you deserve. It truly is a special day for you. And for him."

With a swift move, from a lifetime and helltime of surgeries for the pure sake of inflicting pain, the doctor began to surgically remove the man's nose. Victor cut swiftly upwards, slowed momentarily as the scalpel struck a sinewy piece of cartilage under the first layer of skin, and then brought the knife across and back down the man's face. The man screamed a quick, curt sound as he involuntarily flinched and stepped backward from the doctor's knife. His nose gushed a shooting stream of dark, thick, more-orange-than-red blood across the room, which struck Victor in the face and mixed itself up with the vomit from Byron. The cut off nose promptly plopped onto the floor.

The Doctor then pulled his scalpel down to the where the orderly's stomach was and with a quick, precise strike movement cut a clean, twelve inch incision across the length of the man's stomach. The orderly grimaced and shrieked as the blood rushed out of his stomach cavity. Victor dropped the scalpel to the floor and, while still holding the orderly's throat with one hand, deftly reached into the incision and pulled back the top layer of skin.

Worming his fingers under the skin, and pushing hard, he shoved his entire hand into the opening. The orderly grunted, grimaced and whimpered as his blood fell in streams onto the tiled floor.

Grasping the upper portion of the stomach cavity from the inside, Victor ripped outward and yanked the stomach of the orderly outside of his body as the man's legs gave way and he screamed again. Having completely pulled the stomach out, the Doctor turned it upside-down and emptied the contents onto the floor.

"This is how you empty a stomach completely, you asshole, so that the pain babies don't fucking puke on me ever again," he said.

Squeezing the stomach like he was wringing out a wet mop, Victor twisted the orderly's stomach into a perfect figure eight knot and then while the man screamed and rolled on the floor, he again grabbed the incision and shoved the now empty stomach back inside. The whole procedure took less than twenty seconds.

Victor pulled back and didn't bother to wipe any of the hanging fluids or food from his face as he watched the man now on his knees, scampering through his whimpers to grab his nose. He might have need of it later.

Pointing at him, Victor said, "You will leave the operating room never to return. Be glad your nose is all I have the time to take off today."

The orderly stood up and nodded, holding his bleeding nose, and then turned and left the operating room as quickly as he could. He didn't want to arouse any more of the doctor's wrath.

Victor straightened his jacket and then turned his attention to Byron, who had gone quiet and completely still watching the spectacle.

"You will notice, Mr. Michaels, that the orderly picked up his nose, or what was left of it, and carried it out of the room. I can assure you it was not because he was worried about the health department coming down on us. Here in the City, if you lose an appendage, you can never get it reattached, but because we come into this world with no possessions and all we have is what we were born with and quite literally the clothes on our backs, it is best to keep everything you've got. You never know when it may come in handy to trade for some service somewhere down the line."

Byron tried not to think about what he might have to pick up and carry around for the rest of eternity. He thought everyone here still had most of their arms and legs and other things attached, as far as he could tell. The idea of eternity in this place, and he hadn't even seen what this place was beyond this room, could not have frightened him more. He vomited again.

The doctor put the scalpel down on the table beside where Byron was lying and picked up something that looked like a cross between a hammer and an ice pick. It was long, polished with dried blood, and came to a razor sharp point on the end.

"You will also notice, Mr. Michaels," Victor said as he easily fell into his role here in the operating room. It was like riding a bicycle after having left it alone for many years. It came naturally to him and all the eyes staring at him from above and behind the glass window couldn't bother him now. He was an artist about to paint with Byron Michaels' blood. He continued, "We don't have much need to sterilize the tools of our trade. Infection doesn't play a role here."

Victor leaned over Byron and whispered. "And we never use anesthesia."

With that last word and a horrified look on the face of Byron Michaels, the Doctor took the ice pick-looking instrument and dug it lovingly into the corner of Byron's left cheekbone, directly under the ear. Placing his feet squarely on the floor and using all of his one hundred and seventy-five pounds, the Doctor then shoved the ice pick as hard as he could into Byron's head.

Byron gasped briefly and then, sucking air as deeply into his chest as possible, let out a blood-curdling scream that only made the nurse's grins grow broader.

Victor used the scream as a sign of progress and worked the pick back and forth before he at last had a wide enough hole to wrench it back out. He then dropped the instrument to the floor and kicked it absent mindedly farther under the table.

"Damn, Mr. Michaels," the Doctor said as he surveyed the hole he just made. "Your fucking ear got in the way a little bit. Made the hole a little bit bigger than I needed. But don't you worry. I can work with it."

Byron had felt the cold metal tip of the ice pick as it first slipped under and then through his skin and his blood flowed freely from the new hole. The first sensation of pain hadn't been that bad, but the further the Doctor drove the pick in, the more the pain intensified. Byron silently wished he would pass out and not feel anything until he woke up from this nightmare.

Victor stepped back to the table of surgical instruments such as it was and picked up a roll of duct tape. He pulled a long strand free from the roll and then cut it quickly between his fingers and teeth.

Byron slipped into unconsciousness as his brain tried to take over the situation and save him from some of the pain. Motioning to one nurse with his head and then nodding at the one remaining orderly, Victor indicated they should wake Byron up so that he wouldn't miss any of the pain. Wouldn't miss any of the fun. The nurse took a pail of water that the orderly handed her and threw it into Byron's face.

Byron coughed and awakened immediately to an intense searing of pain where his left ear had been ripped upwards and the hole underneath was bleeding like a fat squashed tick on a concrete driveway. He tried to raise his hands to defend himself and stop the pain, but they were tied securely to the pallet. Wailing now and sobbing openly, Byron tried to beg.

"Whatever your name is, please, don't take it. Please. I beg you..."

"Oh, I won't take it. That never entered my mind, Mr. Michaels. Did you ever study physics in school? I used to love the experiments we did in class. But the ones we did after class were even better. Take this next one, for example. They would never have sanctioned this where I came from. But first we have to finish the job."

The Doctor taped the end of Byron's nose closed with the duct tape and then, cutting another couple of pieces, he covered his mouth and both ear holes. Byron's head lifted momentarily off the pallet as he tried to reduce the strain of the pounding on his face and head as the tape was pulled tightly. The pain was like someone was hammering him repeatedly on the front part of his brain with a ball peen hammer. He couldn't stop crying.

Victor continued, "I always liked the experiments we did with compressed air. It's amazing how strong something invisible like air can be when you compress it and then restrict the access. You'll see. Or more appropriately, you'll *feel*."

Picking up a two-inch nipple attached to a mechanic's air hose, Victor placed it outside of Byron's view and against the opening of the hole under his ear. He could feel the tip of the nipple pressing against the edge of the hole.

"Damn again, Mr. Michaels. I didn't use a big enough ice pick and now the nipple is a little bit bigger than the hole. The good news is that the nipple has threads on it that are designed for just this sort of problem. I'll just have to improvise."

Victor turned the end of the nipple in a clockwise direction, and the nipple sliced into the hole with a crunching sound. The threads gripped the sides of the hole and, ripping the skull and skin apart, the nipple threaded its way into Byron's head. The doctor kept the pressure up and twisted and corkscrewed the nipple one slow inch at a time until it was buried up to the hilt.

Byron screamed at the first twist of the nipple as it cut, and he didn't stop screaming. The deeper it went, the harsher the sounds that came out of his mouth. His vocal cords got sore, and he went hoarse from the guttural cries that were escaping his mouth. The pain was like nothing he'd ever experienced and felt like a truck was driving over his head, crushing his skull into the asphalt.

Victor motioned to the nurse to keep Byron awake should he be lucky enough to pass out again, and then grabbed the end of the air hose and turned the power switch to the "on" position. The machine rumbled slightly and then moved to full power as the air tank filled with compressed air.

He stopped to look down at his patient. He felt no mercy. No sympathy. This bastard deserved to be here, and the Doctor was only doing his job.

Victor checked the connection between the air hose and the nipple and then reached back to the compressor and dialed the pressure knob up to full strength. It would deliver one hundred and twenty pounds per square inch of air directly through the hose and into the side of the patient's head. Byron screeched as he filled up with air and all the natural openings that were taped left no release point for the air to escape through.

Suddenly the pressure in his head became an insurmountable and uncontrollable amount of pounding like a jack hammer on the inside of his skull trying to get out. From every square inch of bone around his head, Byron could feel the pressure pushing as the air looked for an escape hatch. Even though his ears, mouth, and nose were securely taped closed, the pressure forced the blood vessels in all the orifices to burst and an incredible amount of blood shot out through the new openings in his skin.

Victor and the nurses took a quick step back and laughed hysterically at Byron's pain. He was screaming and twisting as much as he could move against the restraints until the physics of air pressure in a compacted space took over and both of Byron's eyes flew out of their respective sockets as far as the optical nerves would let them.

The air "whooshed" out of the newly opened holes where his eyes had been and were now dangling on both sides of his face. The air compressor again ramped up more pressure to replace the now missing square poundage and Byron immediately felt what little sanity he had left slipping away. This simply could not be happening.

Grabbing the pick once again and flipping it over on its side, Victor held the instrument down in front of Byron's eyes, where he could see it. With a smooth butcher like motion, Victor cut through the cord that connected the left eye to the brain, and then held the dangling eye and optical cord up for Byron to view. Byron stared through a swollen eye and an empty eye socket at the doctor as he held up his eye. The Doctor was extremely proud of his handiwork today.

Victor threw the eye and what little cord was still attached to it across the room and onto the floor, and Byron couldn't help it as his head turned and followed the flight path of his eye. The cord hit the ground and bounced twice before awkwardly rolling on its side against the wall and coming to a stop. As he watched, a small, fat rat appeared out of the wall and, gliding across the floor, came to a rest and then nibbled at the ends of the bloody cord.

"Stop that fucking rat! Stop that fucking rat and get my eye back you assholes!" Byron yelled at anyone and everyone.

The doctor shook his head. "Even rats need to eat, Mr. Michaels."

Byron turned what was left of his face towards the doctor. "You had better kill me, asshole, because if I ever get out of here, I will kill you."

A curious look crossed Victor's face as he considered the remark. It'd been a long time since one of the pain babies had threatened him. This man was obviously strong and had a high tolerance for pain because he was still lucid enough to threaten him. Interesting. Victor sighed. It was always difficult for them to understand at first. But they got used to the idea. Eventually.

After all, they had all the time in hell.

"You don't understand, Mr. Michaels. You can't kill me. No one dies here. Ever."

"What?" Indecision and fear thundered into Byron's mind. "What the fuck?"

"We're all dead already. You are in the City of Hell. You are dead. I can only have fun with you, but not kill you again. What would be the fun in that?"

"How can that be?"

"Mr. Michaels," Victor said again slowly. "One more time. You are in Hell and I am Hell's Doctor."

Pain is the only Pleasure.

Hell's First Mantra

INTERLUDE ONE: THE ARCHITECT EVOLUTION

The Architect designed the furnace to burn. What began as a simple oven with rotating knobs on the front and a viewing glass in the center to watch the ingredients cooking became an enormous thing. There had to be simmering and basting, as well as straight roasting. The heat needed variances and controllability in order to prepare the meat. Shelves became a necessity. Lots of shelves.

As he studied the final product, he realized the uncertainty of the whole thing. It seemed like a good idea. But as with most ideas that get acted on before they're completely thought out, this oven wouldn't really serve the purpose of its creation. Perhaps on a smaller scale.

The problem with the oven became apparent quickly during trial runs. Uneven cooking. Red centers. Hot spots. Shelves that didn't hold the meat completely and let some fall to the bottom. Too many problems and not enough positive results.

The Architect noted the oven's strengths, however.

After all, this was the City of Hell, and The Architect handled the prisoners.

The oven was large enough to be almost a five story brimstone apartment complex with no exits. The prisoners assigned to his furnace were systematically tortured with a simple but effective heat that resonated from the center of their stomachs and basically burned them from the inside out. It wasn't a natural fire; it was like being in a microwave. The heat started deep within the bowels and grew until it became an intestinal inferno that consumed the prisoners until they couldn't stop screaming. And itching. The more the heat ravaged them, the more they itched. Many of The Architect's prisoners scratched off significant sections of their arms and legs, trying to stop the pain.

As he watched the latest batch of new arrivals shoved into the oven, he shook his head. Turning from them and walking away while they screamed, and the heat was increased in small increments, deep thoughts occupied his attention. He no longer heard the screams or the pleading. It was just part of the job. His job. He could deal with that easily enough.

He was a young man with a tremendous responsibility. It'd been handed down to him and though his shoulders were narrow, his wisdom and fortitude were on an immense scale. He neither asked for nor deserved the burden.

He jumped down, using a hanging rope to descend to the next level. This whole thing wasn't working anymore. He'd have to be more creative in his efforts or at least get to a place where he felt he was truly appreciated. The oven was only a small stepping stone in a stream that wound around the world.

He didn't devise The City of Hell, or simply "the City" as the prisoners who resided here called it. There were many names handed down through the ages: Hades; Styx's Garden; the Underworld; it was all the same to him. Naming something like this was like a prom date with your mother. For no reason other than a show.

He knew that no matter what the designation, the result was still predictable: if the prisoners ended up here, they earned it.

And there was never any escape.

The Architect moved to his left to avoid an influx of prisoners on a wagon. He didn't see them as humans anymore. He viewed them as either customers or patrons of his art. They squirmed and moved, and many bowed their heads or reached out their hands to touch him like he was some kind of rock star, rather than a design man with an agenda. He never understood why they'd want to touch him. He wasn't big on physical contact, anyway.

As he stepped aside, he noticed the soulful look of despair in the eyes of a couple of the people lying in the wagon on the way to the kiln. The City was what it was: no one lingered around looking to get off for good behavior. There weren't any conjugal visits earned by bribing guards. No chance of parole. Hell was, by design, a continual place. And nowhere in the description that he'd ever read did the words "resting place" fit in. There wasn't any resting here. Rehabilitation wasn't a concern. Eternity was a cage without bars or windows. It was just one thing: long.

The Architect pulled open a hidden door in a secluded hallway where many of the others weren't allowed to go. He needed to rest and to think. The last shift of screamers in the kiln hadn't really been up to his standards.

He noticed the screams were shorter than normal for the oven temperature that he'd set, and they'd also gone quiet too fast. He'd probably have to tweak the system again.

He never knew their names. Hadn't bothered to even look at their faces anymore. For a while he used a system of numbers, but that dropped by the wayside. It wasn't like he had to count them or anything. In the City, the prisoners didn't have to be fed or clothed. Supplies were never a problem. There wasn't any reason for the basic necessities of life because of one simple fact: all the people were already dead.

There was, however, one serious problem with being dead: it didn't end. Ever.

Stretching out on a lounge chair and picking up a discarded magazine for a second, The Architect let his mind ponder the dilemma. He had the tools he needed. It was just a matter of bringing it out and using them.

He closed his eyes while his mind searched. Each of the new arrivals to the City were processed the same. From the very beginning of the place, it'd been that way. They brought nothing of significance with them other than a set of clothes on their backs.

First problem: physical pain had limits.

The prisoners were resilient, if nothing else, and with plenty of time to practice on them, he'd noted on many occasions that humans acclimated their senses to whatever was being thrown at them. Many of his experiments proved the axiom. If the eyelids of a prisoner were burned off with a branding iron, then the brain would shut down his retinas to save his vision. Some of the other senses would then try to compensate for the lack of eyesight, no matter how far off kilter it was originally. Blind prisoners could hear better. Skinless prisoners saw better in the dark to make up for their nerve endings being seared. People with their tongues cut out increased their hearing tenfold.

The Architect's endless experiments on the prisoners at first concentrated on the five basic senses: touch, sight, hearing, smell, and taste. Most of the senses weren't necessary in the City, but each of them contained unique qualities and if the situation required it, their individual strengths could be varied. Proven to be effective was blinding a prisoner while increasing his sense of touch to better feel the needles penetrating his skin. Or suturing a prisoner's mouth shut and taking away his ability to scream while turning up his sense of smell while his flesh burned. He found out that if he turned off their senses, most people would bury their parents to see or regain their sense of touch.

He'd tried other things after the oven in the early days. It was sometimes quite amusing to watch prisoners squirm under the weight of rocks, drown in a river, choke on vomit, puke until their intestines came up, have their heads crushed, break apart sensitive bones, cut off appendages, rip off skin in sections, crush testicles, sew up key openings, and on and on.

Maybe he was approaching it all wrong. Maybe he should have been using the senses *against* the prisoners.

He scoffed at that idea and almost chuckled. Amusement wasn't something he allowed himself to relish. The whole thing needed an overhaul. From the bottom up. He had to adapt. He revamped his original mandate of pure torture and instead inflict *punishment*. A new drug of choice.

Pure punishment. It had a resolutely kinky ring to it.

In the turmoil of delivering pain for many years, he had to deal with the process of the tediousness of it all. A passionate amount of his time was spent designing systems that resulted in a punch, poke, prod, hit, smash, pull, tangle, shock, kick, yank, or bludgeoning to the customers. His input was the originality of the delivery.

If this was going to be any fun at all, he'd have to get more interesting ways to extract payment from the sinners. Any idiot could design a furnace. Any fool could burn a carcass. But only someone with a truly extraordinary imagination could make people *suffer*.

He jumped up from his chair and strode purposefully to the door. Turning left and then left again, he dropped through a chute and then climbed a ladder, getting him back to the first of the floors. The Architect ran past the first of several small doors on the top level. He sought a place he hadn't been for a long time. The room directly above the oven. To rejuvenate.

He ran past the tool shed containing the various implements of the City's workers. Pain and torture needed tools and most of the readily conceivable ones were contained here: hockey sticks, baseball bats, hammers, golf clubs, tire irons, desks, barbells, shelves, dishes, books, sticks, and rocks became the standard for pummeling a prisoner; tie rods, electric probes, batteries, wires, and assorted computer chips for electric shocks; fire hoses, filled bottles of maggot eggs in wine, and high pressure washers all specially designed for drowning and choking; various surgical instruments of finely polished, honed and tempered silver to perform surgeries; and acid, for the truly brutal.

He stopped at the last of the doors on his right and quickly entered the room. He alone knew the combination of the locked door. He preferred to keep most of his assistants out of this room. It was his place of inspiration. It's been a long time since he'd been this excited.

Lighting a candelabra leaning next to the doorway, he watched as the room lit itself up from many years of disuse. The quiet glow of the red wax candle spread about the room and bathed it in a curious light, one that danced and leaped through the distant shadows where it couldn't quite reach. It was good enough for him.

Walking to the table in the center of the room, he studied the balsa wooded mock-up of the City of Hell. The design was easy enough to understand. There were five levels laid out like an upside-down wedding cake. The most rooms were on the top tier and each descending level got considerably more cramped for space. There were trap doors, chutes, ropes, and rudimentarily constructed stairways that allowed movement in either direction.

When he'd originally laid out the design, he'd set it up that the lower the tier on the cake, the higher the status of the prisoners. Just the opposite from the surface, where the kings and queens sit on the highest thrones to look down on the peons. In the City, the lower the level the customers attained, the higher the perception by the others. It wasn't that the levels were better the lower they went; it was just that the prisoners *perceived* them that way. Misdirection at its finest.

He chuckled softly, remembering the first time he'd realized that the prisoners were actually competing among themselves to get to a lower level, regardless of what they'd encountered there. They figured it had to be better than where they were, no matter the facts. All of his customers started on the top level of the wedding cake and tried to work their way down. Lower. Until it took on a life of its own and the lower they got, the better it was for them.

He walked across to the rows of bottled wine, hesitated just for a moment, and selected Sangria. Popping the bottle open, he picked up a glass, blew the dust off, and then poured himself a full dosage. He swirled the soft taste in his mouth for a moment while he considered his options.

Physical torture had its limits. Emotional terror was often clipped.

But psychological punishment had no boundaries.

Pure adrenaline-laced psychological terror.

If he could arrange the levels based on perception, and use what the prisoners already gave him, he could break the boundary of punishment that he'd strove so long to attain. Large or small, wide or narrow, black or white, red or neon, the size of the room didn't matter; what did matter was what happened once the door was closed. To destroy the mind in little chunks, like breaking off pieces of old cheese from a moldy wheel.

To destroy their hope.

Downing the Sangria with one last gulp, The Architect went back to the mock-up table and rearranged the sections, one at a time. He had a lot of work to do if this was going to be done correctly.

This had to be *eternal*.

CHAPTER FIVE

David Masters heard before he saw. He heard the scurrying of what sounded like rats on cobblestone. Their little paws scraped across the rocks and seemed to David to be going as fast as they could possibly go. No, not scurrying. Running. As if in terror.

David opened his eyes and blinked several times. He couldn't see a damn thing. His eyes were open and he could gauge a short distance in front of him, but otherwise, the room was completely dark. Like being in a tunnel under a cemetery. Just the rats and him. After dinner, perhaps?

He was momentarily confused. He knew the triple cocktail he received was permanent, yet here he was lying awake in the dark. There wasn't supposed to be anything else. But he could remember the sand running into this mouth and nose and filling his lungs and then everything went black.

Until now.

But this was a different blackness. There were shadows all around him. He could just make out something directly in front of him, like a black wall. It looked like it was made of black felt and that was why he couldn't focus on anything else. Someone had propped him up in front of a black wall.

No. Wrong again. As David tried to move, he quickly realized he was tied up and lying down. He could feel the pressure on his stomach and on his feet and legs, as the wall was pressed up against his face and he pushed back. He wasn't sure what caused the sensation, but it was putting a tremendous weight on his back. There was definitely something strapped to his back that kept him against this wall.

David tried to move his head and then stopped. It had no effect and whoever strapped him down on his stomach in this position had securely restrained his head from movement. He wasn't going anywhere, anytime soon.

"Mr. Masters."

David heard his name for the first time, and it sounded like the sweetest thing he had ever heard. Like the first time someone in the morgue where he worked called out his name in ecstasy as he rammed her over and over again. Thrust and withdrawal. Thrust and withdrawal. David felt some comfort as the memory lingered. He was back at home, if only for a second. The triple cocktail had obviously failed, and they were taking him back to his cell to figure out what to do with him. That had to be it.

Nothing else made sense.

"I see that you were a forensic physician in your previous life. That will serve me well, I think."

Previous life? What in the FUCK was that all about?

David tried to clear his throat and answer. "I'm not quite in a position to work this out with you at present, asshole, but if you would flip me over so I could see your fucking face, then maybe we could discuss my previous life."

David heard a deep, spirited laugh. It didn't sound pleasant.

"Listen, asshole, when my lawyer hears how you transported me back to my cell on my face, I'll make sure the whole world finds out. I'll have him put it in every paper in North America. I'll get you fired, asshole. What kind of warden are you anyway?" David was getting mad. He had rights and deserved to be treated better. He knew that someone with the ACLU or OSHA or some other agency would love to get their hands on this lawsuit. First, the triple cocktail failed and then being treated like this. It was inhumane. Hell, if it worked right, David might get out of the needle. How many times can you execute one person? There must be double jeopardy somewhere in this mess.

With a new found strength and a glimmer of hope from that argument, David tried to take control of the situation.

"Listen, warden, or whoever the fuck you are. My lawyer will have a fucking field day with this one. Now you turn me over and treat me like I deserve to be treated, or your next assignment will be in fucking Antarctica putting suntan lotion on baby seals." David almost smiled.

"Mr. Masters. I'm not a warden. And you aren't headed back to your cell," Victor stated flatly as he picked up the chart lying on the pallet next to David. "I do, however, like your attitude. Perhaps I will keep you around as one of my higher beings after the operations."

A slight shiver wracked David's body. The voice was so *cold*.

What operations? David fidgeted mightily and pry backwards against his restraints.

Threaten him, David thought. Get control. "Tell me who you are and where I am, asshole, or I start screaming. Now."

The Doctor ignored him for a moment. "I always like to give the pain babies a little idea of what's coming. It really helps the terror kick in. What fun would this be if you didn't know what was going to come?"

David suddenly decided he didn't like this one bit.

"Oh, yeah. Mr. Masters. We also like you to scream. In fact, we encourage it. To ensure that you scream as loud and as long as possible, well, we won't even use any anesthesia this time. Nurse, the four inch scalpel." Victor said as he laid the chart back down and now focused all of his attention on David.

He continued, "You're securely tied down on a conveyor belt. I had the orderlies flip you over on your stomach so I could cut into the back of your head and expose your miserably small brain. As soon as I saw you were a physician, I figured you'd have some knowledge that could help me out from time to time."

Victor licked his lips. He loved the feeling of power, the incredible feeling of dominance he got from the fear of the pain babies as they realized he was going to cut into them. The feeling was better than an orgasm with ten hookers after a margarita shower.

David cried. Where was his lawyer? This couldn't be fucking happening. Could not.

"Hold on one second, will you? Please?" David begged. It was all he had. "I am a highly respected forensic physician. I can help you in your operations. Just check out my record. It's got to be something we can talk about," David said as he sobbed. He had a terrible feeling. He did not know where he was and no idea why this animal was going to do this to him, but he knew he didn't deserve it. He was slurring his words through his tears.

"Not today. Not tomorrow or the day after either, come to think of it. Everything I need from you I will get during the operations. Notice the word 'operations' is plural, Mr. Masters. There will be more than one. When I'm finished with you, you'll be like a neutered dog in the streets. Very docile; no bite and no balls."

Victor laid the scalpel against the base of the patient's head and, using a practiced, perfected movement, pushed the scalpel just far enough in and under the hair to make a small incision through the skin. The scalpel was a dull, as Victor preferred that to a sharp one, so he had to tug and push at the same time to get it to slice all the way through the skin and strike the skull bone underneath.

David jerked as the scalpel, the same goddamn scalpel that he used on his patients, ripped into the back of his head. The pain felt like a molting kind of burning, and then his head jerked as the Doctor pushed down and cut clear through to the bone. David opened his mouth and let out one of the most impressive screams Victor had ever heard.

"Truly remarkable, Mr. Masters. Truly." Victor was grinning. He swelled with pride. This was going to be one of his finest pieces of work as Hell's Doctor. Wait until the council hears of this. The screaming power of this pain baby may be all that he needed to gain a demotion. He was almost giddy.

"Mr. Masters. I'm going to be cutting deeply into the base of your skull and then peeling aside the bone so that I can get my hand inside your skull. I wish to feel your brain."

David could feel the blood flowing down around his shoulders and could see the red drops pool below his face on the conveyor belt facing him. He screamed again and then he threatened, "Cut me loose now, you fucking asshole. Cut me loose now!"

The Doctor pulled the scalpel back across his first four-inch incision and made a cross out of the two cuts. He laid the scalpel to the side and then, pushing his fingers under each of the folds of hair and skin; he pried the four flaps backwards. When he encountered a modicum of resistance because he hadn't cut completely through the muscle, he placed his weight against the pallet by moving his hips to the edges and then he simply yanked with all of his strength.

With a sickening sound like a piece of wax paper being ripped in half, David's skin pulled itself away and clear of his skull until the base of the bone was completely exposed.

David hadn't stopped screaming and had given up all hope of dealing with these people. Whoever the hell they were, they were beyond his abilities, and he knew pleading didn't work. Maybe this was some kind of new procedure to neuter him like the Doctor said? Make him sexless without a pedigree. The pain and suffering he experienced was the most unbearable thing. Someone was pulling his skin off of his skull and David felt every single inch of pain. It was like nothing he ever imagined. Like holding his head to a cast-iron skillet and searing his skin to the pan. David thought he could actually smell his skin and muscles being pulled apart. The pool of blood on the conveyor belt in front of David had grown to a large enough spot that he was inhaling his own blood with every breath.

The Doctor was momentarily satisfied with the section of skull that he exposed and motioned to the nurse to get him the next tool. He said, "This next bit might be a little painful, Mr. Masters. I'm going to be using a drill to open your skull and a palm sander to clean out the mucus and muscle bits that get in the way. But the good news, at least from your point of view, should be that there are a considerably smaller number of nerve endings in the bone itself, so most of the pain will probably be inside your head." With that, Victor and both of the nurses broke into a belly deep laugh from the pun. "Pain in your head! Hell, that's a good one!" Victor was very pleased with himself today.

David could hear the sander rev up to life and then he smelled the distinct odor of burning flesh. His flesh. It filled his nostrils and even though the Doctor had said it wouldn't hurt, it hurt like hell. What kind of doctor was this guy?

Victor purposely let the sander linger way too long on the exposed areas of the skull. He could have done it quickly, but that was not in his demeanor. Nor would it keep him his job. It was always about the pain. Victor dusted the hair and skin and as much muscle of David Masters as the sander could accommodate. The smell was almost intoxicating to him.

David promptly passed out and as soon as he did, one orderly reached down and squeezed his testicles as hard as he could squeeze. David's body involuntarily reacted from the pain of having his balls shoved up inside his stomach and then he tried to retch, but the conveyor caught it all and it stayed directly in front of his nose for him to breathe in. David had given up anything other than crying. The screams didn't help either.

The pain was burning itself into him. He had imagined nothing could be this painful.

Victor next switched the drill on and adjusted the drill bit. He would have preferred a larger bit, but this one was three quarters of an inch in diameter and would just allow Victor enough room to wiggle his fingers into the inside of David's skull. Victor pushed down and threw all of his weight into the penetration as the drill bored into the bone.

The drill bit was far from sharp by design, and it kept catching on its own shavings and grinding to a halt. Every time it jerked to a stop, David's body would convulse, and Victor had to pry the drill bit against the hole to get it moving. One time, he actually took a small hammer and pounded the base of the drill to get it loose. And then it finally penetrated completely, and Victor pulled it out and clear to reveal a quarter-sized hole that gave a nice unobstructed view of the bottom side of David's brain.

David squirmed as best he could as he felt Victor's fingers probe inside his skull and then insert themselves into the base of his brain. It was like someone had shoved a probe up his rectum and David could feel it entering his body. His body twitched and convulsed of its own accord as Victor pushed his fingers deeper still.

Victor straightened up and shook his head. The drill bit just had not given him enough room to get his whole hand inside David's skull like he wanted, so pushing two of his forefingers back inside David's skull, Victor pried away at the sides of the hole until he felt the bone break and he could pull several small pieces of David's skull back and away from the hole to make it bigger. It was like pulling plaster from the wall of a house as bits of bone and sinew fell to the floor at his feet. Quite a bit of fun, actually. He would have to try this procedure more often.

Victor widened the hole to a size large enough that he could wedge his fist inside and then pushing with his fingers like he was giving a pregnant woman an obstetrics exam, Victor pushed the tips of two of his fingers inside the brain of David Masters. The feeling reminded Victor of when he was a child and had played with silly putty on the table at his parent's house. There was substance there, but it was pliable and could be easily manipulated.

David's body convulsed without stopping as the fingers dipped farther and farther inside his brain. His eyes rolled up into his head to see what was going on, his mouth drew the lips back over his teeth and gums as far as they would go until they eventually ripped at the sides of the mouth, and his arm strained so hard against the conveyor belt that his shoulder separated. David immediately wished he could die. Again.

CHAPTER SIX

Randi and Mack both sat staring at each other in silence for the last several minutes. Annicka was gone and Mack had taken a little time to compose himself and gather his thoughts. He had no idea where this was going to lead him or why exactly he'd been chosen, but he knew for certain that there would not be anything about the conversation he just had with Annicka that he could rely on. He'd seen this game one-too-many times before.

There was a crisp knocking at the door and then the door swung inward and both Mack and Randi watched as a man dressed in a bloody suit and coat entered cautiously into the room.

"Pardon me, sir, I'm looking for Mack Teacher?" the man said with his gaze cast downward. You never knew what kind of reception you were going to get in the City.

"I'm Mack Teacher," Mack said as he stood up from behind his battered desk. No amount of paint could hide the abuse it had taken over the years. Mack didn't know who owned the desk before him. He wasn't really sure of either how or where it came from to get to him, but it was one of those questions he refused to ask. Not knowing could be better.

"I was assigned to you," the man said.

Mack looked at him and quickly sized him up. He was tall and strong. Well built. Probably a weight lifter at some point. He also was a new arrival and had just come from the chute. He'd been humbled pretty badly and Mack could immediately sense that he was very uncomfortable and unsure of himself. There was so much for him to learn.

Mack didn't move. He didn't reach out his hand or offer anything to the man that might resemble an introduction on the surface. If he didn't have to touch someone, then he didn't. It could always turn out badly if he did, and Mack never knew how long someone would be around. Obviously, this was the help Annicka promised him. Hopefully, he still had some of his brains to go with his muscles.

"What's your name?" Mack asked. Randi had said nothing yet and Mack wasn't sure if the guy had even registered that she was sitting there.

"Byron Michaels."

"You can come in and take a seat across from this lady," he motioned to the chair directly across from Randi.

Byron nodded and then quickly and quietly took his seat as indicated. He did not wish to upset anyone.

"Did Annicka assign you to help me?" he asked Byron.

"I'm not sure who exactly told me to come here. At some point, I woke up, and the nurse told me where to go. She just pointed down a hallway, and I followed until I got to your door."

He pointed to Randi, "This is Annicka's daughter, Randi. We'll be working for her and her mother from now on until I hear differently."

"Yes, sir," Byron nodded.

Mack looked at him again as he sat with his legs crossed underneath him on the chair. He was trying to make himself as small as possible and not to attract any attention. One of his eyes was taken from him and Mack could see his optical nerve hanging loosely out of his other eye socket. It seemed to swing gently back and forth when he walked. A small trickle of blood was hanging from the end of the exposed nerve.

Randi immediately dismissed Byron from her thought process and looked back towards Mack. "Are you ready to get started, Mr. Teacher?" she asked.

He nodded. This was going to be painful. He knew Annicka was right.

Moving forward in her chair, Randi slipped one of her arms into the inside of her shirt and, as Mack watched, her left breast became completely exposed. The breast was covered by her shirt until now, but when she pulled her arm inside, it just popped out. He looked away immediately, but not before he saw the breast was not beautiful at all. It was old and wrinkled, more in the tradition and style of an eighty-year-old woman than a young woman in her early twenties. In the middle of the breast, Mack noted her nipple was gone, and it'd been replaced with a black scar. He also saw that there was so much hair on her breast that she could have passed for part gorilla. It seemed in that one glance that the hair was still actively growing. He was always good with details, but this he would rather forget.

Randi didn't hide her nudity. No one cared in this place. Modestly did not exist at any level.

Byron looked up with his one good eye and as Mack turned to face him, he could see that Byron wasn't afraid to look. He'd have to learn it was best not to stare. Ever.

He turned to Byron. "I'm not sure what you know, but Annicka is a council member. She has ordered me, and now you I guess, to find something called the 'Black Rose.'"

Byron nodded, but said nothing. If he was going to help, Mack would have to get him to talk, but he wasn't sure to what extent his brain power ran. He would have to wait and see about that.

Randi pulled aside her shirt and, from out of a pocket that was covered up, she produced a rolled-up piece of colored paper. It was old and yellowed by many years of use or misuse, and could've been stored somewhere down here for ages. Mack couldn't even fathom a guess how long it might have been here.

She adjusted her shirt back into place and covered up her exposed breast. He was at least grateful for that. She then moved forward and laid the parchment onto the end of the desk.

He reached out and motioned for Byron to get closer and look at the paper with him.

"Do you have any kind of investigation skills, Byron?" he asked as he grabbed the paper and fingered it gently.

"I was a cop in the narcotics division of Los Angeles for thirteen years before this."

Mack nodded. He had run across more than one former police officer in the City. But this might be a solid find. If Byron could help at all, he would be much closer to finding this thing Annicka wanted.

"Where did you get this from, Randi?" he asked as he slipped the tie off the end of the parchment.

"My sister gave it to me to keep several years ago. I've been hiding it ever since."

"You mother knew you had this?" Byron asked as he stood up to look over Mack's shoulder.

"She knew. But she wasn't sure what value it had until recently. We're still not sure. Not completely."

Byron glanced quickly at Mack at the same time that Mack looked at him. If they weren't sure of the value, why have the scroll looked at now? They obviously knew the value and what the scroll signified. Mack knew Byron read her lie. That was a good sign that he retained some of his cop's instincts. He would need them later. Mack was sure of that.

Mack looked at Randi before he unrolled the scroll. "I didn't know you had a sister."

Randi shook her hair back. "She's my twin sister, actually. Mother has plans for her, also."

He didn't doubt for one second that statement was true. Every council member made plans for everyone they came into contact with. One continuous scheme. Otherwise, they wouldn't last long on the council.

He unrolled and spread the faded yellow paper out to its fullest length on the top of his desk. It probably measured about sixteen by twenty inches when it was originally produced, but all the time hiding somewhere shortened the length. The edges were frayed and torn away in several spots. Mack couldn't hazard a guess as to its age, but the writing on the paper was still fairly legible.

Across the scroll was a relatively clear picture of two roses wrapped around each other. They were entwined down the length of their stems and at the top the petals faced each other like the heads of two snakes squaring off against each other:

At the center of the scroll, there was an extensive poem or limerick. He couldn't be sure which, but he knew immediately that he was going to have to solve the riddle to find the rose:

To touch the petals
Of a Rose made of sin
The answers increase
Under folds of human skin.

A key to the hunter
On bloody wheels of steel
Rides a corpse without an eye
Who becomes the meal.

Some rats in a maze
Who dine on bone marrow
Will chew off their legs
And the heads of dead sparrows.

Red blood and black night
Take a risk before
Chances are won
In a circus of gore.

When the Rose becomes one
And the black burns bright
Havoc is foretold
And change destroys the night.

Mack read it out loud slowly a second time and then looked first at Byron, who shook his head back and forth, and then towards Randi. She lost interest, as she apparently had read it many times before.

"You have no idea what any of this means, do you?" he asked her.

"If I fucking knew some of this, we wouldn't have come to you, would we?"

Byron kept reading the scroll as she stood up and headed towards the door.

"I will not be accompanying you on this journey, Mr. Teacher. But I will be looking in on you from time to time to see how you are progressing. I have other matters that require my attention. You will search for the Black Rose. It means a great deal to my mother, so I would suggest that you and Mr. Michaels begin immediately. I will let you keep the scroll to use as you see fit, but I expect to get it back after this little adventure."

Already a problem. Annicka told him that Randi would accompany him on the journey. If he showed up and Randi wasn't with him, it wouldn't be good for him.

She opened the door and then stopped one last time and looked back at him. "We've been looking for this for some time, Mr. Teacher. Trying to figure out what it all means. Be aware that other council members are also searching for the Rose and even as we speak, their search has started. If you don't find the Rose first, my mother will deal with you very severely."

"One more thing, Randi," Mack said as an idea hit him. "If you've been looking for this for some time, where would you suggest we start?"

A chilling smile crept slowly across Randi's face as she looked first at Mack and then at Byron.

"Try the Funhouse. There's something in the Machine Room you might find interesting."

With that, she left the room and the door quietly closed behind her.

CHAPTER SEVEN

As Victor curled two fingers delicately around the brain stem of David Masters and then pushed the fingers as far as they could go into the lower portion of David's brain, he couldn't help but smile. This was an old technique that was taught to Victor by the previous doctor in this ward. Victor figured the procedure was as close to being a "perk" as the fucking ingrates that ran this arrival wing of the City could muster for one of their doctors. If he could find the right ganglia to attach his primary fingers to, then Victor could garner all the information that the patient had gathered during his time on the surface. It could be passed onto the Doctor through his fingers in one glorious moment. Like drinking a refreshing glass of wine from the blood of one of his patients and keeping all the secrets that the blood holds.

Only this type of gathering proved considerably more painful for the patient. Not to mention the enjoyment for the Doctor. Victor always liked this procedure. He didn't think he would ever teach anyone else how to do it. The idiot that taught him had only enabled him to take over his role as arrival doctor. That guy wasn't the sharpest pitch fork in the City.

David's eyes rolled completely up into his head and the only thing anyone looking at them from underneath the table could have seen would've been pure white eyeballs. The pupils had turned completely around and gone inside his head to see what was going on in his brain. David hadn't passed out because of the orderlies continually twisting a small pair of pliers around his right testicle. Whenever it seemed like he would succumb to unconsciousness and pass out from the pain, the orderlies knew how to keep him awake. It was their only job.

The orderlies had tightened down the straps that held his arms and legs securely to the conveyor belt at Victor's order. The Doctor didn't like the patients flopping around as their bodies invariably convulsed. They could push against the nylon straps all they wanted as long as they couldn't move their heads and possibly move his fingers out of position. Once he found the correct spot, he didn't want to have it moved and possibly lose the connection. Like moving one of those old rabbit eared TV antennas and watching the picture fade out.

David was moaning now and occasionally letting little sounds escape his throat. They were scratchy sounds like sandpaper on a chalkboard and satisfied Victor that he was aware of what was going on.

The Doctor moved his two fingers slightly left and then right, looking for just the right set of nerve endings and synapses inside David's brain. He was almost gleeful with anticipation. This kept him going day in and day out. Taking something from some poor bastard that had no hope of stopping the process and could only suffer underneath his hand. Like sex with a virgin on prom night. Oh, so sweet. Chocolate over strawberries and bloody panties all at once. It didn't get any better than this to him.

Just at that moment, Victor shivered as a small electrical impulse rushed down from the ends of his fingertips into his wrist and he knew he found the entrance to the deepest memories of David Masters. All the knowledge the patient possessed would now be his.

There was a small gasp of air released by the Doctor as he clamped his two fingers around that particular nerve, and then closed his eyes and let the feeling overwhelm him. It was like an avalanche of sensations as his arms and legs went limp and the electrical energy from deep inside David Masters' cerebellum rushed up the fingers and into the bloodstream of Victor Stevens. His very essence became a part of his very being. The two were merged as one, and all that was David became a part of Victor. They were separate, but still tied together. The tiny shocks of electric energy inside David's brain fired and released all of their endorphins into his bloodstream to relieve the pain as his life was sucked into the Doctor.

Like the purest heroin on the streets, Victor felt revived. Every sense he owned screamed for attention. He kept his eyes locked tightly and let the life of his patient flood his mind.

David Masters sat in front of the dead body on the gurney in his lab. It'd been a strenuous day to say the least. The police were hounding him and he could feel the net snaring itself with him inside. He never needed this. He didn't think they were smart enough to catch him, but somehow it happened. It had all come crashing down.

When he was originally hired, he knew his job was a perfect fit. Unlike most of the people who went into the forensic pathologist profession, David felt a genuine affinity for the dead bodies on the slabs. In fact, that affinity caused him the most problems.

At first, he would lovingly undress the bodies brought to his morgue. It had become a ceremony, almost. The hospital people or the police or whoever the lackeys were that deposited the newly dead onto his doorstep had no idea of the painstaking steps he would go through to make sure that each and every body was treated with love and respect. Most of the other pathologists would roughly handle the bodies like they were raw pieces of uncooked beef that had no sensitivity. But he knew differently. They had been someone when alive; in his morgue they were again someone.

And the stupid hospital staff had grudgingly come to admit David's genius with the bodies. The way he posed them after the autopsies was pure poetry. An artistic expression by any stretch of the imagination.

And David had truly stretched his imagination as he dealt with the bodies.

At first, he hadn't enjoyed being left alone with all the bodies on the night shift. The ones that died of natural causes were the easiest to deal with because they died without any visible markings. When he undressed them for the first time, they looked like normal people. Cold, but normal.

The gunshot victims were the first ones to turn his head. When he got used to the frozen strands of blood that coagulated outside of the bullet holes and also on their clothes, David would clean it up and then take pictures.

Oh, the pictures. What he could do with those.

The first time he went home and masturbated to one of the pictures he took from the night before had been traumatic. He closed the drapes at his apartment after a tough night with three gunshot victims. One victim was an elderly woman who smeared on makeup and plastic surgery like the rest of the world drank water. But she was pretty in her own way.

The pictures of her were truly magnificent and he couldn't help but take a couple of extra for himself. One or two for a home collection wouldn't even be remotely missed. When he pulled out her picture that morning in the dark of his apartment, his hand simply strayed to his penis and then before he knew what had happened, he orgasmed with the intensity of a bullet shattering a glass cabinet. This was something he would have to do again, no matter the consequences.

The pleasure overtook the shame by leaps and bounds. There was really no comparison.

What had started at home became a nightly event in the hospital morgue. The lights would go down around two am when the last of the regular staff left and then he would be alone. Just him and the bodies. New ones and usually pretty fresh.

The masturbation turned to oral sex and then to straight sex. Men and woman. Black and white. Lukewarm was alright if they were really fresh, but David liked them the best when they were ice cold. The feeling was indescribable and sent him on a sexual adventure that he hadn't anticipated or could have possibly imagined.

But then David noticed something. The warmer the bodies, the more the corpses seemed to react to *him*.

Oh, the bodies were all dead alright. Some bodies he had sex with were several hours dead and in a couple of instances, some of them were several days old. The stench didn't affect him because he could cover that by placing a small amount of candle wax directly underneath his nose, and then he could smell lilac or the scent of vanilla the whole time.

But some of the fresher corpses, especially the middle-aged women, actually responded to his sex acts. Oh, the movements were never visible to the naked eye, but still he knew. He could feel it as he grunted over them and then released his semen deep into one of their body cavities. Any cavity was alright. After all, he was the one who would write up the report on their death. He could easily overlook some small trace amounts of semen in their eyes, noses, ears, vaginas, anuses or whatever.

But when he realized the cadavers responding to him, the curiosity overtook him. At some point, he'd been a trained and dedicated doctor of pathology who looked for answers in the flesh. This was no different. There were answers he had to know. He was like a pit bull with a crushed larynx in its mouth. He just couldn't let it go. He had to know. Had to find out why.

The initial search led him to expect the freshest arrivals at the morgue. He was like a child with a new toy every time the ambulance pulled up to the back dock, and the paramedics unloaded the body. He looked forward to it.

He pulled the gurneys in and then quickly assessed the body. He took the temperature anally because that was the most reliable and also the best indicator of time of death. If there was any warmth left in the body, he would immediately climb on top and insert himself into the body somewhere so he could enjoy it while being always conscious of the reaction that followed.

The warmer the temperature, the more they reacted to his thrusts.

Thrust and withdrawal. Thrust and withdrawal.

Such ecstasy.

David learned that if he got the body at the right temperature, then he could feel the sensation that drove him into a frenzy. But it only lasted six or seven minutes. That wasn't long enough to satisfy him completely, so he looked to prolong the warmth. Prolong the sensation. Prolong the *reaction*.

He pored over all the books he could find on pathology and the effects of temperature on the decaying body. And then he found it. It could only be one thing. Had to be one thing. Had to be it.

The six to eight minutes the brain lived on after the body died.

It was a well-documented fact that the brain stored enough blood and oxygen to support itself in the event that the body died. The brain was the most selfish of all the body's organs. It knew that it had to survive and did everything it could to ensure that. Storing blood and oxygen was like a mountain climber that took extra supplies in case of a disaster. It just made sense. The brain had to insure its own survival.

So, the brain could live on its own, and David could use that to his advantage. Especially if he could extend it.

The results of his find only made David realize he had to get the corpses at the freshest point possible. The only way to do that was to be there when they died, and since David wasn't that lucky, he would have to kill them himself.

That's when he abducted the girls and when the state trooper saw the piece of clothing hanging from the trunk of his car.

It all went badly after that.

Victor withdrew his two fingers from the brain of David and then shook away the hanging shreds of his brain cells that clung to his fingers. He grabbed a cloth and wiped some of the gray matter off of his fingers and then summarily wiped the rest of the cells and hanging ganglia on his pants and shirt. He stood up and took a moment to compose himself as he came down from his high.

He focused his eyes and stared at the now convulsing body of his patient tied to the table before him. This was an interesting subject.

On the one hand, he was a trained pathologist and would have information about some of the finer points of death that Victor could probably use in the doling out of the Doctor's service to the pain babies.

But David Masters had so much more going for him that Victor could use. He had worked on extending the time the brain was alive after the body died. That could prove to be an invaluable fact to know in the City. If he had extended the time until brain death, it could theoretically keep the portal between the surface and the City open longer.

Possibly open the portal on *command*.

Opening the portal for even a minute more could please the council members so much that they might even demote Victor to a lower level. If Masters had been successful, then the Doctor could use that to improve his standing in the City. If the time the brain was alive could be extended, then the portal that allowed the new arrivals to be dragged to Hell could also be extended. Theoretically, at least.

Deciding on which path that he'd now go after, Victor realized that he would have to take special care of David Masters and not let him get out of his sight until he got all the secrets out of him.

"This man was a forensic pathologist in his former life. I will make him my personal intern and train him to use his skills to the benefit of the council members here in the City," Victor said out loud to no one in particular. He knew that anything proclaimed would find itself glued to the ears of the council members. They had minions everywhere and were always watching. Almost everyone in the City was scared to open their mouths at all for fear that they would be noticed and punished even more. Open proclamations were always an event.

The Doctor bent back over the body of David as he continued to twitch on the table. Reaching two fingers into the hole in the back of his head that he just pulled them out of, Victor searched for and finally found the pieces of David he was trying to find.

Victor wrapped his two fingers around the brain stem of David, and then, sliding them down precisely three and a half inches, he let his fingers probe the C1 and then the C2 vertebras at the top of David's spinal column. He positioned his fingers in the small section at the back of the vertebra and then, twisting slightly and tugging, he promptly pulled the vertebra loose at first and then finally completely free of all restraints from the brain stem and then the other vertebra. He twisted his hand back and forth and then pulled the vertebra out of the hole in David's head.

Pulling the bloody and freshly freed vertebra up to look at, Victor surveyed them. They were of normal size and color, and as far as he could tell, smelled alright. He flicked his tongue out quickly and ran it over the out rims of the vertebra. Even when he was on the surface, he liked the taste of blood. There was nothing like it. Rich and salty in some pain babies, dark and sweet in others.

David's was a little of both. Just right for the Doctor's pallet.

Dropping the vertebras on the floor and then kicking them under the operating table, he stepped back from the table. David's body stopped moving momentarily and seemed to relax against the nylon bindings. Victor nodded to the orderlies, who stepped up and then untied the patient. The operation and his official welcome to the City were over.

Victor would take care of David from here on out.

He looked over at the orderlies standing to his right. "Bring this man to my office," he said as he walked away from the table and left the operating room. Victor's mind was alive with all the possibilities this presented.

CHAPTER EIGHT

Mack looked over at Byron after Randi left and motioned to him they should leave. He nodded and fell in step. He didn't know where they were going, and he sure as hell didn't want to lead. He would have preferred to be completely invisible.

"Would it be okay if I asked you some questions, Mr. Teacher?" he asked without looking up as they walked down a hallway. Mack had taken the scroll with him and was reading it as they went.

He stopped reading and looked ahead, not really acknowledging Byron's question. He knew Byron had just arrived. The pain babies were always terrified, as well as they should be. No amount of comforting or answering of questions could change that. Mack had been here a long time, and he was terrified. So was almost everyone.

Byron had said nothing else and took Mack's silence as meaning that he shouldn't have asked the question. He hoped he wouldn't be punished for opening his mouth.

"It's okay, Byron. I know you're scared shitless. I am too. This isn't going to go well for either of us. I'll try and answer your questions as best as I can, but I've survived here by not asking too many questions. It's best not to be noticed."

Byron nodded as the two of them walked. He assumed the hallway was covered with black windows, and that no one could see out. They were all smeared with some kind of residue that reminded him of a house after a five alarm fire. There were white and black ashes everywhere and he couldn't see a damn thing. The windows had molten shit hanging all over them. There was nothing to look at, anyway. He could only imagine what image someone had placed the windows here to view.

"There's nothing to look at. The windows don't go anywhere. They were probably a cruel joke at some point. If you could see out some of them, whatever you saw would scare the hell out of you," Mack said.

"How'd you know what I was thinking? Can you read my mind?" Byron asked, perplexed.

"No. I don't have that ability. But trust me, many people and things here do have that ability. I just haven't been given it. I just remembered what I thought the first time I went down this hallway."

Byron nodded. "I know where we are, but where are we really? I mean physically? Like in the center of the earth or something?"

Mack shook his head. "I can't begin to answer that, and I'm not sure anyone we meet can answer that. Haven't really thought about it, actually."

"What did you mean when you said 'things' a minute ago? What kinds of things can we run into?"

Mack stopped and turned to face him. "What I can tell you for sure is that the physical laws from the surface don't apply here. There isn't anything like physics that controls movement or ability. You can't count on anyone or anything here."

Byron nodded. "Can I trust anyone?"

Mack shook his head. "We're all here because we deserve it for some reason or another. There is no honor among thieves. Nothing like that. No friends. No relationships. Hell, you could meet your mother here and she'd cut your balls off if it meant she wouldn't have to endure another punishment for three minutes."

Just then, a loud, long wail pierced the hallway. Byron was reminded of a hunting trip he'd taken and, in the center of the woods, he'd come across an animal trapped in a bear trap that was chewing off one of its legs to escape. Same kind of forlorn sound. No hope. That was the sound. He shuddered involuntarily.

Mack stared hard at him. "We aren't friends. Nor will we be. We have a job to do and if it means we won't have to endure direct punishment, then that's what we'll do. Don't count on anyone but yourself here."

Byron looked down at the floor with his one eye. The other eye he had retrieved from the rats that were chewing on it and stuffed it in his pants. "Pain babies?"

Mack turned around and started walking again. "A general term used to describe all the new arrivals. The pain seems to be the most intense for them. They start at the top level where the physical torture takes place. You can hear them scream from clear down here sometimes. They progress down to the next level after a while, I guess. I'm not sure how it works, really. You get used to the screams. It doesn't faze me anymore."

"Levels? Like floors?"

"Yeah. Five of them. The top level where all the patrons first enter the City is called 'Havoc.' Physical pain and continuous torture. Dismemberments, burnings, water tortures, flesh eating, skin peeling, and general things of that nature. Things to avoid. Below that's the 'Funhouse.' Physiological torture. We're on the third floor called the 'Womb.' Like with a protected fetus. Generally they keep you here if they can use you in some form or another. Below us is where the council members are. The lowest level is reserved for him."

Byron shuddered involuntarily. He knew who Mack meant. "Which is the worst?"

"Probably the 'Funhouse.' Cardiac arrests are daily events. Many of the patrons are driven mad within hours of arriving. Totally and utterly insane."

"How long have you been here, Mr. Teacher?"

Mack shook his head. "I have no idea. The passage of time doesn't exist here. There isn't any way to gauge it. There are no clocks or doors to the outside to estimate sunrise and nightfall. You won't need to sleep here, so you can't tell when a day has passed. Time is one thing I don't like to think much about."

The hallway widened slightly and as Byron looked, there didn't seem to be any end to it. As far as he could see, the hallway went on. Like looking into black mirrors that were facing each other and gave off the impression of infinity. There was black shit hanging on the walls, and as he turned and looked closer, it seemed to descend. Rather, it appeared to be sliding down in one continuous motion. Not stopping, but just disappearing into the side of the floor. But there were no cracks. Nothing determined where the walls stopped, and the floor began. The physical lines didn't exist.

And the smell was like nothing he'd ever imagined. It was like someone had combined three or four different chemicals together and mixed them up in a jar before throwing the contents up into the air and letting them drift on the winds. The smell was everywhere and likened itself to old dog shit that clung to your shoes for a couple of days and the smell just followed you around. Wherever you went. Always with you, but just under the surface.

"No physical rules. So I guess the things you referred to earlier are...."

"Monsters. Whether you believe in them or not, you're going to encounter things here that just shouldn't *be*. Should not exist in this or any other world. Designed for one thing - to terrify anyone who encounters them. And they will reach into the darkest corners of your psyche and pull out your deepest fears. That's how they work here. If you ever imagined it, the council members or administrators or room mothers will somehow conjure it up to work on you specifically. There is no absence of terror or imagination here."

"Room mothers? Council members? Is there a hierarchy here?"

Mack thought for a second before he answered. He didn't know this pain baby and didn't, for one second, trust him. He could work for Annicka as easily as being sent here to help him out. There were no good alliances here.

"Room mothers handle the individual rooms. They are the first line of administration and their only job is to get the patrons to scream as loud and as long as they can. Room mothers are what the patrons call them. It's short for room mother fuckers."

He paused and then continued, "Each of the five levels have a floor administrator. They keep an eye on the room mothers and look for new pain babies to promote to room mothers. If the screams from the room are loud enough to get noticed, the floor administrators take a look inside to see what's going on. You can't imagine some of the depravity that's a daily event here. You're going to see some of it as we search for this Rose. If it even exists."

"I don't understand, Mr. Teacher. Why wouldn't the Rose exist? Why would they send us on this if we aren't able to find it or it didn't exist?"

"You need to keep four numbers in your mind at all times here, Byron."

"What numbers? Will they help me?"

"5317," Mack said as he stopped and held up his hand for Byron to stop also. There was something up ahead coming towards the two of them at a rapid pace, and Mack was obviously concerned.

CHAPTER NINE

Annicka glided along. She was not hovering per se, nor was she floating, but riding effortlessly and soundlessly along the corridors. As she moved, small eddies of dirt and garbage that were scattered along her path swept themselves out of the way.

The corridors were empty and Annicka made her way with purpose. She'd been summoned and must answer the call, but she had business before that required her attention first. She knew that not going to one of the council meetings immediately could end up unpleasantly for her, but the information she sought was worth the pain. It might prove helpful to her at some later point, and in the City, information was a powerful bargaining tool.

Gliding and turning, she made no announcement of her presence to anyone. She transcended to a lower level than she normally visited and although she held no fear on this level, caution was still necessary. This was the fourth level and the council's home. There was danger and discomfort everywhere and she had neither the time nor the inclination to partake of it. Not now. Maybe at a later point she could handle it. But not at present.

She closed her eyes that had turned to coal black and seamlessly let herself move among the patrons at this level. Those that she ran into would realize her status as a lower being and move out of her way. Most would not even risk a glance up at her, fearing her wrath and their pain, but those who were protected by one of the other council members would not avert her gaze. They harbored no threat from her, but they still must respect her presence.

Stopping herself with her subconscious completely in control of her movements, Annicka entered a doorway that was invisible to the naked eye and left the corridor. Her eyes reopened into the total blackness of the room, but she could see easily. Lights were not needed for the council members.

She hovered above the ground approximately two inches and waited silently to be acknowledged. It was not her place to speak first to the man in front of her. If she truly felt like pressing the issue, she could have treated him as any other higher being and demanded what she wanted from him or simply took what she needed as she saw fit. But this was no ordinary patron in front of her. His ability to provide information made him a formidable foe, and she didn't know who protected him. When dealing with him, caution was the best practice.

The patron did not look up from the book he was studying at the moment. This room was as close to a library as could be found in the City and there were several old parchments and badly damaged books in apparently random order strewn about the shelves and on the floor. She knew this patron continually read all the information in here and could recite verse upon verse when needed. His memory was never questioned and he would never lie to a council member. It was the insurance that kept him in this place and relatively unpunished.

He looked up at her for the first time, stopping his reading. "Annicka," he stated simply.

The Professor was as near to a normal-looking man as you could find anywhere in the City. He retained all of his appendages and carried very few scars from punishments. His mostly bald scalp ended with a very shiny forehead, although it was dusty from years of not washing. He had little white tufts of hair encircling his ears and pointing upward in different places. He wore broken glasses that were taped in the middle a long time ago, with one lens clearly missing. He wore a tattered and ancient tweed suit with a bow tie that at one time must've been white with brown polka dots. The Professor also sported severely yellowed teeth that showed through when he spoke and a faint mustache and goatee that turned to gray many years ago. In short, he looked like a typical college librarian that you might encounter on the surface in any number of places.

"Professor," Annicka replied.

He nodded at the simple greeting. Neither of them deferred to the other. It was a simple game replayed many times in this room, with each of the council members at one point or another.

"What do you want? As you can see, I am clearly busy."

"You will address me correctly, Professor, or I will take actions," Annicka stated.

"I will worry about that at another time. Do you not have a council meeting to attend at present? I am surprised to find you here instead of there," he replied.

Annicka's eyes flared to a callous black as she thought about his comment for just a second. His knowledge of the meeting only further showed that one or more of the council members was his sponsor.

"Your knowledge appears to be quite extensive, Professor. I must be gone from here quickly. What can you tell me about the Black Rose?"

He nodded as if he expected the question and then turned his back on her. Normally this simple act of defiance would have enraged her and she would've instantly struck him down, but the knowledge he could give her and the advantage she'd gain from that information was critical and worth the temporary snub. She would, however, not forget it. Revenge could be a long time coming.

The Professor turned back around towards her as he pulled a simple tome from some hidden shelf that Annicka hadn't seen. Whether the book was hidden didn't matter. He was in charge of the information, not the books.

He opened the book and began leafing through long aged pages of yellow and streaked black, as well as partially missing pages. Entire sections were ripped out from several of the tomes in the library, but what was there was accurate. It was one of the few things he could count on.

"The Black Rose..." he started and then let his voice trail off. "It's considered to be one of the great prizes in the City. Whoever possesses it will control great power."

"I am aware of that, Professor, but what power does it grant specifically?"

He looked down again and a small amount of spit from a long dead saliva gland fell off his mouth and onto the pages of the book. He continued without noticing or stopping as he flipped through the pages, slowly at first and then more rapidly. With a triumphant "Aha," he at last stopped and pointed to one of the sections. His fingers, gnarled through the ages and curled up under themselves from bad arthritis, followed along with the words as he read them to himself. One of the few pleasures he got was when a council member needed him.

He sighed and took off his glasses and then rubbed his eyes, savoring each and every moment of Annicka's impatience. He put the broken glasses back on the bridge of his nose and then looked into the dark eyes of Annicka.

"The Black Rose, according to this tome, can help to manipulate the portal."

Annicka nodded and her red, black and white hair seemed to flow out farther behind her. As she levitated and thought about what the Professor said, a small glow, like firelight, illuminated behind her. "Manipulate it how?"

"Well, as you know, Annicka, the portal allows the pain babies to be summoned to the City. The portal opens and we extract them. It has always worked like that."

Annicka was quickly growing impatient, both with the continued use of her name by this higher being, and the time it was taking him to get her the information. She wouldn't forget this transgression. If she could get rid of his sponsor on the council, then she could deal with him. Perhaps, she could even turn him to become one of her minions.

"Continue," she said as the fire behind her grew and branched out and was now putting out a considerable amount of heat into the room. The darkness dissolved and a soft glow hung between them from the light.

"Well," he paused for effect, "according to this passage right here, the Black Rose allows the portal to be reversed."

"Reversed?" Annicka had risen farther off the floor and the colors that illuminated from behind her back had alternately changed like a kaleidoscope. The higher she levitated, the faster the colors changed. First red, then black, then gray, yellow, orange, and blue. The colors became increasingly intense and crystal clear. And then repeated. A personal rainbow.

"Annicka. The portal only goes down. To the City. It was designed that way. The Black Rose has the power to reverse the direction. The portal could then go up."

Annicka's colors were coming so rapidly that the room was a virtual carousel of color. "Up?"

"Yes," the Professor said. "Up. To the surface."

Satisfied, Annicka glided away through the unseen door and back into the corridor as the Professor stood silently. He was waiting for him. He knew he would come in just a moment. He always came.

From behind where the Professor stood, a shimmering wave appeared, and the shape advanced into the room. The Professor stood silently and waited for him to assume the form of his choice.

"Have you been listening?" the Professor asked.

Stapleton nodded as he silently crawled around the room like a sliding slug. He seemed to be everywhere at once and nowhere in particular. He was pleased. Very pleased.

"You have done well, Professor."

"I am sure she will intensify the search now that she has the knowledge. The power of the Black Rose is immense."

Stapleton nodded. He was well aware of its power.

With a flick of his transparent head, he dismissed himself and left the room.

He had much work to do.

CHAPTER TEN

Mack heard it before he saw it. The first of the noises hit him as he was facing Byron and trying to answer some of the simpler questions. Answers he was fairly sure were correct. Although most of the patrons in the City would lie to a pain baby for the sheer pleasure of it, that had never been one of Mack's strengths. He would at least call it like he saw it until he had to lie, then it would be whatever was needed for survival.

Mack turned to look further down the hallway in the direction they were traveling. He at first thought he heard distant drums like an army approaching, but as the sounds got closer, he could clearly make out the whine of a machine. It was moving towards them at a steady pace and would be on them in a few minutes. He could see something like a headlight illuminating the tunnel and coming at them.

CLUMP. CLUMP. CLANG.

Mack thought it sounded like a steam furnace that they used to put in some of the old-fashioned hotels in New York. The damned things never worked quite right and when they weren't making noises, they were hissing steam at you. He had never forgotten the sound of those furnaces.

CLUMP. CLUMP. CLINK.

The machine may have been moving steadily towards them, but Mack knew it didn't sound like a finely tuned instrument at all. Some gears were obviously grinding themselves to dust and making more noise the farther the damn thing went. It announced its presence for all to notice.

Mack turned to Byron and motioned for him to lean back against the wall and to make himself as small as he could. Byron didn't need any more encouragement than that and flattened himself up against the slimy wall as best as he could. He wanted to be about five inches tall at that point.

CLOMP. CLOMP. CLANG.

As it got closer, Mack could see that the machine was hanging upside-down from the ceiling and making deep tracks into hard tile. Large clumps of dirt and debris fell behind it, and it looked to Mack like the thing was being driven by a single horizontal tank track. The track ran the length of the machine from front to back and churned at a steady pace.

The machine was a long cylindrical tube that literally hung suspended from the ceiling. It was an odd color of school bus yellow and rust and blood stains that covered it from the front to the back. Hanging from the center of the cylinder and directly in the middle was a tarnished cage of rusted metal. It looked to be about five feet tall and a couple of feet wide. A driver sat there and manipulated some kind of control panel.

The machine driver was wearing a torn black cloak that covered his body from head to toe and hid every visible part of the driver from prying eyes. But it seemed to Mack that the driver, though his face was invisible, was thoroughly enjoying himself.

With a couple of practiced and precise movements, the driver rapidly massaged his panel. Mack couldn't see what he was doing exactly from his vantage point, and could not even guess what the control manipulations accomplished, but it appeared to be almost a sexual bonding. As if the driver and machine had become one.

In front of the machine were three completely naked people, two men and a woman, running as fast as they could along the ground. They were all roped to the machine with a heavy, industrial strength chain like someone would use to pull a tractor. The chains were attached directly to a manacle that encircled the necks of each of the three people.

CLOMP. CLOMP. CLINK.

The two men and one woman were desperately trying to get away from the machine as it continued to churn ever forward. They had strained the chains as far as they could, out until the chains were taught against both the machine and the necks of each of them. Mack stood staring when he heard a distant sound, like a school bell ringing. It rang and rang.

The three people on the chains wrenched themselves in fear at the sound of the bell and strained even tighter. They were facing away from the machine and each of them struggled to break the chains. They would alternately claw at the manacle around their neck and then pull against the chain itself. All to no avail. The manacles were clearly cutting into the skin around each of their necks, but it didn't stop their desperate actions. Mack could see that they were terrified and were trying to run away from the pain like dogs on leashes.

With another deafening squelch as if metal were hitting metal, a door on the bottom of the machine opened and then a large, three-pronged metal set of fingers stretched out from the base of the machine. The fingers flexed themselves and made a screeching metal on metal scraping sound as they stretched to their full lengths. The three fingers then reached out like the tines of a fork and planted themselves into the ground directly behind the chained patrons.

The woman shrieked and struggled mightily against the chain and the manacle that choked her throat. She had to get away. She was screeching like a cat in heat as she struggled to get as far physically from the tines as possible.

The tines extended themselves ever nearer to each of the patrons, and the machine kept advancing with a steady clanking sound. CLANK. CLANK. CLINK. With a last lunge, the woman turned around and nearly strangled herself on the manacle. She coughed once and Mack got his first chance to view her back and also the backs of the other two as they ran past where he and Byron were hiding.

The woman's buttocks and back were completely devoid of skin and reduced simply to hanging muscle. The entire image was like looking at something from an anatomy book on muscles. The skin was still hanging on in some places, but for all intents and purposes, it had been stripped away, inch by inch. Her buttocks had been carved into portions of meat like a grinder might produce for good hamburger, and they were bleeding. Pieces of flesh were everywhere.

Byron had melted into the wall as far as he could. He wanted no part of this and wanted neither the machine nor the dark driver to notice him. As he pressed farther back against the wall, he felt something wet. It started at the base of his spine and then progressed upwards slowly, and Byron realized it was *inside* his shirt. If he didn't know better, he would have been certain that the wall had opened and was licking him. The wetness continued up to his neck and then stopped and made a small circle and then descended again. Like someone tasted him for later on.

Byron tried to pull slightly away from the wall but faced with a choice between what he was witnessing in front of him and what was happening behind his back, he thought it might be to better to let the wall lick him. If that's all there was.

The first fingers to reach inside the back of his shirt, and then snake themselves up his back along the trail of the wetness, did more damage to Byron's psyche than he could have thought possible. He didn't know where the hands had come from, let alone whose body they were connected to, and he didn't want to know. He would have to move a little farther away from the wall. Being close was not good.

As Byron tried to step away, the fingers became arms and quickly encircled his chest and hugged him to the wall. He was trapped and glanced over at Mack, who was in the same predicament. There were three pairs of arms holding Mack up against the wall. Neither of them could get free. They would have to endure whatever was going to happen. Getting away was not an option as Byron felt a second and then a third pair of arms encircle his legs and then his head. He was effectively pinned.

Byron looked back as the tines stretched themselves to the perfect height and angle to slice cleanly through the woman's buttocks in a downward motion. The tines were stationary for just a second and then they were raised again and planted firmly on the ground. The length had been exactly measured to allow the three patrons to be just inside their cutting zone. The machine was deftly accurate and precisely designed. The tines were raised and lowered by the shadowy driver in the black cloak and with each downward slice, the tines would implant themselves into the flesh of each of the patrons to a deliberate depth. The more the patrons ran away, the more the razor sharp tines sliced off the meat from their backs and buttocks. If they fell to the ground or quit running, the tines would slice cleanly through them and cut them in half. A perfect machine for what it did. Simple and painful.

One of the two men stumbled for just a second and the tines promptly sliced through his left foot and cut off all of his toes. He screamed and scrambled to grab them as the motion flipped the toes behind the machine and out of his view. He could not stop for even a second to try and get them back as he turned and struggled to keep running away.

The machine CLANKED, CLANKED, AND CLOMPED one last time as it passed Mack and then Byron. The three people could be heard screaming down the hallway and Byron turned his attention the other way as the arms loosened their grip and he fell into step behind Mack.

With a last glance at the driver, Mack pulled back suddenly and pushed himself against the wall when he realized the driver had turned and was staring directly at him. The driver had no face, and as far as Mack could tell, no eyes or facial features at all save for one: a large gap-toothed split grin. Here was a man who loved his job.

CLANK. CLANK. CLUNK.

Mack shuddered and watched as the parade disappeared into the darkness and the screams of the three patrons died down to silence in the distance.

It was an image that he wouldn't forget for a long time.

CHAPTER ELEVEN

David Masters couldn't help himself. He sat in a chair in Victor's office on the other side of the desk facing the Doctor. He had taken no time to analyze his situation and think about where he was and what exactly was happening to him so far, but that moment would just have to wait. At present, he was trying to figure out how to stop the convulsions.

He sat as straight as he could manage in the high-backed chair. But sitting wasn't really the correct word. He didn't just sit; he flopped. He wiggled. He squirmed. He moved and twitched. His body did whatever the hell it wanted and he couldn't control it any more than he could control the weather. He was like a Mexican jumping bean hyped up on an adrenaline shot. He could not stop flopping, no matter how hard he tried.

David would stand up and then sit down. His leg would stretch and convulse and then release as his other leg moved. His right arm was curled into a ball and kept slapping back and forth like a chicken wing. His spine would shake and then shudder and his head would throw itself side to side with each shake of his back. He couldn't stop any of it.

Victor sat across from him behind a small and aged desk that had seen better days. He inherited this office from the previous doctor and the desk with it. They were both small and decrepit, but served a purpose. It was the only place in the City that he could have five minutes alone without someone wanting something from him or needing some kind of attention. It was the reward that he earned from all the services he performed on the pain babies and the other times when he'd done things for the council members.

The Doctor really had only two primary purposes that he served in the City. He was the introduction for the new arrivals, whose specialty was maiming without scarring so that the room mothers could leave all the permanent marks. He was given enough liberty that he could inflict the first suffering on the pain babies and leave small marks, however. It took him a long time and many operations to win that right. Many of the scars he left were so tiny that the room mothers didn't complain when they saw their new arrivals. Most of the time, they were so happy to have new pain babies assigned to them they didn't bother to say anything to him at all. Some would occasionally say that he'd overstepped his edict, but none of the council members ever came back on him about it. After all, it was all about the punishment.

His second primary purpose was to bring back to consciousness and basically revive the patrons who succumbed to the punishments and the suffering. Here was usually the biggest challenge that any doctor could face. The patrons deposited at his operating room could have any conceivable amount of appendages missing, brain parts gone, facial features rearranged or hand carried, bleeding sores and holes that were as thick as their body and frequently went all the way through, or anything else that the room mothers could think of to give them. Victor was expected to repair the babies to the point of being able to feel the next round of pain. It didn't matter if it took surgical skill or lots of duct tape to do the job; he was just supposed to get them back onto the playing field like a football trainer. Turf them.

Some cases required more skill than others. It was simple enough to put duct tape around their intestines after he shoved them back into whatever hole that they fell out of and then to pump the cavities full of the blood it so badly needed. That was the elementary stuff.

The challenges came when they arrived from the Funhouse. When the patients were certifiably insane, then no amount of duct tape would do any good. And nearly everyone who came to the Doctor from the Funhouse ended up insane. It was a real bit of operatic magic to convince these patrons that they were basically okay, or to detox them, so that they could go back to the Funhouse and get abused again.

So much fun and so many new ways to do it.

Victor looked over at David as he flopped around in his chair. It was annoying the hell out of him. He reached into his pocket and fondled the two vertebras that he took out of his spine. Before he left the operating room, he had stooped over and picked them up. He thought it might be kind of fun to have them in his pocket to play with whenever he wanted to play with them. There were any amount of toys that he could've gotten a hold of here in the City, but the toys you took for yourself were always the best. And the fact it came from another doctor only added to the game.

David continued to twist and jerk until Victor had had enough. He looked around the office and spied a six foot long shovel lying against the wall that he kept for sport. Victor walked over to the shovel and picked it up.

"I can't. I can't. I can't...," David stuttered and flopped into his chair.

Victor took quick aim and, with a roundhouse blow and two hands on the shovel, promptly hit David on top of the head as hard as he could. He connected cleanly and squarely in the center of his head.

David's head snapped downward from the blow and the lower part of his brain where the two vertebras had been taken from connected instantly with the other vertebra. Like two electrical wires touching and the current jumping from one of them to the other, there weren't any disconnects now.

David sat upright in his chair and moved his head back and forth to the left and right. It would have been a lie to say that he had a neck because the missing vertebra took care of that, but when Victor hit him, the brain could now talk to the spinal cord and he could put forth at least a semblance of intelligence.

"I can't understand what happened," David said as he reached up and massaged what was left of his neck.

Victor put the shovel down behind his desk and then took his seat across from David. "Shut up, asshole," he said as he glared at him.

David quit rubbing his neck and instead rubbed his head where he'd been hit. Victor hit him with the flat part of the shovel for maximum effect but still spilled the scalp and it was bleeding. Patchy but consistently.

"Listen and don't speak. I am a lower being than you. I'm not in the mood for a bunch of questions, but if you have any of the sense, I think you might have, you'll figure things out quickly enough, anyway."

"Why can't I speak or sit upright like this all the time?" David asked as he surveyed the office. "And who are you?"

"That's two questions. I told you not to ask any." Victor promptly stood up and grabbed the shovel, and with one swift and smooth move, hit him over the head again.

David shrieked as much from the surprise of the move as from the pain and then fell off the chair and onto the floor. He lay there for a second, looking up at the ceiling, and decided not to ask any more questions. Placing his hand on the chair, he got back to an upright position and then sat down without another word.

The Doctor put the shovel back against the wall and then stared at David for a minute while he thought. "I removed two of the primary vertebras in your neck, C1 and C2. That's why you can't stop convulsing or make a fucking coherent sentence. I'm beginning to wish I hadn't removed them after all as you'll be a bigger pain in my ass without them than you would've probably been with them."

David was dumbfounded and stared open-mouthed at Victor. "Bullshit. That's simply bullshit. You can't remove C1 and C2 and expect to live. Let alone talk and walk."

"Things operate differently here as you'll see, but right now, I want to focus on some of the things you did on the surface."

David sat back in the chair. "What surface? What things?"

"Jesus Christ. If you don't stop asking questions, I'm going to hit you again. Are we clear on that?"

David nodded. He could wait. He was a patient man. He had always been before.

"This is the long and short of it. I am the Doctor in residence here. You have died and been sent here. Your punishment will be less severe if I can use you for some of the technical knowledge that you apparently gained on the surface during your late night visits when you weren't fucking the corpses in your morgue."

David didn't say a word as he processed the information. This guy was obviously nuts, and he was in an insane asylum where the inmates were in charge. He would have to figure it out as he went along.

"I have to reconnect your cerebellum to the spinal cord if I want you to be useful to me. I'm not sure how long it will last, but hitting you with the shovel does essentially the same thing. We'll have to wait and see about that one."

David nodded. This guy was certifiable. That was the only thing David knew for sure.

"When you started the experiments prolonging the length of time until brain death, what did you find out? Were you able to extend the time the brain remained alive after the body died?"

David was dumbfounded. He hadn't made any notes, and he'd done the tests completely alone and in the privacy of the corpses. There was no physical evidence of any kind to connect him to that research. It made little sense. How could this guy know?

Victor said, "One more time because it is always hard to swallow. You were executed by the state of Florida. Your last physical memory was probably some arms extending and pulling you downward. You have arrived at your final resting place and it is the City of Hell. I know everything about you and I am in charge of you. And your punishment for the time being."

David nodded.

"Try this, asswipe. I made a four-inch hole in the back of your head and opened your skull and took out your vertebra. But before I pulled them out and threw them on the floor, I probed your thoughts by sticking my fingers inside your brain. Remember?"

David blinked three times in rapid succession as the entire memory of the operation and the hideous feeling of the Doctor's fingers inside his brain flooded back to him. He reached around the back of his head and let his fingers trace the opening that had dried and was now covered by caked-in mucus and blood.

David pulled his fingers back and looked at the old blood on them before he said anything. Now was not the time, but he wouldn't forget this guy. Ever.

"I was able to make some positive results. The brain can be kept alive for up to twelve minutes, if properly medicated and prepared."

Victor sat back in his chair. *Twelve minutes*? Jesus Christ. If that was true, the portal could be open twice as long as anyone else knew, on the surface or in the City. Victor might figure out a way to use that extra six minutes.

Six minutes. That was an eternity.

CHAPTER TWELVE

"Do we get to see a lot of those kinds of things?" Byron asked as they turned after watching the machine go down the hallway. It wasn't a sight he wished to see anytime soon.

Mack nodded. "Unfortunately, I can absolutely guarantee you that we'll see more of those kinds of things. And other things you can't quite put an easy description on. This place has things that you couldn't image in your worst nightmares."

They were walking down the hallway again when a thought occurred to Byron, "What level are we on and where are we going? I'm afraid of the Machine Room and I haven't even seen it. Have you been there?"

"There are so many different kinds of rooms on the top two levels here. Remember, the higher you go, the worse your status here is. In other words, whoever is at the top is in the worst situation. The lower we go in the levels, the better it is for the patrons. That's you and me. Or I guess that's what they call us. Patrons. Like we agreed to pay for this shit," Mack said, slowly shaking his head. "The one thing you can count on is that everyone we run into here, even that guy driving the cage on that machine a minute ago, is here because he belongs here. No one is even remotely innocent. No one here got screwed by his lawyer or the judicial system."

"When I spent some time on the surface in jail, the unwritten rule was that you never asked the other guys what they were in for. I have to assume that it's probably that way here?" Byron asked. He couldn't help but wonder what landed Mack in this place. Mack didn't seem like the typical patron. Everyone belonged here, so he knew Mack did, too. There were no admittance mistakes. No delivery problems from the post office. No early or late arrivals.

"That's as good as any way to put it, I guess. I've always figured that the less I knew, the less I could be held accountable for. I never really spent much time on the top two levels - we're on the middle of five levels here - and I don't want to. The council members and other lower beings always felt I could do something for them. Remember. Always remember. If you can't serve a purpose on the third level, you will get kicked upstairs where the punishment is more severe."

Byron looked back over his shoulder. "I would imagine that no punishment is not an option?" he said hopefully. He still maintained an iota of hope that he could find a place where they'd leave him alone.

Mack shook his head "no."

Byron nodded again and thought for a second. "You didn't answer my question. Do you know where we're going?"

The hallway had changed texture and decoration, if it could be called that, again. The lights had brightened as they approached the end of the hallway. It resembled some kind of train switching yard. There were various hallways heading out of the central "station" they were standing in. The light was bright enough to count seven different branches. There was no telling how many limbs each of the hallways broke into, and those could have branched out as well. It was mind boggling how Mack knew where he was going and could find it.

There were train tracks that appeared to begin and end in the same place. There wasn't any as they walked, and then it was as if a train developer had started one right here. Each of the branches had train tracks that went nowhere.

The interior of the switching yard was painted old baby puke green with splotches of orange scattered about the walls. It looked like something a three-year-old had rejected after several attempts to eat. The walls smelled like old piss. Cat piss, specifically. It was a faint undertone of smell that Byron noticed earlier. Not something to get used to quickly.

"I'm not really sure," Mack said as he stopped and faced one of the switch yard branches.

"Not sure of what?"

"Not sure of where we are or where we're going. I have a general idea of where to start, but I'm being led."

"Led?" Byron asked "By whom?"

At that moment, from down the train tracks to their immediate left, Mack heard a scraping sound as someone walked or was dragged towards them. It was the sound of gravel being moved by someone with a large club foot. Like a gorilla walking without really picking up his feet, but sliding them along the ground. And pulling something large.

"Really, Mr. Michaels. I would have expected you'd at least figure that out by now. Who is interested in you?" Randi said as she appeared out of the dust and walked towards them. Her feet were normal size and nothing was being pulled. The sound of normal footsteps replaced the dragging sound just outside of their eyesight. Whatever she was dragging, she had obviously dropped it and left it by the side of the tracks.

Byron shrugged his shoulders. "Sorry. I should've known."

Her answer was swift and sure. Without so much as a second between the end of his apology and her retribution, Randi threw something directly at him that pierced the middle of his chest. He screamed once and fell forward, clutching his chest.

Mack never saw what it was or where she pulled it from, but he guessed it was some kind of carving knife from Byron's reaction. Something small and sharp that she could send his way with little physical movement on her part.

Byron rolled over on the floor and grabbed at the end of a large spike that had penetrated his chest to the hilt, leaving nothing except a wooden handle sticking out. He stopped moving and lay still on the floor as Randi stepped around Mack and immediately in front of him.

"You must learn never to speak unless it is requested, Mr. Michaels. This was a very small sampling of what can happen. We have so many wonderful things to show you here. This is a knife," she said as she reached down and gripped the handle of the knife and then wrenched upwards. "A special knife that has little fish hooks along each of the sides. See, it goes in smoothly, but the coming out is a little trickier."

With that said, she yanked the knife out and Mack could only watch as Byron writhed on the ground. The knife came out, making a much larger hole in his chest than it made when it went in. The hooks on each side of the knife served only to rip apart the tendons and muscle from the inside out, causing excruciating pain. He couldn't help screaming out loud as the end of the knife finally left his chest amid a pool of fresh blood and cartilage. More of Byron Michaels on the floor.

Randi, who until this time hadn't displayed those kinds of tendencies, seemed momentarily satisfied and wiped the end of the knife off on his cheek and then put it back to whatever hidden fold it was in before she pulled it out. Mack couldn't see where she kept it, but he knew better than to speak, anyway. The pain babies always had to be taught the hard way.

Stepping back, she eyed him. "Mr. Teacher. Please don't disappoint me and tell me that you didn't know who was leading you?"

"I knew it was you or your mother."

"Have you been to the Funhouse before, Mr. Teacher?" she asked, like an innocent child. Her face had turned to a creamy skin color, pale and white, and she was looking at him once again from beneath her hair that at present was a golden-orange color. She was far from innocent. At anything, he knew.

"A while ago, I did some work for some of the other council members that required me to go up to the levels. I've seen some things. Some of the sights."

"And you're not afraid?" It was a simple enough question. One that, until now, Mack preferred not to think about. The horrors he knew were coming he'd been able to avoid most of the time. But no longer.

"Yes. I'm afraid."

"Of what, specifically?"

Byron gathered himself together and now stood quietly to the side of Mack. If there was any good news here, he thought, it seemed recovery was a pretty quick thing. That was both good and bad. The patrons recovered fast so they could be punished again.

Mack thought for a moment before answering. Randi was enjoying this. "I don't want to be left there after we find the Rose you seek."

Randi threw her head back and Mack could see both her eyes again. She laughed a deep and hearty laugh. "I won't leave you there, Mr. Teacher. The City has plenty of patrons to keep on those floors. I prefer you where I can use you. Like a little lap dog. Perhaps a Pomeranian?"

Mack noticed she didn't speak for her mother. Just because she wouldn't leave him on the upper floors didn't mean that her mother wouldn't leave him there. Not to mention that Byron hadn't been through the levels yet. Hadn't earned his scars, so to speak.

She turned to Byron, "Did you like the machine?"

He looked down at the floor. He would not speak to her without being prompted again. His chest stopped bleeding, but he was still holding it for fear that something might fall out.

"You may speak to me now, Mr. Michaels."

"I'm not really in a position to judge other than I haven't seen anything like it before."

Randi took that as a compliment and stared at him through one eye again as her hair fell partially over her face. It was an effective trick because she could hide her emotions easily that way.

She turned suddenly to Mack as if she just remembered something. "Did you like having your back licked?"

"I figured that was you all the way. Not doing the licking, but at least making sure the driver didn't get too near us. The protection was needed."

Byron hadn't asked Mack about the licking, but guessed since it happened to him, it must've happened to Mack. This was proof that at least Mack was going to get whatever Byron got. On equal footing.

"What have you figured out so far?" she asked him directly.

"I've been thinking about what you said and also what the scroll says. You said we should start at the Machine Room. Have you sent someone there before who failed?" he asked.

"Excellent, Mr. Teacher. The information we have on you may prove to be correct. The patron we sent on this errand failed quickly last time. He started in the Machine Room. He never got out."

"Thought so."

"So where will you start?"

Mack unrolled the scroll from his left hand where he'd been carrying it. He wiped a spot clear on the floor with his foot and laid it down on the ground between the tracks. As he read, Byron looked over his shoulders, hopeful that he could help without attracting attention.

Mack pointed to a passage. "Here it mentions something that stuck out to me when I read it."

Red blood and black night
Take a risk before
Chances are won
In a circus of gore.

He continued, "It seems to me that I've heard of a red and black room in the Funhouse. I think we better start there."

Randi was obviously pleased. The others, and there had been many more than the one she told Mack about, showed no understanding of the scroll. Randi pointed down the hallway to her left. "Take the river and then walk up the stairs at the first bend. Once you are in the Funhouse, the room you seek will be shown to you."

Mack looked down the hallway. It appeared to be swimming with eels or maybe squids continually moving back and forth on the walls and floor. Squirming would have been a better word for what they were doing. There were tentacles and suction cups making a continuous "popping" sound as they flexed back and forth. He couldn't tell what it was from this distance, but he knew he was about to step near something very much alive. What kind of river had been conjured here?

"You will be protected to a certain degree, Mr. Teacher. Where and when, you won't know, as my mother likes these kinds of games. Make no mistake, though. If you appear to be lost or are losing the trail, if she cannot see the Rose in sight at some point quickly, she may well leave you to be handled by the room mother who has you at the moment."

With that, Randi turned and left down the train tracks she came from and in less than a minute after she disappeared from his sight, Mack could hear the scraping sound again. She was definitely dragging something. It sounded heavy, like perhaps a body.

Byron raised his head and watched her leave. "I guess I learned a pretty good lesson there. Has this happened to you before?" he motioned to the hole in his chest.

"Several times, in fact. Each of them different from the previous one and more painful. It's best to maintain a very low profile. The less people look at you, the better."

"Before we go down this hallway, I have to ask you something that has been bugging me for a little while, but I haven't gotten the chance to ask you about it yet."

Mack stopped and faced Byron at the entrance to the tunnel. He could hear something "hissing" at them from inside. "What?"

"What did you mean earlier when you said I needed to remember 5317? Is that a code or something that can help me out if I get into trouble?"

"It's not specifically a code. It's rather a rule of thumb that I live by down here. Or rather, it has helped me survive."

"And what does it mean?"

Mack had a serious look on his face. "If we're to do this, I'm going to need your help. We're going to get into some things that I can't imagine at present and some other things that I don't have any idea what they'll mean. This scroll," he held the scroll up in front of Byron's face, "is the only thing that can save us from ending up on one of these bad levels. We may never be able to get out of the Funhouse, or in my opinion away from the much worse terror on the Carnage Level. We're going to have to work together."

"Okay. What can I do?"

"You can remember. Always remember this." Mack leaned in very close to his face. Even though one eye was missing and he still had a bleeding hole in his chest, Mack had seen worse. Much worse. And these were the cards the council dealt him. "5317. Remember 5317. It will keep you on track and quite possibly out of serious harm's path."

"Okay. But why?"

"5317 is a number that I remembered from when I was a kid back in Michigan. We used to say that when we didn't like the answer we got from our friends, parents, whatever."

"I still don't understand. How did you know not to start where Randi told us to us to start?"

Mack bent back down and drew the numbers 5317 on the ground in large block letters in front of Byron. He then motioned for Byron to walk around to the other side and look at the numbers upside-down.

Byron held his breath as he instantly understood. Written in the dirt was one word:

LIES.

He looked up at Mack. "So Randi was lying to us when she told us to start with the Machine Room?"

"Everyone lies here."

Mack turned to the hallway and began walking. "Everyone."

CHAPTER THIRTEEN

Victor spent the last several hours digging deeper into what exactly David learned in his studies in the morgue. The job of forensic pathologist had proven to be a perfect setup for this kind of study. Nobody bothered him on the night shift when he worked and, of course, the corpses never complained.

The study into the six minutes that the brain lived on after the body had already died wasn't a new thing to science. There were numerous experiments and articles published in various medical journals through the years, but they all lacked the one thing that David Masters had recreated: the freshly dead. In all the studies prior to his work, the scientists and doctors had to rely on data they got from cadavers that had been dead several hours and then kept "on ice" to make the study as fresh as possible. When a human consented to be studied for the advancement of medicine and it was dissected their brain for knowledge, then as soon as they were pronounced clinically dead, the team of doctors in the operating room would systematically try to keep the brain alive.

The first school of thought proposed to rapidly drain the body of all fluids like a typical autopsy, and then the blood was replaced with a synthetic blood that was kept at a considerably cooler temperature than the ninety-eight point six that the body had thrived on during its life. That system was a good start, but not really practical because the fastest the fluids could be replaced with the synthetic blood were three and one-half minutes, so over half of the brain's life was already spent by the time the synthetics were introduced. It just wasn't practical.

Especially to someone like David, who experienced life and death every day during his job. He could get the freshest corpses when he wanted by killing them and administering his own cocktails directly into the bloodstream while they were still *alive*. It might have been uncomfortable for the humans being tested under his program, but a true scientist didn't let comfort affect his work, regardless of the outcome, including being put in jail for murder.

The absolute favorite thing that had happened to David during his trial was a motion filed by a group calling itself the ETC Group. The group claimed that David Masters should receive the death penalty for his actions against the dearly departed. He found out that the ETC part of the slogan stood for "Ethical Treatment of Corpses." He sneered at them in court. Ethical treatment of corpses? What could be more absurd? Every time someone read a statement from one of the lawyers of the ETC Group, David would burst into uncontrollable laughter. That didn't help his case either.

But Victor saw the true genius in the work of David as soon as he extracted parts of his memories from the operation. Victor may have been a singularly depraved individual, but he was smart enough to recognize an opportunity when it came his way.

And this idea was an opportunity.

Victor didn't know exactly how the portal worked, as it had been stricken from his knowledge by the council members some time ago, if he had ever even been privy to it at all. They chose who would and would not be allowed to know those kinds of secrets about the City.

But he knew that the ability to control the length of the opening of the portal could give him incredible bargaining power.

He turned his attention back to David who started flopping again. Every couple of hours, because the intervals were irregular and unpredictable, David would shake and then his limbs would start flipping this way and that and then he'd stutter as his head slowly but surely pulled itself away from the connection between his cerebellum at the base of his brain and the closest two vertebras that they could contact.

Victor would simply grab the handle of the shovel and, with a pronounced "WHACK" deliver a blow to the top of David's head and then they could resume their conversation. David proved to be an intelligent physician and Victor knew he could use him successfully to gain a demotion in the City. If he played his cards right, David could take over for him as Hell's Doctor and Victor might gain a council seat from this. The idea was positively orgasmic.

They'd been having this conversation from the time that the Doctor first brought David to his office. It had been a revelation for him.

"So, back to the question of the cocktail. Can you tell me what we could use to cover the substances? We haven't got the kinds of drugs here that you had access to on the surface. We're going to need to improvise somewhat," Victor said as he sat back in his chair.

"I can't. I can't. I can't…" David stuttered again.

Victor grabbed the end of the shovel and promptly hit David hard and square on top of the head. The sound echoed in the rounded room and "WHACK, WHACK, WHACK," could be heard as a dying sound in the dimly lit office. In any other setting, it would have been immensely comical. Nothing was funny in the City to the higher beings. Only the council members had anything to laugh about.

"I can't be sure until I've studied the drugs you have available," David continued as he rubbed his head where Victor hit him. The hole in the top of his head had gotten bigger and Victor was actually trying not to crack his skull when he hit him, at least until he got all the information out of him he needed. Then he'd decide if he wanted to crack his skull clear through or not. Split the sucker wide open.

Victor nodded. David would have to be taken to the drugstore and given liberty. It could be easily arranged. The council members left him alone to do as he pleased, as long as he did what they wanted first.

"I'm going to take you there right away and I want you to match the drugs, or at least try to match them. Something must be able to work. We've got to keep that portal open."

"That's interesting, Doctor Stevens."

Victor looked up as Eikken appeared in the room. He had not been there, and then he was. Like an explosion of fury that overflows an opponent and then suddenly fills the surrounding air, Eikken was there. It wasn't like him to show up suddenly like this. Victor knew better than to think he could keep anything from the council members, but he didn't anticipate this. Didn't want this. He liked to be left alone.

"Why would you want the portal open?" Eikken floated around the room. David stared at him because he hadn't ever seen anything like a floating body before. It didn't matter what Eikken looked like, but it was not something David could truly wrap his mind around. This was unbelievable.

Eikken was simply a presence. He had form and rigidly defined lines to make it easy enough to see him. But at some point along the way, as he was continually shaped by the events in the City, Eikken had somehow lost his permanent form. He was like a floating apparition. In modern terms, David would have called him a ghost, but not like any ghost he had heard of or read about. This kind of shit just didn't happen.

Eikken was transparent in places but clearly solid in others. He seemed to open and close holes in his body, or as David would have called it, his abdomen like on an insect, at will. One minute, David was looking at the center of his chest and then the vision seemed to shift and he was looking through a hole and directly at the wall behind. It reminded him of one of those nets they used to catch crabs in Alaska. Solid on one end and completely see through on the other.

And Eikken's face was another matter altogether. He had one, but not at the proper angle or the proper height for the rest of his abdomen. An insect with a small head and a large abdomen. Kind of like an ant. With pincers and tentacles.

His head held his mouth and his eyes, but no nose that David could see and still had the solidarity problem. Holes appeared and then disappeared. A pepperoni pizza face with severe zits. Holes all over the damn thing.

He smelled too. Like a chicken coop after a heavy rain in the spring, when the chickens had gotten dirty all winter and the farmer hadn't cleaned the bottom of the cage for three months. It was hideous.

Eikken floated across the room and landed on David before he could speak or react. David felt a tingling sensation all across his body as Eikken settled around him and basically laid his form on the lap of David. Little electrical shocks pulsed all across David's body and then Eikken connected with him and the two were momentarily one. He felt like he was being raped from the inside out.

Eikken probed all of David's thoughts and orifices with his essence as he let the shapeless formations of his floating body wind themselves around, down, and into his body. He would get to know this man whom Victor had taken such an interest in. He would learn his secrets as well.

But something odd occurred as Eikken tried to join with David. He was probing, touching, feeling, sanitizing, writing. But the man's thoughts were being blocked from him. Eikken had sensed this on only one other occasion.

Eikken shrieked a howl of irritation at being denied that which was rightfully his, because he knew who was blocking him. Eikken disconnected, and David's body slumped to the floor and convulsed again. Victor simply looked on. He had been silently pleased when he realized Eikken was unable to read David. It would keep the secrets of the portal unavailable to Eikken. Better for the Doctor to use later when he needed a bargaining chip.

Eikken floated towards Victor and in a very threatening and menacing voice from a newly formed hole where his mouth should've been, growled at Victor, "You would be wise to remember your place in the City and its structure, doctor. I keep you at my pleasure."

With that, Eikken enveloped Victor and wrapped his essence around him and covered him in a blanket of electric particles. Lights flickered and went out and then Victor felt the constant shock of electric wattage being forced down his open mouth and into his body from all sides at once. Whereas he had been small and select in shocking David, he was using random and intense electrical currents positioned at the mouth and temple of Victor. A burning smell consumed the room as some of the hair on Victor's head smoked under the strain, and then the Doctor was instantly transported backwards. He screamed as Eikken sent him to the place where it all began for him and left him on the road to the City of Hell.

The lamppost was decorated with gray paint dulled from years of misuse. It started out to be a glossy sheen at one time, but through the years and with all the rain that this part of London received in the springtime, the weather faded it from glossy to plain. It still held some of the original sheen, but it wouldn't be long before that was gone completely. Several of the locals had also added their personal decorations as graffiti on the post pretty much anywhere that they could find an open spot.

Victor Stevens walked the streets alone tonight. It was an unusually cool time of the evening for this part of spring, and the rain let up earlier in the day, so all that was left was the shroud of fog. And it was dense tonight.

The fog never bothered Victor. He grew up on the streets of London and as a kid he never fully understood it, but once you get used to something, if it is taken from you, then you actually miss it. Even the damn fog.

He wasn't in a hurry tonight. The air was heavy, and the lights had just turned on like they did every night at exactly nine o'clock. The current prime minister had instituted this policy a couple of years earlier to save some of the taxpayers' money. Even though it probably didn't save shit to have the lights come on at a prescribed hour rather than at dusk, it made the prime minister look good in the papers. It was all about image, anyway.

Victor probably understood that simple maxim better than anyone else in London. It didn't matter the job you did; it mattered the job the client perceived he received. Such a simple concept, really.

There were no hookers anywhere tonight. Victor had taken lately to picking them up in the alleyways and then using them for a mere pence or two. The weird thing to him had been when he got to like the bartering over the cost of the sex as much as actually having the sex. It suited a purpose to him, much like his wife. She was a wife in name only and the sex he got on the street was considerably better than anything he even attempted at home. She said no, so he took it anyway. With Victor Stevens, no one ever said "no."

His wife would lay there on the bed with her dress bunched up around her thighs and one of her large breasts bared as he took her at will. He liked the power of the moment much more than the release and with his wife, it quickly and regularly reminded her she was his to use as he saw fit. No excuses.

But the hookers. They were almost exceptional to the core. They would stand facing him or with their back to him and he would take and use them as well. It was a good transaction for both of them. If he could get them to squeal like a baby as he pounded them, it only helped him finish.

As he walked down the street, a smile crossed his lips. This town was his. He was a prominent doctor in the heart of the world itself, the business and fashion capital of all Europe. And he was the highest paid doctor in the area. The rich Brits sought his advice in every aspect of their medical life and frequently in the political arena as well. He was never wanting for money, and never unable to give opinions. Opinions the wealthy craved. Even though the rest of London was mired in a deep depression and the lowly scum were now living on the streets and creating filth for all the good people, he rose above it all.

He pulled his cloak a little tighter around his waist and then straightened his top hat. With a clink of his polished cane on the cobblestone street, he turned left onto Hanbury Street and walked toward his favorite pub. He would check here for a quick fix from a hooker and if there were none, he would head home to his dreary wife.

Something to his immediate right caused a momentary startle, and he stopped in his tracks. He heard a sound like a door being closed quickly as he passed. And it seemed to Victor that the door closed because he had passed. Of that, he was sure.

Looking to the right and then behind him, he couldn't see into the shadows the lampposts cast nearly as well as he would've wished. The lights weren't the best on Avery Street anyway, and it could've helped him if they were. He could at least see who was standing there.

The doorway that the sound came from appeared to be empty and with a shrug, Victor turned and continued his walk. The moment had passed. He was hearing things.

But the next sound he heard was not his imagination. The same thing as the last time, the sound of a door closing directly behind him, although this time the sound was followed by a soft but firm slap of a boot on the wet street. It must have been halfway immersed in a puddle because the boot made a sloshing sound and then stopped. Whoever it was had noticed him and stopped his movement. He was directly behind Victor.

Pulling the hand holding the cane up and then releasing a catch under the handle, Victor withdrew a hidden knife from its sleeve in the cane. It was a sharp and polished six-inch shiv that, if wielded correctly, could do a considerable amount of damage. He put the knife back under his cloak before he ever turned to the sound. It was a good idea to be prepared in London because of the thieves.

What happened next was so fast that Victor never really reacted at all. The door to his left opened and when he turned to look at the shapely lass coming out from inside the hostel, Victor felt the first searing pain as a knife was cutting expertly across the backs of his ankles and effectively slicing his Achille's heel. He howled in pain and dropped his cane and knife as he fell and realized that the lass who came out of the hostel was now standing over him and around her were three or four other women. The women magically appeared out of some hidden archway nearby. It was hard to count them and he was having trouble keeping conscious as the blood ran out of the deep cuts on his ankles. He couldn't possibly run and he was in trouble. Deep trouble.

The shapely lass that was staring down at him lifted her leg and with a strong downward motion kicked Victor squarely in the face, effectively breaking his nose and all the cartilage in it and driving some of it towards his brain. He howled again and tried to shrink away from the women standing over him, but as he looked up through a bloody broken nose, it seemed like the number of women had multiplied tenfold, and now they were everywhere and engulfed him.

The cobblestone street was wet against his back and his nose was bleeding a tremendous amount of blood along with his ankle. He couldn't stand up and run away because his ankles handicapped him. Victor didn't see an opening anyway to run toward. The women were on all sides of him. There must have been upwards of twenty of them standing over him and looking down as he sat up, still holding his nose. He did not know what they wanted.

All at once, they fell on him like rabid dogs on a piece of meat and he literally was thrown backwards against the street as some of them sat on his chest and others sat on his legs. They pinned his arms back, and a woman sat on each of them. They held him securely in place from the sheer weight of their bodies. The total weight combined was like having a thousand pounds suddenly constricting his chest. He was gasping for air with his broken nose and all the blood running into his throat, and with the weight on his chest, Victor thought he would surely suffocate.

The women stopped moving for a moment and everything went deathly still.

Victor gasped a deep breath as one woman shifted her position slightly off the center of his chest, and he took that moment to beg for his life.

"Please, me lasses, whatever I've done, I'm sure we can work this out. I've got money in me pocket. Take it, but please leave me here. No charges will be filed against ye. Let's end this and let me make my way home to me wife. Please, she's a waitin' for me. She'll be worried."

With the last statement, Victor suddenly knew he was going to die as surely as he knew it would rain tomorrow in the streets of London. The crowd parted slightly and his wife, whom he thought was waiting at home for him to come through the doors, walked up and looked down at his pathetic form lying prone on the ground.

"I'll not be waiting for ye anymore, Victor. You'll be in Hell, where you belong," she said as she bent over him and with a long horizontal movement sliced a fifteen inch cut from his throat down to his belly. Victor screamed and his eyes widened in terror as he felt his life drain into the streets.

Victor's wife stood up and handed the knife to the first young lass that cut his ankles. She took her turn, cutting directly across his chest from shoulder to shoulder. She then handed the knife to another lady and then to another, and Victor faded from this world as the pain cut deeper and deeper into his chest. He could hear the women cackling and laughing as he bled to death on Avery Street.

The last thing he heard was his wife saying something about getting even for all the women in London.......

Victor was curled up on the floor of his office shaking and sweating as the memory of each of the deep knife cuts that sent him to the City came back. It wasn't just the memory, but Eikken had made him relive the actual sensation of each of the cuts that killed him, from the first ankle cut to the broken nose to the last knife slice. The pain was as real today as it was so many years ago.

"Get up, doctor, for I have work for you today," Eikken said as he removed himself completely from Victor and now floated easily across the center of the room. He'd been enraged when he was blocked from reading the thoughts of David, but the Doctor would've felt his wrath, regardless. It was important to dole out punishment, so they never forgot who could give it to them. At any time.

Victor stood up, shaking his head, and took his seat behind his desk and awaited Eikken's orders. He would have to put his plan on hold for a little while.

"What am I to do?" Victor asked.

"I'm not sure exactly what is happening, but I've noticed some of the council members are exercising their abilities more than usual. Something is going on. I want you to use your considerable talents in the metering out of pain to figure out what they're engaged in."

Victor thought for a second. "I will follow your orders, of course. I'll begin immediately. My assistant will be invaluable and will accompany me, if you wish."

Eikken floated away. He had another matter to attend to at present. A meeting. "I will check on you soon and be watching, Doctor. Do not fail me. I require this information. And quickly."

Victor watched him disappear into thin air. He'd not been used for this kind of task before, but it would have to wait until he finished his own search. With that, Victor swung the shovel again, WHACK, and then motioned for David to follow him. They were headed for the Havoc Level.

But first they were going to stop and get the drugs David needed to keep the portal open.

CHAPTER FOURTEEN

Stapleton called the nine of them together. It was rare for him to do it anymore, and even though most preferred never to be summoned because it was beneath them, they knew the meeting had been a long time coming. He expected them to respond and quickly be at the table. Their presence was required.

If this was simply a town meeting or a collection of city council members, then someone would've called the meeting to order and recorded the events. A duly appointed secretary would read from the notes, and there would've been a certain amount of pomp and circumstance. Things like roll call, quorum established, members in attendance, and the usual requirements set up somewhere along the line during the establishment of the council's charter would be followed.

But what happened here was never recorded and seldom forgot. No ceremonies. No elections. No side bars and legal consults.

Only dark deals struck. The kind no one wanted recorded.

This council comprised the nine administrators that were demoted at some point. It was a tentative position that existed purely in the minds of the council members. The positions held no official title. They didn't get a red sash or a broach to proclaim who they were. There weren't any press releases.

It was just what it was.

Because he was the lowest member of the council, and by the rules of the City, Stapleton was the leader. He sent the word out without using verbal commands, and then the eight others stopped whatever they were doing and appeared. It was almost immediate and never more than a few moments from when he summoned; they appeared.

Stapleton found it relatively easy to locate the eight of them. There were many, many places in the City they could hide out in or perform their respective duties, undefined as they were. Since he knew they were always engaged in the same activity with varying degrees of success and disorganization, he knew where to look. Each of them had but one driving thought: building their own personal case for taking over for him as leader of the council. It was an accepted, and even an expected, practice.

Stapleton counted on it.

He'd been on the council and taken the bottom position from the previous leader so long ago that he couldn't even remember how it happened. It took deception that he was proud of but now he couldn't recall either the time or the incident. Now he watched the others and waited for them to make their move. Openly acknowledging a plot to overthrow him and take his post was nothing new. It was the only game in town.

And it was the only game he liked.

As he entered the chamber of the council members, he didn't bother to acknowledge their presence. Normally, they would've taken their places around the table and he would have entered last, as was his due. But this meeting had a pressing problem. It required his attention, and he felt slightly distracted when he became visible to the others.

Looking around the table and letting his eyes rest for a moment on each member, he knew they deserved their positions, and all had a right to be here. At least until someone else could figure out a way to get rid of them and claim that position for themselves.

"Normally, I would not be speaking aloud to you. As you know by now, I do not like verbal communications, but we will use our voices so there can be nothing misunderstood about our presence here today. No separate treaties while we speak. That is the rule," Stapleton began. Many of the council members were known to make agreements during the meetings with the other members when communicating by thoughts alone. He needed to prevent that.

Stapleton was an enigma, even to most of the council members who watched and plotted against him. He'd been given the power to change his shape at will. At present, he preferred to float above the ground and have no solid form. Like a black cloud of dust, he simply remained motionless, but in motion. He stayed in one place, but vibrated slightly, like there was a breeze in the room.

There was a general agreement and a nodding of the heads. The members came alone to the meeting and left their seconds at their regular posts. It was not unusual to have at least one supporter in attendance.

Stapleton mandated them to appear alone. What he had to say was not to be repeated to the higher beings.

Annicka hovered immediately to the right of Stapleton. That was a small approval of her past accomplishments and depravity. There was nothing but pure, unbridled hatred from each of the council members to each of the other council members. But many times, enemies could prove useful. The only goal was to be in the last seat. Like Stapleton.

Next to Annicka was Callen the Beast. Known simply for his ability to invoke pain from the prisoners in the City, he was a brutal and mindless mass of flesh. Not to be trusted by anyone or anything. He held no contracts and was unreliable. But he was probably the most vicious of the eight. Stapleton was glad he was also the stupidest and the easiest to control.

On the left side of Stapleton was another male, Eikken the Lion. The rest of the council comprised Abbas, Magnar, Witter, Helga, and Isa. There were three women, and the rest were male. The women hadn't dropped as quickly to positions of prominence, and only one woman had ever been the lowest. It wasn't a sexist thing, Stapleton knew, but simply a basic DNA problem. Males were simply more ruthless and could be counted on to eviscerate their opponents, while the females in the City were more devious. It just took more time, even though there were exceptions.

Most of the members preferred to remain near their stations, either sitting, standing, or hovering near their designated spots at the table. Stapleton took this as a small sign of defiance, but let it pass. He didn't wish to get caught up in battle along those lines. Not at this moment, anyway. That could be handled later.

Since he knew each of the members possessed unique abilities and strengths, then the competition to oust him evolved into learning to use the various abilities, while limiting their opponent's strengths. Some of the most compelling theater Stapleton witnessed involved a council member's inability to harness their particular strength fast enough to use it against another member. He saw many times that strength turned to weakness.

Isa spoke first. She was seated at her regular place at the table and preferred to use verbal communications, anyway. On the surface, she'd been a lawyer for the mafia and had no reservations about using a convenient wise guy technique of dismemberment for her gain. She particularly relished pain babies getting their legs cut off early in the game and then spending the rest of their time sliding along the ground like slugs. The trails of blood they left were always easy to follow.

"Perhaps you've called this meeting for your amusement again, Stapleton? It is not unlike you," she said to no one in particular. "When aren't these meetings designed to strengthen your position and remind us of who holds the lowest seat?"

Magnar agreed. "Isa is correct, as always. I'm very busy at present and do not like these kinds of petty interruptions from you anymore, Stapleton." Magnar closely resembled a rhino in his physical adornments. He was large shouldered and burly, with a full mane of hair and a long growth of beard. He'd been on the council for the least amount of time and hadn't firmly established his position in the pecking order. He despised all women, Isa in particular, and made a point of letting each of them know. On this council, it wasn't what happened in view that was a problem; it was the steps taken behind the scenes that secured positions and made alliances. Hate was only an emotion. Emotions were like butter. They ran between hard and melted, but neither had any real texture.

Abbas, the council member given the ability to arbitrarily determine the placements of the new arrivals to the City, spoke up. "It would be wise of you, Magnar, to hold your tongue until it is requested that you speak. Perhaps I could assist you and have one of my administrators cut your tongue out, so it isn't such a nuisance to the rest of us?" The threat was overt, but not malicious. Threats were common at the council meetings, but none of the members could use something as simple as physical pain to get rid of their contemporaries. The immortal laws of the City forbade the council members to use physical force on another member to remove them from their seat. It wouldn't work, anyway. They'd each endured so much physical pain that it didn't faze them anymore and was an empty threat. It was just the only way they could communicate on an equal level.

Stapleton held up his hand. He'd already heard enough. "I'm here to discuss that which we do not discuss."

"Sure we will. How do we know you will speak to us as the equals that we are, Stapleton?" Helga asked. The challenge was on the table. If Stapleton couldn't back up his statement, then the other members would know that Stapleton feared one of them. Each knew they weren't equal to him. Perhaps an opening could be created.

Stapleton roared out loud at the slant from Helga and with a sudden move of his left hand threw her back against the wall and pinned her in place. He'd crossed the distance between them before she could react and pinning his body up against her slight frame, he stared deeply into her eyes and drew his face to merely an inch from hers. He waited for her to speak.

She stared defiantly back at him even though she was held securely in place, and then with a flick of his black tongue and quick movement of his form, Stapleton bit a sizeable chunk of her cheek off of her face and chewed it up. Slowly. Like he was savoring each morsel.

Helga's eyes flared, and then she quickly returned them to their normal color. She had openly threatened his position, and he'd reacted. It was to be expected. Another hole in her already pockmarked face was not even a consideration at this point. She would handle the situation between her and him at a later date. Not in this council.

The other council members didn't stir from their places. They'd long since passed the stage of being impressed by simple anger or outbursts from the lowest. It was just a reaction to the slight. The result was quick, but not insurmountable. Stapleton's seat had been precariously close to promotion recently. The rumors foretold a falling out of favor. But apparently, not at this moment.

Stapleton retraced his steps and took his position at the last seat of the table again. He summarily spit out the last remaining part of Helga's cheek he'd been chewing, and, satisfied that his authority wouldn't be tested any farther at this meeting, proceeded. "I've been informed that some of the council members have recently started a quest to locate some hidden items in the City. The items need not be discussed here, but they've been hidden for centuries for particular reasons. Their locations are only known to a few select members."

Witter agreed. He was a mousey looking man and could have been less than twenty three on the surface judging by his smooth skin and clean features. He was also one of the most homicidal maniacs in history and claimed on his resume the deaths of thirty-seven people through a well-placed fire bomb. He had a thing for fire. He mandated that his administrators burn. Just burn, baby, he was fond of saying. "If it is hidden in the City, then there is a good reason and perhaps it doesn't want to be found. It would be best to leave it alone."

"Why?" asked Callen. He was a South African with a taste for flesh. He never spit out the ones he ate. "If something is hidden, then it must be found. To hide it precludes the reasoning that someone else will look for it. That means it has value, whatever it is."

Annicka said nothing up to this point. She was uncertain who knew of her quest to find the Rose, but wouldn't be surprised if Stapleton knew. He had a way of finding out things. His minions had saved his ass and hence his position before. "What are the items you are referring to, Stapleton?" she asked openly. She could be alternately beautiful and youthful in appearance when it favored her outcome. She never forgot her own abilities.

He decided. "I will say only this. It is only one item in specific, although others exist. This item is important to the function of the City itself. Of an unknown power. But many think it has something to do with the portal. That's why its location has been hidden for so long. I would prefer to make it known to the council members who are looking for it here in the City, that I will be watching you. If you get too close, I may have to take action. I may prevent you finding it or I may aid you. In either case, I will gladly make sure that you suffer for going after the item in the first place. Promotion to the Havoc Level is always an option."

"So you know where it is?" Abbas asked. "Why should we look for it if you know where it is?"

Stapleton didn't flinch. All the council members watched him closely. "I do not know where it is. But I will know when you are close. The City will tell me."

He looked around the table at the eight other members. They were scheming as he spoke. He wasn't sure what he started with this meeting, but he knew that now all the council members would be after each other. He'd have to make sure that none of the others gained enough power to get demoted to the last seat. His position.

All eight members looking for the same thing. And Stapleton, right in the middle of them, making sure that they didn't get it. He would have to use all of his considerable cunning to win this battle. It had been brewing for a long time.

Let the games begin.

Since Eternity is incomprehensible and no prisoner can experience death again, time will be measured in stages of dismemberment.

Hell's Second Mantra

INTERLUDE TWO: THE ARCHITECT
PAIN BABIES

The Architect wasn't exactly sure where the term "pain babies" originated. He hadn't coined it, nor did he order it. Sometimes there was a classic moment even from Hell's viewpoint, and something became imbedded in the lore of the City. The term for new arrivals who screamed the loudest when they were given a little welcome just stuck in the evolution.

An epiphany while drinking Chardonnay brought him to this juncture. "Eternity" was never truly appreciated. Mortals had no comprehension of the enormity of such a word. It was like estimating darkness; it couldn't be done. The concept was impossible to grasp. Let alone endure.

The Architect kept coming back to the central idea of what exactly constituted "eternity"? He decided that the measurement of punishment had to relate to eternity, at least in the minds of the pain babies. The more the pain, the longer the duration. Eternity could be measured by never ending punishment, if doled out correctly.

And the only way to do that was to kick-start the pain babies' arrival program.

When a patron was dragged down to the City, the level of consciousness was always in debate. He'd noted that most were busy screaming, crying, chastising, cursing, begging, promising, demeaning, cajoling, floundering or whimpering. Conscious thoughts couldn't be controlled. The arrivals to "The Havoc Level", or "The Funhouse", were too preoccupied to think. It was a luxury they couldn't afford. They conserved their strength for more important things: like diverting the punishment to other patrons.

The Architect stepped back from his model of the City. He knew physical laws didn't always apply, but sometimes, had to be followed. His creation, "The Welcome Cruncher," might stretch the limits.

It was destined to leave the pain babies without hope.

He picked up another bottle of Chardonnay before proceeding and took a long congratulatory swig. The process was simple enough to understand, yet brilliant in scope. He'd invented a new beginning for eternity.

The selection procedure had to be dealt with, of course. He had no control over it, nor did anyone else in the City. During the last six minutes of a potential's life, the City was given its chance. If the person wasn't taken up, then he was going to be coming down. Property of the City and guest of The Architect. No middle ground.

And the pain babies cried. Oh, did they cry.

The City owned them.

The Architect's original arrival process was to let them sit while they awaited their turn in the furnace. His new program would revolve around deception based on their core belief that a place like Hell didn't actually exist. He could alter their minds just by letting them watch others go into the furnace first.

He turned and left his room and headed for the fourth level. The first thing he needed was help. The plan wouldn't work without something to assist him. He could rotate the knobs on the furnace easily enough, but for something this extraordinary, he needed assistants who could keep up with the demand.

Jumping through a couple of chutes and down a third ladder, he quickly arrived at the lab. His experiments would commence immediately. DNA manipulation was a specialty.

The Architect needed something small and nimble, without complications. It had to be mindless and appreciative of the task it was given. His first merge involved a DNA strand from a monkey with a leftover dwarf, but the results were stupidly comical. It wasn't smart enough to speak and couldn't see very well, nor move around quickly. So he added a touch of bat DNA for mobility and vision and the matrix strain was formed.

He produced a species of unimaginative creatures that were about three feet tall and bent over from spinal problems, possessed gigantic eyes and ears with an elongated snout and mouth, and had large teeth and hoofed claws that gave them some balance. They could walk and talk, and see relatively well in the dark recesses, but they weren't very smart. Not very smart at all. Perfect assistants.

The Architect added a second strain of bat DNA to increase their resistance and intelligence and hopefully give them some kind of radar, but it increased their defenses, made them sniveling crybabies when things went wrong, and gave all of them incredibly long and thin phalluses. He laughed out loud when the phalluses protruded more than ten inches. When the phalluses weren't fully erect, they dragged on the ground and caused scabs to form, which caused the monkey-dwarf-bat things to cry even more.

He used double helixes and strands of DNA to make sure each was a twin, anticipating a lot of work that needed done. When the helix was split evenly, instead of one stupid monkey-dwarf-bat thing, there were always two.

The first sets of twins came out angry, which wasn't expected, but he could deal with it. He needed their minuscule brains focused on his requirements and not angry at the DNA merging, so he placated them. His first thought was simple but elegant: cover their heads. Then give them something to do with their phalluses.

The Architect located a couple of baseball hats to stop them from crying and whining. It was like appeasing an infant with a bottle of milk and it seemed to work, so now all the monkey-dwarf-bat things had to wear some kind of hat. It was a status symbol that comforted them. They could function in the task they were given, no matter how simple it was if they had a hat and could mate continuously, whether as a prize or reward. He could also use it against them to not let them mate.

The more they wanted to mate, the more they dragged their phalluses around on the ground, until it became a common sight to see them constantly holding it in one hand while they worked with the other hand. It wasn't a sexual thing; it was more of a necessity that kept it from dragging on the ground. The scabs made them cry all the more.

For some unfathomable reason, one of the DNA fuckup twins, as they were originally called, could not utter a sentence without lying. That was anticipated behavior and accepted. But one monkey-dwarf-bat thing twin would tell the truth. Every time. That was not accepted. And they didn't know the difference between truth and lies.

The Architect thought this was a potential disaster. How could he figure out which was which? One was telling the truth and one was lying. If he knew it was lying, then he could count on the answer; same thing if he knew the truth was being told. But if the stupid monkey-dwarf-bat things didn't know which was which, how could anyone else?

Distancing himself from the process of DNA building, he inadvertently named the monkey-dwarf-bat things by stating he should have used "more bats" for a better mix of species. The name "morebats" promptly stuck.

The morebats became the workers of the City and handled everything that no one else, except the pain babies, were ever assigned. They could be counted on for simple tasks, and they were incredibly loyal, like a good lap dog.

He accepted what he'd created and moved on to his task at hand: the arrival of the pain babies. He focused on procedures and tactics and then went to work on details, with an eye towards fear.

First and foremost was the design, of course. Casting logistics aside, he set to work conjuring up something both terrifying and dangerous. One or the other fell easily enough into place, but the combination of the two seemed like a task best left to desperately fertile minds. The Architect quickly delivered a few prototype "monsters," and sent them to the various welcoming rooms. He watched amusedly as the patrons scurried like mice away in terror from some of his more imaginative creations.

But the monsters themselves had to be fed, maintained, and controlled, which proved to be the biggest problem. They were always hungry for flesh, or for blood, depending on which model he produced. But the control made him decide they weren't worth the trouble.

The morebats couldn't control them when they got out of hand. The patrons would simply be crushed in the onslaught and although that wasn't a bad thing, it wasn't exactly how he'd drawn the script up. He couldn't count on them to behave when he wanted and not necessarily when they wanted, which required constant damage control.

The defective ones were by far the hardest to control.

It's almost an oxymoron to develop a "defective monster." But there was nothing else he could really call these things. They were all hybrids of other failed experiments, and ended almost as badly as they started.

Some freaked out from the onset and immediately turned on the morebats and started to eat them. Others went berserk and ran through the halls of the City breaking down doors and disturbing and consuming both the room mothers and some patrons. And then he had to replace the morebats.

So the Architect sent out an evisceration crew. The morebats quickly figured out that if they put the pain babies out in front of their approaching columns of razor wielding lunatics, the defective monsters came out of their hiding places. They smelled the bait; it turned out. Pain babies made great stink bait. The worse they smelled, the faster the defective monsters came out to eat, and the quicker the morebats could cut them to shreds.

So the whole experiment with "monsters" in the City of Hell was put down as a "misstep." He knew he'd return to that form of terror at some point after he had time to straighten out the design flaws. But for the moment, the whole monster idea was shelved.

Which left the machines to welcome the pain babies. The degrees that modern machines could be constructed to were truly frightening, both in appearance and in performance.

Some of the machines could be constructed by the morebats in the factory and put to use immediately. Others could be tested and then tweaked on the new arrivals until they delivered the desired results. Imagination and machinery without physical limits. Every engineer's dream. Every pain babies nightmare.

He envisioned it all. Machines that pulled apart bodies. Machines that skinned heads without searing. Machines that could cut at precise angles, delicately stripping the skin off by millimeters over a thousand years. Machines that crushed the bodies to a pulp but didn't permanently dismember. Machines that could simulate, stimulate, destruct, explode, ravage, contrive, convince, puncture, devour, chew, juxtapose, or just intimidate by sheer vastness.

The possibilities were endless.

The Architect drew up plans and then ordered construction on Welcome Crunchers. He realized that functionality was more important than aesthetics, so the prototype lacked smoothness and made hacking and coughing sounds as it moved. The jerkiness reflected something caught in the spokes, causing it to slink instead of roll. It sat upon a single drum-like wheel of a discarded barrel. The central part contained a "cruncher" that was a twisted and reshaped missile from a world war one silo that had exploded partially and still contained original Russian markings. The missile housing had been cut away in the center and sat at an angle on the barrel, off to one side.

He added a disassembled merry-go-round attached to the outer section of the missile, and as the Cruncher moved, the merry-go-round portion rotated around the machine. On each of the places where a wooden horse had once rested, now stood the rotting carcass of an animal at different stages of decay. There was a dog here and a horse there; a rhino here and a tiger there; an eagle here and a panther there. Turning at a steady pace with every movement that the Cruncher took, the decaying animals rotated. He kept them all alive and shrieking. Alive enough to scream out about the indignation of their predicaments. About the pain they must have suffered being put on this turnstile.

Under the carousel of still live animals was a hole located directly in the center of the machine, positioned between the missile and the barrel underneath. The hole was shaped specifically like a wide open mouth and contained thousands of razor-sharp teeth that sparkled and shined no matter what direction the machine faced. The mouth flexed and yawned as it approached the new arrivals. It was laughing, knowing it was about to eat.

And the Cruncher really only did one thing well: it ate. And it was always hungry.

The Architect finished his work and led several of the twin morebats out of the lab. He mandated the construction of a delivery chute and a well, and then used a few machines to welcome the new arrivals.

Taking a seat in a viewing room at the center of a command console, he waited for the next pain baby to arrive. He knew it wouldn't be long.

A chime sounded, and the morebats scurried around him to take up their places and prepare the new procedures and bring the machines to life. It was a glorious moment in the evolution of the City of Hell.

And he'd done it all himself.

Watching through a window, his plan took immediate effect. As the next nameless pain baby arrived coughing and hacking from the sand in his lungs, The Architect made sure he could see clearly. After being dragged to Hell, his vision improved rapidly. He needed to see what was up ahead.

And then the terror took over.

Like being dropped into an arctic lake in the middle of winter, the new pain baby was dropped onto a cold, hard canvas of nothing. Pure nothing. The light was gone and there was only darkness in its place. The arms that dragged him down were torn from around him. The man stood up and vomited. He was small and had a head full of bushy black hair that he parted on the side. The floor was ice cold, and he reacted like he was naked, even though he wore pants and a shirt. He reached up and pulled his clothes tighter around himself to ward off the frigid air, as he instantly knew this wasn't a good thing.

Whipping his head nervously back and forth, he squinted into the darkness. Seeing nothing, he shrunk down a little, trying to get his bearings. His fall was broken by a hard floor, but he didn't think he was hurt, as he rummaged his hands up and down, searching for broken bones. He heard nothing, but knew he was being watched, even though he couldn't see *them*. The room was completely devoid of sound or sight, and the only thing present was his own breath sounds. Like being under water in the darkness and not being able to feel anything, his breathing became more and more labored.

The Architect had no idea who he was or why this man arrived in the City. It wasn't his concern. He was just the first to get the new procedures, and for that matter alone, The Architect was interested in him. Nothing more. He was surprised at the sudden gasping for air that he knew wasn't there. The new pain baby, his first test subject, had no reason to be gasping for air. There wasn't any air here, anyway.

The Architect leaned forward and put his hands against the glass. The moment he was waiting for was just about to happen. It was almost excruciating slow with this one. The moment of realization. The second the man grasped his predicament.

It was simply the best theater imaginable. After all, who really thinks that when they're on the surface, they might actually end up in Hell? Leaning up farther and pushing his nose against the glass window, The Architect smiled. Any second now, he knew.

They always got religion.

But no one answered their pleas.

The Architect was gauging how much time to leave him in the room. It was an interesting phenomenon. He motioned to the morebats fiddling with controls that he couldn't possibly comprehend next to him in the booth. He mandated the time that this arrival remained in the dark and cold depended on how long he spent wailing. If he settled down, the morebats were to move forward to stage two. If not, there wasn't any hurry to get him out of the room.

The man with the bushy eyebrows quieted down, and The Architect pushed a button to show one of the twin morebats which sequence was next. The floor dropped out from underneath the man and he fell into a pit of murky water that bubbled around him. He splashed once and then surfaced quickly, scratching at the slick walls. He didn't know where he was, but he wanted out.

The twin morebats got excited watching the new arrival splash and try to grab a non-existent hand hold as he sank into the frigid water. He would sink and then surface again as he gasped for air that didn't exist. The pleasure came from watching him drown over and over.

The wailing and crying stopped completely, and he treaded water while he assessed his situation. He knew he was in a well. A deep well with cold water that sloshed. He also knew he couldn't tread water for long.

The Architect showed the twin morebats another slide switch and a door in the well's bottom opened and, like a swirling funnel, the well water drained. He hadn't meant for it to happen, but The Architect thought of a flushing toilet bowl as the water made a circular motion and descended into a whirlpool. The bushy eye-browed man got sucked down hard. He fought against the pull of the water, and then screamed as he entered the funnel.

Turning to another flip switch, The Architect expected the man's reaction and turned the strobes on. Piercing beams of red light cascaded around the falling man on all sides and highlighted parts of his anatomy like a target on a firing range. Small, distinct laser beams of light would dance on his chest and head as it looked for a suitable spot. The man tried vainly to grasp the light as he fell. It was the only thing he could focus on clearly as he descended and the freezing water fell with him.

The Architect showed the morebats how to move the lasers and light up different parts of the pain babies' body. He made sure the morebats understood to move the lights constantly so that nothing was solid. Nothing could be counted on. He wanted the mind of this man conditioned to unending terror. That was the key. The new arrivals needed to know it was always going to be this way.

He left nothing out of reach or off limits. He was welcoming the new arrivals to an eternity of pain and punishment without restrictions. This was simply the entrance point.

Pointing to another set of controls, The Architect watched as one morebat flipped through the images on a kaleidoscope. Across the walls, images appeared. Still pictures of the bushy eye-browed man's life on the surface. The walls would alternately light up, and a slow-motion movie played. Gruesome details of why the man was here.

Instantly, the bushy eye-browed man *knew*.

Throwing his head back, and letting out a chest full of energy, The Architect clutched at the moment. The new arrival understood. He owned him now.

The man wailed again. Whoever was doing this to him and whatever lay at the bottom of the pit knew what he'd done on the surface. Knew what crimes and sodomies he'd committed. Knew about the torture.

And it wanted revenge.

A full color still of him plunging a knife into the neck of wheelchair bound women flashed across the wall. On his left was the time he had to cut off two fingers of a man to steal a wedding ring. It was all here in glorious three dimensional vision. The pictures came complete with the cries of terror of his victims and flowed by a stopgap style pacing.

The Architect had the morebats fill the bottom of the welcome pit with stalagmites filed to razor sharp points. He didn't want this man impaled, but just pierced in several places. The stalagmites were honed thin to accomplish the task.

The water made a loud splashing sound as it hit the highs and lows of the perfectly placed stalagmites. The new arrival looked downward to the sound and the small light, momentarily drawn away from the scenes on the walls, as he sensed the bottom of the pit looming.

A sudden array of lights lit up the stalagmites. The busy eye-browed man hit the rocks with full force and was instantly pierced through until the points protruded from his back and legs. He screamed and wiggled to get free, but a couple of broken bones slowed him down. Every movement of his arms or legs caused excruciating pain.

With a sudden start and then another intake of air, he realized he wasn't *alone* on the rocks. To this point he'd been engrossed in himself, he now knew it was worse than that. Much worse. The new arrival went completely still, even though he was encased in pain from the rocks, and listened.

The Architect adjusted his seat and wrenched his neck to make sure he had an optimal view. He wanted to watch the man sweat. He needed to see the complete terror. His drug of choice.

It was a gasping, wheezing, coughing sound that seemed to come from the ground itself, but in reality just echoed off the rocks. The wheezing was deep and guttural, like it emanated from deep inside a cave. It rumbled and rolled at a steady pace, slightly increasing in intensity. It was clearly a breathing sound. From something large. Very large.

And it was getting closer to him.

The Architect could feel the man's fear. Actually feel it.

The man violently tried to free himself from the stalagmites. It didn't matter at this point what bones he'd broken or how badly he was bleeding or how many spears had gone through him; he was getting out of there *NOW*. He kicked and wrenched at everything around him.

But The Architect had the morebats grease the rocks to make it impossible to do anything but slide farther down.

It needed a name.

The Architect needed something profound to announce through a loudspeaker to the new arrival. Something sinister that conjured up an image unthinkable before by the new pain baby. He wrestled with some controls as he let his mind wander. Names like "Eater" or "Digester" or "Baby Crapper" didn't really do his creation justice.

He smiled. Picking up a microphone and leaning forward to watch the reaction, he whispered one word: "Cruncher."

The bushy-eye-browed man watched as it rounded the corner and came into full view. What looked like a claw came out of the top of the missile, slammed its pinchers together a couple of times for effect, and then reached for him. Grasping him around the waist, it stuffed him, screaming all the time, directly into its mouth. The jaws collapsed and bones broke and flesh tore off in pieces as the machine chewed. Good to the last drop.

And The Architect could tell by the look on the pain babies' face he'd done his job.

CHAPTER FIFTEEN

"I guess somebody, probably one of the council members, at some point thought this'd be a lot of fun. It's called the lazy river. It's a little bit hard to imagine, if you haven't actually seen it," Mack said as he and Byron stood at the edge of what appeared to be a flowing river.

"I thought most rivers had water in them. I'm not sure this constitutes water," Byron added as he watched the rocking of the river below them. They had moved off in the direction Randi indicated and only walked a short distance before they were standing at the riverbank.

"The patrons call it the 'River of Sleep.' Once you get trapped in it, you never get out. Like going into a coma with your eyes open."

Byron nodded. He had seen nothing like this before. Not even in East Los Angeles, where the real perversities could be found.

The river itself, if it could be called that, was a continuous motion display. It looked to be only four or five feet deep from Byron's vantage point and was flowing in a left-to-right direction. It meandered as far as he could see down the tunnel at a slow but steady pace. Mostly straight, but with some natural bends and breaks as it navigated around the various rock outcroppings in the tunnel. It may have been six feet across at its widest point.

But it wasn't filled with water. Whatever was filling up the river and sloshing against the sides of the tunnel was thick, like a snot kind of mucus after a bad summer cold. It was a green color and meaty, very meaty. It also bubbled and popped at various points like there was a boilerplate on the bottom and it was heating the mucus to a boiling temperature and the steam inside needed released. Pop pop here. Fizz fizz there. The river listed with its own sounds and movements. With its own life.

The mucus-snot water was fairly transparent, and that was good to a degree, as far as Byron was concerned. At least he could see what was in the water, even if it reflected a dyslexic appearance that anything under the surface of water showed. Shimmering at one point and moving at another, the shapes were indistinct and hard to accurately define, but the general nature of what was in the river was fairly easy to identify.

As the two of them stared into the current, several bodies floated just at the top of the surface or just beneath it. Because the river wasn't deep, the bodies of the unlucky patrons who were placed here or had fallen in and couldn't get out would bob and weave in a continual display of buoyancy. Some were floaters and others were sinkers. There didn't appear to be anything other than randomness in whom or what was floating or sinking.

The patrons would surface, cough and hack for a moment as they cleared themselves of the snot-mucus from their lungs and airways, and then they'd just float past Mack and Byron. Most would glance up and look at them as they stood there, but no one said anything. They didn't ask to get out or to be helped. They just floated on past. All very much alive and all very much trapped. One would bob up and take a mouthful of air and then disappear beneath the surface as he continued down the path of the river.

But the bodies weren't the only things to float past them. There were thousands, maybe hundreds of thousands, of partial bodies. And body parts. It was like the City had decided the river was its own dumping ground for bodies. Mack and Byron watched scalps, eyes, ears, tongues, feet, legs, fingers, testicles, breasts, and every other imaginable body part, bob and weave its way along the path.

And all of it was alive. Every single part twitched.

The eyes stared. The chests heaved. The nostrils flared, and the teeth chattered. The fingers wiggled, and the toes stretched. The breasts and their respective nipples quivered for attention. The testicles dangled and swayed with the movement of the current. The tongues flicked. The arms wavered, and the legs tried to run. It was an overwhelming spectacle of movement as the river swallowed the parts up along with all the bodies and hurtled them all forward.

"It looks like we'll have to ride this river for a while," Mack said as he tentatively put one foot in the snot-mucus and then stepped inside. He quickly pushed off from the bank and let the current carry him along. He turned to look back at Byron, who was watching him from his one eye, and motioned for him to enter the river. "Come on. The bend can't be too far up here."

Byron shrugged and stuck his foot in to test the river before he jumped in up to his hips. The snot-mucus was warm like molasses and thick, like an over-ripe oyster. As he surrendered to the stream, he thought he wasn't drifting along in the river, but riding the stench and the oysters.

He pushed his foot farther down and easily touched the bottom. But then whatever was under his foot shifted and Byron knew he placed his foot on top of one of the body parts and not the bottom of the river. He refused to look and see what it was.

Mack had traveled a little further ahead. He was uncomfortable, but not afraid. Things kept bumping into him and then sloshing away. Occasionally he heard of grunt of protest when one of the patrons with a voice and full body stumbled into him. It reminded him of one of those lazy rivers that wound themselves around amusement parks. It just kept flowing, and everything and everyone in it rode with the current.

Byron resigned himself to riding the snot-mucus and tried his best to keep his single eye trained straight ahead, looking for the bend that Randi mentioned. He couldn't get out of this fucking river of snot fast enough. Every time he took the chance and looked down to see what was passing him, he cringed and wished he hadn't. He could deal with the bodies as they popped up to get some air and coughed and hacked, because they barely seemed to notice him.

But the parts were a different matter altogether. Not all of them were recognizable. He could see what looked like whole intestines stretched out beside him, snaking their way right along down the river. Here was a blood red heart still beating. There went an aqua blue pair of lungs, still breathing. Here was what he guessed was someone's gray matter brain. He had to look away and concentrate on the bend and the staircase that couldn't get to him quick enough.

Up ahead, he glimpsed the river bend and watched as Mack grabbed a hold of a railing from the staircase. It protruded directly down to the bank of the river, but not into it. The design was obviously to give a patron the chance to get out of the river, but not necessarily the permission to do so. Byron wasn't entirely convinced that this river might not have been one of the lesser of the punishments in the City. It was certainly the tamest he'd seen so far.

He only had another couple of moments to ride the current to where Mack got out when he felt something attach itself to the front of his pants. It felt like something was tugging at his pants and had somehow gotten a grip on his zipper. He reached down and outlined an arm without a body attached to it. He ran his fingers up the arm to the end until he found the fingers.

Byron grabbed the hand as the zipper on the front of his jeans was being pulled down. As quick as any hooker he'd ever paid for, his zipper was down and the hand reached inside his pants and was rapidly stroking his penis in an up and down fashion. It was the most erotic touch he'd ever felt. Whoever had owned this arm and hand must have at one time been an incredible massage therapist that excelled in happy endings. His penis stiffened of its own accord.

He shook his head and seized the fingers with both of his hands. Mack stood watching his ministrations from the river bank with a perplexed look on his face as Byron ripped the hand and fingers away from inside his jeans and then pulled the arm above the snot-mucus and threw it as far as he could down the river. He watched as it plopped downstream and then bobbed once before disappearing from sight.

Mack reached down and grabbed his outstretched hand as he drifted to the railing and the staircase. With a pull and a grunt, Mack helped him out of the river. There was a slight belch as the river gave up one of its prizes with little indignation. Byron stood up and looked back down as another body popped to the surface for air.

He nodded at Mack and then looked down at his still open zipper. All of his clothes were covered in a thick meat sauce and a significant portion of it had penetrated inside his pants and was sliding down his legs. Wriggling its way down like it had purpose. He shook first one leg and then the other.

Mack motioned for him to follow and climbed up the stairs in front of them. They weren't very steep and ended abruptly in a brightly painted red door. Turning, he put his hand out and placed it in the center of Byron's chest, motioning for him to stop for a moment. They were standing on the top landing directly in front of the red door.

"I need to remind you of a few things before we go in. First, the room mother fuckers will try to trick us into staying in the rooms with them. Or they will point us in the wrong direction. Remember, they're always being watched and will do or say anything to get out of that room and demoted. Do not fucking trust anything you see or hear."

Byron nodded his agreement.

"Second, we've got a scroll that I'm not sure helps us or misleads us. Annicka and her daughter wanted you and me together to find this Rose, but there's more to it than that. We just don't know what it is yet. They will gladly sacrifice us if it benefits them," Mack glanced towards the door.

"Third, and this is the one that we have to pay attention to and get right. Absolutely right. There's only one exit that's the correct way out of each of these rooms. There's no place for errors."

"What happens if we pick the wrong exit?"

"This City was set up to receive, not release. Each of these rooms has several doors that lead into and out of them. Only problem is, it's like a never ending maze of trouble. One door will lead us in the right direction and to the next room, and another door will lead us into trouble. We pick the wrong door and go into the wrong room and the room mother will try to keep us. The doors will swing shut behind us, and it's almost impossible to reopen them. No handles on the doors behind us. Only on the doors in front of us. On purpose, of course. We won't be able to get back where we came from. An architect's nightmare. If we chose the wrong door at any time, then the journey will be over and we won't get a second chance. We'll be trapped in the wrong room and we might be given to the room mother fucker. Each of our choices of exits has to be exact."

"Doesn't sound like a high probability for success, Teacher."

"No, it doesn't. I know why they choose me, I think. I've always been good with puzzles, and this is going to be a difficult one. Something they haven't been able to figure out before. I also have experience in the City."

"That doesn't explain why I'm here, does it? I'm not real good with puzzles, but at one time, I was a pretty good detective. Maybe they thought you needed help?"

Mack nodded. "Maybe."

He turned and put his hand on the door knob. "We're about to find out," he said as he turned the handle and pushed the door open with his foot.

CHAPTER SIXTEEN

Mack opened the door and walked tentatively into the room, followed closely by Byron. The two of them were separated by about three feet, and Byron had edged a little closer to make sure that Mack didn't accidentally let the door close behind him and leave him on the outside of the room. Being left behind in this place wasn't something that he wanted to even contemplate.

Mack's eyes adjusted quickly to the dim light emanating from some low wattage fluorescent bulbs hanging from the ceiling. He'd never been in this room before and he wanted to stop for a moment and get a sense of exactly where he was and what was going on in front of him. He thought it best to move at a snail's pace until he located the potential danger signs ahead. He knew there'd be plenty of them.

Mack could feel Byron slide in behind him. He was bunched so close that Mack could feel breathing on his shirt collar. The door behind them closed with a rush of putrid air and slammed shut. There was no going back now. A slight tremor of fear wiggled itself into his brain.

The room was circular and seemed to be perfectly symmetrical on all sides. It didn't have a high ceiling, and the roof appeared to be just above six feet, giving it a cramped feeling. Byron could barely pass underneath it without scraping the ceiling with his hair. The room resembled a bass drum laid on its side. Everywhere Mack turned and looked from the front to the back, there were no corners. Perfectly round.

The room was painted in two alternating colors. First red and then black, touching each other in perfectly straight lines running from the ceiling to the floor. Bright red next to glossy black. Even in the dim light, it was an unsettling room. Something he didn't want to spend a lot of time in.

Byron positioned himself evenly next to Mack and within an arm's reach away. He, too, surveyed the room and took everything in. Standing in this room was like being trapped in a fish bowl.

He nudged Mack on the arm and pointed directly in front of them and then back across to the wall behind. He mouthed the word "doors" silently, and Mack nodded. The walls were doors. About three to four feet wide and stretching the length of the room from ceiling to floor, the walls were made up of doors. Each was painted in the red and black color patterns and came equipped with a doorknob. Byron let out a very soft whistle as he contemplated the dilemma they faced. How in the world were they going to figure out which door to leave from?

"Gentlemen! Gentlemen! You must be Teacher and Mr. Michaels? We've been waiting for you for some time. We heard you might join us. Please be welcomed to the red and black room!" A booming voice across a crackling loud speaker addressed them. The words were alternately loud and booming and then crackled and popped like an old radio program from the nineteen thirties. Mack couldn't tell where it came from or in which direction because the sound of the voice echoed off the round walls.

"I am the Ringmaster and you have entered my room. Please feel free to stay as long as you like! You might like it so much that you'll decide to stay with us permanently!" The loud speaker belched at the two of them.

"Remember Kmart shoppers, only three minutes left before the wheel goes round and round again!"

Mack heard a sound like a small whimper from a child and realized it was a female's very weak voice. Until now, he'd been so caught up in his bewilderment at the very structure of the room he hadn't even noticed all the patrons lying on the floor. The sound of the voice, soft but obviously in pain, drew his attention to the center of the room.

Mack looked down at the floor and, with his eyes finally adjusted to the lighting, could see several bodies, both men and women, lying on the ground a few feet from them. He glanced at Byron and saw that he'd already noticed them.

The people were arranged in various positions across the floor. There were so many of them they covered the decking almost completely, but he could still see that it was painted black. Many of them were moaning softly, like they were only mildly injured, but Mack knew that this was a complete deception. Whatever had happened to them stopped a couple of minutes ago, and this was the recovery period.

"One minute! One minute, my very dear pupils. The Ringmaster will make all your dreams come true in one minute! Teacher! Mr. Michaels! You are going to enjoy the show we put on for the pain babies here in the red and black room. I'm sure you will love the design! I am very pleased to present it for you. Please take your places as the show is about to begin!" The loud speaker crackled to a silence with a last hiss and a pop.

Mack motioned to Byron and with the one minute left before whatever was going to happen happened, he studied the nearest door to his immediate left.

"Look." Mack pointed to the door directly in front of him. "Each of the doors has a name and a number on them."

"How in the hell are we going to figure out which door to go through, Teacher?" Byron scanned all the doors. "There's sixteen of them."

Mack was studying the lettering on the door to his side. It was labeled "RED 3." Next to it on the immediate right was "BLACK 3." He pointed to the numbers. "Look Byron, they're in sequential order." He pointed to the left of the door in front of them. Next to "RED 3" was "BLACK 2" and then next to it was "RED 2." He quickly located the door marked "RED 1" and made Byron move over and stand in front of it. He had no idea which door they entered through, but he knew their search had to start with the beginning.

On the immediate left of "RED 1" was "BLACK 8." Byron pointed to that one. "There are sixteen doors, Teacher. RED 1 through RED 8 and BLACK 1 through BLACK 8. We have to figure out which one..." his voice trailed off as the loudspeaker interrupted him.

"Time's up patrons of the red and black. As your Ringmaster it brings me great pleasure to bring you the next round of fun! Round? Did I just say that? Well, I guess it fits, huh? Ha, ha, ha, ha," the voice trailed off with a deep, disgusting laughter.

Mack heard a clear buzzing sound like someone had turned a machine on, and then he quickly steadied himself as the floor shifted. There was mechanical latch or two that unhitched underneath him, and then the floor rotated slowly. He grabbed a hold of the wall the best he could and looked across to see that Byron had also taken up a position against the wall for support.

The floor started slowly but quickly gained momentum and as Mack and Byron pressed themselves up against the doors behind their backs, the room accelerated. The patrons of this room who'd been lying on the floor were thrown outward against the walls as the centrifugal force of the rotating floor caused them to be hurled tightly against the walls.

Mack felt himself being pulled to the center of the room. He shook his head, as this was physically impossible. If the floor was rotating underneath him, then he'd have to have been pinned against the wall by the force. But it was not to be.

As some unseen force pulled them both into the center of the room, it also pulled all the other patrons in with it. Mack fell to his knees as he realized that the floor hadn't been moving at all, but the *walls* were spinning. As he laid down, the speed of the walls picked up and seemed to spin so fast that Mack could no longer discern the separation of the red and black doors at all. The room was revolving at an incredible speed, and he was lying on the floor in the middle of the room watching the red and black doors rush past his field of vision.

Red. Black. Red. Black. Red. Black. Red. Black.

Each one of the doors became a blur of motion and color as they flew past Mack and Byron. The image of the spinning room and the red and black colors rushing past his limited field of vision was making him nauseous. Very nauseous.

He closed his eyes tightly in the middle of the floor as the room spun mercilessly around him. Byron had melted into the crowd of the pain babies who'd been drawn to the center of the room with them. It was a mass of bodies heaped upon one another as the room continued to gain speed and spin.

Mack looked up and he could no longer read any of the words on the doors. He could see bits and pieces as they rushed past him. R2. B3. R8. B1. R1. Then the numbers themselves disappeared as the room gained maximum speed and spun round and round. He squeezed his eyes shut again.

Most of the people that Byron could see were hiding their heads under their shirts or arms so that they didn't have to see the red and black colors rushing past their eyes. He looked up long enough to realize that he was losing his mind.

The colors were mesmerizing. As he stared at them, they actually seemed to slow down. He could see the numbers clearly. Red and Black. Red and Black. It was so beautiful.

He let out a howl when he realized that he'd been hypnotized and did not know how long he'd been staring in rapt attention at the passing colors, but he knew that if they didn't stop immediately, he might kill whoever he could reach. He was having an epileptic seizure brought on by the constant barrage of colors on his senses.

He lowered his head and promptly vomited all over the entire group of bodies lying below him. As soon as the other patrons heard him retch, all of their respective stomachs convulsed as one and they all vomited uncontrollably. One after one would bend over and then empty the contents of whatever was left in their stomachs all over the other pain babies assembled around them. Mack held out for a few seconds and then he joined him on his hands and knees and vomited until he couldn't breathe. He could not stop his stomach lurching as all his sensory organs of balance were thrown out of whack.

Mack and Byron vomited along with everyone else until there was nothing left to spit up and then several of the pain babies bowels' let go directly into their pants. So much shit was expunged that it invariably worked itself out of their pants legs and onto the other patrons and the floor. Another round of vomiting followed.

Mack curled himself into a fetal position and silently wished for it to end. He looked up one last time to see what happened to Byron, but as he did, the pain baby on his immediate left let his bowels release onto the floor next to Mack and then he vomited again. His stomach felt like a tied up slip knot that had lunged its way up to the back of his throat.

With his eyes closed and his body exhausted, he at last heard another buzzing sound and then some more mechanical latches and he knew that the red and black room was slowing down. He didn't even attempt to stand up because he couldn't have anyway, so he lay still until he was sure the room no longer moved. Opening his eyes once again and looking at the red and black doors, he saw the numbers go slowly by without the words attached. B 4. R 5. B 7. R 3. R 1.

The walls came to a complete stop with a whine and then a hiss as somewhere steam was released. An old locomotive pulling into the station and dumping its load.

Byron had not raised his head yet, and Mack struggled to stand up. There was vomit and feces everywhere, and he was covered in some kind of bile that he couldn't possibly identify. But he knew for certain that the stench alone would make him vomit again if he didn't get out of there. Now.

"Ah. Teacher! I see you survived. Do you know where you are? Some of the pain babies forget after the first couple of spins. They forget where they are and what they're doing. Some even forget who they are. But one thing is for sure, Teacher, this will drive you insane! Perhaps Mr. Michaels would like another go!" The ringmaster blared out of the speakers at Mack, who stood groggily on his feet and tried to find his balance. He spied Byron trying to stand, and after stopping to retch one more time, he walked over to him. His head was clearing just slightly enough to help.

"Enjoy yourselves, my pupils. You have ten minutes! What's that you say? We don't have clocks in the City? Oh shit! I forgot! I'll just have to guess!"

Mack leaned against a door and Byron stood next to him. Byron's face looked terrible, and Mack saw that the vomiting was harder on him than it had been on Mack. He reached into his back pocket and pulled the scroll free. He quickly unrolled it and read the words about the red and black room again. It was all he could do to see the words.

Byron tried to be some kind of assistance. He continually wiped his mouth with the sleeve of his shirt and blinked his eye to focus. It wasn't much, but it was the best he could do. He leaned in over the shoulder of Mack and read in silence.

"Whatever we figure out, here, Teacher, it better be quick. I'll be damned if I want to go through that again."

"I know. Me neither. Let's take a look at the stanza again. Right at the moment, I have no clue."

Mack held the scroll for both of them to read. He didn't think he could figure it out before the room mother fucker turned the machine on again. If he couldn't get it done, they'd have to go through it again and make sure he didn't lose the scroll while puking his guts up.

"The answer has to be in this one stanza," he said, pointing at the only stanza with a reference to red and black in it.

Red blood and black night
Take a risk before
Chances are won
In a circus of gore.

Mack shook his head. He had no clue.

"My children. My children. The clock that we don't have in the City is nearing ten minutes. I can feel it. Can't you? What fun we are having and I think our guests, Teacher and Mr. Michaels, are staying for another round. May I buy the round this time, Teacher?" The cackling voice across the speaker was having a huge time.

"I really would like to take this guy out. Wouldn't you?" Byron said under his breath.

Mack didn't answer and refocused his attention on the scroll. The answer had to be there. He looked at the doors and the numbers and labels on each of them. RED 1. BLACK 1. RED 2. BLACK 2.

Mack closed his eyes and could see the numbers and letters on the doors flying by as the room spun a minute ago. The labels had been reduced to mere fragments of words. The numbers indistinguishable from the other numbers. They were like strobe numbers and letters in Mack's mind as he replayed them flying past him when the room was spinning.

Red. R. Black. B.

R1. B1. R2. B2. R1.

He suddenly opened his eyes and read the scroll again. Byron could sense a change in Mack. "What? What is it? Jesus Christ, hurry."

"Time is up my children! The round's on me this time! Come to think of it, the rounds on me every time! Who will vomit first? I cannot wait to see! Who will shit themselves first? Teacher, will it be you and your friend this time? The ringmaster has spoken!"

Mack read the lines again.

Red blood and black night
Take a risk before
Chances are won
In a circus of gore.

"Look, Byron. It's right here. It was right in front of me the whole time, damn it!"

"I don't see it, but I don't care. Just do it, Teacher. Whatever the choice is, we need to make in now." Byron said as he heard the buzzer go off and around them, a dozen of the patrons groaned loudly.

"Here. Right here," he pointed. "The chances are won. It's not 'are won.' It's R 1. The individual numbers on the door. I saw it as they spun around."

"Let's get out of here. Now!" Byron tugged on Mack and headed off to the door marked RED 1. They crossed the room and Mack put his hand on the door and was about to turn the handle when he heard the first of the latches unlock on the floor beneath them. The room slowed to a crawl.

Mack stopped. It was wrong.

"What? What? Open the fucking door, Teacher! The room is starting to spin again. We don't have any time." Byron put a hand out to the door as it moved.

Here comes the first of many rounds on me, my children! Hang on! Hang on! Wait! There's nothing to hang on to! Ha, Ha, Ha, Ha....." the Ringmaster was laughing hysterically at his own joke.

Mack pulled the scroll up as the room shook beneath his feet.

"Teacher! We don't have time. We have to go. Now!" Byron grabbed his arm.

"We can't be wrong. We can't go back." Mack shook his arm free. "5317. Remember? 5317." He quickly scanned the stanza again. Then he saw it.

Take a risk before
Chances are won

The walls of the room were speeding up. Mack said, "It's not R 1. It's the stanza above it. It's not R 1."

"What? How can you be sure? We have to be sure." Byron said as he let the door handle to R 1 fall from his grasp and the door moved away from them. "What fucking door is it?"

"It's here. It's B 4. In the stanza above the 'are won' stanza it says 'Take a risk before.' Everything is backwards here. It doesn't mean 'before.' It means door B 4. It doesn't mean there's a risk at B 4. It means the opposite.

There isn't a risk at B4! It's referencing the path through the B4 door. That agrees with R1. Chances aren't won with R1. It's backwards. It means no chances are won with R1. You have to trust me."

Byron wasn't sure and had never been good at this type of thing, but he knew he couldn't stay where he was at the moment. "I do. Let's go!" Byron shouted. "Here comes Black 4."

The room walls had gained speed, and Mack and Byron tried desperately to keep their balance. As the door got closer, Byron grabbed the handle with one hand and, with the other hand, grabbed Mack. He opened the door and stepped through, pulling Mack close behind him.

"*Fuck you assholes! Fuck you, Teacher! You'll never get back! Never!*" the Ringmaster screamed at them through the loudspeaker as the room hit maximum acceleration and all of the patrons were again thrown into the center of the room. He was enraged that they'd left him.

As the door slammed and clicked behind them, all Mack could hear was the Ringmaster screaming, "*You picked the wrong door, assholes! You picked the wrong door!*"

CHAPTER SEVENTEEN

Victor and David traveled to the drug store of the City and picked up the supplies to concoct his own personal cocktail that could extend the time the portal was open. Although David had been fairly precise in what drugs were needed, and with his forensic and physician's background, he could make an excellent case for knowing what would and wouldn't work, Victor knew he hadn't gotten the prescription exactly right. There were always complications here. This was just one of those that he'd have to deal with for the time being.

To start, the City didn't keep an extensive amount of drugs on hand. There was no pharmacy per se, but there was a place where drugs could be obtained. Victor led David there, knowing what they were going to find would not be what they were going to need. The City wasn't set up to relieve pain. The entire purpose of existence was torture and maiming, which eliminated the need for most drugs. The enigma of actually having a drugstore in the first place made no sense to anyone. However, some things were kept available.

None of the drugs in the City were used to heal. They were used simply to prolong an existing high from some previous drugs or to induce one. Being Hell's Doctor, Victor was a regular sight at the drugstore. He frequently liked to shoot up whatever they had in stock before he operated on the pain babies. He never knew exactly what he was injecting into his veins or snorting up his nose. If there was an advantage to not worrying about the effects a certain drug could cause, it was that since overdose was impossible; it didn't really matter what was snorted or shot up. A basic perk.

Generic equivalents didn't exist. The quality was pure and uncut and the Doctor was given the liberty of deciding if he gave the drugs out or used them on himself. The stocks were meager and no one really gave a shit one way or the other, as long as some were available when they wanted to use them. The drugs were his to use as he saw fit. Why they even had a morebats to control giving them out in the first place made no sense to Victor. Why block control of who got the drugs when no one cared what they were used for? It wasn't something he thought about, anyway.

David had requested what he regularly used on the surface or an equivalent, but Victor ended up with a hodgepodge of what was available. A true cocktail. He'd gotten some of the right ones and just grabbed a handful of others. Maybe it would work. He had little faith, but stranger things had happened. Especially here.

Victor was playing a dangerous game, and he knew it. Eikken the Lion left specific instructions on what they should've been doing and so far they had gotten nowhere near close to even asking for information. He'd taken the turn to the drugstore and now they headed to see the doorman. Neither of these tasks was he supposed to be doing. If Eikken found out, and he was sure that he would eventually, he'd be in trouble. Retribution here was not a simple task. But if he had bargaining power, then it might prove worth it.

"I'm having trouble understanding how we're supposed to reproduce my laboratory experiments without having the proper drugs, Victor," David said as they walked quickly through some terrifyingly dark hallways to some unknown location. He was blindly following the Doctor and trying to make sense of the package of drugs given to him. "I mean, half of this stuff. I don't even know what it is, let alone what it does. How can I possibly recreate my findings in this type of environment?"

Victor was walking at a hurried pace and not really in a mood to stop and explain at all to him. David was a higher being. First, and second, he didn't answer to him. He damn sure would not tell him what he was planning. "Listen, asshole. I got you the best they had. You're going to have to learn to work it out and handle it like it is. We don't get a lot of second chances to get it right here."

Victor turned to the left and then to the right, like he knew exactly where he was and where he was headed. David was trying to keep up but kept slipping on the slimy flooring, if it was even flooring at all, and also trying to read the labels on the packages in his hands. He could make out some words on the labels, but this wasn't an easy task.

"I can't even tell what I've got here, Victor," he was almost pleading as they walked. "I can't read the labels."

The Doctor whirled on him and grabbed him by the throat, lifting David completely off the floor. "One more time, asshole. This isn't Walgreens. You *will* recreate the brain death extension drug from your lab, and you'll do it with what I've given you or I'll remove another couple of your vertebra and toss you to the next higher level and leave you there. Are we clear on that?" He pulled David up close to his face and hissed at him through yellow teeth.

Tossing him back on the ground, he watched as David dragged himself up and wiped his nose with his sleeve. "I can't. I can't. I can't...." David started stuttering again.

WHACK!

Victor hit him with the shovel and David collapsed on the ground because he hit him harder than normal. He shook himself to clear the cobwebs and resumed what he was saying. "I'll do it. I won't complain anymore." He looked down at the drugs in his hands. He'd have to make do with what he had. It was going to take some adjustments.

Victor nodded and resumed his march down the smoky hall. He noticed David stuttered more when he got nervous. It was a 'tic' that he could use if he had to later on. Like during a poker game when someone has a good hand and then rubs their fingers or arching their eyebrows to give it away to all the other players at the table. David's stuttering meant he didn't know or have what was needed. Victor could use it to tell if he was lying to him. It'd prove to be useful later, Victor was sure of that.

Turning down a last hallway, they came to a metal door that was closed and appeared to be rusted shut from many years of disuse. Victor stopped for a moment and then, without thinking further about what he was going to do, reached for the iron handle and heard the tumblers groan from years of dust and mold, and then finally flex and give way. He tugged the door open and went inside.

David followed him as closely as he could without touching. He didn't want to bring the wrath down on him again. The Doctor had a hair trigger on his temper and seriously needed anger management classes as far as David could tell.

The room was small and, like every other place in the City, dimly lit. There was some light from behind a small podium that sat at the far facing wall across from the door they'd just entered, but it was more for the patron who stood at the podium than for any visitors. He had to see; the visitors didn't. By design.

The man standing behind the podium was not surprised to see them. Even though the door had opened slowly and with some small metal complaint from lack of use, it seemed like they'd been expected. Like the man who stood there welcomed guests to this place every day, and they were his morning appointment.

He was dressed like he'd been a monk or perhaps a brother at a sanctuary on the surface. He wore a tattered floor-length robe of gray that was wrapped around his waist with an old rope. He had a few tufts of salt and pepper colored hair on his head that stood straight up. He was portly and solid, but the years in this cavern made him speak in a nasal voice through what was left of his blackened teeth. He obviously didn't get to talk to many people.

The Doctor stood in front of him, not sure exactly how to proceed. He'd come here on purpose and not without a lot of prior thoughts on the matter. There was the issue of who was the lower being to be considered that Victor wasn't clear about to begin with, and what he wanted to do probably would not go over very well either. A terrible combination.

But he'd come here for a reason and wouldn't be dissuaded by nuances and pettiness like correct decorum and protocol. He would use bribery. That was always an excellent tactic.

"You're the doorman?" Victor asked.

"I am. What do you seek?" The monk replied.

"I came to help you," Victor said.

The doorman laughed. No one comes to help anyone. "Horseshit," was all he said.

Victor nodded. So much for that approach. Persistence instead might work.

"I need to try an experiment. I am the Doctor, if you do not know."

"So?"

"I require entrance to the inner workings of the portal. I believe I can aid in the expediency of the new arrivals, thereby aiding my own service to the council members."

"So?" He was obviously unimpressed.

Victor thought for a moment. Name dropping wasn't working, nor was this guy impressed with him. He tried his staple.

"I could cut you. Into many small pieces."

The doorman didn't move at the threat. He wrinkled his fat face, and his nose seemed to disappear entirely into the folds of his skin. His neck had bulged, and he was turning a distinct shade of red. He was already bored with this man.

"You will not threaten me. It will do you no good. Try stating your reason for coming here or be gone."

Victor had never even considered telling him the truth. It wasn't an option.

"I can't. I can't. I can't...." David had started again.

Victor took the shovel and, turning to David, swung the shovel in a wide arc, but deliberately missed David and hit the monk on the side of the head before he could react and get out of the way. No one, at any time, had ever come into the portal and tried to force their way in. It made no sense to go into the portal; it was an "Exit Only" place. If there'd ever been a way to get back to the surface, this wasn't it, so there'd been no reason to guard the entrance. The so-called doorman simply controlled the movement out of the portal. There was never a reason to go in from this entrance.

Victor hit the man lying on the ground again and again until he could no longer form a coherent sentence and blood shot forcefully into the air from his neck and head. He rolled on the ground and cried softly through his fat cheeks, but no one was coming to help him.

Victor motioned to David, and the two of them slid him out of the way and against the wall. Grabbing the door handle behind the podium, Victor pulled the door open and for the second time in the last several moments, they stepped through a seldom used doorway.

CHAPTER EIGHTEEN

Annicka glided through the rooms of the City. Her mind and her demeanor were in a calamitous place. She was seething inside and trembling on the outside. It would not do any of the higher beings any good to come into contact with her at this moment. The Professor's information had set her off on this journey.

It wouldn't have been her place to find the Black Rose on her own. No one of her status in the City had ever taken it upon themselves to do the work of a higher being when it could be doled out. The council members were continuously in a quest to either maintain or expand their power realm and domination of the higher beings through either direct intimidation or trickery. It'd been that way from the beginning. She had enough to keep her busy without adding a journey.

As she glided, her thoughts were solely concentrated on the power of the Rose. The portal had one purpose and one purpose only: to bring new arrivals into the domain of the City. There had to be a way for the new denizens to arrive, and the portal was established a long time prior to Annicka's arrival. It was just the way it was. Like so many other things in the City, it was simply accepted.

She had arrived through the portal, as had every other patron in the City. She held no memory of the majority of the events since her arrival. It suited most of the patrons to retain very little memory. There wasn't anything they even wanted to remember from their time spent being punished. It served only as a reminder of what they didn't need. A horrible memory was considered best left under the carpet.

Annicka's memories of her time in the City consisted mostly of vague images that swam somewhere under her consciousness. She retained glimpses that startled her sometimes as she glided along, administering over her higher beings. Things that could bring her to a stop in motion and cause her eyes to change color from red to black and then back again. Images from both the surface and from some of the time here. Since she had no idea how long she'd been here, as did anyone else, memories were not a luxury that she would have to handle.

But the power of the mind, and of the subconscious mind in particular, was an overwhelming thing. It was always there, just below the surface, like something hidden in a shallow pool in the forest. There was something always swimming in the pond, but never defined. And the subconscious was arbitrary when or where it brought those memories to the surface. If the subconscious mind decided it wanted to remember an event and bring it to the forefront of the mind, then nothing could stop it.

It was like that for all the patrons. The memories could have been manipulated by the lower beings, and to a certain degree they were, like when a council member invoked a punishment memory unto one of their higher beings, but mostly the memories of the patrons were off limits. Uncontrollable. And that had also been by design.

It didn't take very long for the council members to realize that the longer the patrons retained their original memories from the surface, the more chance it would be that they would also retain some of their ability to *conceive*. Not conceive like reproduce. But rather to conceive a plan. To formulate an idea. An original idea that hadn't been seen before, and possibly use this to usurp the council members' position of authority. To gain the council position for themselves.

That could not be tolerated. Not by any council member who wanted to retain their position, as they all did. Higher beings were better controlled and punished by limiting their memories. If they couldn't remember their life on the surface, then they couldn't try to get back to it. They would only know a life in the City. An excellent premise.

Annicka had been no different when she'd first been a pain baby. She spent a considerable amount of time on both of the higher floors, one after the other, sometimes moving freely back and forth. She was cunning enough to understand her placement and vicious enough to earn her demotions.

She got noticed quickly.

But not all of her memories could be easily erased. Her subconscious mind had a will of its own sometimes and as she glided along in search of one of her minions, she came to an abrupt halt. Her eyes swapped color, and she was drawn back to the time when she was on the surface.

She stopped her movement when she sensed, rather than remembered, that she'd been in a hallway like this one in a previous life. The hallway was lit up by hanging candelabras that each contained a single burning candle swaying at a slight incline. The flames danced around and across the brick walls from a warm breeze blowing in from an open doorway. Even though that was impossible because there were no open doors anywhere, the flames still moved.

But the memory flickered across the vision of Annicka's eyes like a warm ray of sunshine she hadn't seen in so many eons. She was a little girl, maybe seven or eight years old, and she was running through the caverns of a castle. She could hear her name being called by her mother, although she couldn't see her. Her mother kept calling her, and she ran faster and faster. Her mother was a duke's wife of some status in Europe, but Annicka couldn't remember either her home country or her official title. She just knew her father was a revered duke from the old country.

Her footsteps echoed off the bricks and mortar walls of the castle where she lived and played. Her father was seldom in attendance because his business and position in the hierarchy of the country's government kept him away from Annicka and her mother frequently. But he was arriving home today, and the castle was alive with anticipation. All the servants, from the lowest serf to the chambermaids of her mother, were bustling about the castle this day. There was laughter and gaiety, and the entire castle was alive.

Annicka saw see herself running through back rooms and climbing the stairs towards the sound of her mother's voice. The voice was clipped and strong, like perhaps she was tired of calling for her daughter. Annicka had wandered far away from her mother and probably would've been punished for that at another time, but not today. There was too much to do before the return of her father.

As Annicka mounted the steps, out of breath and as excited as she could possibly be, she didn't notice that one brick had come loose from the step she was about to land on, and as she laid her foot upon it, the casing gave way and she tumbled backwards from her momentum and then fell. She heard a distinct snap as her ankle broke cleanly in two pieces, and then she cried out and fell to the ground in pain.

Within moments, she was swarmed by the servants of the castle as they rushed her to her mother's arms. Her mother reached out to take her, and

Annicka could see the warmth and concern in her eyes. Her tears would not fall on deaf ears this day.

Annicka's eyes rolled back to their normal color of black as the memory receded from her conscious. She didn't like these temporary interruptions when she needed concentration. Her path wasn't clear at present, but fraught with her concern for her position and likely demotion to the head of the council to replace Stapleton. That was what this truly was about.

She pushed the momentary memory of her mother's face and her broken ankle from her vision and thought no more about it. Distractions served no purpose here. It only weakened inner strength, and if any of the other council members could use it against her, they most certainly would do just that.

The portal was her chief concern at the moment. The Professor had clearly told her she could use the power of the Black Rose to reverse the direction of the portal. If that were true, then Annicka could control who came down to the City, and more than likely send herself back to the surface. It wasn't a unique idea, she knew, but she also knew that whoever had tried to gain this advantage before had failed.

There'd been stories of the Black Rose for many eons, and the resultant pain that the possession of the Rose would cause the owner. The history was not clear, but it was delicious with intrigue. And power. Always about the power.

Returning to the surface was not something Annicka even contemplated until this moment. What would be the purpose in that? Why wish to be among higher beings than herself who simply could not or would not envision the depths of the richness that awaited them once they expired from their insignificant lives and were transported to this Hell? It made no sense.

But controlling the movement across the portal could add to her stable of pain babies and increase her concentration of power. The more patrons above her, the better. And she would be perceived by the other council members as having special favors, which she could use. Plus some timely deceptions to remove Stapleton from his seat at the bottom of the council table. It would be a considerable coup. She could increase the number of her servants, have the ability to control the very number of new arrivals and possibly the timing, control the movement across the portal, and be demoted. It was simply the lowest form of reward she could envision.

She resumed her gliding among the rooms of the City. She enjoyed watching the higher beings receiving their punishment. Their screams could be refreshing to her and helped her to concentrate.

She held several advantages, even though she knew that her visit to the Professor, and what he told her, would be common knowledge among the council members soon enough, if it wasn't already known at this point. She had something that none of them had: the scroll.

It hadn't been easy to locate, and when she first heard of the existence of the Rose, she instinctively knew that it would be hidden somewhere within the many cracks and crevices of the City. Hidden well, because if any of the rumors of the power of the Rose were even remotely true, then no one would want it found any time soon. It would be found when the City deemed it necessary. Possibly to change the status quo.

Annicka hadn't stumbled upon this knowledge through blind luck. She'd spent her time using her considerable abilities to ascertain the truth behind the story of the Rose, and once she became convinced of its existence, she had to figure out how to find it, and at the same time make sure that none of the other council members found it before her.

When she got demoted to the position of council member, the ability to project her mind ahead and around the City without having her physical presence actually following was her gift. Like smoke wafting through the ventilation system, she sent her vision out to seek while she was physically somewhere else. It was an advantage none of the others possessed. And it proved quite valuable over the many internal wars she'd participated in. Quite valuable indeed. It enabled her to be in two places at the same time.

She sent her essence out in search of the Rose when she first learned of it. Unknown to the others, she'd canvassed many rooms and levels trying to locate it. But the Rose was hidden well.

She did, however, find the scroll.

She came across the parchment while searching for the Rose on the Womb Level of the City. It hid in the internal workings of the City. One place no one would've had any reason to search for anything of value. It was guarded by morebats who had no idea they were guarding it. Hiding in plain sight for anyone who was looking.

When she first learned of the scroll, she didn't make the immediate connection between the Rose and the scroll. The Rose was almost impossible to imagine in length and breadth. It might have been just a rose, or perhaps the term "Rose" stood for something else entirely. Annicka had no idea, but she knew she must possess it.

The scroll came into her possession while looking with her mind's eye. Her essence was probing, pushing, and pressing into the darkest corners of the Womb when it spied the scroll sticking absentmindedly out of the corner of some machine's center. The scroll was rolled up and looked like a page of an old yellow book catalog that someone used to look up phone numbers on. It was aged and crackling when her essence noticed it being used to wipe up an old blood spill by one of the morebats on the machine. He had the scroll tucked into his back pocket and would occasionally take it out and wipe either his brow or the blood off of the machine. He had no idea of what the paper was or what it contained.

But the essence of Annicka that was searching for the Rose immediately recognized that something wasn't right with the picture of the morebats wiping his brow with a yellowed piece of paper. Not that they didn't wipe down the machines or wipe the blood and spit and other things off of themselves, but the way the morebats handled the paper was the problem. He would open it slowly, Annicka noticed, and then look around to see if anyone was watching him or his movements before he used it. Like the paper might mean something to someone, and he wasn't supposed to use it for that purpose. Or that he was doing something he wasn't supposed to do. The child with his hand in the cookie jar stealing a cookie.

Annicka sensed that the parchment was more than he pretended it was, and when she approached the morebats in person soon after that, he denied he owned the parchment. She dismembered him immediately and tore the paper from him. He'd rolled it up and stuffed the entire thing in his anus, and when she pulled his intestines out, it came out wetter than it went in. The fact that he hid it there confirmed it's worth to someone in the City.

Annicka took the paper from him and melted his mouth shut with a hot iron poker so that he couldn't tell anyone what happened to the scroll and who had it now. Morebats couldn't be trusted and would fold up to the first patron that pressured them for information. Normally reliable, they were superb at not keeping secrets. They wished for no pain, ever.

Annicka took the parchment and, after reading it and trying to decipher it, knew that she couldn't figure it out. But she also knew that it was directly related to the Rose itself. The scroll had a drawing of the Rose on it and some strangely confusing lyrics written underneath. It proved the Rose existed somewhere in the City, if she could find it or figure out what the clues contained in the scroll meant.

The first couple of attempts to find it were handled by her minions, who quickly failed. They possessed neither the intelligence nor the overwhelming desire to get involved. The promise of less punishment did no good when the total of their brain power was less than a low wattage light bulb. She couldn't convince them or encourage them or even threaten them to perform a task they were incapable of doing.

To care for the scroll, she gave it to her daughter Simone, who'd proven to be fantastic at becoming lost in the City itself. Many times Annicka herself couldn't even find her. If Annicka didn't have the scroll, then the other council members, when they heard she found it, wouldn't be able to trick her out of it.

And it would give her time to figure out the clues contained inside and then to recover the Rose.

Annicka picked Mack to solve the puzzle for her. Randi knew of his reputation in the City, even though Annicka herself did not. She considered it beneath her to involve herself in the normal comings and goings of the City and the higher patrons. They didn't matter to her. They were like bugs on the ground to be crushed.

But this one did interest her. Mack Teacher. He must be watched and protected from the other council members, who would try to turn him if they sensed him getting close to the answer. Since the idiot Stapleton announced the search at the last council meeting, Annicka knew her time was growing short. One of them would figure it out, if they hadn't already.

Annicka decided to follow Mack and Byron closely as they went on their journey.

CHAPTER NINETEEN

Eikken should have been the lowest member of the council a long time ago. He'd earned it, or so he thought, and it was rightfully his because of that simple fact. The position didn't bestow itself on those who thought it should've gone to them. It went to those who earned it. The City knew who'd done what and when and to whom, and would reward them with the demotion to the last seat at the appropriate time.

Eikken could easily bide his time until that moment came. He'd waited so long, and this was no different.

Eikken left the council meeting intent on discovery of this mysterious object of Stapleton's. He started with a slow tour of the Womb Level. He had nowhere precisely to go at present, and instead preferred to drift along like a sea breeze. He moved like a squid moved under the ocean, riding the currents of the City like waves against the shore. He would alternately extend his tentacles across the room and then pull himself to the other side as he latched on to something physical. He needed no momentum, nor did he need legs and feet to traverse the areas he wished to cross. His strength lay in his ability to move effortlessly and soundlessly around the City when it suited him and be, mostly invisible to all, except those who had the sight of eternity. Nothing was invisible to them. Nothing.

So Eikken drifted across the shallows and depths of the Womb. He neither pretended to be seen nor allowed himself to be seen by the patrons and morebats who passed. They were as oblivious to him as to the surrounding air. They would have been forced to do his bidding if he presented his material form to them, but at present, he was sleek and covered. He preferred it this way.

As he drifted, his mind was in a torrent of upheaval. When the patrons and the others didn't know he was there, they would, and often did, pass along tidbits of information that he could use against them or against the others at some point. The future frequently depended on who he could use and how he could use them. It suited him at the present to swing from side to side along the murky hallways. He'd never dwelled on the physical shape of the City for any length of time before, but at present several things occupied his mind, all of them troubling him.

The incident in the Doctor's office unsettled Eikken slightly. It was rare anymore that he couldn't read the thoughts of a higher patron, especially a new arrival, and that he'd been blocked from this one made no sense. It was something he would have to investigate further to come up with an adequate explanation. Obviously, whoever was blocking this particular pain baby from him wanted some information kept secret. An interesting puzzle.

Eikken heard the common sound of a quarrel up ahead of him, quickly followed by a pleading and then a soft scream and exhaling of breath as another of the denizens was punished or tortured or whatever. It didn't concern him at present.

He stretched his shapeless, bulbous-like form across the breadth of the hallway, and then pulled himself to a small inset into one of the tiny crevices. He didn't really pay attention to where exactly he was at the moment; he was just drifting along on the current of the City. He liked to let it take him to where it chose when it wanted.

Noticing a body under him that someone forced into this space many years ago, he gracefully settled himself down upon the unmoving carcass. It'd been a woman at some point and her bones were brittle and dried up and she was gasping for a decent breath of the dirty, musty air. There wasn't ever a good clean breath of air here, but the patrons frequently clung to the gasps of breath. Eikken gave that up with his material self when he'd been demoted to council member and given the privilege of shapeless materialism. He no longer formed a solid being unless he chose to do so, and that was rare. Very rare. Material beings were so fragile.

As he settled on top of the prone outline of the old woman, his tentacles completely encompassed her and, like a squid settling over its prey, the woman disappeared underneath the form of Eikken. He had no genuine desire or reason to even notice this decrepit woman. He didn't know who she was or why she'd gotten herself pulled down to the City. He didn't know how she came to be curled up inside this little inlet in the cave of this hallway. He simply had nothing else to do other than think through some of the actions of the council members, and this looked like a suitable spot. She was convenient.

She stirred as her eyes opened, and she felt him stretch out his tentacles and probe all of her openings simultaneously. She arched her back as she felt him enter her nose and mouth, and then her vagina and anus all at the same time. It wasn't something she liked or envisioned happening to her, but also not something she could consciously avoid or struggle against. She just resigned herself to the inevitable, and let Eikken probe her.

Eikken let his tentacles caress her like she was a pet he'd found in the yard, and then he pushed farther. He felt the old woman. She was probably in her early seventies when she arrived and might've been here for a thousand years. Eikken noted she wore a loose fitting loin cloth and a small top across her shriveled and hanging breasts. She shuddered and then completely surrendered. Her memories and thoughts opened to his every desire, and the tentacles pierced in as he delved deeper into her being.

Eikken hit the nerve he was searching for and though the eyes of the old woman relived her last actions. He moved and probed and discarded the things he didn't care about until he found memories of interest. He wasn't looking for anything in particular; he was just reading her like an old novel he found in a junkyard. She was open like a new-born child.

He passed over the last several moments as she lay bunched up in this crevice and then moved on to some more recent memories and noticed she'd been one of the wall beings. Assigned to be a piece of the City hallways themselves. One of those nameless patrons who lined many of the darker alleys, resigned to an existence of staring out and watching traffic move by. It was a place for those who'd been punished for so long they were temporarily moved aside for the new pain babies. There was only so much punishment to go around, and sometimes the simple logistics of the operation required movement from the front line to the waiting list. Those that were put along the walls were basically hammered into the wall itself. They became a part of the plaster and mortar, and could spend dark eons waiting for a room mother to notice them and pull them back into the mainstream. They were always found and never forgotten, just temporarily put to the curb.

This woman, whom Eikken found out was called Doris at some point in her existence, was part of the wall until just recently. A floor administrator dragged her out and was going to promote her back to the Havoc Level soon. Very soon.

But while she had lain here, Eikken could see that her eyes, though old and gray and covered by numerous cataracts, noticed two men cross in front of her. The men stopped almost directly in front of her, and although she couldn't hear everything they were saying, she could see they were gazing at an ancient piece of paper. It was tattered and yellowish and one man unrolled it so that the two of them could read the contents.

Eikken did not know who these men were, but his instincts told him they were important and he should hold this memory for a second longer, so he wrapped the tentacle that landed on the nerve tighter around the ganglia itself, and squeezed. The woman let out a "grumpf" kind of sound and relinquished.

Eikken could see the men reading the paper and on the top of it, there appeared to be a picture, like a flower, but he couldn't be sure. He then heard someone called "Teacher" and the two men turned and left the eyesight of the women as they went farther down the hallway. Eikken heard them discussing the location of a Black Rose of power clearly.

Eikken pulled his tentacles from the woman and lifted himself up into the air. This was the prize that the council members were seeking. He was positive about that. And it looked like someone held a map. These two men, and the member they were supporting, held an advantage. There were no coincidences in the City. He'd stumbled across the two seekers, whoever they were. He would have to find this Black Rose.

Leaving the woman lying there in the wretched cavern, he drifted on a course after the seekers, trying to feel and smell their trails. He hadn't tracked like this in a long time, but he could find out who the "Teacher" was from some of his minions. If he couldn't locate them, he would let the Doctor find this Black Rose for him.

It would not be easy, but now he knew what he needed to find. That made it possible.

CHAPTER TWENTY

The Doctor and David walked through the metal door and into a wide room that stretched as far as they could see. Unlike most of the rooms he'd been in before this, where the motion was often listless and detached, Victor watched a beehive of activity. There were morebats on each side of a wide aisle and as they entered, only a few them stopped what they were doing and took any notice of the two of them standing at the entrance to their room.

Victor straightened up and walked confidently along the aisle that ran through the middle of the room. It effectively separated the two halves into equal parts and, although he couldn't tell it, the room was oblong and not rectangular. It was well lit, unlike pretty much every other place in the City, and the amount of activity going on resembled his operating room on a busy day. The morebats were moving and grunting as they worked diligently at their assigned tasks.

The two men walked forward several steps until the entrance door was well behind them. Victor was assessing the activity the entire time and trying to understand just how it all worked. If he could gauge how it made itself run, then he could figure out what he was looking for and the most probable place to find it.

On the left of him was a row of morebats, each standing next to what looked like holes in the walls. The holes were cylindrical and deeply black, with no light either emanating from them or going into them. Even though the room itself was lit up and Victor could clearly make out the features of the morebats working and the holes themselves, he couldn't see into the depth of the hole at all. Not even three feet into them. It was cloak black.

He could, however, hear screaming. Lots and lots of screaming.

Not the sort of screaming he'd usually hear when he operated on the pain babies. This was a different pitch of screaming. He'd ferreted out some of the deepest and most delectable screams imaginable on more than one occasion. Some of the pain babies were incredibly adept at letting out a truly deep scream from their bowels themselves, but this was different.

This came from their very souls. It was a more of a tearing wail than from those patrons that were enduring physical pain. It resonated and echoed outward from the very depths of whoever was actually doing the screaming. Victor couldn't see anything or anyone in the holes, but could clearly tell the screaming was coming from inside the holes and filling this room. It was a perfect background noise for the work that was going on and apparently was a common occurrence as none of the morebats even seemed to take notice. They were used to these kinds of screams. Victor would've set up a tape recording machine to capture some of this stuff and use later if he'd been in charge.

But the holes themselves, even though they had no light and depth, and were impossible to gauge, did indeed have complexity. And it was considerable. There was no shallowness here. These went a long way. Down into the blackness.

Victor stopped in front of one morebat who had just shifted his baseball cap over to the side of his head and wiped his brow from the effort of his work. They never complained about any of the tasks they were given, instead seeing their job as a means to complete their day and get to time off so they could mate with something. This particular morebats had a New York Yankees' hat on its prism-like head. It had no other clothing and was a purplish and orange color. At present, it was studying what looked to Victor to be an old transistor radio with the back panel removed and the batteries exposed.

"What you got there, morebats?" Victor asked as he motioned for David to stop and sit down on the floor behind him. He was going to do a little negotiating. David had quietly been contemplating the drugs he'd received and trying to make some common sense out of the ingredients. He knew what he needed to make the serum, but this wasn't it. Not even close.

"Benny not sure. Not sure at all. Other morebats give to him. Benny try to figure. Might be good. Might be bad. Benny not know."

"That your name? Benny?"

The morebats nodded vigorously. He was deeply concerned with the inner workings of the radio, even though he couldn't possibly have the intelligence to fix it or make it work. He might impress someone with it, though.

"Benny, what's your job?"

"Guard portal. Wait. Benny always waiting."

"What're you waiting for Benny?"

"Puller bring Benny pain baby for City. Benny wait until he arrive. Know what to do, Benny good at his job. Best in portal area. Best."

"How long until the next pain baby arrives, Benny?"

Benny looked at his wrist, an old watch strapped to it. The watch hadn't run for many years, but it was a status symbol among the morebats themselves, so he wore it and looked at it frequently. It was important that the other morebats knew he owned a watch. Whether it worked was immaterial. He could look at it anytime he wanted. They could not.

"New pain baby come in any minute now. Any minute now. Benny ready."

Victor stood in front of the morebats for a moment and thought. He would appeal to the only thing that made sense to the morebats. He needed an opening and this might serve. He peeked around the room and noticed that none of the other morebats had even so much as noticed him. Apparently, they got some visitors here. All the portals had a morebats in front of it. One for each. What exactly they did, Victor didn't know, but he figured he could get around this one.

"I heard you were the best Benny. That's why I've come to you. With a gift."

Benny stopped his fiddling with the radio, deciding it was a ridiculously complicated instrument and not that attractive anyway, and looked up at Victor. "You heard of Benny? That's good. Good for Benny. Might get to mate."

Victor nodded. "That's what I've brought for you. A present."

"Benny like presents. Not get many here. What present?"

Victor motioned to David, who was sitting on the floor pouring some of the contents of the drug packets into a syringe. Crude, but possibly effective. "You can mate with this one, Benny."

David looked up, immediately sensing that he was being talked about. He hadn't paid much attention to the conversation to this point, but now it had his full attention. Victor had just said this monkey-thing could mate with who?

"What? What did you say, Victor?" David asked as he stood up and pushed the glasses back up his nose to see better.

Benny regarded them suspiciously. This didn't happen to him. Others got to mate during work, but not him. "What wanted by you? You need what?" he said to the Doctor.

Victor nodded to the portal. "I know how good of a job you do here, Benny. I came to give you a gift. And in return, while you mate, I will look into the portal. For just a second."

Benny shook his head "no," vigorously. "Is not allowed. No one goes into the portal. Is a rule. Everybody, even pain babies, know. Nobody in portal from this side. Never."

Benny was quite sure of himself, but Victor could see that he had reached down and was stroking his ten-inch long phallus. Victor simply said nothing and waited. As he watched, Benny stroked it a little faster and then a little harder and it was rising to its full length. He'd counted on this.

Stepping quickly to the side to get out of the line of sight between Benny and David, he said, "Well, Benny, I understand. They told me you were the best morebats at your job and I just wanted to see the portal for a quick minute. I thought maybe I could make a deal with you, but now I can see that you're too devoted to your job. No wonder you're the best at what you do. Everyone knows that."

"Benny the best. Benny the best. Everyone knows," Benny was shaking a little as he stroked his phallus faster and faster. He was drooling slightly and his eyes had gone to tiny slits as he stared at David. "But Benny must mate. He must MATE!"

Victor nodded. "I know," he breathed. "I only need a minute in the portal. No one would ever know."

David was staring at the monkey-thing in front of him. It was salivating openly now and grinning at him like he was a virgin on a wedding night dressed only in garters and lace. "I can't. I can't. I can't....." he stuttered.

The Doctor knew an opportunity when he saw it. David convulsed and shake and Victor sat his now ever present shovel aside. He wouldn't bring him out of it this time, instead preferring to see what the convulsions would do to Benny. He thought it might excite him even further.

Benny was rapidly stroking his phallus and lusting openly for David, who was flopping around like a pinball in a broken machine. The movements only heightened the intense sexual excitement of Benny, as he took the flipping and rolling of David to be some kind of lust dance.

"Benny must mate, must mate. Benny must mate now."

"Can I go into the portal while you mate?"

"Is okay for a minute. Benny must mate. Must mate."

Victor reached over to David and grabbed the syringe from his clenched fingers and Benny set upon him like a dog on a piece of meat. The speed that Benny crossed the space between himself and David amazed even the Doctor who'd seen these things mate many times with whatever was available.

As Benny crawled over David, looking for any opening to insert his erect phallus into, Victor turned from the scene and stepped through the portal.

Eikken increased his speed and roamed through the hallways. He'd gone to the Havoc Level and then down to the Funhouse and hadn't located anyone he was after. He was furious. As he rushed from room to room on the different levels, he knew he couldn't possibly go through them all, but he knew where they should be. And they were not there. It only increased his anger.

As he moved, his color across the vaporous part of his body changed constantly. Like a never ending rainbow as he passed from room to room, the colors changed themselves to mask his appearance, like a crude form of camouflage, except it was not intended this time. It happened when he was enraged.

And the patrons were going to pay for it.

As he went from place to place, he would alternately envelope a room mother or pain baby and quickly electrocute them as he probed their thoughts. He'd found no trace of either the two men the old woman had seen or the Doctor and the idiot, and that's what made him the most furious.

The fucking Doctor should have been on the Havoc Level looking for the information and he was not. He had gone off on his own, with that sniveling imbecile beside him, and not done as Eikken bade him to do. It was almost inconceivable to Eikken that he hadn't done what he was ordered.

Eikken saw two prisoners writhing on the ground in front of him. He swooped over them and settled down on top of both of them at once. He let his full cape of tentacles flow around them and over them, and then he ran electrical currents through their bodies as he probed them for answers. Had they seen the Doctor or the two men? Where the fuck were they? Eikken was getting madder by the moment and his colors were changing so rapidly that they were becoming a blur to anyone looking at him. If they even dared.

The pain babies under him were cringing from the shocks and rolling under his weight. He stretched his tentacles out and covered them both like a blanket as they yelled. He pushed a tentacle inside one of the open mouths of the two men and gagged him momentarily as the tentacle snaked its way down his throat. He wretched involuntarily and Eikken shocked him from the inside of the man's esophagus, alternating the current. The pain seared his muscles to the inside wall of his esophagus until it bubbled up of its own accord and the man tried vainly to roll away from the tentacle shoved down his throat.

Eikken quickened his shocks to both of them and then he stopped. The one man had seen the Doctor. He released the useless man and as he rolled away screaming and moaning all of Eikken's tentacles came to the task at hand and completely ensnared the man who'd seen the Doctor. The shocks were coming without interruption as Eikken sought to get the last ounce of information. He'd seen the Doctor recently on the way to the portal cage.

Eikken released the man, and he fell unconscious to the ground in a limp pile of human remains that still breathed. He was smoking and was charred over three quarters of his body. If it had ever been anything else, his brain was now a vegetable.

Flying rapidly from the hallway, he aimed for the portal cage on the Womb Level. The Doctor should not have been there.

Eikken would have something to say to him about that.

The portal was not really a doorway or even an opening, as Victor noticed the second he stepped through. It was like a gelatin-kind of blackness. It had substance and a jelly like feeling as it washed itself around him. He tentatively pushed first his head and then his entire body through the opening. The bleakness surrounded him and encased him in dark. It wasn't an unpleasant feeling, but resembled a steaming hot shower that cascades and then covers the skin. All the parts get saturated slowly but evenly. Except this wasn't water, and it was thick. Like day old coffee thick.

He couldn't see anything as the opening closed behind him after only a few seconds. He was looking for the place where the new arrivals were first grabbed and pulled down, but he had no memory of it at all from when he'd been taken, and neither did anyone he'd ever come in contact with in the City. He was going to have to do this one alone.

He heard some sort of noise as he sloshed forward through the murk. The darkness was total, and he had no forward vision, so he stepped one foot in front of the other and tried to walk in a straight line. He would have to get back out of the portal the way he came in and didn't want to lose his direction.

The sound came from his left, although he couldn't be sure because it also echoed slightly and that could've been because of the thickness of the jelly surrounding him. It played on his face and seeped into his nose and mouth and had a sort of spicy taste. He didn't think it would be a good idea to drink the shit, though.

He followed the sound as best he could, because there was nothing else to follow, and after only a couple of steps, he saw a small, blue light. It wasn't hanging or coming from a light bulb. It was more like a light that had no origin and was always just up ahead. He walked towards the blue light and watched as it got a little bluer with each step.

The noise became louder as he trudged, and the light got brighter. He felt something brush across his left leg, and then across his right leg and before he could react, something with a thousand rigid arms grabbed him from behind and placed him into a vise-like bear hug.

Victor was momentarily immobilized and couldn't move his arms or his legs as the thing that grabbed him squeezed tighter and tighter. He felt his breath escape in a gasp, and then heard one of his ribs break with a distinctly clean snapping sound.

He'd located the "Puller."

He wretched his head from side to side and struggled to get some air into his lungs as the Puller closed the vise around his torso. He heard two more ribs snap in half and he let out a small howl from the pain. He was in deep trouble and he knew it. He didn't want to be processed again.

All at once, the Puller completely relaxed its hold and all the arms that wrapped themselves around Victor flexed and fell from his chest. Victor looked back into the murk, couldn't see what happened or why he was let go, but heard the creature scurry away from him. It circled him and then Victor saw the trailing end of the millipede-like thing head for the blue light. It was moving quickly and was obviously going to work. It had completely forgotten about him for the moment because it had something else to do. He stepped quickly behind it and watched. This was the moment he'd been waiting for. Even though his newly broken ribs protested, he knew they'd be alright. He just had to get to the pain baby before the Puller completed his task.

The Puller twisted and wound its way like a slinky going down a stair step. It moved and weaved through the slime and the jelly parts of the darkness as Victor struggled to keep up. He was just behind it and almost running through the stuff.

The Puller stopped suddenly and then reared up on its hind legs in a vertical position directly in front of the blue light. It then opened its arms wide as it simply waited for the right time to grab the new arrival. It stood probably six feet tall and had dozens of arms. Victor guessed there must have been a thousand of them protruding out from a skinny, scaly body without a distinguishable head. It served one purpose and one purpose only: to get the pain babies and drag them to Hell.

A clock ticked each second off somewhere beside Victor's right ear, counting down, getting louder with every passing tick. He had only a few moments to complete his task. He had no idea how to do this, so he did the only thing he could do right then: he just tried something. Anything. It would take a bit of improvisation to be the right combination, and he wouldn't get another chance to prove this worked.

Victor stepped in front of the Puller and thrust his right arm with the syringe directly into the blue light. His arm encountered a resistance, like he was pushing it through a piece of aluminum foil, but then the foil gave way and he broke through. He dipped the syringe into something soft, not understanding what it was, and pushed the plunger, emptying the contents into whatever the needle had found. It felt like an overripe peach. It was soft and squishy and flexed backwards against the syringe. He quickly withdrew his arm and stepped out of the way to see what would happen.

Victor glanced behind him and saw the Puller had become very agitated. Its arms were flailing backwards and forewords and moving up and down, all at once. All one thousand of the arms were in rapid motion. It seemed to

Victor that the Puller was in a heightened state of excitement. Like it was about to feed.

The Doctor quickly moved out of the way and the Puller reached all of its arms into the blue light and Victor watched as the muscles on the arms flexed a couple of times and then tightened up on something. Obviously, it'd found what it was looking for and was gripping the thing in its bear hug. The ticking clock had chimed loudly. It was time for the new pain baby to be welcomed to the City of Hell.

All at once, the Puller went rigid and stopped its movements. It straightened up slightly and then relaxed and simultaneously pulled its arms completely back to itself and the shoulders, if that's what they could be called, slumped forward. This one must have gotten away somehow. The Puller wasn't used to losing the prey and was clearly disappointed. It'd never been denied before.

Victor had altered the sequence somehow. Whatever the cocktail of drugs that David had prepared, and he'd injected into the new arrival had done this. What exactly the effect was, he couldn't be sure, but it had done something. Changed something.

Victor looked to his right where the sound of the chimes had stopped and heard what sounded like gears of a machine unwinding and clashing against each other. There was a momentary pause and then the ticking resumed at a quieter pace, but still steady. It was like time had been reversed. He'd heard this countdown before.

The cocktail worked. The pain baby's brain must still be alive and the Puller couldn't take it yet.

Yet.

Victor didn't know how long it would last, but he wanted to get out of that portal before the Puller got bored and turned its attention once more in his direction. He walked backwards in as straight a line as he could imagine, always trying to keep the blue light directly in front of his eyes. As he backed up, he noticed the Puller was moving its one thousand arms rapidly again and the ticking clock had grown louder. The time was again near for the pain baby.

Victor moved as quickly as the murk and jelly shit would allow him to move. He carefully placed one foot in back of the other until he felt the jelly soften against his back and neck and his breathing became a little easier. The blue light disappeared into the darkness and he backed out of the portal.

He wiped his hands and face free of the jelly shit and then blinked his eyes in the light of the portal cage. It was as he'd left it. He had no idea about how long he had been gone, nor did he care. He'd done what he set out to do. David's cocktail worked perfectly. The only question was how long it lasted. How much longer the portal could be kept open.

He turned to see David flopping around on the ground in front of him and directly attached to his right leg was Benny. He still had all his clothes on and was rolling around on the slick ground, trying to keep Benny from mating with him. The morebats had obviously given up on finding one of David's orifices readily available and were instead desperately hunching David's leg like a dog in heat.

Victor grabbed the shovel and swung it until it compacted squarely with David's head, and he immediately stopped twitching and flopping. He kicked out with his right leg and threw Benny off and against the nearest wall.

"Stay off me, shit bat," David said angrily as he stood up.

"It worked. The cocktail you made somehow kept the portal open for a little longer."

David nodded like he expected it the whole time. "How long?"

"Don't know."

Benny got up and was running to the front of his portal. He was very upset and stopped only to fix his baseball cap. "Something wrong. Benny not know what. Something very wrong." He was pointing at the portal. "Puller never fail. Never fail. Where baby? Where baby?"

Victor shrugged and turned to leave. It was no longer his problem. He grabbed David by the shoulder and dragged him behind. "Let's get out of here," he said.

He opened the door to the outer room where they'd left the monk guardian curled up on the floor. The monk had resumed his position behind the podium and eyed them warily through blood encrusted eyes as they walked past him.

The monk pointed at them from his podium. "You do not scare me, Herr Doctor. We will meet again."

Victor nodded. "Yeah, yeah. Whatever. Go fuck yourself, monk."

He opened the outer door and walked through to the hallway from where he first entered and directly into the floating face and body of Eikken.

Victor was instantly startled. He hadn't expected this. Eikken was hovering directly at the entrance to the outer room of the portal. Eikken said nothing, but simply glared. Victor could see that the colors of his vaporous shell were rapidly changing like a kaleidoscope with crossed wires. The colors were intense and brightly lit up and rapidly firing.

Without a word, and before Victor could react, Eikken swooped over him and covered only his head with his tentacles. He sat down directly atop the Doctor's head and as David watched; the tentacles entwined themselves over, around, on, and under every square inch of his head. Victor screamed momentarily until it was cut off with a choking sound as a tentacle was shoved into his open mouth and then up each of his nostrils, digging directly into his brain. He staggered once and then twice and then fell straight down to a sitting position with Eikken covering his entire head. David couldn't see even one eye through the moving, circling, squeezing tentacles.

Eikken wrapped his tentacles securely around Victor's head and neck and then tightened the noose twice before cutting off all of his air supply. Victor gasped loudly and then his eyes bulged out of their sockets as he tried desperately to gather a straw of air. Eikken only increased his grip. He was going to make this higher being pay for his disrespect.

Victor saw only blackness as he was completely engulfed in tentacles and slime from the moving arms of Eikken. Shooting white lights crossed the field of his closed eyes, and he teetered on the verge of unconsciousness from the lack of air and the pressure on his head. The grip was vise-like and increasing.

Eikken felt Victor slump, and he released just enough pressure from the neck to allow him to gasp for a breath of air. The air rushed into Victor's lungs and bloodstream and revived him momentarily. When Eikken felt him stir slightly, he tightened the noose again and choked him back to the rim of unconsciousness. He kept choking and releasing Victor. Just on the edge.

David stood stunned in terror at what he was watching. Victor was sitting cross-legged on the ground and his body would alternately straighten up and then slump back down with every breath Eikken allowed him to get. David had seen enough choking victims during his time at the morgue to know the incredible pain that Victor must have been going through. He was scared he might be next.

Eikken relaxed his grip around Victor's neck and allowed him to regain complete consciousness and when he was fully awake, Eikken adjusted his position on top of Victor and sent out tiny needles from the center of each of his thousands of suction cups on the tentacles. The needles pierced Victor simultaneously over every square inch of his head and then inside his mouth, nose, and ears. The needles were about six inches long and a quarter of an inch round and drove small stakes into his brain from the inside of his head.

David couldn't see what exactly Eikken was doing, but as he watched, Victor screamed in agony and then started prying against Eikken to get him off and rolling around on the floor like he'd just caught fire. Blood was pouring out from under the tentacles as Eikken tightened his grip around the Doctor's head and drove the needles in farther.

The battle lasted only a few seconds more as Victor finally quit screaming and came to a complete stop on the floor. David assumed he was either unconscious or incapacitated. Either way, he was totally fucked as far as David was concerned.

And then Eikken looked directly at David.

"I can't. I can't. I can't...."

"Shut up you idiot!" Eikken screamed as he disengaged himself from a now perfectly still Victor.

Eikken floated above the room, close to the top. David couldn't quite concentrate, but he could hear him.

"Get the Doctor up and get back to the task I have given you."

"I can't. I can't. I can't....," was all David could manage.

Eikken turned his attention back to the Doctor. Eikken closed his slotted eyes and threw his oblong head back and then released pent up air. He looked down at Victor. "You will now get up and serve me as I instructed you earlier. I've found out what the council members seek. It's a Black Rose. I must have the power of the Rose to myself. You will find it for me. Now."

It took a moment to concentrate through the pain long enough to answer. "What is the Black Rose? Where should it be? How will I ever locate it?" Victor gasped with each word. He was bleeding and felt like his head exploded. He'd never been given this intensity of punishment before now. It smelled of more trouble coming.

"It's a Rose, you imbecile, and it rests somewhere in the City. I believe it resides on the Havoc Level, but I haven't been able to find out where exactly. It's the only place that makes sense to hide something like this because the council members keep to the lower levels and don't venture up there very often. It is beneath me to stay on that level. I imagine that is where it hides. You will use the information from the room mother fuckers to guide you. They will assist you at my direction, and of course, you are to use your surgical skills to extract the information from any of the pain babies you think can help you out."

Victor nodded. He would do this and then get back to the portal.

"Make no mistake, Doctor. There are other council members taking a different pathway to find this Rose. They have also begun a journey, but I must gain possession of the Rose before them. The Havoc is where it rests, I'm convinced. Follow your instincts, and take this idiot," he motioned to David who was stuttering again, "along with you. He might come in handy. You will leave at once."

Victor stood up. He could continue his work soon enough. He had plenty of time.

"The Rose holds one key to the portal, Doctor, but this knowledge will not help you as you cannot know the power or how to use it. Be gone now," Eikken the Lion said as he disappeared like smoke wafting out of a room.

Victor couldn't believe what he'd just heard. Even through his intense pain, he knew he'd heard it correctly. The portal? The fucking portal? This couldn't be a coincidence.

Victor knew three things for sure as he grabbed the shovel and prepared to stop the stuttering idiot. The Black Rose had some kind of power over the portal. David Masters had given him knowledge to keep the portal open and no one in the City but Victor knew that information. And Eikken hadn't discovered from David what he wanted when he was in his office. The doctor didn't know how or why Eikken was so enraged, but he knew he didn't get what he wanted from him when he tried by merging. Which was good for the Doctor.

He was sure he could figure this thing out and use all the pieces of the puzzle, pieces that he alone had knowledge of, to be demoted and get a council seat.

And he'd try his damnedest to get rid of Eikken if the opportunity presented itself.

WHACK.

Victor struggled to keep his balance. He stood awkwardly for a moment as he sought to concentrate on what Eikken said. His feet shuffled because he couldn't lift them off the ground. His head was bleeding like a water dam broke inside. He moved towards the hallway with David in cowering tow.

Eikken watched them leave for only a moment. When he was satisfied that he'd delivered the proper message to the two higher beings, he turned and quickly floated away. He had to get to the Funhouse. There was something he had to do right away.

The game was in full swing and he couldn't miss out on this opportunity.

CHAPTER TWENTY-ONE

Mack and Byron stood completely still, staring at the picture in front of them. They'd run through the black door and left the ringmaster behind and now they stood facing what looked like a circus tent. It was tall and billowing in a non-existent wind. The tent was painted a red and off-white striped color, and had an open flap, inviting them to step inside. There was music playing somewhere in the background. Mack was reminded of the organ music that used to play outside of the circuses his parents had taken him to when he was a kid. This looked as open and welcoming as any Barnum and Bailey's on the surface.

But Mack knew better.

There was nothing warm and inviting here. Nothing. It was all a facade.

"Howdy, boys," a voice said directly behind them.

The two turned at the voice and were surprised by who greeted them. She was small, being only about four feet tall, and quite a stunning blond.

"I'm Daisy Mae. I'm the room mother here. I run the circus."

Mack nodded. She was a beautiful girl, with golden blonde hair and bright blue eyes. Her hair was pulled behind her in a tight ponytail, and rested on her shoulders. She wore a red and blue checked open-collared shirt that showed off a curvy figure under it. Her pants were blue jean cut-offs that had frayed at the ends and were snug fitting.

The perfect country bumpkin girl. Except that the reason she was only four feet tall was that her legs had been cut off at the knees. She stood perfectly upright on what should've been her feet, but that part of her legs had somehow been ground down to a flat spot and she maintained her balance on her knees. She stood perfectly erect, not swaying. No feet, no problem.

"Don't mind my feet, boys. They've been gone longer than I've been the room mother," she stated simply.

"I'm Mack Teacher. This is Byron Michaels."

She nodded and reached into a back pocket in her cutoff jeans and pulled out a straw, which she promptly put into her mouth and chewed aggressively on the end. "I know who you are. I've been told you might be comin' my way. Don't mind me," she continued, "I like to put things in my mouth."

She grinned at Mack and then Byron, taking the time to look separately at each one of them. "Would either of you like to put something in my mouth?"

Mack shook his head "no" and Byron did the same.

"How about a straight old-time country fuck, then? I'll do both of you. No problem. Same time, if you want."

Again, Mack shook his head "no." This was only an effort to throw them off, he knew. The room mothers didn't normally act this nice or look this good. For all he knew, she might be a man or something worse, like a made-up morebat. Definitely stay away. Far away.

"Since I can't interest either of you boys in me, I guess you're both gay? Is that it?" She was just asking. More from a curiosity standpoint than anything else.

"We're trying to find our way through here as part of a job dictated to us by a council member," Byron said.

"I understand. No time for little ole me," she sighed.

"You said you were told we might be here. Were you told we also might not?" Mack asked.

She tilted her head and arched her eyes at him. "Can't rightly recall what I was told," she said.

Mack knew she was lying. Byron knew too. A set up.

"If ya'll want to go into the circus, I'd guess we'd better get started. I'll guide you, cause there's some things you're going to see that are just amazin', if I do say so myself. Designed this whole place myself and some of my guests have been here a long time. Nobody seems to want to leave little ole me."

Mack nodded. She would've been cute if he knew what the hell she was. Or what her real purpose was for wanting to guide them. She wasn't here to help, he knew that.

"Ya'll do realize that I can't exactly lead you through here, but I can give some information, as best as I can."

"I know."

"If ya'll get lost or turn the wrong way or take the wrong door, I'm fraid that you'll be staying with me fer quite a while. Then we'll see iffin' you really are both gay or straight." Her accent was getting more and more country by the moment. "Could be a lot of fun fer ya'll."

Mack didn't think so. Nor did he see a reason to get into a deep conversation with one of the room mothers whose only interest was adding to their stables. They might make two more pleasant additions if they screwed up and chose the wrong way. He was sure that she'd be glad to trade them out for something like a demotion for herself. Only after, of course, they'd been adequately punished first.

"Let's take another look at the scroll, Byron," he said as he pulled the scroll out and unrolled it. Daisy Mae moved up behind them. She was deft in her movements for someone without feet. Her legs were just short and stubby, nothing else. Still functional, obviously.

He laid the scroll on the ground and pointed to the stanza above the red and black one. "Here, I think."

Byron nodded. "How can you be sure?"

"I'm not. Just nothing else to go on at present. And something Daisy Mae here said." He motioned to her, and she grinned broadly at being mentioned.

"She said it was going to 'be amazin', remember?"

Byron nodded. He'd heard her say it.

"The scroll said something about a maze. Here," he pointed at the stanza.

Some rats in a maze,
Who dine on bone marrow,
Will chew off their legs,
And the heads of dead sparrows.

"I'm not sure about the stretch for the word 'maze.' But I don't know anything better either," Byron agreed.

Daisy Mae had gotten to a point where she could also read the writing. "That sure is a pretty picture you got there. Like the words too, if I do say so myself. I know where a maze is."

Mack and Byron looked at each other. Byron mouthed 5317, and Mack nodded.

"Don't ya'll look so suspicious now. I got no reason to lie about this, cause it's right here. In the tent. I call it the circus maze. What kind of Funhouse doesn't have a maze inside somewhere?" she said.

"You mean that there's a maze inside the tent?" Mack pointed to the open flap.

"Yeah, iffin' that's what you want to call it. Once my patrons get inside the open door there, they gets to choose the doors to get out. Lots of doors. It's amazin'. Like I said."

"We're at the right place, Byron. Let's go." He picked the scroll back up and tucked in his back pocket.

"What about the other three stanzas in that rhyme? We have no idea what they might mean."

"I know. I'm hoping we find out before it's too late," Mack said.

"Too late for what?"

"Remember ya'll, once you go through a door, it don't reopen. Careful how you chooses," Daisy Mae added.

Mack nodded and walked towards the open flap of the tent with Byron beside him. Byron had unconsciously reached into his pants pocket and was furiously stroking his eyeball. This could get ugly, he thought as he stroked.

CHAPTER TWENTY-TWO

Daisy Mae moved quicker than Mack would've thought and got in front of them. She was obviously proud and wanted to at least lead them into the maze, if only for a moment. Mack knew that once inside, she would hasten to the rear of the procession. She couldn't influence their choices, but she could mislead them. He wouldn't let that happen.

The two of them stepped into the tent and were greeted by more music coming softly across hidden loudspeakers. The music was standard organ grinder music that Mack had heard outside the tent, but now it seemed to be quieter. Like someone had turned it down for them so they could enjoy the coming show. Three rings and all.

Daisy Mae pointed to an opening directly before them. It was narrow and rectangular shaped and even though she fit comfortably through it, both Mack and Byron had to duck just slightly. There were no other doors or exits that Mack could see, so he followed her inside.

The opening led to a plain, balsa constructed hallway. The workmen who did the construction in this hallway were not very skilled or didn't give a damn about it, because it was tall and mostly lopsided, being six or seven feet tall and about three feet wide. It was covered with various shades of brown and dark crimson stains, like the workers started painting and left in the middle of the job. Mack wouldn't have called them back. As he looked farther up in front of them, he could see the hallway narrowed at both the top and the sides, giving the whole hallway the look of a descending cave. There was no light, but some filtered in from behind them. Probably built by morebats, he thought.

Daisy Mae led them to the end of the hallway and then slid aside. She pointed to the door at the end, and then opened it and motioned for Mack and Byron to precede her. Mack hesitated only for a second. This was too up front to be a scam, and he stepped through the door and into a wider room. Since there was only one way in or out so far, no other passageways, Mack knew it was alright. But he damn sure didn't trust the bitch farther than he could throw her four foot frame. No feet and all. He would watch her.

The room they stepped into was miniature, just wide enough to hold the one patron who was standing there looking at them. It had a row of old telephone booths on one side of the room, five phone stalls in all, like Mack used to see in train stations. The other side of the room was a lit up and plugged in computer terminal. The lone man was standing directly in the center of the room, between both the phone booths and computer terminal.

Byron whispered to him, "This doesn't look too bad. So far."

"Give it a minute. Remember, this is all bad. All bad," Mack replied.

"What the hell do you want? I don't have time for any of this," the man said to them both. He glanced from the phone booths to the computer and then back to them. "Get the hell out of here!" He was dressed in a blue suit with a red spotted tie and a recently starched white stained shirt. His pants had been pressed, and he wore black, polished shoes. A high-class executive, obviously.

He was bald, almost completely, but had a small tuft of white hair and white, bushy eyebrows that flexed when he talked to them. His eyes were a piercing blue. He was a man who was used to giving the orders from a penthouse somewhere, Mack guessed.

"This is Ken Lay," Daisy Mae said from behind them, as if she was introducing them to each other.

Byron's one eye grew a little wider, and he turned to Daisy Mae. "The Ken Lay? Of Enron fame?"

Daisy Mae nodded and pointed at him. "Kenneth Lee Lay was found guilty on several counts of fraud related to the company he was CEO of in Houston, Texas, during the early 90s. He systematically committed fraud and perjury, and bilked several thousand of his employees and the taxpayers out of millions of dollars and almost all of their pension funds. He is a true corporate genius and one of my personal prizes here in the City. His true beauty lies in the fact that he had a heart attack and died on the surface before he could be sentenced. In the courts, that means his verdict was set aside. Is that beautiful or what? Not guilty by reason of death. Is that a great country or what? A true master of imperial fucking of Neanderthal employees. I am personally in charge of his rehabilitation." She shrugged her shoulders. "It's a perk."

"Did you know him, Teacher?" Byron asked softly.

Mack shook his head. "It was after my time on the surface. But trust me on this, there are a lot of famous people here. You won't want any autographs. Not a one."

Byron couldn't help but wonder when Teacher's time in the City started, but he bit his tongue and didn't ask. Probably sometime in the thirties or forties, would have been his guess. "I think you're probably right," was all he said.

"Stop talking! Stop talking now!" Ken pointed at them. He was clearly distraught. "The only one who talks in my board meetings is me! Me! Do you hear me?"

Daisy Mae continued while she chewed on the straw ever more vigorously. "His body was supposedly cremated somewhere in the mountains. Supposedly. But we found him."

Byron nodded. "Everyone here deserves to be here, I guess,"

"Don't question what you see. Try not to get involved. We have a purpose," Mack said.

"What is his punishment, exactly?" Byron asked.

"You'll see. Any minute now, would be my guess." Daisy Mae could only grin. It must have been one she concocted herself.

Just then, one phone in the booths to Ken's immediate left began ringing. Ken stopped pointing at Mack and Byron and lost all interest in them. He whirled and ran to the ringing phone.

"Hello? Hello?" Ken picked up the receiver and shouted into the phone.

"Mr. Lay?"

"Yes. Yes. This is Ken Lay. CEO of Enron Corporation."

Mack and Byron could hear both ends of the phone conversation through the loud speaker system. Mack didn't know if it was like this all the time or only for their benefit.

"Mr. Lay?" the voice on the phone asked again.

"Yes. Yes. It's Ken Lay for Christ sakes."

"I'm sorry, Mr. Lay. It isn't the right one. But thank you for answering the phone, anyway. The next call will be the one you are waiting for and you will be released. Talk to you in just a minute."

"Fuck you! Fuck you! Fuck you!" Ken screamed into the now dead phone. The line had gone dead and was just buzzing. Ken slammed the phone down on the hook and walked back to the middle of the room.

He pointed at Mack and Byron again. "Are you people still in my meeting? Alright. One of you get me something to drink. Anything. I need it now. Not tomorrow or in ten minutes. Now. Do you hear me?" He was pointing at them again and literally screaming.

Neither Mack nor Byron moved as the computer monitor buzzed on the other side of the room, and Ken rushed over to the screen. He turned it to face Mack and Byron. They could see that the screen was loading and had one of those little clocks going around and around on the screen itself. In a red-lined box under the clock was a message that said simply "Please wait while the screen loads."

After a few seconds, Ken stood up and hit the top of the computer. He screamed again and whacked the top of the computer again. It wasn't loading fast enough.

"Any minute. Any minute now and I'll have it. The key is right here. As soon as it loads," Ken intoned as he studied the screen and waited.

The screen changed colors, and another box appeared. This one said clearly that the program was experiencing an internal error and needed to close. Would the user like to send a report? It asked. Please hit the send button now.

Ken screamed and pointed the mouse over the box marked "send" and clicked the mouse. And clicked the mouse. And clicked the mouse. The box would blink but not change.

"You fucking piece of software shit! Send this report now! Now! Now! Damn it!" Ken clicked and clicked, but to no avail. He was shaking and had turned a purplish-red and brown color under his collared shirt.

Just then, another phone rang.

"Christ!" Ken pointed at Daisy Mae. "Would you get me some fucking help in here?" He rushed back across the room. "Hello? Hello?" Ken picked up the receiver and shouted into the phone.

"Mr. Lay?"

"Yes. This is Ken Lay. CEO of Enron Corporation."

"Mr. Lay?"

"It's Ken Lay damn it to hell!"

"I'm sorry, Mr. Lay. It isn't the right one. But thank you for answering the phone, anyway. The next call will be the one you are waiting for and you will be released. Talk to you in just a minute."

Ken screamed into the mouth piece again and slammed the phone back down onto the hook. "Do you see what I have to put up with? Do you see? The incompetence. The fucking incompetence!"

Mack turned to Byron. "How in the hell are we supposed to figure this one out?"

Byron pointed first to the phone bank and then back to the computer. "Look, Teacher. There are two doors. Two ways out of here. One behind the phones and one behind the computers."

Mack looked again and saw what he'd missed while watching Ken run back and forth. They hid in plain sight, and he'd completely overlooked them.

The computer to the right of Ken buzzed, and the screen changed to reflect "loading" again. Ken rushed over from the phone and stood waiting expectantly.

Mack turned to Daisy Mae. He took a shot. "Incredibly ingenious Daisy Mae. An executive that is caught between a ringing phone that says nothing and a computer that won't load the screen he needs. How long has he been at that?"

Daisy grinned. She was very pleased that his punishment had been clear to the two visitors. "Psychological terror is far worse than physical. You can get used to the pain. But a patron's brain cannot wrap itself around the constant barrage of one thing. One thing will always drive the patrons over the edge and into the abyss."

"What's that?"

"Hope."

Mack nodded. Might be a country girl on the outside, but smart as anyone he was likely to meet here on the inside. He would not forget that fact.

The computer screen went to the "Please send an error message" again, and Ken whacked the hell out of the top of the computer. He had apparently had enough of that message. He picked the computer up and threw it to the floor.

The phones started ringing again, and Ken ran back across the floor to answer it. As he must have done repeatedly. Mack shook his head. This was a different kind of pain. A bad kind. He had to have gone insane by now.

Ken screamed at them before he answered the phone to get him something to drink, and then he slammed the phone back down after hearing the same message. It was always going to be the next one. The next phone call would be the one that set him free.

The computer buzzed again, and Byron noticed it had somehow been repaired and stood back up. Daisy Mae waved it off, noticing where he was looking. "We keep it repaired so his therapy isn't interrupted by a system malfunction." She laughed out loud at her own joke.

Mack took the scroll out from his pocket again. How was he supposed to pick one of the two doors from this shit? He had no clues for this one. No clue at all.

Byron ignored another ringing phone and looked at the scroll. It had to be there. "This is a maze. Seems to me that we're going to see a lot of these kinds of things in the tent here. I doubt the answer to each door is in there, Teacher. Whoever wrote this scroll probably didn't count on Daisy Mae keeping the same punishment over and over again. I'm going to take a chance here and figure the scroll was built and works regardless of the maze itself."

"You might be right. Makes a little sense, I guess. But there has to be a clue. It has to lead us. We guess and we're wrong. I don't want that. It'd be bad." He snapped his fingers. "The phone message says something about being the right one. Could that be a signal to us and not to him?"

Byron turned to Daisy Mae. He knew she'd lie, and he didn't think Ken would be sane enough to give them a straight answer. He tried Ken. "Hey, Mr. Lay. Is the message on the phone the same every time?"

Ken stopped and straightened his tie for a moment. "Finally. One of you fucking ingrates recognizes my importance. What the message says is for me and me alone. But if you have to know, it changed just now."

Byron nodded. He turned to Mack. "Probably the truth. He doesn't care about us. He wants out of here."

"I agree. What did the caller say exactly?"

"It isn't the right one."

"If logic holds true, and that message was for you and me, then I'd say we need to take the door on our right?"

"You're asking me, Teacher?"

"What do you think? It's reverse logic. It isn't the right one means that it's the left one. The left door. But if it's a lie, then it means it's the right one. The right door."

Byron shrugged. It could be right. He looked back at the two doors. Ken had stopped and was staring at them for a minute. The phone was ringing again, and Mack and Byron could see it was taking every ounce of willpower Ken Lay had not to run to his left and answer the phone. Every ounce.

Byron pointed. "Our right or his?"

Mack rolled the scroll back up. "Has to be our right. The caller couldn't know which way he'd be facing. Only thing that makes sense."

"Nothing makes any sense here, Teacher."

Daisy Mae nodded. "I have to agree, but I will say that I appreciate you noticing the great care I took to arrange Mr. Lay's therapy. Good work is always appreciative of someone noticing."

Mack pulled on Byron's shirt. "Let's go. To the right door." He pointed to the one behind the computer and Ken couldn't stand it anymore and broke into a run to answer the phone before it quit ringing. What if this was the call that released him?

Byron spotted it first. "Look Teacher," he said as he pointed to the door they were headed toward. "There's some kind of Greek symbol over the door itself."

Mack stopped and looked up. He then looked over at the other door and saw it had a symbol over it as well. "Oh shit," was all he said.

"I don't like the sound of that," Byron commented.

"Since I'm not an expert on Greek symbols, I'll guess we'll have to stick to the original plan."

"We're not even going to try to figure them out?"

"Why? I have no chance of telling what a random symbol might or might not mean. If it isn't straight forward, then it's leading to something else. Or a part of something else. We could be in the middle of the riddle, at the start, or at the end. Anything."

"True enough," Byron said.

Byron stopped and was standing before a door. Like all good mazes, it had two ways to turn at every intersection. To get the rat trapped farther and farther inside the maze with no hope of getting out. No hope.

The symbol over the door was more than likely Greek for something, Byron guessed. It looked like a large block letter *N* but slightly tilted to the side. Like it was off balance or something.

Byron looked at the other door. Over it was an obvious symbol of the letter *W*. "Women's restroom? Women go this way? Could be anything. Your plan is good by me."

Daisy Mae was close behind them as Mack opened the metal door behind the computer and walked through it. She had a knowing smile on her face. This was all she lived for in the City.

Ken Lay was slamming the phone down as Byron stepped out of his sight. "Nobody said you could leave, you assholes!" he screamed. "Get back here and get me something to drink! Now! Did I tell you I loved raiding your pensions? You fucking ingrates!"

The last thing Byron heard as the door shut was the phone ringing again.

CHAPTER TWENTY-THREE

Daisy Mae was conspicuously hanging just behind Mack and Byron as they entered the next room of the maze. This room, unlike the previous one, was small and very cramped. Byron's six-foot frame was a tight fit. He figured it would only be a moment before they were out of this room, so he wouldn't complain. Complaining wasn't something he thought he would ever do again.

The walls were completely devoid of color and furniture. Overall, it was more like a box than a room. It was small with a low ceiling and housed only two occupants. They didn't look like they needed a lot of space. By design, he was sure.

In the center of the room stood two people, one man and one woman, dressed in an older set of clothes, possibly from the late 1800s. The man wore a pair of brown pants and a white ruffled, long sleeve shirt. The woman had on a simple yet relatively clean dress with hoops underneath the center section that made it stand out farther from her waist. They stood about four feet apart from each other and the man had his back turned to the woman.

"Here we have Mr. Karl Grossman, from Germany. A particular vile and disgusting man. He was convicted of killing several women and cutting them up into little pieces in the early nineteen hundreds. A good candidate for the Funhouse and my maze."

She waved her hand at the man with his back to Mack and Byron. "He isn't without his strong points, however. My personal favorite fact about Mr. Grossman was that during World War I, he was known to have set up a small hot dog cart on the corner of the streets in his German homeland and sell hot dogs to support himself. The real fun comes when you stop to wonder about what ingredients he used to make the hotdogs? They were always top sellers."

Mack didn't want to think about that at all.

"I'm told that some of his hot dogs were particularly spicy. Like they were made with Brazilian women instead of fat frauleins. Something to chew on, don't you think?" Daisy Mae burst into laughter again. She was having a good time.

Byron realized he was so far out of his league that he couldn't have possibly descended any further, regardless of what the room mothers said and what Mack told him. He had sunk to the lowest level. This was too real to be fiction. He turned his eyeball over and over in his pocket. The more nervous he got, the more he seemed to finger the eye. A round, pliable worry stone that just happened to be a human eye.

Mack looked back at their guide and saw that she'd chewed the straw to a tiny fragment of its original length and had just a little bit left hanging from her mouth.

"Do you have a question fer me, Mr. Teacher?" she stressed the "Mr." part and grinned up at him from her viewpoint. She was baiting him, but he wouldn't rise to the occasion.

"No," was all he said.

"Then enjoy the show, Mr. Teacher. Mr. Grossman here spent several rotations on the Havoc Level of the City, but we felt he deserved to be here, where I could work with him personally."

At that moment, Karl Grossman turned around and looked directly at both Mack and Byron. He had a sharp-featured face with coal-black eyes, through which he stared hard at them. His mouth was a black hole that was closed firmly and looked to Mack to be unable to be opened. His eyes said he was completely and utterly insane.

"To make this little scene work well for Mr. Grossman's therapy, you'll notice we had to cut out his tongue and suture his mouth closed," Daisy Mae said nonchalantly. "It helps him and one day he may realize the error of his ways." She giggled convulsively. She didn't get audiences like this often. "We stapled his tongue to his chest. It's under his shirt, so he can wag it if he feels the need to say something."

As Grossman stared at Mack, the woman talked to him. If she noticed the others in the room with her, she didn't reflect it with either her actions or her body language. She was devoted to talking to Karl.

"You never take me anywhere. You don't really love me. You never help me with the kids. You never do right by me. Never. You don't help with the housework. Just look at this place. I work and slave all day to keep the place clean and you don't appreciate it at all."

Grossman turned and looked at her as she continued talking. The words came out of her mouth at a decibel level just below a runaway freight train, and Mack was tempted to cover his ears from the sound. Karl turned his back to her, but she deftly moved to his left and got back in front of him so he could see her clearly when she spoke.

Daisy Mae continued. "The girl was one of his victims. The one he hated the most. We got a pretty good copy for him to look at, don't you think? He gets to see her every moment of every day until I get tired of the scene."

Byron couldn't resist. "Why doesn't he attack her or choke her or something to make her shut up?"

Daisy Mae grinned. "If he touches her, we cut off something of his and feed it to her. He never really liked that." She pointed to the corner where an unseen morebats stood holding a sickle, waiting and hoping that Karl Grossman laid a hand on the girl. It was a prime-time slot for a morebats.

"You never take me anywhere. You don't really love me. You never help me with the kids. You never do right by me. Never. You don't help with the housework. Just look at this place. I work and slave all day to keep the place clean and you don't appreciate it at all."

Karl turned to them and Mack thought he had a pleading look in his eyes for a moment instead of pure insanity. "Does she always say the same thing to him?"

"Sometimes I very the speech a little bit, but it's essentially the same."

Mack nodded. His eyes roamed the little room and located the two doors. He nudged Byron. "Two doors again. Go figure."

Byron pointed at the top of the doors. "More symbols. The one over there looks like an *O*, and the other one looks like a *C*."

Mack nodded as he looked at them, tearing his eyes away from the scene in front of him. Grossman turned around again, and she cornered him. Her voice had risen an octave and was now not only loud but high pitched. Like a soprano opera singer. It sounded like someone scraping their nails on the chalkboard.

"Hey Teacher. The last room had a *W*. This one has an *O*. There's a *W* and an *O* in the word sparrow. If you spell it backwards."

Mack nodded as he thought for a moment and ignored the screaming girl. He shook his head "no."

"It doesn't sound right, Byron."

"Why not? It's backwards and a puzzle. Just a little one, but still a puzzle."

"Because you figured it out on the second clue, for one thing, and it disregards the third line of the stanza. Remember? *'While cutting off their legs.'* I have to think that's not there for window dressing. It means something. We just don't know what. Not yet, at least."

Daisy Mae darted her head up and down. "They said ya'll was smart fer sure, Mr. Teacher. I'm rite proud to be here listenen' to this."

Byron turned to Daisy Mae. A thought struck him while looking at her. He pointed. "Is it possible that she had her legs cut off at the knees?"

Mack blinked his eyes. Was it right in front of him? Was it possible? All he had to do was spell it out? She did have her legs cut off. He looked at the symbols over the two doors again. It didn't feel right. That also meant they took the wrong turn in the last room.

Mack closed his eyes while the woman turned the decibels up another notch and stood directly in front of Grossman's face, practically screaming at him. Mack didn't know how much torture he could take.

"You never do right by me. Never. You don't help with the housework. Just look at this place. I work and slave all day to keep the place clean and you don't appreciate it at all."

Mack looked at the woman. He could see her mouth moving, but no longer hear her. Blah, Blah, Blah, Blah. Her words turned to a dull recording in his mind. Never do right. Never.

He opened his eyes and turned to Byron. "Daisy Mae said they change the words every now and then. Think about it. If we go with the premise that we were right the last time about the words over the loudspeaker being altered for us, then we have to think we're right again. Never do right. If you never go right, then you go to the left. If it's a lie, then we take right again."

"Why wouldn't they alter the words to throw us off track? 5317."

"I'd normally agree with you, but I think the scroll doesn't lie. Not if we can figure it out. The symbols lead me to believe that we're right more than what the loudspeakers are telling me, anyway. If I'm right, then the loudspeakers and this woman are leading us away from the spelling of the word 'sparrow' in reverse, like you said. If I'm right, then we take the door with the *C* over it. The door on our right. And we try and figure out what the hell a *C* means in the stanza on the scroll. Wasn't the other letter over the door we went through an *N*?"

"I think so," Byron said. "But tilted or leaning. Something like that."

"I don't 'member exactly," Daisy Mae added. Another lie. Mack knew she was too sharp to forget this soon.

"If we stick with what we did and try to figure out the scroll, then we take the door with the *C* over it. Same as last time. And I hope we're right. I think we are. It feels right to me. If the loudspeakers and her words weren't in agreement with this, then I might agree with you."

Byron nodded. "Okay."

As Byron and Mack opened the door with the symbol *C* above it, the woman could only ask Grossman why he didn't take her out anymore. Byron hoped for their sake she wasn't lying.

CHAPTER TWENTY-FOUR

Victor and David were walking, or more precisely, shuffling along through the lazy river. They climbed one set of stairs and immersed themselves again in the river on this level. David had no idea where Victor was leading him, but he struggled mightily to keep up. He hadn't dared to open his mouth after the scene with Eikken a little earlier.

Victor was moving at a relatively slow pace for him. He desperately wished he had time to snort down some of the blue and white powder from the supply closet near the operating room, but he was too far away physically and two floors above the Womb Level where his stash was kept. It was an impossible want at this point.

He turned to David, who was sloshing through the bird-shit like mucus that comprised the lazy river on the Havoc Level. The river was thick and composed of three primary colors: black, white, and green and looked all the world like the biggest pile of bird shit that might have fallen from a pterodactyl three thousand years ago. David thought it smelled horrible and was particularly ripe. He walked with his hands above the flow of the bird-shit river holding what was left of the cocktail of drugs he put together for Victor back at the portal cage. He was keeping it as safe as he could.

The Doctor moved through the river a little easier than David at the moment. His head had turned to a black and purplish-crimson color and had bloated considerably from the pain that Eikken put him through. Victor knew it was stupid to have defied a council member, but now that he thought about it, he figured it was well worth it.

He turned to David, trudging steadily behind him and making his own way through the slime. "Hey, asshole."

"Yes, sir," David replied meekly. He had gone to a semi-state of consciousness as he tried to deal with everything that had happened to him. Not to mention the things that might bump into him and touch him all over underneath the surface of this river. He was weak anyway, and this just kept it out front for all to see. If he got too nervous and didn't control himself, he was sure Victor would hit him again with the shovel.

"You make sure that cocktail is protected from whatever happens to us until we find this fucking rose that Eikken wants us to find. You hear me?"

The threat was clearly there. "Yes, sir," was all he could muster.

"Good," Victor nodded. His head was still smoldering and little wisps of smoke rose from several places, like the embers of a fire had been put out on his head somewhere. His head felt like a truck drove through it.

"I have something in mind that will require us to use that cocktail of yours at a later point." Victor turned back around and continued his way through the bird-shit.

"I don't think it's a good idea to do anything other than what Eikken wants. Don't you? Victor?"

Victor whirled to him. David had stared to crawl up his ass the last several moments and now he was regretting ever having brought him along on this journey. He needed the cocktail. He didn't need the man. As soon as he learned what exactly was used to make it, he would dispose of David Masters completely. "I will tell you what to think and, more importantly, when to think it."

"Yes, sir."

"What I need to know from you is how much more of that cocktail we have?"

David looked down at the empty vial in his hands. There was barely a trace, and he knew it wasn't enough for even one injection. Opening his other hand, he counted the rest of the ingredients still leftover from the drug store.

"I've been meaning to tell you, sir. I don't have enough here for another injection. And we don't have enough of the ingredients leftover to make another." David shrunk back from the on-coming wrath of the Doctor.

Victor scratched a piece of hanging flesh on his now smoking scalp. "What do you need to make more?"

"I need the same as before, I think."

"Can we use other things as substitutes? Think about what's available around here before you answer."

David studied the vial and what was left in the packages he carried. He thought about all that he'd seen since his operation at the hands of this mad man. He nodded slowly and then more rapidly. "I think I can replace some of this stuff, but I'll need specifics that have the same base of genetic structures." He nodded again. "Yes, it might work."

Victor was actually patient for a moment. He hurt too badly to hurry, and he was trying to focus on what he needed to find. And how he was going to torture Eikken when he got the chance. "Go ahead and tell me what you need."

"I think I can make it work with four things, if we can find them. One, I need the blood of a virgin. That might be difficult in this place. I don't know."

"Keep going." Victor's mind was scanning the various places in the City he could turn to find that level of blood.

"I also need an enzyme that breaks down carbohydrates. Some kind of powerful digestive enzyme would work just fine. Number three is a high concentration of female hormones. The last thing I need is melted follicles of protein. Like in hair."

The Doctor thought for just a minute before climbing out of the lazy river. An idea formed in his mind. "I think I might be able to find those things for you and then you can make more of the cocktail. Correct?" "Yes, sir. It should work. Feasibly, anyway."

"If it doesn't work, I'll cut you into tiny pieces and feed you to this river." Back to his normal self. "We're here ass wipe."

"Yes, sir," David said as he followed Victor up and out of the river.

He had no idea where *here* was, and he was deathly afraid to ask just why it was named the "Havoc Level."

He was just about to find out.

CHAPTER TWENTY-FIVE

"May I compliment you, Mr. Teacher? Ya'll are very smart. At least I thought so anyway. But you just made a mistake back there. I think you're going to regret it later," Daisy Mae said.

Mack looked back at her and noticed the straw had disappeared completely and she had resorted to chewing on her fingernails. Her thumb protruded from her mouth and it looked like she was pouting. Her expression said all he needed to know. He'd made a living from being able to read people. He leaned over to Byron. "I'm sure we're on the right path now. Daisy Mae here just slipped up. She's lying, and it's making her nervous that we're on the right trail through this little party tent of hers. I'm damn sure she doesn't want us to succeed."

Byron glanced at her and then back at the new room they'd entered. Here we go again, he thought.

"Can you introduce us to the denizen here, Daisy Mae?" Mack asked.

Byron looked to see why he'd suddenly changed his attitude toward Daisy Mae, but he couldn't read Mack. He hid his thoughts well. Byron thought he'd be hell to face in a poker game. Like they were playing now.

"Don't rightly know what a denizen is, Mr. Teacher."

Mack pointed to the only man in the room. "That guy."

"Oh shit, Mack. I know him, too. That's Ted Bundy."

Daisy Mae nodded. "Very good, Mr. Michaels. You get an A+ for serial killers. This true revolutionary in front of you is the one and only Theodore Robert "Ted" Bundy. He was only really tied to four murders and rapes, but we know he was far more resourceful than that. We're convinced that he's a true City hero and can be linked to more than thirty killings of women all through his active adulthood. Alas, the state of Florida executed him before we could tie them all together. He's been with us for quite some time and I'm afraid his rehabilitation isn't going very well. He just doesn't seem to get any better. I don't know why. It certainly isn't my fault." She raised her eyebrows in total innocence. "I've tried everything I can think of. But this is new. I hope you'll like it, Mr. Michaels. Perhaps you'd like to stay behind and share this room with him?" She blinked her blue eyes at Byron and smiled sweetly.

Byron turned away from her and watched as Mack took it all in. This was another case that made Daisy Mae extremely proud. Her accomplishments in psychological warfare were indeed impressive. Byron never wanted to end up in her tent. He might enjoy the throwing up room more than this shit.

This room was taller than both of the first two in the tent put together. It was at least fifteen feet tall and towered over the two of them. It was also quite wide, and even though he couldn't guess just how wide, he figured it had to be to do what it was supposed to do.

The walls were covered from floor to ceiling with what looked like state-of-the-art plasma televisions. Each of the walls contained two screens, one on top of the other, and each of them stretched the length of the wall. Eight screens playing simultaneously in high definition and liquid crystal display.

Each of the televisions was turned on and playing an incredible close up of pornography. The entire room looked like an up close orgy of the highest quality. On one screen there was a blond with huge boobs riding a cowboy. Another screen held a redhead riding the cowboy's horse. There was anal sex, oral sex, vaginal sex, animal sex and every other thing Byron had ever seen or imagined playing as loud and as wild as it could. The sound was turned up on all the screens and it sounded like a football team had just run ten miles with no breaks in full padding by the sound of the gasping.

In the middle of the room sat a dejected looking Ted Bundy. He was sitting on a metal bench and he was completely naked. He held a flaccid penis in one hand. Or at least it looked to Byron like his penis.

As Byron looked closer, he could see that there was a jar of cream on the bench next to Bundy, and what he'd taken for Ted's penis was anything but. It was flaccid, but apparently the cream hadn't worked and the penis was obviously rubbed raw from many sessions of masturbation. Many, many sessions.

Bundy looked up at Mack and Byron as they entered the room, and then immediately dismissed them from his mind. He had other issues to contend with at the moment.

Daisy Mae said from behind them, "Ya'll have to excuse Mr. Bundy. He's a little upset. That's all."

"Okay," was all that Mack could think to say. He licked his lips as a small amount of sweat ran down his forehead. He had no idea what was going on and didn't really want to know. He immediately started looking for the two doors to get out of this room and away from this scene.

"Ya'll see what's going on here?"

Mack shook his head "no" but couldn't take his eyes off of Bundy sitting on the metal table. At that moment, the sound of ecstasy from all sides of the room were halted and a voice over a loudspeaker broke in on his thoughts.

"Mr. Bundy. Your break time is up. Please proceed to watch screen number three. It's the one to your left. I think you'll enjoy the show."

Mack and Byron watched as Bundy swung his eyes over to the screen and the scene changed from the redhead riding a horse to two men having a mutual masturbation session.

"Mr. Bundy. Mr. Bundy."

Bundy's head snapped up to look at the loudspeaker in the top corner of the room.

"If you don't begin, we'll send in Hannah and she'll help coax you to nirvana. Please begin."

The loudspeaker voice was almost singsong and pleasant, as if it were talking to a favorite pupil in kindergarten.

Byron whispered to Mack, "What the hell is a Hannah?"

Mack shook his head silently. He had no idea.

Bundy grabbed the jar of cream sitting on the bench next to him and unscrewed the cap. He reached in with his left hand and pulled out a small amount of what looked to Byron to be white paste. Possibly some kind of putty or chalking that could be used in a bathroom. It was thick and gritty with the consistency of sand.

"Sorry, Mr. Bundy. Here comes Hannah!" The voice said gleefully.

Bundy screamed "No!" and started vigorously rubbing the putty paste onto his penis, or what was left of his penis. His penis had been rubbed so raw that there was no skin left on it at all, and was in reality a red mass of muscle and nerve endings with something white and putrid-looking hanging off the end where the tip should've been.

Daisy Mae explained. "Ya'll see? We let him get all excited. We encourage him in various ways to relieve himself. What with all the images in front of him and all the sexual tension Mr. Bundy must have built up while on the surface, I thought it would be good therapy to let him get close to the release he needs."

"Close?" Byron asked as he involuntarily gulped.

"Well, now we can't give him everything he wants, can we? Not even a City hero like Ted Bundy gets everything he wants."

Mack knew what was coming. He didn't have to ask.

"We don't let him come. We just let him get close, is all. We never left him finish himself off."

Byron shuddered at the thought of always being on the verge of a sexual release and constantly having it taken from you. No wonder Bundy's penis was raw, red muscle.

A small door opened, and a dressed up morebats entered. The morebats had a yellow wig on and was dressed in silk stockings and a black brassiere.

"You get the fuck away from me, Hannah!" Ted yelled as the morebats licked it lip's and its twelve-inch penis rose from underneath the stockings. Bundy masturbated furiously and Byron saw that the cream contained some rather large chunks of sand mixed in for added effect.

The closer the morebats got, the faster Bundy pumped a still flaccid penis. He was cringing and screaming alternately between pumps, as it must have hurt with every stroke. He started to breathe harder and deeper, and then he threw back his head and closed his eyes. Bundy was getting close.

The screens in the room went suddenly deathly still and then an audiotape of the Barney the Dinosaur song played. "I love you. You love me...", and all the screens changed to show the grinning dinosaur.

Bundy screamed as he lost the moment and the red muscle in his hand slipped out. It fell against his leg and didn't move or twitch. His head slumped to his chest.

Hannah, the dressed up morebats, receded into the background with a deliciously deep chuckle. She'd done her job. Bundy hadn't been allowed to finish, but only brought to the brink.

"This time, I guess we better go with what we know. I didn't hear anything or see anything on the screens to indicate which door we should go through. Did you, Teacher?"

Mack pointed to the image on screen number three that was brought to Bundy's attention by the loudspeaker. "I might be wrong again, but I think that screen is showing us the way to go."

"What did you see?" Byron asked.

Mack shook his head. "I didn't see anything. It's what I heard, like in the last two rooms." He turned to Daisy Mae, who resumed chewing most of her fingernails off and was now down to the last finger. "Didn't you say that Mr. Bundy has been here with you for quite a while?"

Daisy Mae shook her head "yes" as she chewed. Mack figured that particular fingernail must have been extra tasty because she was savoring each bite.

"If Bundy's been here for a long time, then I assume he'd know which screen was number three. Wouldn't you?" he asked Byron.

"You're right. Yet I remember the speaker telling him specifically 'It's the one to your left.' I think he said it like that."

Mack agreed. "That's exactly how he said it. So I have to assume it was meant for us again and the door we want is on our right. Not our left."

Byron had seen enough. "Let's go," he said.

Mack tugged his shirt. "Notice the symbols above the doors again. On the one to right we're about to go through, it looks like the letter *P*. The other one has a clear letter *R*."

Byron stopped short. "I'm not sure this is right anymore, Teacher. *W-O-R* so far on the doors we haven't chosen. It clearly spells Sparrow backwards."

Mack pulled the scroll back out. He could hear Daisy Mae breathing hard behind him as she munched away on what was left of her nails. He looked and could see she was sweating slightly. He spread the scroll on the floor and Byron leaned over him.

"*And the heads of dead sparrows.*" Mack read out loud.

"What about the third line?"

"I've been thinking about that. I don't really think it's Daisy Mae here. Do you? What if there was a different room mother? The scroll has to work for all situations."

Byron looked at Daisy Mae. Mack had to be right. It made sense in a world that made little sense. And she looked nervous. She was chewing everything she could fit in her mouth. He'd seen it on the streets enough to know.

Mack looked again at the words. *"While cutting off their legs."* What the hell? he thought. He looked up at the doors again as the screens broke into another animated display of raunchy sex for Bundy's enjoyment. Or rather, punishment. Mack looked over to see Bundy hanging his head. He didn't want to look up at the screens.

Mack stared at the symbols over the door. It was right there in front of him, he was sure of that. But yet....

His head snapped back to the symbols over the door they were about to go through. The letter *P* stared back at him. He was so close he could feel it.

"I don't know. But I think it's getting close. I say we stay with what we've done."

"Right. We go." Byron headed to the door on the right and watched as Hannah headed over to help Bundy with his flaccid problem. Bundy was screaming with each stroke of his hand, and Hannah was salivating the closer she got.

CHAPTER TWENTY-SIX

Victor and David stopped at the fourth door they came to after exiting the lazy river. The Havoc Level was encircled by the lazy river, so the Doctor didn't think it would matter where they got out of it and started their search. All roads would eventually lead to the same place. He did not know how they were going to find this damn rose thing anyway, but he figured they may as well start here. If they asked questions while getting the ingredients for the cocktail, Eikken would never know. It was a little dangerous for them, but Victor could search for the Rose and get his ingredients for the ass wipe at the same time.

He opened the metal door and pulled David through behind him. David hesitated ever so slightly. He was in no rush to see what other things had been conjured up here.

"Gentlemen, Gentlemen. Welcome to my humble home! New guests are always welcome here." The man approached them with his arm out to shake the Doctor's hand. He had an award winning smile like he was selling them a used car, and a mouth full of teeth. He had a head full of black, oily hair that'd been plastered back with grease, two large blackheads on each cheek, and no eyebrows. He wore a blue and green plaid suit with an off-colored checkered tie accentuated with a red kerchief in the pocket. Just a sleaze ball that belonged where he was at the moment.

Victor looked at the proffered hand sticking out for him to shake, and then back at the man's face. No one in the City shook hands because it could lead you to be thrown down to the ground or cast into some other kind of room He didn't offer his or take the one thrust out to him.

The used car salesman ignored the slight and clasped his hands together as he looked over at both David and Victor. He had pulled two new prizes in from the pond and he was going to enjoy it. He started clapping.

"What can I do to help you gentlemen today? I'm absolutely sure that we can accommodate you here. My room is better than any of the others, and I know that if I treat you right, you'll tell the floor man all about me and my friends here." He motioned to the patrons behind him.

Victor moved to the side so that he could better see the room and the people behind the Welcome Wagon Man. The room itself was large, far larger than he'd first thought when he walked into the alcove. It was covered in rocks, like it was bricked many centuries ago, and the rocks were covered in a moss colored slime. It was green and looked and smelled like fresh algae that was just pulled from a river bank. The walls oozed the algae, and it moved constantly downward and disappeared into the ground beneath the floor. To where, he had no clue.

The room had no ceiling, but revealed a smoky-like fog shroud that covered it from end to end. If there was a ceiling, it was completely obscured by the bluish smoke. The smoke billowed slowly back and forth, giving the room a feeling of motion, even though Victor knew he wasn't moving and it wasn't moving around him. Like low clouds on a foggy morning in London somewhere in his past, he thought.

"Would you like to meet some of my customers?" The used car salesman was only too happy to show them his customers.

Victor still hadn't spoken a word, nor indicated that he'd heard the man. He knew the room mother would try to trick them in one fashion or another, depending on how original the guy could be, but he also knew that he was more than likely considerably smarter than this room mother. If the guy had been very smart at all, he probably wouldn't still be on the Havoc Level dressed in a suit from long ago. He would've been demoted by now.

"I can assure you that all of my patrons are ready to scream at the top of their lungs. Would you like a demonstration?"

David walked close behind Victor. His eyes grew as wide as saucers at what he saw displayed in front of him. At the moment, it was relatively quiet, which was also a surprise because what he was looking at must've hurt like hell.

Victor stopped in the first row in front of him. He adjusted to his left and then to his right so that he could see down the row upon row of patrons in this room. There must have been a couple of hundred of them, at least.

"I have to ask a couple of questions. I want to speak to some of your patrons who have been here the longest. If you fuck with me, I'll add you to this last row here." Victor pointed to the row in front of the salesman.

"I can guarantee that my customers will answer all of your questions, sir. There is no reason to threaten me with my own creation, now is there?" He asked as he slid a little further away from the Doctor. He'd been right up in front of the two of them, proudly showing off his room. He knew the rules here. If a patron came walking in through the front door like these two did, then they obviously were lower beings and not here to join his herd. If they'd been carried here by morebats and were screaming their indignation at the top of their lungs, he would've been free to do as he wished with them both. These two were not bleeding, even though the one who led them was smoking from his head and had obviously been burned recently. They didn't look like the usual pain babies. These two would make a lovely addition to his herd, but he had to be careful. He had to think how best to get them to stay with him. They wouldn't do it voluntarily, but if the salesman could add them, he might get a demotion for out-thinking two lowers. It was an interesting prospect.

Victor led them past the first row. "What do you call this place?" he asked.

The used car salesman grinned broadly. "The Stake House."

Victor nodded. Made sense. He knew the one he was looking for was here somewhere. He'd heard.

Row upon row of wooden stakes standing approximately seven feet tall and planted into the ground, beckoned to Victor. Each was firmly drilled into the floor, which was just mud and sand. Early concrete. The stakes numbered twenty across and stretched back to the wall as far as he could see. They were spaced evenly apart at about six foot intervals throughout and looked to be militarily regimented.

The stakes themselves were polished a deep brown color and honed to a very fine point on the top. The bottom was rounded out and looked to be about three inches across at the widest point, just prior to entering the ground. The stake tapered off from the bottom to the top, where the point was located.

On many of the stakes, but not all of them, as there were several that were empty, was an impaled person. The people were at various levels of stake depth. Some were completely impaled and the top of the stakes had come out of either their shoulder or the top of their heads. These patrons slowly rotated around their stakes like puppets on a string. The others, who were being completely impaled, were resting with the stakes shoved up inside them to different depths. While some stakes had most of the seven-foot lengths showing and very little of the points hidden inside the patrons, the other stakes ranged in depth from thirty percent to almost one hundred percent imbedded. Victor figured the depth of impalement depended on how long the prisoner had been in the room.

The patrons themselves were in various stages of dress. They were all nude from the waist down, but several still had some semblance of shirt attached. The stakes entered from either the anus in the men or the vagina in the women and proceeded up through the body slowly. Excruciatingly slowly.

All of the patrons were spread eagled out like a large letter "X." Their individual arms were chained to the smoky ceiling by skin tight manacles. Their legs were spread as wide as could be accommodated, and each of their individual ankles was attached to a crank and pulley with a lever of some sort that the Doctor figured was a tension device. The more the pulley was tightened by turning the metal crank beside it, the more the legs were pulled downward, impaling the patron on the seven-foot stake by driving the person down on it. The crank could be turned so that the stakes were driven in inch by agonizing inch. Simple, but very effective.

There should have been an endless amount of screaming from the pain, but at the moment, it was fairly quiet as the patrons caught their breath for a second.

The salesman looked at Victor as he surveyed the room. "Wondering why it's so quiet? Trust me, my newfound friend. It'll get loud in just a minute. When the pulleys begin to turn." He clapped his hands and several morebats appeared from the shadows of the room. They moved clumsily towards the various pulleys and cranks and took up their positions. As soon as they shuffled to the cranks, the screams and wails from all those impaled howled loudly across the room. They knew what was coming.

Victor put his arm out and signaled to the salesman to stop for just a minute. "I need to ask a couple of questions before you start turning the cranks. I'm looking for someone. Although, I admit, I would enjoy watching this," he said wistfully, letting his eyes roam across the men and women.

The salesman was happy to oblige. "Yes, Yes. Let's try the third row. I have a very special man there." He turned to his right and then his immediate left, and walked past the first two rows of patrons.

David walked directly behind and to the right of Victor. He would not be left here. He struggled to keep up with the pace of the Doctor's stride, as his head swung nervously from side to side. He didn't like this room at all. There was a considerable amount of blood and intestines strewn about the floor and, with every step, David could hear something "crunch" beneath his feet. He had no idea how it would feel to have a seven foot wooden stake slowly driven up his butt, inch by inch over the millennium, but he had no reason to ever find out. If he could manage it. He was quite amazed that they could ever be quiet with the pain that they must be feeling. All the patrons were awake and watching them through blood-soaked eyes.

"Here we are. A perfect model of a patron for you to question!" The salesman grabbed a busy morebats watching them next to an adjacent crank and pulled him over to the stake where the three of them were now standing.

The man the salesman stopped in front of was fairly youngish looking, and dressed in some kind of ceremonial robe. Victor could tell that at one time he had been royalty, but a present, he had the majority of a seven-foot stake rammed vertically up through his chest and protruding from his left shoulder. His head was lolling from side to side and his eyes were half closed in a vision of pure agony. He wore a cap and looked vaguely familiar to Victor.

"I am most honored to introduce you to the imperial ruler, Vlad Dracul." He waved his hand like he was introducing a world leader. His grin was as broad as his face was wide.

Victor nodded. He remembered Dracul from some of the old pictures in books he'd read as a kid. He knew immediately where the impetus for the Stake House had come from. Dracul's favorite way of ridding himself of various challenges to his throne during his reign in the 1400s had been to impale his challengers on six-foot stakes he called tzapas. Turkish word for stake.

It was, in some weird way, almost fitting that the inventor of the impalement had ended up on one himself.

Victor shook his head "no." This wasn't the one he was looking for and sought to ask questions. He didn't think he could help him. Victor didn't know why he felt that way, but he was sure of the feeling.

David's eyes had gone as wide as small pies at the mention of the name "Dracul." He certainly knew who he'd been on the surface. He felt humbled to be in the presence of greatness.

The smile on the face of the salesman quickly faded when he saw Victor didn't want to talk to Dracul. He thought he might be interested in the more famous patrons he had on display.

Victor scanned the aisles of bloody people and pointed at a shapely red headed woman who was impaled about half way up the length of the stake. That was her, he was sure of it. She was conscious and had an eternal look of pure fear in her eyes as the men approached. The stake disappeared in her spread open vagina.

"An excellent choice. I can tell you know exactly what you want!" The salesman led them straight to her and the grin returned.

Standing directly in front of the partially nude woman, he continued. "This is also a famous patron of the Stake House. She's been here only recently however, transferred from a nearby room when it was determined by that room mother that she could no longer properly care for this woman."

David moved to the front. He stared up at the redhead, who looked back at him with what looked to be very sad eyes. The stake, being driven slowly through her entrails, was bleeding profusely onto the ground under her. David thought she was incredibly lovely.

"This fine specimen of the Stake House is none other than Elizabeth Bathory. The Blood Countess. The one and only!"

Victor looked up at the impaled woman. Exactly who the Doctor sought. He knew she was here somewhere. The used car salesman was obviously disappointed at his lack of excitement.

"You don't know who Elizabeth Bathory is? Well then, I shall be most glad to tell you. Elizabeth was known as the 'Blood Countess.' She was most famous for draining teenage girls of all their blood and pouring it into her bathtub and then bathing in it. She then drank it without exception and with every meal. An incredible talent to have in my showroom." He was obviously proud.

Victor pointed at her. Here was his virgin. He motioned to David. "Ass wipe. I figure if she ingested all that blood of the teenage girls, some of them must have been virgins. Perhaps some of that blood made its way into her stomach and we can get a vial of it to use. It might be the closest thing we'll get here." He turned back to Bathory. "I want to ask her a question. You said she came from another room here on the Havoc Level?"

The salesman nodded vigorously. "The Crispy Critter room."

Victor turned and looked up at Elizabeth. "Did you come from there?"

She raised her head and let her eyes drift from David long enough to look at Victor. "Why should I answer you?" Her eyes showed defiance even in her predicament.

The salesman looked horrified that one of his patrons would address a lower in that tone. He snapped his fingers and the closest morebats, who had a straw hat on his pointy head, grabbed the crank next to the feet of Elizabeth and before anything else could be done, turned the handle one full rotation.

David watched as her legs were yanked down suddenly, and the stake was pushed another two inches up inside her intestines. Judging by the length of the other stakes and the amount of stake that had to be inside of her at the moment, David figured the point of the stake was piercing the outer lining of her stomach.

Elizabeth let out a blood-curdling scream that seemed to come from the depths of hell itself. She threw her head backwards and her whole body reacted violently against the chains that held her. She threw herself forward, and David watched as she tried mightily to move up and off the stake that was driving itself into her. She lunged and twisted, but her chains wouldn't budge and blood gushed out of her vagina, along with several small chunks of intestine.

After several moments, she stopped wailing and dropped the crescendo into a small howl. The salesman waited patiently for her to get a grip on herself. "Answer his question or I will have the morebats turn the wheel again."

Elizabeth raised her head and looked past the Doctor to David. Something seemed to pass between them and even Victor noticed she had eyes for no one else but David. He stared back at her.

"It'd be unwise to get a schoolboy crush on anyone in the City, ass wipe," Victor said, but didn't take his eyes off of Elizabeth. "Have you been in the fire room?"

She struggled to raise her head, but nodded. She'd been there.

Victor continued. "I'm looking for a rose. The Black Rose that's housed somewhere on this floor. Did you hear of anything like that while you've been here?"

"I have heard," she answered.

"Tell me."

"It is a rumor. Nothing more. Supposed to be powerful. The room mother in the fire room spoke of its power a couple of times. I know nothing more." She took her eyes off David and lowered them to the ground again.

"I can't. I can't. I can't..." David stuttered.

WHACK.

"She helped us, Victor. She should be rewarded."

Victor turned to David. He made sense when he wasn't an idiot.

The salesman chimed in, "I make the determination who is rewarded and who isn't in this room."

Victor sprung immediately at the salesman. He'd had enough of this guy. He grabbed him and savagely pounded him with his bare knuckles. Once he got him on the ground, Victor kicked him until his face was almost unrecognizable. Grasping his arm and wrenching it behind his back, the bones in the salesman's wrist snapped. He curled up into a small ball and started crying.

"I helped you. I helped you. You shouldn't do this to me," he pleaded.

Victor grabbed the morebats who'd turned Elizabeth's crank and pointed at him to move the body of the salesman to one of the empty stakes to the right of Elizabeth. Realizing what was about to happen to the room mother, all the patrons in the room cackled and screamed with delight.

The morebats and Victor lifted the pleading and struggling form of the salesman, and placed him into the chains. They shackled first his legs and then his arms, and as he cried about the indignation of this moment, Victor turned the crank attached to the pulleys and the salesman was lifted into a perfect position of impalement, directly atop the sharp end of his stake.

The entire room was hooting and laughing, and as Victor turned the crank again, the salesman was instantly impaled on the dagger. He let out a soul deep, gut wrenching scream as the stake pushed past his anus and into his lower colon, tearing all the time like tiny shark's teeth on human flesh. The blood flooded the ground beneath the salesman and flowed rapidly into the cracks in the mud.

David walked over to the crank at Elizabeth's station and released the tension pulley. She thrust upwards and pulled herself off of the crank, immediately using her arm strength. She would not let this moment pass.

Victor watched as she lowered herself to the floor. He wasn't going to help her. "We need a vial of blood from your stomach," he said.

She would have given them anything for this release. Especially for the little one. She motioned to David, and he sheepishly handed her a syringe. She plunged it into her flesh where David was pointing and then drew a full capsule. Handing it back to David, she made sure her hand brushed his.

As he turned and left the room, with David looking back over his shoulder and walking behind him, Victor couldn't help but be intrigued. He'd doled out some just punishment and gotten some information all at the same time. And the first of the four ingredients.

Elizabeth would do a fine job in her new position as room mother of the Stake House. She was headed for the crank on the stake of the salesman. David figured she had some revenge issues built up that she was about to even out.

CHAPTER TWENTY-SEVEN

Mack and Byron stepped aside as Daisy Mae nudged her way past them. "What you are about to see, gentlemen, is one of my favorite rooms in this here amazin' maze."

She motioned for them to keep up with her and to get a good look at what was waiting for them. Mack already ignored her. He was concentrating on the third stanza of the scroll. He was convinced the answer to the path was right there in front of his face. He looked to the sides of the circular room they were in and his eyes searched for the symbols over the doors. His face fell when he realized that these two doors did not have symbols over them. Nothing on either door.

Byron noticed also that there was nothing on either of the doors or over them. He scanned the dimly lit room to make sure the symbols weren't hidden somewhere else.

Daisy Mae motioned to the lady sitting in the center of the room. "Either of you detectives recognize her?" she asked.

Mack stopped searching the walls and doors to look more closely at the woman on the floor. She appeared to be wholly intact, which was good for her. She wore a simple yellow flowered dress with a green checkered scarf around her neck. She sat almost completely still, and neither moved nor made any sign showing she recognized that they'd entered the room.

The only distinguishing mark on her was the fact that she was, quite literally, at least four hundred pounds. She was incredibly obese and was probably one of those people they had to bury in a piano case because of her size. Her arms were hanging globs of skin and long since dead muscle, and her legs under the dress were blue varicose veined monstrosities that couldn't possibly have held her frame up even if she could struggle to a standing position. Her neck was so fat her head seemed to rest on a tire of blubber. Mack didn't know who she was.

Daisy Mae shook her head back and forth rather vigorously. "No, no, no. She isn't here because she's so fat. They had to use a crane to bury the bitch. We're not like that," she said rather indignantly with a flip of her golden hair.

"Then why?" Byron asked. He was fascinated by looking at her. She seemed to be immobile, but he knew it was more than that.

"This is the infamous Belle Sorenson Gunness."

Mack blinked his eyes. He knew that name but couldn't place it. "You know her Teacher?"

Mack shook his head "no." He waited patiently for the explanation that he knew was forthcoming. Daisy Mae had her own stage here and wouldn't relinquish the role, no matter what he or Byron knew. It was her show.

"Belle was responsible for killing over forty people that we could tie her directly too. She was amazing in the fact that she also killed at least one of her two husbands and a couple of her children."

Mack nodded. Now he remembered. From the late 1800s. He'd studied it at the FBI academy.

"If her damn husbands had done what she wanted and not fucked with her, she probably wouldn't have killed them."

Mack turned to Daisy Mae. "You're saying she killed people who deserved it?"

"In my opinion, Mr. Teacher, everyone deserves it."

Mack turned back to Belle and saw immediately why she hadn't moved. He saw something on each side of her on the floor that he hadn't noticed before. Belle turned her head and followed Mack's gaze as he stared at the tiny brown thing on the floor.

A cupcake. Just out of her immediate reach.

Belle stretched a tentative arm from its resting place on her stomach and crept her hand towards the chocolate cupcake sitting next to her. As her hand neared the cupcake, the cupcake inexplicably moved, as if by its own will. It moved a centimeter at first and Mack wasn't really sure he understood what he was seeing. Then Belle moved her hand closer to the same cupcake again, and it moved noticeably this time. Just out of her reach.

Belle pulled her hand back to her stomach and reached out slowly with her other hand. The cupcake on that side of her slid deliberately away from her. Belle quickly threw her body on the side and tried to trap the cupcake, but it was faster and moved just beyond her extended grasp.

Daisy Mae laughed hysterically as she watched Belle roll over on her back and lay prone on the floor. The two cupcakes were at the very ends of her fingertips and she could just barely scratch the icing on the one, but not on the other one.

Belle screamed a cry of anguish and fought to right herself. She would not be bested by these damn cupcakes again. She turned and stared directly at Daisy Mae. "But I'm *so* hungry," was all she wailed. It was more of a plea rather than a statement. Daisy Mae knew she was hungry. "I will get one of these fucking cupcakes. I will!!"

"Good luck, Belle. Good luck."

Belle lunged at the cupcake to her left, only to watch as it moved the perfect distance away from her.

"I'm fucking starving, you bitch. I will have the cupcake. I will. I will," Belle screamed.

Byron pointed at the cupcake on Belle's left at the moment. The two cupcakes had been moving ever since they'd arrived. Belle would never get to eat, but instead have to look at them and salivate for a long time. Psychological torture at its finest.

"Hey, Teacher. Those cupcakes. Do they look like they have writing on the top of them?"

Mack squinted. It was hard to be sure because they kept moving, but he thought Byron was right. "I can't quite make out the wording, but someone has written something in green icing on top of both cupcakes."

Byron grabbed his shoulders. "It's the symbols, Teacher. One on each of them. The two symbols."

"What are they?"

Byron squinted. He had the better angle to see the writing at the moment. "One is a capital *A*. The other looks like a *V*."

Mack sighed. Here we go again. An *A* and a "V." What did it mean? As he watched, Belle screamed another cry of anguish and lunged as the cupcake in front of her turned away from her. It was the one with the *V* on it.

"Shit! That's it. How could I have missed it for so long?"

"What? What did you miss, Teacher?" Byron asked.

"It's not a *V*. Not at all."

"What? The hell it isn't. It's very clear."

"It's not a *V*. It's an upside-down *A*. *With one leg missing*. Here look. We've been following the letters without the legs from the beginning. It wasn't until Belle turned that *V* upside-down that I saw it."

Mack spread the scroll out one more time. *"While chewing off their legs,"* he read. "The first letter wasn't an *N* tilted. It was a *W* without one of the legs. Like this." He drew the *N* in the dirt floor and then added the extra leg to make the *W*. "The second letter wasn't a *C*. It was a half enclosed *O*. Then came the *P*."

Byron saw it then. "The *P* was really an *R* when you add the leg. Whoever wrote the scroll is spelling 'sparrow" backwards, but without the legs." Pretty good puzzle. Difficult but solvable. He looked up at Mack with renewed respect. This guy was very good. How did he end up in Hell?

Mack stood up. He had it figured now. "We don't have to go on with this show of yours anymore, Daisy Mae. We can just go straight through the doors that lead to the next room, if you don't mind?" Mack turned and looked at her. "If I'm right, the next letter we're looking for is a *D*."

Byron nodded. A *P* without the leg makes a *D*. It was easy now.

Mack looked once more behind him. Daisy Mae was no longer chewing on her fingernails, but had taken her shirt off completely, exposing her rather large breasts. She took one of them in her mouth and was chewing the nipple off with several gulping, slurping sounds. She wanted to give the boys a good show.

Mack moved to the door nearest the cupcake with the upside-down iced letter *V* on it, and Byron followed. Belle had taken up a sitting spot in the middle of the room again and was patiently planning her next assault on the cupcakes on each side of her. An assault Mack knew she would never win.

Byron frowned as he followed. They may have solved the riddle of the stanza. But that didn't get them out of going through the rest of the maze. Unfortunately.

He figured there were still some surprises that Daisy Mae had prepared for them.

The cavern contained no light. There was occasionally some filtered fluorescent light that wormed its way into this part of the cavern when a door nearby was opened. But at the moment, the door was closed, as it'd been closed for many years, and the cavern was in almost total darkness.

Behind a grayish-black rock that rose from the floor of the cave like a mighty stalagmite about to pierce a fierce enemy was a small opening in the cavern's side. It was cylindrical, honed out through many centuries of constant water dripping and erosion. To anyone passing, the crevice was completely hidden from view. The combination of no light and a perfectly formed slit up the side of the wall of the cavern made it nearly impossible to see. To find this crevice, someone would have to know it was here. It would've still been a challenge.

Inside the crevice in the darkness of this cavern, there was a stirring. Not the like the wrestling of a wind, but a simple stirring. More like a sleeping bear awaking from a long winter nap. First, one part would move and stretch, and then something else would take a clue from the first stretching and respond. Soon the sleeper would be completely awake, but it'd take a little time.

The stirring continued as some of the dust on the floor of the crevice momentarily scurried, flew up in the air, and then settled back to the ground around the movement. There was something coming alive in the crevice. It was simply letting the world know it was here.

Under the dusty foundation, in a world devoid of beauty, a single seed germinated. The seed unfolded long dead and clenched roots as it struggled to survive, if only for a moment. It must live. It had to live.

The seed found its strength from an unknown resource. From someone it didn't know existed.

In the darkness of the cavern, in the blackness of Hell, a Rose grew.

CHAPTER TWENTY-EIGHT

Annicka had not spent the time since leaving Mack and Randi doing nothing. She'd found a place to perch her physical self and not be bothered as she sent her essence out and wandered the hallways again. She was looking for something.

It'd been too easy and as she sat there with her eyes closed in a quiet corner of a darkened chamber, it just didn't make any sense. Her cat, stretching and moving from one of her shoulders to the other, hissed even when it was content, but more so when Annicka was at rest. The cat considered its job was to watch the outside and the immediate surroundings as Annicka went into these fugue states. The cat wouldn't let her be bothered or attacked while she roamed the City with her mind. It had its job to do and would instantly dig its claws deep into her shoulder and wake her if there was a threat.

Annicka was still hovering, as she preferred never to rest directly on the ground. She considered the floors vile from centuries of spilled and dried and caked and clustered blood spume coverings. She would always glide over and past anything that was in her way and that included when she was resting, as now.

Her arms, the one good one and the one tentacle, were curled over her chest while she searched and thought. Her eyes were closed, and she appeared to be in deep slumber to those who faced her. Her mind was awhirl and awash with the activity and the complications. She may have been a council member, but she was still vulnerable. They all were.

This entire process had bothered her from the start of this journey for several reasons. Foremost, nothing came easily in the City of Hell.

That she had got this far led her to believe that she was being helped, or more than likely pushed, in a certain direction. Led like a dog on a chain to where she sat presently.

As she rested and let her essence search and roam the nooks and crannies, she could only wonder how she came to be this close. It made little sense to her. Not really.

Annicka found the scroll eons of time ago and had been wise enough to recognize the importance and to hide it. But the locating of the scroll still irked her to a degree. If it hid such a dark secret of the City, why hadn't it been hidden better? Hidden where she or someone else wouldn't have been able to find it, no matter how hard they searched? If the Lowest didn't want you to know something, he certainly could block their thought processes or abilities with a simple wave of his hand.

But the competition often fostered itself when things got boring. Annicka had seen it on more than one occasion during her time on the council. Although she'd mostly been left alone, perhaps the time had come to test her. Her resolve. Her abilities. For whatever reason.

Perhaps this was about something else altogether.

That thought was certainly delicious. How would she handle the power of the Black Rose once it was in her hands? Once she owned it. Once she controlled it. And she would have it. Probably sooner than later.

The tiny higher being she had picked for the job was considerably resilient and had the right make-up to find the Rose, she was convinced.

Still, the whole thing bothered her.

She'd watched them maneuver through the red and black room and easily solve the riddles where the others she'd sent before them failed so miserably. She watched, semi-amusedly while they struggled through the maze. An ingenious puzzle had been figured out, and they were definitely on the right track. They were getting through it and were about to come out the other side. Definite progress.

If she was being observed or led, then she was doing fine. If she was being pushed to the ending, then she was a fool.

The scroll held secrets she'd been unable to comprehend since she first acquired it. Yet, this higher being, this puny human with the pathetic excuse of suicide as his ticket to Hell, was doing just that. He was solving the riddle.

It had been Randi's idea to use him. She'd heard of this man before Annicka had known of him and his work for some of the other council members. He would've been used at some point to be stationed on the

Womb Level. And she would have eventually heard from her sources, her highers, of his abilities. But Randi led her to him.

If he could solve the entire riddle of the scroll and continue on this journey, then she would need to be ready for him to make the discovery. She would need to be in place to protect her find from the other council members. They would begin circling like sharks in the water when they heard what she was about to own.

Her mind wandered as she rested, but now it stopped of its own accord. Like when she spotted the scroll for the first time. As she scanned, her mind knew there was something out of place with the picture it was drawing.

Annicka kept her physical position, but her mind was instantly awake and sharp as she pushed all of her senses outward to the edge. Her essence had picked up a bizarre sound on the Havoc Level. At first, Annicka couldn't identify it. She concentrated fully on the location and her mind moved to the outside of the door from where the sound emanated. It took her a second to recognize the sound.

It was *laughter*.

Annicka instantly knew something was wrong inside that room. She allowed her essence to seep through the cracks in the hinges of the metal door and she crept inside, without being noticed, like a wisp of smoke.

She recognized the room at once, having journeyed here many times over the years. It was one of her favorite rooms. The Stake House, she seemed to remember, as it was called by the patrons.

She was met with a bizarre scene, even for the City. It had been so long since she'd heard these kinds of cat calls and the sound of laughing from the patrons that it took a full couple of minutes for her mind to register exactly what it was witnessing.

There was a partially clad redhead who was systematically turning one of the cranks. She would turn the crank one full rotation, and then she would cackle and point at the patron on the stake as it pushed itself further and further into his body. She was loving every minute of the pain he was experiencing. Every time he shrieked and struggled against the stake being driven through his body, she laughed.

And the other patrons laughed as well.

Annicka's mind watched and then withdrew. She'd seen enough to know that the redhead must have recently taken over as room mother and the prisoners on the stakes were enjoying the tables being turned on their tormentor. It sometimes happened that way. But as her mind receded from the room, she couldn't help but wonder what had caused the changing of the room mothers. It wasn't a regular occurrence, and she usually was aware of the comings and goings at the Havoc Level. She didn't really care who gave out the punishment or who served as the various room mothers, but she was usually aware of a change, as it meant something extraordinary had taken place. Something she would have wanted to witness.

But she hadn't been alerted to the change. Which meant it hadn't been planned, but rather had just happened.

Annicka's essence left the room and reversed its course. She called her mind back to her physical presence and awoke herself with a start as the cat sat back on its perch on her right shoulder. She had to catch up with whatever had caused the change to happen in the Stake House. She had to know why it happened now. The coincidence with her getting close to the Rose was not an accident.

She sensed it was something that she would have to know about.

CHAPTER TWENTY-NINE

Mack and Byron walked through the metal door and heard it close and latch shut tightly behind them. Daisy Mae stood silently at their heels and even though Mack knew he didn't need her help through this maze anymore, she might come in handy if they ran into something they couldn't maneuver away from on their own. She was like a little insurance policy as far as he was concerned. If he didn't have her along, it would probably be alright, but it was definitely better to have the insurance if something went awry. And her introductions and background to the maze and the denizens inside had proven helpful. So far.

An immensely tall mirror faced the three of them, and Byron was entranced as he stared hard at his own reflection. He stood just behind and slightly to the side of Mack and this was the first time he'd seen himself since he became a permanent resident in the City. He didn't think it was a beautiful picture he was painting.

Daisy Mae had chewed her entire nipple off of her breast and was rolling it around in her mouth. She would alternately suck and lick the sides as she tasted every part. Byron watched her take it out of her mouth a few of times and inspect it like she'd never seen it before, and then pop it back into her mouth like a pacifier. She stopped what she was doing as she looked up at him again.

"What kind of amazin' maze would it be without a hall of mirrors?" was all she said.

Byron looked at the group of mirrors in front of them and on all sides. The entire room was comprised of floor-length mirrors that were about three feet wide apiece. Some were slanted at various angles and some were bowed in the middle, either concave or convex, to change the images they projected. There didn't appear to be anyone else in the room with them, and he could clearly see all of their reflections readily reproduced in color right in front of them.

Mack stopped and was assessing himself, much the same as Byron. He hadn't seen a full mirror for a long time and, as nearly as he could tell, he still looked the same as when he swung from that noose so long ago. There were some physical scars that were apparent in the mirrors, but nothing else that really shocked him. That was a small victory. That he had to look at himself at all may have been the worst thing Daisy Mae could've done to him. He didn't want to see. It would only make him remember. To think of how it had been with Melody so many years ago.

The mirrors appeared to be sharper than anything Byron had ever seen. They reflected the outer appearance as all mirrors did, but the clarity had to be the punishment. He saw he'd lost weight and was gaunt from the loss of blood. He was also still bleeding from his one eye and from his nose where the Doctor pumped air into his head. It seemed like a long time ago, but Byron really did not know how much time elapsed since then. He couldn't have imagined himself looking like this. He had an optical cord hanging out of its socket, blood running down both sides of his face, and vomit on his shirt. If he'd come across himself when he was a detective, he would've shot himself without another thought.

Mack walked forward. The mirrors quickly enclosed themselves on him from all sides, so he wasn't really sure which way to go. He reached out a hand and touched the mirror, only to have his hand go past the outside of the mirror and slip directly into the inside of the mirror. Like a pool of shimmering water, the mirror rippled, and his reflection rippled with the waves. He tried to steady himself and feel his way through the hall.

"We're looking for the symbol I told you about. It'll look like a *D* and will be hidden in one of the mirrors, Byron, so as you pass, look at your reflection and anything else that's displayed. It has to be here somewhere. I'll lead you through the opening between the rows of mirrors as best as I can. It would probably be a good idea for you to grab the back of my shirt, so that we don't get separated."

Byron didn't hesitate. With one hand, he reached out and grabbed Mack's shirt, and with the other hand, he reached into his jeans pocket and rubbed his eyeball again. Daisy Mae latched onto the shirt of Byron.

Mack tried not to think about his reflection. It'd been so long since he'd seen himself, seen what he had caused by hanging himself, that the thought of having to look at himself again made him want to puke. He'd done this to himself. But not being able to view it was reassuring. If he never had to look himself in the eyes, then he really didn't have to accept what he had become. The image of reality was so much worse than the thought. To actually see himself, to actually have to answer his own reflection in the mirror, was a terrible punishment. Mack couldn't look into his own eyes.

"Why don't you look up at yourself, Teacher? You're a fairly handsome man. I would still love to have sex with you. We could do it right here in front of these mirrors and we could watch ourselves. Surely that turns you on?" Daisy Mae asked.

Mack felt along the pools of shimmering water that were mirrors as best as he could without really looking at them. Every time he glanced up at himself, he quickly averted his eyes. He didn't want to concentrate on what he'd become. What he had done.

He felt the steady pressure of Byron pulling his shirt behind him and following. They walked at a snail's pace as Mack felt each mirror looking for turns in the hallway. He'd let his fingers trace the ends and the side of the mirrors until they came to a definite angle, and then he would push his hands down the angle to verify it was a place they could turn. He wasn't concentrating on anything other than the turns and looking for the symbol.

"Would you like to taste my nipple?" Daisy Mae offered to Mack.

He was having trouble shutting out the sights that forced themselves into his brain at every turn. The other rooms were meant to torture the patrons placed in the rooms themselves. But this was different. It was intended to torture him and Byron directly. It had been placed here for their benefit alone. By whoever was pulling their strings at the moment.

Mack felt the back of his shirt lose its constant pull and he looked in the mirror beside him. Byron's hand had dropped from his shirt and he was staring at a different mirror than Mack. He'd turned his back and was intently watching something that had him transfixed.

"Byron. Byron. Are you alright? You need to grab my shirt through this. Have you found something?" Mack asked.

Byron didn't answer, but stared hard at the mirror in front of him. Mack could see nothing other than Byron's reflection, but he didn't know *what* Byron was seeing. As he watched, Byron shook.

Byron could not tear his one good eye off of the mirror. It was right there. Right there. He could touch it. Touch *her*.

She was about five feet six inches tall. Long shoulder-length blonde hair with highlights of black strewn throughout for good measure. Her hair was tied back, and she was pulling a brush through the loose strands. Her eyes were a devilish blue color that was so piercing Byron thought he could feel them bore into his flesh. She was smiling and a perfect dimple had appeared on her cheek. She was stunningly beautiful.

She was the girl he had met and married directly out of high school, in all of her beauty.

Sitting next to her on the vanity top of a dresser was a small child, possibly three or four years old. The child had bright green eyes and black hair that needed to be combed. His smile was missing two front teeth but stretched from ear to ear none-the-less.

Byron knew instantly that the child was his son.

He stood riveted to the picture show in the mirror as he watched the son that he never held laugh and play with his wife. They were only married six months. He hadn't known she was even pregnant. Not until now. She never told him.

He reached out and put his hand through the surface of the watery mirror. He watched it ripple and the image of his son and wife floated like waves on a pond.

"Byron. Byron. You stop that now. We have to get you ready for school. And we can't do that until we get me ready first," his wife said to the child.

He tried to reach into the mirror as far as he could. His hand disappeared up to his wrist and all he could feel was cold. Ice cold.

The picture faded out of view.

Byron screamed, "No!" and tried to grab the image before it was completely gone.

The girl in the mirror and the child blinked out like the lights of a theater going off and he watched as they disappeared. Possibly forever.

Byron put his head down and cried. A deep, wracking sob escaped his throat as he realized what he'd done. And where he was. And the life he had wasted. He sat down on the floor and put his head in his arms and cried like a baby.

Mack grabbed Byron by the shoulder and pulled him out of his trance. He yanked him to his feet. "Whatever you saw, Byron, it wasn't real. It's not real!" Mack shouted.

Byron sobbed and nodded. "Yes. It was. These bastards." He turned to Daisy Mae, who was quietly smug and smiling at him. "You fucking bitch!" Byron screamed and lunged at her.

Mack moved quicker than even he thought was possible and jumped on the back of Byron before he could reach Daisy Mae. Byron rolled over and tried to punch him, but the fist found nothing but air and Mack moved and lowered his weight onto Byron's back, forcing him to the ground.

"This is what she wants. Byron. Listen to me. This is what she wants," Mack yelled as he sat on his back and tried to calm him. Byron struggled to throw him off, but his fight left him and all he could do was cry into the slime on the ground in front of his face.

Mack was quieter this time. "This is what she wants. What they all want. If you harm her in any way, she'll be allowed to keep you here with her. To torture and punish you as she sees fit. For as long as she wants. Until she grows tired of you. Then she'll cast you off in some place worse. She baited you. They baited you. Don't believe anything you saw. Nothing."

Byron stopped squirming as he accepted his fate. He knew inside that Mack was right.

"Are you alright? Can I let you up?"

Byron nodded. He stood up and looked at Daisy Mae, who hadn't moved and was now sucking on her other nipple.

"Almost got you, Mr. Michaels. Almost." She seemed a little unsatisfied.

Byron turned away from her without answering and grabbed the back of Mack's shirt. He looked up into the eyes of Mack and nodded, even though he had no clue why.

Mack glanced once at Daisy Mae and resumed his searching of the mirrors with his hands. He palmed first the ones on his left and then the ones on his right. He let his hands probe and explore as he felt his way through the maze.

Moving the three of them several paces forward slowly, he paused. He stood in front of a tall, oblong water-mirror that was concave. Byron saw him gazing into the mirror.

Oh shit, Byron thought.

Mack didn't move a muscle. He didn't twitch a finger or flex any part of his body. He was rigid and perfectly still as he stared at the image in the mirror. Byron didn't know what he saw, but he knew it wasn't good for them.

Melody stood facing Mack. His Melody. She was dressed in a dirty and disgusting dress that she wouldn't have been caught dead wearing. She was beckoning. Calling to him. He could hear her voice. She was disappointed in him.

"Come to me, Mack. Come to me," she kept calling to him.

He couldn't tell what she wanted. Couldn't run to her and solve her problem. Couldn't be there for her.

"Mack. I need you. Come to me, Mack."

He cleared his mind. They were baiting him. Knew they were using the one thing he couldn't just disregard. Couldn't just forget. They could abuse him all they wanted. But they were using Melody.

She walked towards him. Getting larger and closer. She was waving at him to come to her. To join her. To be with her.

In the mirror.

Mack saw it then. It was on her chest. Right below a torn pocket. Right there. He had to go to her now. She was leading him home. He didn't know how or why, but Melody was helping him.

He turned and motioned. "Let's go, Byron. The symbol is here. In the mirror. I can see it."

He pointed to a place and a spot in the mirror where only he could see the symbol awaited. Just as he envisioned the next symbol to look without the leg attached, it was there, and it was staring directly back at him from the torn pocket of Melody's dress. The letter *D* was right there for him to follow. And she was calling him.

He put his hand through the water-mirror and tried to touch Melody, but she backed away. Byron moved to the side of Mack and looked. He wanted to see the symbol himself. He strained his eyes. He couldn't see what Mack was looking at, but he could see the symbol. Right there in the middle of the mirror.

"I see it, Teacher. Let's go."

Mack walked into the mirror itself. To let the cool waters of the mirror swallow him and lead him closer to Melody. Closer if only for a moment, even if only in his mind. He didn't care either way. This was the right way, and he was sure of that.

Byron heard Daisy Mae make a short, curt-like kind of growl sound that came out of her lips as he got close in behind Mack to enter the doorway disguised as a mirror. She would have to follow on her own.

Byron stopped. It wasn't a coughing sound she made. It was a laugh.

She was laughing at their choice.

This wasn't correct. How could he be so stupid?

Byron reached out to grab Mack's shirt just as he was disappearing inside the water-mirror. Byron could just see the back of his shirt as the water tried to close in behind and cover him completely in the doorway. With a sudden tug, and using all of his strength, he yanked and pulled Mack back through the door to where he was still standing. He pulled him out of the mirror and away from the door.

Mack howled at him and whipped around. "What are you doing? The symbol is right there. Can't you see it?" He was extremely pissed off at Byron for stopping him. He looked back and Melody was quickly disappearing into a murky, dark pond behind the surface.

"It's a mirror, Mack. It reflects what's in front of it."

Mack's eyes flew open wide as he realized Byron was right. The mirror was showing Mack what was directly behind him. Mack moved him to the side and watched as the last embers of Melody's visage fall away to dust. He turned and saw the symbol on the mirror behind the two of them.

He reached out and touched the top part of the mirror, that was a wooden border of the mirror itself. It was painted nickel chrome and black and didn't sway like the mirror. The symbol *D* was directly in the center on the top. It'd been painted there many years before they were here. The other mirror, the one Mack tried to go through, had been concave and the parallax from that mirror moved the symbol from the top of the mirror across the aisle to its center. Anyone looking at it from the front of the mirror would see the symbol residing directly in the center of the mirror. It was a perfectly envisioned puzzle to make the seeker misstep and go through the wrong mirror.

Stepping around him, Mack walked through this water-mirror and Byron followed.

Daisy Mae quit laughing.

CHAPTER THIRTY

David couldn't quit looking over his shoulder. The farther he walked and the closer he got to Victor, the better he liked it. He felt some regrets leaving Elizabeth, but he knew that his place was beside Victor. He had no idea what the outcome of this attempt to find the rose-thing or finish the cocktail would be, but he knew that if he could, he would go back to the Stake House and seek Elizabeth.

Victor said nothing to him since they left the Stake House. He was walking rapidly and kept his head down, like he was deep in thought over something, but David could only guess what was preoccupying him at present. He was brooding and he never let David know anything, anyway. It was probably best this way for David, as long as he could keep up.

The Doctor stopped in front of another metal door that had strong, rusted hinges on the outside and a castle era slide lock. He removed the bar that held the slide in place and pulled the door open. He obviously knew where he was and where this was leading them, because this didn't look like a random entrance to David. Victor had been here before. He knew so much more about the City than David.

As soon as David entered the room, he felt a wave of intense heat swarm his face like locusts eating the ground. It was a strong based heat from a large burning house, but it was different because of two things he noticed immediately: first, there wasn't any smoke. None. No black, billowing smoke causing his eyes to water or making him cover his mouth to breathe; and second, there were people in the room. Tons of people and they were all on fire. And screaming loudly. Very loudly.

He tried his best to melt into the walls of the place so he wouldn't be noticed by anyone, including Victor, who might suddenly decide he wasn't worth the trouble and leave him here. He also didn't want the patrons, the room mother, or anyone else to even know he existed. He'd been deathly afraid of fire and getting burned since his father used to put out cigarettes on him when he was about five or six years old. His father used to climb the stairs with the burning butt of one of his three packs a day cigarettes still showing the red ash, and seek him out. He'd learned the best place to face his father when he was in this kind of mood was in the bathroom. After his father put the cigarette out on his back, he quickly lost interest in him and would retreat in a drunken stupor to some other part of the house, and David could get the water from the tub to cool the burn. The quicker to stop the pain and start the healing process.

David shrunk down as far as he could and tried to minimize his entire existence. The scene being played out before him was something out of horror magazine that should've been trashed many years prior and never made it to print, he thought.

There was a solid gold chain stretching across the room from one end to the other. The chain was anchored about halfway up the ten-foot walls on both ends and stretched fairly taught as there wasn't any droop in the line at all. It looked like fourteen carat gold and shone so brightly from the lit fires all around it he felt like putting on sunglasses to look at it, if he had any.

The chain served as a sectioning rope. As he squinted into the room a little closer, he could see the chain not only ran length-wise across the fire room but also from front to back and divided the room into four sections of different sizes. Little rectangular pens to keep the animals at bay.

In each of the four sections, the patrons were at various stages of burning. The first, to David's left and directly in front of him, looked to be the tamest, as each of the several hundred people inside the chain borders were only a little on fire. David blinked his eyes as he stared and a thought came to him. A little on fire? If that wasn't an oxymoron, then he didn't know what the hell an oxymoron was. How could anyone be a little "on fire"? Either you were burning or you weren't. Either fucking way, it was going to hurt.

The patrons in this first section had some specific part of their body on fire, like an arm or a leg or their hair. He watched as one man, an older man with a crew cut and black square framed glasses like he just stepped out of the nineteen sixties, kept trying to stop his jacket sleeve from burning. It was almost comical and reminded him of one of those candles that kept relighting themselves and couldn't be put out. Blow and relight. Blow and relight. The jacket would light up, burn, catch a blaze of quick, white hot fire, and the man would frantically try to pat it out. And then the sequence would start all over, with the man stopping only long enough to scream and roll the arm on the ground. Or try to cover it with dirt and smother the flame. He tried to take the jacket off twice, but the zipper was welded to his chest and he had no hope of ever getting it off, even though he kept trying. Every time the sleeve lit itself up, David would hear him scream and curse and desperately try to put it out before the flame jumped up his arm and onto his face. His face had a smoldered-ash look and his hair was steaming from the residual heat.

David wiped his eyebrows and face with his shirt and looked to the right at the second group inside the rope-chains. They were more on fire, if that was even possible. Maybe half of their torsos were encased in flames that couldn't be snuffed out. All the prisoners here were running around and screaming at the top of their lungs. Some of their heads would be entirely in flames, snapping and crackling like popcorn on a skillet. They ran around in circles and kept wrecking into each other. Fire, so simple a thing and one of the four basic elements on the surface, was an incredibly painful punishment.

The third sectioned group in the far back seemed to jump around like their feet were on fire and nothing else. As he watched, they would alternately jump and scream, jump and scream, and David couldn't tell what exactly was on fire or what was burning them, but he could see ashes everywhere around this group. As he watched, one woman in the group jumped up into the arms of the man next to her and let out a blood-curdling cry, and he threw her on the ground away from him and tried to stand on top of her. At that instant, David saw what exactly was causing them to jump around and scream so loudly. Their legs had been slowly incinerated inch by inch every time they touched the ground. It was so scorching hot that whatever part of them touched the boiler plate surface instantly smoked and puffed before turning to ash and floating away into the air. The longer they were touching the boiler plate, the more of their bodies turned to ash. David fixated on a tiny prisoner who jumped from body to body and carried an armful of pure ash. He tried to step on everyone else and use his small size to his advantage. Supposedly, the parts of his body that already melted away were in his arms. It was a losing proposition, even though there were a lot of people in this section, because some of them had to be touching the ground.

They were fighting among themselves and screaming and falling down, and as soon as one went down, several more would jump on top of the body and try to pin that person to the ground until there was nothing but smoldering ash and they looked for another. It was the only way they could survive for a few seconds more intact.

The fourth area looked to be the worst. This one held only about thirty or forty prisoners, from a quick count. They weren't screaming, nor were they even running around like maniacs. Most of them were simply walking in circles and staring open-mouthed at the other three areas. They appeared to be wholly intact and with some sort of intelligence. Once or twice David saw them glance his way, but only quickly and only for a second. The people in the section didn't like to take their eyes away from the man standing at the edge of their section. They were whimpering like puppies at an abandoned house, trying to get the door to open so they could go outside.

David knew instantly that they were the next to be divided up and go to one of the three fire stations. Lambs in a pen waiting for the butcher to slaughter them.

The man leaning against the gold chain in front of it all looked to be youngish, possibly in his early forties. He wore denim jeans and a cowboy hat. He looked like he was at a rodeo and he was trying to decide which contestant got to ride the bull next.

He turned and walked to where Victor and David were standing. "Howdy, folks. Slim's the name. From southern Wyoming. Had a little place there, about six hundred acres. Best cattle man you ever met. Best steaks you ever ate."

Victor looked at him and then said, "You must be the room mother here?"

"Yes, sir. What can I help you with? I figure you must be a lower cause you entered the main door. Only lowers do that. The rest we get here come down the coal shoot over there," he said as he pointed to a previously unseen four-foot door nestled in the middle of black ash on one wall.

"I'm looking for the previous room, mother. I was sent to find something she might know about."

Slim pointed at section number three. "She's over there. If you hang on a second, I'll go and dig her out. I'm sure she'll be happy for the break. That section's fairly nasty, I think." He turned and walked over to the chains and the patrons in section four momentarily stopped their jumping and begged for him to take them out of the section and move them to another one. He pointed to an old woman that basically looked to David to be half a person. She was small, maybe three feet tall, and had been riding on the shoulders of some man who stood on top of another body. The woman had half of her face burned off and most of her legs. Her dress and hair showed signs of being recently scorched off. There were ashes all over her face.

Slim lifted her over the ropes and carried her over to where David and Victor were standing. He set her on the ground and she stared up at David from blackened eyes. She looked like she was grateful for the respite.

"Gentlemen, this here's Marie Madeleine Marguerite d'Aubray, one of France's legendary female serial killers. As I'm sure you're aware, female serial killers are somewhat of a rarity, so I'm awfully glad that she's stopped by my room to spend a little time in my corrals. Madame d'Aubray was found guilty of poisoning her father, daughter, brother and even a couple of sisters. She got the whole family, and guess what? It was all just to get her hands on their property. She was burned at the stake in the late 1600s and came to us. She was so prolific with her artwork of poisoning her family, that the council members demoted her to room mother, but I wrestled that away from her some time ago."

Victor looked down at the pathetic form of a half-burned woman. Some of her prominent parts were crispy. What was left of her didn't seem to be very threatening. But he knew better. Patrons had a way of resurfacing in this place. A lower could demote someone anytime they wished, so it was always possible to run into a patron again under different circumstances.

"Madame d'Aubray. I'm Hell's Doctor and a lower being. I need some information you may possess."

She nodded up at him. If she helped him, he may reward her. She didn't know, but not helping him would get her thrown back into section number three immediately.

"Are you aware of the Black Rose?"

She nodded again. When she opened her mouth to speak, a raspy sound, like crumbling aluminum foil, came out. Her voice box was desperately burned and probably raw. Beyond repair. "There were some rumors I heard when I first came to the City. Rumors of the Black Rose. I thought it was a chance for me to get out of here."

Victor's ears picked up at that. "Tell me what you know. I will speak to Slim here for you, if you tell me everything you know."

Her eyes brightened a small amount. "The Black Rose has something to do with the portal. It can reverse the direction was all I ever heard."

Victor was stunned. Reverse the direction? "What do you mean reverse?"

She seemed to perk up slightly at the attention. "I'd always heard that the Rose could make it possible to move the portal in the other direction. Going to the surface instead of from the surface."

"Did you believe it?"

"Yes, sir, I did."

Victor squinted his eyes. "Where can I find it? This Black Rose?"

The Madame shook her half burned head. Parts of her skin fell off to the ground and some of her hair with it. "I'm not sure, but I've had some time to think of where I would put it, if I'd wanted to hide it."

Victor nodded vigorously. This was going better than he planned. "Where would you put it?"

"I would hide it on the Havoc Level. In plain sight."

"What the fuck does that mean? In plain sight of what?"

"The best way to hide something is where no one can see it. In plain sight, I always thought." She seemed to shrink away from them. She could sense the Doctor didn't like her answer.

Victor motioned to Slim. "I need a small sample of her burned hair for one of my experiments. I'm going to take it now." He reached down to her face and scooped a significant amount of burned hair and skin up and then handed it to David, who quickly added it to the syringe of ingredients. They were halfway there. Only a couple of items left. Victor turned his attention to Slim. "I'm done with Madame d'Aubray. Put her back where you want her."

Madame d'Aubray screamed and Slim picked her up and, turning towards corral number three, pitched her up and over the golden chain and watched as all the other patrons got out of her way so she could fall to the ground. She shrieked again and then David heard a searing sound like eggs on a fryer as the other patrons scrambled to stand on top of her and she disappeared under their weight.

"Maybe now she'll be enlightened?" Slim asked as he turned back to section number four and signaled to one of the men to move to section one. The chosen man howled and tried to run. A morebats appeared and then another one and they promptly grabbed the man by the legs. Kicking and screaming, they dragged him to corral number one and threw him inside. As the man landed, he hit the ground and rolled to a position where he was up off the floor on his knees. His left leg promptly burst into flames, causing another screech to come out.

The newest addition to corral number one added his scream to the surrounding others, and as they turned to leave, David could only wonder at what Slim had meant by "enlightened".

An inside joke, he thought, as Victor went through another hot metal door and David followed.

CHAPTER THIRTY-ONE

Daisy Mae was in a state of unrest. She spit her nipple out onto the floor and dragged it through some of the muck and general shit surrounding her legs. After flipping the nipple over several times like a pancake and making sure it was deeply saturated with all the elements from the flooring, she popped it ever so gracefully back into her mouth. Like she was a fine chef from a major restaurant, adding a delicate and exact amount of seasoning. Mack and Byron witnessed this display and knew that her anxiety level had increased significantly, and this was just her way of dealing with it. Her breast, the one without the nipple and with the newly formed hole, was gushing a significant amount of black bile down the front of her chest and it coagulated on the tops of her cutoffs. She seemed neither to be aware of this nor to care. Overlooking the nipple chewing thing, she didn't have any conscious recognition of the pain or what caused the bile. Like it was a normal, everyday event in her life.

But Mack could tell she was clearly agitated. When they first met her outside the tent at the beginning of her amazin' maze, she was coquettish and impish at the same time. Now she was restrained and a little aggressive. A lion waiting in the weeds to pounce. Sitting on a pile of nervous energy and ready for anything. She knew what was in front of them, but she was acting more like she didn't know. Like she was leading the pigs to the slaughter, but they weren't following. Not directly in her footsteps, anyway.

He leaned over to Byron as the door closed behind them and they found themselves inside a brightly lit room. He whispered, "Watch yourself. I don't like how our host is behaving. She knows something's up ahead and waiting for us. Keep on your toes."

Byron nodded. He noticed her getting more aggressive in her demeanor as well.

"You two boys wouldn't be talking about little ole me, now would you?" she asked with a devilish grin on her face, blood dripping down her exposed chest, and a freshly sauteed nipple rolling around in her mouth.

Mack answered before Byron could. "No ma'am. Just wondering what's going on here? This room is particularly clean and shiny."

Daisy Mae's smile broadened, and it looked like something alive was wiggling around the inside of her mouth. Miniature worms or something. They were small and green and seemed to move of their own accord. "Yes. It has to be to welcome our incoming guest."

"You mean he isn't here yet? Are we waiting for him?" Byron asked.

Everywhere they looked, the room resembled a reception room. The lights on the ceiling shined a bright fluorescent. The walls were painted a cheesy yellow color and, from the smell, were freshly painted. There were a couple of tables with magazines on them and a couple of chairs sitting next to them. Mack read three of the titles: *People Magazine: the Insane Edition*, *Surgical Procedures for Dummies*, and *Morebats' Weekly*. A typical dentist's office.

"He's not here yet, but he'll be here soon enough."

"I'm afraid to ask? What do you mean by soon?" Byron asked.

Daisy Mae turned and looked into his eye. "Well now, young man. He's still on the surface, but we know he's coming our way. And we have to be ready. After all, he's a celebrity and all. We want to put our best face forward for when he arrives. They're giving him to me to help him adjust. I can't wait."

Two doors on opposite sides of the room opened and two morebats walked out and over to the center of the room. The doors closed quickly behind them before Mack could get a good look at what was hidden on the other side. The morebats were each dressed in sweats, like they'd just finished running a track event somewhere. Their sweatshirts came with writing on the front of each of them, like a team jersey. One wore a baseball cap, and the other wore a construction helmet. Both were sweating profusely. They each carried in their one hand a bag with the words "Welcome to Hell" embossed on it. Like a Welcome Wagon would deliver a bag of gifts to a new family in the neighborhood. Each of their other hands supported a ten and a twelve-inch penis, respectively.

"Who's the patron you're waiting on?" Mack asked again. He was continually scanning the walls as he spoke to her. His eyes roamed the room, looking up and down for the symbols he knew had to be hidden. The last symbol had to be *C* again. An "S" with one leg missing. He was sure it was here somewhere and would lead them out of the amazin' maze.

"Well, Bernard Lawrence Madoff, of course. Bernie Madoff, as you know him. The man who took the Ponzi scheme to a level unseen before. He bilked millions, if not billions of dollars, from just about everyone he knew." Daisy Mae sounded bored as she recited this.

"He's still on the surface?" Mack asked.

"We don't think prison will agree with him too much and he'll join us soon."

"I must welcome Bernie to the City. I must welcome Bernie." The one morebats proudly proclaimed to them.

Each of the morebats was busy dusting the tables while their "Welcome" bags sat off to the side. One was using his hat to dust, and the other was using his sweatshirt. As Mack watched, one of them turned from his dusting and faced him directly where he could read the letters on the sweatshirts. "Oh shit," was all he said.

Byron saw it as well. "This is not my strong suit, Teacher."

"Whatever are ya'll talking about now?" Daisy Mae asked innocently.

On the first of the two morebats sweatshirts was a simple slogan in large red letters. It said, 'I am not a liar. He is a liar.' And underneath the second "liar" was a letter *C*. The other morebats sweatshirt said, 'I am not a liar. I will show you the door.' He also had the symbol *C* under the word "liar".

Mack stared at them, talking out loud while they went back to dusting. "They let us read their shirts so we could see what was on them. Very nice, Daisy Mae."

She had returned to the impish girl they met many rooms ago, except she still had the nipple in her mouth. She looked innocent enough from where Mack was standing, but she was indeed quite intelligent, if she cooked this up for them.

"So, which one is telling the truth? I have no idea, Teacher," Byron said.

"One always tells the truth and one always lies. It's just the way they are. I guess that's the whole point. We have to figure out which one to ask which door to take and then decide if he's lying or not."

Just then, one morebat piped up. "I am not a liar. I am not a liar. I love your shirt," he pointed at the other shirt, so Mack couldn't tell if he was reading it off the other morebats or it was on his shirt.

"I love your shirt more. It's beautiful." He stroked his twelve inch penis. "I must meet Bernie Madoff. I will welcome him. Then I will mate with him. I must mate with Bernie."

The other morebats, the one who spoke first, said, "I must mate with Bernie, but I don't want to ruin my shirt. I must mate."

Mack shook his head. Each of them had the symbol on the shirt. Each of them could talk. But which one did he ask about the door and which one did he believe? "Oh shit," was all he could say.

He looked to Byron. "There doesn't seem to be any immediate threat here, so let's try to work this out."

"Okay."

"The one shirt says, 'I am not a liar.'"

"Okay," was all Byron could add as he stroked his worry eyeball in his pants pocket.

"If that statement is true, then he'd have to be telling the truth on his shirt, which means the statement is true. He isn't a liar and admits it."

Byron shook his head like there was something crawling up the inside of his nose. "What? You've totally lost me."

"If he was a liar, then the shirt was lying by saying he wasn't a liar. Either case could be true."

"I can follow that. Sort of, anyway."

Mack cocked his head and arched an eyebrow while he thought it over. He knew that one of them was lying and one was telling the truth. He unconsciously started stroking the third finger on his left hand where his wedding ring used to reside.

"I get it. Then one of the morebats is a lair because he wears a shirt that says he is not a liar, which is a lie? But both could be lying with that statement." Byron was perplexed.

"So of the two morebats, one is telling the truth and one is lying? If he is a liar, then the shirt would say, 'I am not a liar.' If he isn't a liar, the shirt would say the same thing. Is that right?" Mack was confusing himself further. Daisy Mae was standing by, enjoying the moment. She could follow their logic, because she invented the scenario.

"But how can we figure out which is which? Neither will admit it to us. And one will surely lie. But which one?" Byron asked.

"Oh shit."

"You keep saying that, Teacher."

Daisy Mae agreed. "Yes, you do."

Mack ignored her. She was only adding gas to the fire. The two morebats were cleaning in a frenzy and signing about how they were going to mate very soon. They had concocted some kind of mating song for Bernie:

We can lube him up;
There won't be a hassle;
You can hold him down;
I'll penetrate his asshole!

Bernie will be proud to hear it sometime soon, they were convinced. A truly proper Welcome Wagon treat.

Mack looked at the first morebats with the words "I am not a liar" written on his shirt. The words themselves were just logic and had to be the key. If he was telling the truth, then his shirt reflected that which a morebats wouldn't willingly do. But a room mother might. Mack turned to Byron. "Try this."

"Okay."

"It doesn't matter which one we think is the truth teller and which one is the liar."

"How come?"

"Try it like this. First rule in the City?"

Byron answered, "5317".

Mack nodded. "Working from that premise, then both of these guys are born liars. Both of them are lying. We know that by rule number 5317."

"I'm with you so far."

"One of the morebats, and it doesn't matter which one, is simply stating a fact on his shirt. He's probably not even aware of what it means to say, 'I am not a liar.' He isn't lying about it. He's not that bright. He's just stating a fact. Something he can understand."

"So if that is true, you're saying the other morebats is smart enough to understand that what he put on his shirt is false?"

"No. But Daisy Mae here is."

"Maybe." Byron was thinking out loud. "Okay. So who do we follow? Which one? Both will lie when we ask them which door and each one will give us a different answer, leaving us right back at square one."

Mack shook his head "no." He understood. "We get one to ask the other which door is right. The first morebats will lie to the other morebats and then when he turns to us, morebats number two will lie to us about what number one said. We then do what number two says."

Byron had a look of confusion written all over his face.

"Like this, Byron. Let's say we wanted to know what color the walls were. We can see that they're ugly yellow. If we get morebats one to ask morebats two what the color of the walls are, then morebats two will lie and say black. Morebats one will turn to us and lie about what morebats two said and say 'yellow.' We then have the answer."

Byron could then see it right in front of him. "The morebats doesn't care which door is the correct door. He only cares about lying to us."

"That's right. If we asked one of the morebats directly, we'd never know if he was lying about the answer or lying because he was talking to us. We let them lie to each other. This eliminates the problem of figuring out which one is lying by working from the premise that they're both lying."

"So why not just ask one and do the opposite of what he says?"

Mack vigorously shook his head back and forth. "Because of what their shirts say. One could be telling the truth and if we asked that one without knowing if he was telling the truth or not, then we'd assume he was lying and pick the wrong door. But getting them to lie to each other solves that problem. Daisy Mae here has one morebats out there that is a truth teller. His shirt says, 'I am not a liar,' which is the truth. She also has one morebats out there that is a liar. His shirt says the same thing: 'I am not a liar,' which is a lie and works for both shirts. It's the only way this thing works."

Daisy Mae coughed several times during this explanation. She didn't like what she was hearing.

Mack turned to the first morebats. "Which door will lead us out of the maze? Ask the other guy for me?"

Morebats one turned to the other morebats. "Lower wants to know which door leads out of maze. You know?"

Morebats nodded. He pointed to the door behind him. "That way is the way out."

Morebats one turned to Mack and pointed to the opposite door from the first one the other morebats pointed to. "He said that is the door out of the maze."

Mack and Byron walked over to the door the last morebats pointed to, and without another thought, opened it and stepped through. As Byron looked back, Daisy Mae was smiling at him, which unnerved him slightly. He could hear the two morebats singing about mating with Bernie as the door closed behind them.

"Bernie be my Bitch. Bernie be my Bitch. Mate every day and night. Every night."

She was following close on their heels, but Byron didn't like her smile. Not at all.

Punishment of prisoners is not a duty, but rather must be embraced.

Hell's Third Mantra

INTERLUDE THREE: THE ARCHITECT HAND ME DOWN SKIN RIPPERS

The Architect began the indoctrination of the pain babies to the technology era with the skull crusher. One morebat positioned the chin of the prisoner in the bottom of a vise made of hard wood and then placed a crossbar over the top of his head. A quick crank downward of a lever and a wooden screw turned, tightening the vise. The more the lever was pulled, the tighter the vise squeezed. The prisoner's bottom teeth would implant themselves in the upper half of his mouth, cutting through the pallet until shattering from the pressure. There was squirming and grunting as the pressure of the vise popped his eyes out of his head and drove the jawbone into the skull.

Directing the morebats as they tightened the vise wasn't working for The Architect. They were efficient at lining up the patrons and strapping them down, but often they pulled the lever so fast the pain wasn't punishment. There was projectile bleeding from the eyes and ears and nose, and most of the patrons were nearly unrecognizable after it was over. Their heads were flattened to where the only visible thing was a patch of hair sitting on a mouthful of broken teeth. The height of the head, from hair to neck was about three inches. He needed to extend the sequence.

Experimenting with a variety of other torture devices, like the rack, the cage of nails, the sanding stone, the hanging breast bar, and others brought effective but predictable results, which were never acceptable. Unpredictability was the driving force.

He added *leverage* to the machines.

There were computers and machines that could be altered. With a mind like his and the advent of technology, there weren't any limits. By using the breadth of engineering, he could dole out punishment infinitesimally and by the millimeter. Now, the dreams were capable, and the pain was intolerable. And it was all recordable on disk.

If he added the morebats' lack of intelligence with the engineering marvels produced on the surface, the results would be complete unpredictability. His aim of never giving the same pain twice would be achieved. He could produce machines engineered by morebats. No matter what the outcome.

Every *failure* was a success.

The Architect worked to provide intolerable levels of pain and discomfort through failure. If a machine produced a wrecking ball of cataclysmic proportions to the patron, it was still a success. All a good failure did was invent a new machine. Several of the most spectacular failures he commissioned as new machines and ordered the production of them in the hundreds. No failures were ever thrown out; they were just given to the higher room mothers to play with as they saw fit. All the room mothers would benefit from an epic failure. Everyone but the patrons.

Starting by connecting a computer screen and a keyboard to the head vise seemed like a logical choice. He merged a sixteenth century pile of wood with a leather strap and then molted that to a computer with an electrical wiring harness. Choosing a former council member who had been promoted to the Havoc Level for deceit, The Architect went ahead with the first trial of the new technology.

The morebats strapped the promoted member's head between the wood and the leather chin strap, and then tied him down to the table, while a host of viewers gathered for the ceremony. There were room mothers and several council members in attendance. It was a historic day in the City.

The Architect ordered a morebats to sit in front of the computer display and input the correct sequence to start the vise. The problem immediately arose that the morebats weren't smart enough to punch in a long sequence of commands. It took about three keystrokes before he realized the mistake and instead of a gentle squeezing pressure; the vise clamped shut with such ferocity that the patron's head was crushed like a steamroller ran over it on a concrete highway. There was a suddenly cut off scream, a crunching sound like two pieces of marble hitting each other, and then the head went flat. The pressure was so intense and the action so quick that the patron's brains literally gushed out of his ears and sprayed onto the computer. At one moment there was a normal-looking head in the vise, and then in the blink of an eye, gray matter and blood were flowing from every orifice. There wasn't even time to finish the scream.

The morebats at the keyboard, to impress his twin, continued to punch in anything he could think of on the keyboard. He spelled his name on the computer screen; he typed in his favorite mating methods; he labeled his twin an idiot and predicted he would mate with a council member and be demoted soon. All on the computer keyboard, which translated to the computer screen, which translated to commands to the head vise which went out of control. It opened and closed. It widened and reduced. It slammed and pinched. It started going up and down like a perpetual motion machine, having no reason to stop. Or slow down.

All of this time, the patron's head remained in the vise itself, being pulled up when the top part separated and summarily crushed when it slammed back down. With a morebats turning the vise crank, the smallest any of them had ever gotten a human head was a little less than three inches. With the computer managing and the morebats at the keyboard completely confused, the patrons head ended up slimmer than a top of the line laptop. An inch at the most.

The patron wiggled and fought to his best, but in the end, his face had been crushed to a pulp-like spaghetti. There was gray matter and splattered eyeballs and bones hanging from everywhere, and parts of teeth shoved so far up into the head that what was left of the brain had a full set of broken incisors in the center. The picture presented when the morebats at the controls finally got the computer to stop hammering the vise down was better than The Architect could have imagined. The patron was thrown into the lazy river after pulling his head from the shoulders because the only thing connecting the two at that point was various string sinews.

He loved the results so much he ordered the correct string of keystrokes be thrown away and the morebats were given free charge to do as they pleased at the controls. If they couldn't spell, it only got worse for the patrons.

The results led to the concept of hand-me-down skin rippers.

Properly pulling the skin off a prisoner took a long time to learn, and many of the room mothers weren't adept at the process. Skin ripping wasn't a new thing to anyone who spent any time on the Havoc Level. It was an accepted practice. Usually, the room mothers devised patterns when pulling off skin, like carving their names into the backs of the prisoners.

Combining what he learned from the head vises and computers, The Architect had a crop combine welded to a computer by the morebats and a patron was thrown into the receiving end. He expected crushing with such force and ferocity that the only thing to come out of the end of the machine would be bone bits and some gold fillings. But what actually came out was a partial patron. Partial in that he was still relatively intact, but most of his skin was gone. Partially ripped off, exposing muscles, but otherwise the body was still intact. Large pieces of skin and not small sections. The skin, or what had been extracted from the body of the patron, spewed itself out of the machine a couple of seconds after the patron.

Tinkering with the controls, a morebats could throw a pain baby into the machine, and in about twenty minutes nothing other than a functioning pile of muscle was left. The skin would be spit out a couple of minutes later, and the patron could still function well enough to pick up the skin and carry it around. The skin was see-through and pliable like a piece of wax paper. It crinkled when they picked it up or moved it from place to place, and it was fairly elastic, but it wasn't going back on.

But The Architect had a problem with the first cut.

If a pain baby was thrown into the machine without an initial splice, then the combine machine wouldn't have a starting point. There was no entry point to make the first separation, and the skin would have to be dragged off the muscle and separated from the bones and then pulled out of a machine made cut. It was messy and often left the skins, although relatively whole, in disjointed conditions. Not acceptable.

The Architect solved the problem by adding a knife to the entrance. The knife was used to rip a solid cut about twelve inches long directly across the scalp of the pain baby. The computer instructed an exact cut that penetrated the scalp of the pain baby to a minimal depth, and then two arms would peel the skin apart like an orange. With a section already flayed apart, the combine then ripped the skin off in one piece.

The first several skin rippers went through modifications and adjustments until the product could effectively handle the complete removal of the patron's skin with minimum waste and excessive pain. If the computer was adjusted to a lower setting, the procedure would take more time, and the skin was ripped off at an agonizingly slow pace. It was deemed that this was the preferred setting because of the level of screaming with each yank and thrust of the machine. The sound of a torn telephone book would filter out from the center of the skin ripper, and then an ear-piercing scream would immediately follow. The pain babies waiting at the entrance to the skin ripper could not only imagine what they would soon be feeling, they could hear it in graphic detail.

The system was adjusted until the speed of delivery was adequate, and the older machines were then discarded. Who would want the old ones when you could have a new and improved skin ripper? The hand me down skin rippers were then assigned to the various room mothers.

The Architect thought about all of this as he moved to an outer room on the Womb Level and surveyed the factory. It had to be done here. The final assembly of prisoner and technology. He conceived the factory as a junkyard of old machines released to the discretion of the morebats, to complete construction.

The morebats lacked both the mental capacity to understand the workings of an advanced torture machine, and he knew they didn't have a snowball's chance in the City to fix the damn thing. He watched them take the machines apart piece by piece, discuss every dissection, and then not have a clue how to put it back together. The machines ended up coming to rest here.

What he needed was a place to reassemble the machines and add the castoffs and rejects. With a general dumping ground of human leftovers that hadn't been collected by their owners and machine parts, the factory was born.

He allowed the morebats to chunk anything into the factory and rather than become just a dead machine junkyard; he achieved a storage house for all the things that didn't work quite right. There were ball bearings, chains, computer panels and wires, steering wheels and parts, motors, brakes, and train tracks intermixed with heads, hearts, lungs, livers, brains, eyes, and intestines.

Deciding to add fresh patrons to the assembly line instead of using discarded parts, The Architect gave the new machines a tighter edge. If a particular part was needed, rather than having a morebats and his twin scour the floors of the factory to find it, they could just cut it out of new arrivals.

The merging of prisoner and machine achieved spectacular results. He relished the pain babies having to endure the pain of their limbs being sliced off and then welded into a machine. Every time the machine went by, they'd be looking at a part of themselves, still attached and working. That the morebats and the engineers, along with some of the finest Nazi concentration camp doctors, could keep the severed appendage still alive and functional, was an incredible coup. The Architect's finest hour.

To finish the welcoming phase, he rearranged the delivery to the factory.

He redesigned the tongue of the Crunchers to snake its way out of the teeth-lined mouth, and wrap itself securely around the new arrivals and then tear them upwards off the stalactites. He implanted reverse fish hooks on the undersides of the stalactites to tear off the flesh as it lifted. Slow was better. Much better. The Crunchers were never in a hurry. It was also systematic so that the pain babies got to watch another new arrival get ripped off the stalactites and swallowed before they did. The terror and screaming was increased tenfold.

The Cruncher would transport and chew, transport and chew, until it arrived at the entrance to the factory, where it would turn around and back up to the unloading dock. The pain babies were then squeezed out of a small opening at the back. The opening was lined with razors and flexed around the arrivals. He wanted the pain babies to know they were "shit" out of the Cruncher.

Welcome to the City, part two.

Morebats collected the discarded arrivals in wheel barrels. Most of them were so cut up and twisted that they couldn't possibly walk. They'd be bleeding out of every orifice they came with naturally and several more that the cruncher provided. Blood on the ground was normally three to four inches thick when the loads were dropped at the docks.

With little energy and no ability to protest, the pain babies rode in the wheel barrels into the factory entrance. Normally quiet at this point, they'd try to take it all in. And since they were heaped upon each other, many times the only thing visible would be a leg or an arm sticking out from under the pile of bodies.

The new arrivals were unloaded without ceremony onto the floor. Each of them was pulled to a standing position and put in chains, arms over their heads and suspended from the ceiling. Legs were manacled and tied to the conveyor belt. Like a slab of meat in a butcher's shop.

As the conveyor belt moved slowly along, the pain babies were conscious and wide eyed. A large powered monocle with a morebats standing behind it, would swing into view and allow the morebats the chance to examine each of them with a jeweler's eye. The pain babies couldn't see who was behind the monocle; the only thing they perceived was that someone was looking them over from head to toe. Closely.

The Architect would sometimes view the assembly line from this point, as the new arrivals swung from the chains in front of the monocle. It was here that they'd be evaluated for parts and needs of the room, mothers and the man-machines. If something was needed, he had it sliced off or cut out by the morebats, who were not very exact and simply made their best effort at getting the complete part out intact. If they failed and only pulled out half the liver, for example, it was okay, because they could get the other half of the liver from the prisoner hanging in chains behind that one. Or they could be bypassed entirely.

Of course, from the pain babies' point of view, the treatment so far was inhumanely unjust and *someone* should have protested at some point. Surely, they believed, some advocacy group somewhere had to be having a meeting to get the conditions improved right at this moment. Surely.

Being bypassed for parts was too good as far as The Architect was concerned, so he added one more step. He had them cleaned off with a scalding fire hose. The force of the water wracked their bodies back and forth in the chains. The water was preset at one hundred and fifty degrees Fahrenheit. The perfect temperature to burn every part of skin or muscle that it touched. The water was tainted with a large portion of crystallized rock salt. If the temperature didn't scald them into fits of madness, the salt in their open wounds would worm its way throughout their bloodstream and burn them from the inside out. With every beat of their heart, and every inch of coursing blood through their veins, they would scream.

Once through the factory and cleaned off sufficiently for inspection, the pain babies that were still relatively intact and had not been scrapped for parts were assigned to a room mother, based solely on their previous life on the surface. All of them, almost without exception, would enter the City on the Havoc Level, in one room that had been chosen for its ability to dole out the kind of punishment the new arrival deserved. At least until they could be demoted.

Sometimes, while under the microscope of inspection by the morebats, certain things stood out. Things that they had been told to watch out for from a lower being. Traits that could be used by the room mothers or the council members. Doctors or lawyers were always taken off the factory line and delivered to the Womb Level. Some policeman and engineers also made the cut. The Doctor got to deal with each of them.

The man-machines were an extraordinary success for The Architect.

CHAPTER THIRTY-TWO

Victor and David stood completely still as they surveyed the scene if front of them. The metal door they exited from the fire station to get to this hallway wasn't the same one they'd entered. One door in, or so Victor thought, and one door out. But the one he'd picked was not the one he wanted. It was just the most readily accessible, and he'd opened it and walked through. Not normally a difficult position, but this time proved to be the exception to the rule.

David stood next to him viewing the long hallway, if that's what it could be called. There was gravel under their feet leading to a paved highway, but unlike any highway he'd ever seen. The highway went off for a distance into a mist that was falling steadily on their faces. He looked up and put his hand out to feel the rain. It was slick and discolored, a dark brownish-red, and he could tell that it was old and smelled like dishwater that hadn't been thrown out after washing the dishes for several weeks. The smell was overwhelming, but the texture was also a little unsettling. As more and more of the rain fell down on him, he felt tiny chunks interlaced throughout. There were vegetable-like substances, red and green cut up pieces, layered inside the rain, but he was pretty sure these weren't vegetables. Not a chance.

The Doctor ignored the rain. He had two more items to gather to complete the cocktail, and he was focused on that alone. Looking down at the black asphalt highway that stretched into the distance as far as he could see made him frown. The rain made it hard to discern, but there was definitely something coming at them from the other end. Something he would've guessed was not there to welcome them.

He motioned to David, and the two of them turned and ran away from the sound. As he ran, he heard the noise gaining on them slowly but surely. It was coming with a sloshing-shoe sound and a steady drumbeat persistence. Whatever place they stumbled into here, it hadn't made the thing on the other end of the highway thrilled. He knew instinctively the thing knew they were in its territory.

Victor looked back at the approaching sound as his mind tried to figure out what was making the noise. It was a hideous sound and reminded him of a dentist's drill when it first fired up before being put into the patient's wide open mouth. It whirred and wheezed, and gained momentum as it neared the tooth. This thing sounded exactly like that.

David proved to be quicker than the Doctor and ran out ahead of him. He obviously had no desire to meet whatever it was and out distanced Victor with every step. He did not know where he was running, but he knew it was away from the noise. The ever-increasing noise.

As Victor turned back to locate David through the mist, he was swept off his feet and hurtled toward the pavement. He landed with a "thud" and rolled for several moments before coming to rest. Before he could sit up, David rolled to a stop up against him with a dazed and confused look on his face. Something had tripped the both of them and made sure they were next to each other.

"What kind of guests turn and run at the first sound they hear before they know what's following them?" a voice behind them asked.

"The kind that knows they aren't supposed to be here," Victor answered as he stood up. His head was no longer smoking, but remained a black color from the electric shocks earlier.

"Well, there are no mistakes in the City. Only opportunities," the voice replied. "I see this as a prime opportunity."

"Well, you can get that fucking opportunity talk out of your system. We're not staying, and we're only looking for information. A council member sent us."

The voice chuckled dangerously. "A council member? Here?"

David answered quickly. "Yes. Eikken."

The voice laughed a little louder and harder. "Where is he now? I can only wonder why he'd send you to me and not let me know you were coming. There are no mistakes."

Victor looked around him to figure out who was speaking, but the voice seemed to echo off the pavement of the road and he couldn't tell where it was coming from, let alone who was speaking to them. "I have no time for games. I'm on a mission for a council member. You will respect that."

"I do respect that. But respect can have different meanings, don't you think?'

"Fuck you. We're leaving. Show me the door."

"Such language from the Doctor of the City. I would have expected better."

Victor straightened up. Here was the respect. "So you know who I am?" he asked.

"Yes," was the only answer he received.

"Then you know I am a lower being."

"Yes."

"You will show me the door. We will be leaving."

There was only a fraction's hesitation. "No."

Victor was stunned. David backpedaled at the strength of the simply stated word. Whoever this room mother was, he was neither afraid of them, nor did he care who they were or what they were doing here. A bad sign.

At that moment, the whirling, drilling sound that had been close on their heels revved up, and both David and Victor took an involuntary step backwards. Victor completely forgot about the sound while he was talking with the room mother, but now he remembered. The noise had gotten closer and was within reach.

The room mother expected the next move. "Running will do you no good." It was a straightforward statement and extremely threatening.

Victor and David stared as the mist parted. Directly in front of them and coming straight at them was something that the factory had produced in the last several years. Something Victor had heard about but never seen. Something that was going to make Eikken's earlier punishment of Victor resemble a slap on the cheek. Something that Victor could truly fear.

As they stared open-mouthed, a voice rang out, feminine and quite attractive sounding. "Gentlemen, may I introduce you to the Leech Blender?"

The voice had to be smiling.

CHAPTER THIRTY-THREE

"This is the room I'm the most proud of in my amazin' maze. Ya'll will like it, I'm sure. Ya'll can rest fer a spell here and get some good home cooking." Daisy Mae was strutting in front of them like the host at a wedding reception. She was moving through a busy throng of morebats bustling all around her.

Mack counted at least six morebats working in harmony. They were running around the room like ants on a farm and the faster they moved, the harder it was to keep track of them. They were all engaged in some kind of activity.

Byron whispered to Mack, "We get to eat? I don't know about you, but this can't be a healthy dinner."

Daisy Mae bent over and talked to one of the morebats. She nodded and then stood up and turned to Mack and Byron. "Ya'll come over here and sit on the couch next to me. While my morebats make us up something to eat."

Mack stood stock still and put his hand out to stop Byron from advancing. He didn't know if Byron would sit next to her or not, but he would not let him if he could prevent it.

Daisy Mae made a pouting face and then turned away from Mack's gaze. "Alright. You can stand iffin you want. But I prefer to sit."

"There wasn't anything in that scroll about this, Teacher," Byron whispered.

Mack nodded. He was sure of that.

The room was cylindrical shaped and painted in yellow and blue stripes. The walls and the ceiling reminded Mack of a circus carnival cage that fell by the wayside. The rides no longer worked, and had been left to decay and rot in a field somewhere, but the lion's cage, brightly painted at one time and on a set of wheels, still stood proudly. Except this room wasn't proud and there were no lions anywhere.

In each of the corners of the room, a small rotating light threw four different colors on the walls and onto everything they touched. The two kaleidoscopes turned slowly and lit the room up in patterns of red, blue, green, and orange. The lights rotated in front of a high wattage bulb that made the room dimensions seem to change. If he hadn't known better, Mack would've thought someone had slipped him a high-powered drug, and he was living through a LSD infused dream. The changing colors made it hard to focus clearly on what was happening in the room itself.

"We call this the John Wayne Memorial room," Daisy Mae said innocently.

That immediately pissed off Byron. "There is no fucking way that John Wayne is in the City. No fucking way!" Byron had stepped past Mack and was ready to fight about this. She was disparaging one of his boyhood heroes.

Daisy Mae seemed upset by the implication. "Not *that* John Wayne. There are others."

Byron backed off for a second. Mack looked at him. "5317. Remember? Nothing is what you think it is here." He looked at Byron's one good eye and then turned back to Daisy Mae.

"Since I was of the opinion that we'd already left your little maze of fun, why don't you tell us what's going on here? I'm sure it's going to take a minute to figure this one out, anyway." He turned back to Byron. "We're out of symbols."

Byron nodded. "I know."

"The morebats pretty much handle the majority of the cooking," Daisy Mae said.

Mack turned and watched as two morebats stood next to each other. They were both stirring large metal pots boiling over a small flame. The morebats would alternately stir the pot with a wooden spoon and then lift the spoon out and take a quick taste.

"They're cooking for our two John Wayne's," she continued.

Mack looked at the two people laid out in the center of the room. Each was completely naked and strapped down to a pallet on their respective stomachs. One of the two men wore a clown mask, complete with a little red ball tied over his nose and green curly hair. The clown also wore a party hat, while the other man was just naked with a look of pure hatred on his face. Their arms were positioned out to their sides at a forty-five degree angle and also tied down.

In the center of the room was a hanging neon light with the words "Kiss My Ass" brightly lit up and flashing. The neon sign would sizzle, and a loudspeaker would boom out behind the men reading the words aloud. In case they forgot what it said, Byron figured.

"Mr. Michaels. You look confused. I would have expected that from the Teacher here, but you should know better." Daisy Mae pointed to the patron wearing the clown mask. "This is John Wayne Gacy. He killed and dismembered over thirty young men and then buried their remains in his mother's house. He hid the smell with acid and lye until he was eventually caught." Just then the words "Kiss My Ass" lit up, and the loudspeakers boomed.

Mack watched as the pallets the two men were on began moving forward slowly.

Daisy Mae pointed at the other man. "This pain baby is John Wayne Glover. He was the notorious Granny killer from Australia, mate," she said as she smiled at Mack. "John here killed six older women by hammering them with a ball peen hammer. To top it off, he then stole their wallets. Got about a hundred dollars from each. Alas, he committed suicide before he could be executed. The state never gets to have any fun."

The pallets inched forward and, as Mack watched, the morebats who were not stirring the pots were running around hysterically, very agitated, like they'd just received some dreadful news.

Daisy Mae continued. "John Wayne Gacy over here, liked to dress up as a clown and frequent kiddie parties in Chicago before killing his male lovers. The state did get to execute him, however, and his infamous last words were 'Kiss My Ass.' We thought it appropriate if he got to hear them played over and over again. À propos, don't you think?" She'd gone back to her coquettish mode.

She pointed to the morebats stirring the pots of whatever was in them. One took a quick taste and made an "okay" sign to the others running around. "What's for dinner, Margie?" Daisy Mae asked one of the cooking morebats.

"Dinner good. Make chili. Old family recipe. Have meat, jalapenos, sugar and secret ingredient. Lots of beans. Make digestion easy for twins."

Mack glanced at Byron at the words "secret ingredient." That could literally have been anything.

As the pallets moved forward slowly, the four morebats who weren't cooking ran over to the cooks with spoons. They each scooped a handful out of the pot and gulped down their dinners. Whatever Margie had used was an instant hit as the morebats grinned and chomped the chili down as fast as they could. Byron could barely keep up with the movement of the spoons. They were so fast. Almost a blur.

"Positions everyone! Positions!" Daisy Mae clapped her hands together twice as the pallets with the two John Wayne's came to a stop, and the morebats took up their positions. Each John Wayne had two morebats standing directly in front of their faces. The pallets were placed at the perfect height to accommodate.

The red neon sign lit up, and the room danced in an array of colors as the loudspeaker boomed, "Kiss My Ass! Kiss My Ass! Kiss My Ass!" repeatedly.

It looked to Mack like something out of a comic book. A decidedly strange and demented comic book, but still something from another planet.

The first morebats turned around and dropped his pants and planted his butt cheeks squarely on the face of John Wayne Gacy. The morebats squirmed a little and flexed his butt muscles and pushed backward until Gacy grunted and his entire mouth and nose were covered with morebats butt. Mack could see only the white painted face of Gacy and the black underlined eyes showing above the butt of the morebats. The other John was in the same position. Nothing but upper half of the face showing as his morebats settled firmly against his nose.

"Let's get the timing right now, morebats," Daisy Mae clapped. The loudspeaker screamed "Kiss My Ass" nonstop, and the neon sign flashed in perfect synchronization. "On my count, now. Just for our guests. One. Two. Three."

At the count of three, Daisy Mae squealed with delight and Mack and Byron watched as each of the two morebats grunted and then flexed. Mack pulled his head back and covered his mouth when he realized they were both defecating directly onto the John's faces. As he shuddered and watched, sudden streams of feces, showered with chili chunks and resonating with undigested red beans and some special ingredient which was probably intestinal parts of dead animals, streamed down the face of Gacy and Glover.

Both of the men retched and violently puked directly into the morebats' butt.

As soon as one had deposited his load, the next morebats walked up and planted himself onto the noses of each of the patrons. The entire process repeated.

"Damn it," Daisy Mae said in mock ferocity. "I wanted you to be more precise with your aim. Look at poor Mr. Gacy. You messed up his clown paint and got some in his eyes. What will we do with two boys who can't shoot straight?" Daisy Mae wagged an index finger at the morebats as they ran back to the cooks for more chili.

"We need to find our door, and get the hell out of here, Teacher." Byron said. He felt very sick. He pointed to the two doors at the end of the room painted in the yellow and blue stripes. "Which one?"

Mack shook his head "no." He didn't know.

"How?" Byron started and then stopped. The pallets were retreating to their starting points. "Look."

Mack turned to see what he was pointing at. "What?"

"The pallets. The bodies themselves. Look at the positioning of the bodies." Byron was getting excited.

"I don't see it. What? What do you see?"

"The bodies of the two John's, with their arms stuck out like that at forty-five degree angles. Don't they look like arrows?"

Mack saw it immediately. "Yes. Yes. You're right. The placement of the arms makes them point at that door over there."

Byron was sure. "That's it. The John's are pointing the way to that one door."

Mack turned to the door on the other side of the room. "We take that one. The opposite one from where they're pointing. Let's move."

He ran towards the door as the pallets moved again and Daisy Mae sat on the coach. "Don't be leaving without eating, Teacher. The meal's almost ready again."

He ignored her and pushed the metal door open and stepped through before he changed his mind. He and Byron were leaving the amazin' maze and Daisy Mae behind.

"Any ideas about what's up ahead, Teacher?" Byron asked. Although it was disgusting and several of the rooms in the maze were coated in psychological terror, he'd survived with just scars. Most of it could be forgotten. Except the mirror. That would stay with him for a long time. What could have been.

"Not really. I figure we're going to come into contact with the machines soon. It has to be. The scroll points that way also."

Byron nodded. He didn't like the maze, but the unknown waiting up ahead could be far worse.

Daisy Mae sat quietly still as the morebats cooks stirred the pots again after she'd watched the two of them exit her maze. She was waiting. It would only take a moment, she knew. She stood up from the couch.

Walking to the center of the room, she "shooed" two of the morebats away. She looked up at the ceiling and then stepped to her right half a step. She watched as Eikken unfolded his tentacles and detached himself from the ceiling corner where he'd been lying in wait the whole time Mack and Byron were there.

Daisy Mae spit her nipple out of her mouth and momentarily forgot it while Eikken descended to the floor and faced her. He was a pale yellow and blue color that matched the ceiling perfectly. He'd been invisible to anyone looking up. He was obviously pleased. He stretched his tentacles out and back and looked at her from about three feet off the floor.

"You've done well, Daisy Mae. I am very pleased with your cunning and your performance as the poor country girl," Eikken said. As he stretched, the red neon sign lit up and reflected off his tentacles.

She nodded and cast her eyes down.

"They made it through the maze and found the door I wanted them to find. They're gone now and out of the picture. They won't be finding their prize. This should prove most troublesome for Annicka," he said.

Daisy Mae had no idea what he was talking about. She'd only done what he wanted. What he instructed her to do. Let the two men work their way through the maze with no interference from her and make sure they picked the wrong door at the end.

"I can foresee a floor administrator position opening up very soon. I will demote you to that level when it opens."

With that, Eikken floated back up to the ceiling and then turned and slid out of the crack in the ceiling. As Daisy Mae watched him go, she was very pleased with herself.

238

Very pleased.

She turned to the morebats standing beside her, burping up their chili dinners. "Move the two John's back to their original positions. Turn them back to the direction they were facing before we switched it. Make sure they're facing the original doors," she said.

The morebats went to work, turning the pallets back to their original directions as Daisy Mae got some tape and put her nipple back on her breast. The hole just wasn't attractive.

Not if she was going to be a council member.

It grew without light and without proper soil. It grew without water and with no one talking to it. It showed a strength not seen for many years in the City and grew of its own accord. As if two different worlds collided, one of stunning cruelty and one with a hope of something better, ran into each other through the infinite ministrations of the cosmos. It was on a journey of its own.

The Black Rose unfurled from a tiny seed to stand alone in the dark crevice that was its home. If there'd been any light available, anything to cling to and cause it to prosper even slightly, it would have radiated and responded like a new beginning. It was life where there was only death.

In the small crevice, behind the stalagmite that the Rose looked upon since its birth, it stood strong, on its own stem as the petals mysteriously unfurled and opened to the world of the City.

Until now.

Sensing that something changed, that something was different and the light it found in the valley of darkness had been snuffed out, the Rose pulled one of its petals back to the center of its depth, and then another followed. The course was reversed and the Rose could no longer draw the strength it needed.

Slowly, achingly, and without awareness as to the why of the equation, the Rose withered.

CHAPTER THIRTY-FOUR

Victor was riveted to the place where he stood up on the pavement. Running was useless at this point and if he and David were going to get out of the predicament they were in, it would take all of his cunning and some luck, he thought.

The machine that came at them out of the mist was a takeoff on a straightforward design from the surface. Some engineer somewhere in the City had to have been very proud of this creation. The vision in front of them would've come from a cruel mind intent on both physically scarring the patrons, and detaching their minds from reality by scaring themselves shitless at the same time. It was a rare work of intelligence that could produce a profoundly different machine. This engineer had done just that.

"Prepare to be swallowed by the 'Leech Blender', Herr Doctor," the mysterious voice rang out to Victor's conscious.

While most machines began with a purpose of aiding man on the surface, what the Leech Blender started out as could only be speculated. The thing was monstrous, and aside from the whirring, wheezing, drilling sound it made as it moved, was relatively quiet for its girth. It looked to Victor to be over twenty feet tall and just as wide. A dozen skinny little bicycle tires moved the machine.

Except for the spokes.

The spokes of the tires, though shiny and metallic colored from a silvery paint, were entirely human and alive. Each of the several spokes on the wheels of the machine was a patron that'd been stretched beyond the normal limits of the human body. After they'd been stretched, the people-spokes were then welded onto the sides of the rim. As the wheels turned and ground on the pavement, the people-spokes would howl from the weight of the machine as it crushed their heads every time they rotated against the gravel of the highway. Their small intestines had been redesigned with an elastic material that allowed the people-spokes to stay in one piece and perform their job, but at the same time be over eight-feet tall apiece.

The main building of the "Blender" carried a house-like structure that was round like a long street pipe and housed the gears that powered the machine. It reminded Victor of a jet engine. It ran the full length from front to back and was transparent, with windows making up the bulk of its round walls. As he looked closer, he saw the windows wavered as the machine moved and weren't solid, but more like saran wrapping. He knew from his many operations that the transparent windows were membranes from the skulls of patrons. They were billowing back and forth and yellowy. Each was attached at the top and bottom of the structure with bloody femur and leg bones.

Inside the cylinder house of the "Blender" rotated the residents of the machine, and although Victor did not know who these people were, he knew they weren't happy to be part of the machine. They'd been stretched and integrated into the machine itself, and all the patrons in the cylinder were working parts. Several of the people inside were shaped like cams and cylinders and were melded into each other. They were intermeshed gears of the machine itself, constantly rotating to push the machine forward. They flipped and turned as the gears moved. The patrons never flinched or blinked and stared mindlessly at Victor and David every time they were turned towards the two of them. If they understood what was going on around them, they gave no sign.

In the machine's front was a pair of six or seven foot eyes that directed the machine which way to go. They locked on to Victor and David and blazed blood-shot red with the prospect of capturing them and adding to the tea party going on inside. It wouldn't be a pleasant invitation.

Underneath the eyes in the center of the hub of the machine was an impeller. It looked like it'd been lifted off of a high powered yacht in the Caribbean and could deliver a significant amount of pulling power. It was rotating faster than the machine was moving, and everything in front of it for several feet was being swept up into the machine like a vacuum. If an unlucky patron got within the cone of suction, they were going to become part of the machine.

Victor backed up as the wind swept over him and the machine sucked him and David into its open mouth. David started blubbering and was stuttering so bad, even Victor couldn't make out what he was saying. At one moment, they were standing on the pavement, and in the next instant, both of them were in a whirlpool of dirt, garbage, smoke, mist, and other prisoners, swirling around and around and being sucked inside an opening in the front of the "Blender."

Victor clutched at anything to hold on to, but his fingers slipped through the gravel. The mouth of the thing opened and Victor was instantly sucked inside and thrown around like a rag doll. He crashed into other patrons and higher beings. He caught a quick glance at David as he flew from side to side in the machine. The mouth opened wider like a yawn, and some gears gnashed against each other as both of them were scraped across the teeth. The gears were razor sharp and cut cleanly into Victor again and again. He screamed as he was thrown over and on top of David and then cut up by the shredder.

Victor reached across and, using what little leverage he could get, he grasped a full set of the gears in his hand. The machine's impeller increased its torque and the teeth immediately clamped downward and tried to cut off Victor's hand directly above the wrist. At the last moment, as he was thrown around like a cat in a dryer, he swerved his body to the right and threw all of his weight to the left and knocked one of the other patrons into the gear his hand grasped. The impeller coughed and slowed down for a fraction of a second. The sudden ingestion of a full body, when it was only designed to munch on some of the parts, caused it to hiccup.

The Doctor had all the time he needed in that fraction of a second. Grabbing David from the swirling bodies in the blender, he threw him feet first past the teeth and back out onto the pavement. He jumped down behind him and rolled around behind the impellers, which negated the pull of the suction. He figured that if he could get behind the impeller, the suction wouldn't be so effective.

He heard the voice that had been speaking to him scream for the machine to turn around, but Victor turned and ducked with it. He pulled David along behind him and when the machine finally got turned around, Victor sprinted away into the heavily falling mist. He could hear the machine grinding its gears against some of the new pain babies it had sucked up and then adding them to either the spokes it already made or some of its precision internal parts. The machine wasted none of the parts of the patrons it ingested. There was a use for all the parts, little or large, and the pain babies made such perfect gears. A little pressure here or there, and some adjustment of the basic structure of the DNA of humans, could produce a perpetual machine. It simply fed itself, making its own part replacements.

Victor knew the purpose of the machine was to use its heavy jaws to stretch the patrons to a length sufficient to serve its purpose, and as he and David rounded a bend and ran away from the turning machine, he was glad that he was still five feet nine inches tall.

She stepped out of the falling mist and popped a lollipop into her child-like mouth. With a flip of her blond hair and a heavy sigh, she turned and walked away. Her job here was complete.

She watched them for a moment as they ran away into the scaly rain and pungent mist. She no longer was interested in pursuing them. The "Blender" did its job and slowed them down for a little while. Her mother, Annicka, sent her here to make sure of that very fact.

Randi left, headed to another task for her mother.

CHAPTER THIRTY-FIVE

There was no light that Mack could see. There was no sound. There was no humming, no filters, no speakers working, no breathing. There was nothing. And a lot of it.

Mack felt Byron reach out and grasp the back part of this shirt and give a little tug. It was so completely pitch black, so devoid of light or sound, as to be death like, he thought. He'd felt this one other time in his life, at the end of a rope. But that ended badly for him. He was afraid that this would end badly as well.

When he stepped through the last door and heard the soft, metallic click of a steel latch on a steel post, Mack knew immediately that they'd chosen the wrong door. For the first time since starting on this trek, he'd made a mistake. He'd been led here by the clues, but something had gone terribly wrong. He could not hear a sound; could not see his hand in front of his face; could not hear his own breathing.

And he was afraid.

For the first time in a long time, he was afraid. He'd never been a vigorous man, but he'd never been weak, either. If he had to describe himself, he would've said in most cases he was stronger than the other men in the room, but that all changed when the lights went out. Ever since childhood, Mack had been deathly afraid of the dark. When the lights went out in his room, he used to climb out of his bed and climb into the bed of his older sister. It wasn't uncommon, his mother used to tell him, for children to fear the dark. To fear what they couldn't see or hear. It stayed with him a long time.

And now it had come back.

"Mack?" Byron whispered.

"What?"

"This is seriously scary."

"No shit. I can't see anything in front of me. Can't hear a damn thing. Can you?"

"No," Byron answered him. He moved a little closer to Mack without realizing it. He'd closed the gap between them to less than a foot, but had no clue, as he still couldn't see Mack. He tightened his grip on the shirt even more. He would not get separated. Not here. Not in this nothingness.

But something else bothered him even more than the fact that he couldn't see Mack. He couldn't feel him in front of him, either. Couldn't feel his presence in the room with him. Like someone had pulled the very air out of this place and rendered all of his senses unusable. He should've been able to sense Mack's presence, but he couldn't even do that.

And one more thing. Byron knew it as surely as he knew he was going to suffer for his surface sins. Knew it inside the very pores of his skin. Like it was a part of his heart beating in his chest.

They had made a mistake.

They'd taken the wrong door out of the last room. Daisy Mae got them both. She got the last laugh while she sat on that couch and watched them walk out of her maze and straight into a trap.

If Mack left Byron, this would be the perfect place to do it. Nothing could be followed here or worked out. There were no scrolls to lead them, and they couldn't have read it if there was one. They were trapped and had done it to themselves.

"We made a mistake," Mack said. He put his chin down against his chest and trembled slightly. He had no idea where he was and no idea how to get out of the spot he was in. It was absolutely hopeless, and he knew it. Knew he caused it. He sobbed softly in the dark. It was the only sound.

Byron moved his hand up and squeezed Mack's shoulder. He'd felt very little kinship since the beginning of their odyssey. Mack had made that quite clear at the beginning. There were no friends here. No ties that bind. But now he felt the same way as Mack did. He felt like crying in the dark, but Byron knew he wouldn't just sob. He would wail out loud in the darkness. He also knew it would do absolutely no good. This was a designed terror. They wanted you to cry out and then realize that you were not going to be rescued.

"I know, Mack," he said.

Mack stopped sobbing. It did no good anyway. It wasn't a cleansing release. It just was a distraction. He needed to think, and this wasn't helping.

"Any ideas, Byron?" Mack had deliberately resisted using Byron's first name until now. It wasn't a good idea to become very comfortable with another patron. They had a way of disappearing in this place and he'd been able to keep him at a distance by not putting a name to the face. It was like showing a picture but not naming the people in the photo. If there wasn't a name, then there wasn't any life in the photo and they were just stick figures on paper. The photo could be quickly forgotten without a name. But he relied on Byron, and he'd been helpful with their task. He was also as close to a friend as he had in the City.

Shit, Mack thought. The task was over. It was no longer in front of them. It was behind them, and now they had to figure out how to survive.

"None. You?"

"Not a damn thing. We failed when we picked the wrong door. We're being left here."

"I'm afraid to ask for how long?"

"Does it matter?"

"No," Byron shook his head in the darkness. Mack couldn't see him, anyway. He might as well cry. "Should we walk?"

Mack just didn't know. "What else do we have to do? It's not like we're going to a dance in a couple of minutes. If we are, the limo's late."

Byron chuckled, a polite, soft laugh. "You told me there wasn't any humor here."

"Did I lie?"

"No. You didn't."

"There is only one thing here, Byron," Mack said as he moved forward tentatively. He would slide his foot forward a couple of feet and then move the other one up to be even with it. He reached up and clamped a hand over Byron's hand. He didn't want to lose him, either. Not now. Not here.

"I'm afraid to ask for the rest of that statement. What?"

"The only thing we have in the City. Despair."

Byron didn't need to see the face in front of him as he lingered behind. He knew Mack would have tears in his eyes. It was impossible not to at this point. What if they had to spend the next one thousand years or so in this nothingness?

They shuffled forward like that for a few moments, each lost in their own thoughts. The absence of everything, of all the usage of their senses, was as unsettling to Mack as anything he'd ever felt or witnessed. Either on the surface or here in the City. It was terrible.

He risked it. Why the hell not? What the fuck else did they have to do? The sound of his own voice and that of Byron's was the only thing he could grasp in the darkness as they shuffled along. He knew it would probably cause him to have to let the truth out. Why not at this point?

"Byron?"

"Yeah?"

"I'm going to take a chance here. Alright?"

"Anything, Mack."

"Want to talk?" Mack asked. It was a simple statement, but so profound for the situation that Byron was floored. He literally stopped his movement.

"You know. Have a conversation. Like people used to do. Hell, I imagine they still do on the surface."

It was something that had never entered the imagination of Byron. He knew that no one just talked here. They were too busy dodging or protecting what they had to carry on a conversation. It was probably unheard of in the City. How could you have a conversation when you were being tortured?

"Absolutely. I think it would probably be the first thing that hasn't scared me since I've been here. No. Check that. I know it would be the first thing that hasn't scared me."

Mack snorted. "I don't know if it's scary or not. But the sounds of our voices are comforting." He slid forward again. He did not know where he was going, but standing in one place didn't seem like an option.

"I'll agree. Talking would help. Let's leave it at that."

"Okay," Mack said. "Were you married on the surface? Was that your family I saw back there?"

"No. Not really. The image was what could have been, I think. Cruel, but effective. I was married out of high school to that girl in the mirror, but it didn't work out. The only thing I'm not sure of is whether that was my kid or they were just pushing me. She never told me she was pregnant, if she was. We split pretty fast when we got divorced. Hell, I wasn't much of a husband to her, anyway. We would have ended up like we were, I think. You?"

"I was married to a wonderful woman named Melody. That was her in the mirror. I hadn't seen her image since I left the surface and was dragged here. Not really seen her other than in my dreams. For that matter, I hadn't seen my own reflection for a number of years. Or longer. Who knows? You can't judge time here. It just passes."

"What passes?"

"Time. Time passes. Nothing else passes."

Byron understood, but preferred not to dwell on that. "How long were you married?"

"Not long enough. She died of cancer. I haven't told anyone here. They know anyway. They use it against me."

Byron took a chance. "I'm not the smartest person in the class, but I figure you were on the surface sometime during the early forties or fifties. Nineteen, that is?"

Mack nodded, even though it was unseen. "Yeah. Late thirties." He didn't elaborate.

Byron pressed the issue. "Why are you here, Mack? You shouldn't be in this place. That I can tell. I deserve what I've been given. But you? I get the feeling that you don't belong here."

Mack said nothing for a moment while they moved deliberately and achingly slowly forward. He knew this would come up as soon as he had a conversation. It was inevitable. No one here really bothered or really dared, to ask why you were in the City. Unless you were famous and the room mothers could brag about you. If you gave out information, it could always be used against you. Like this. Like what he was about to confess to Byron. Who could say if they might end up adversaries in the future? Who could really predict if Byron would use it against him? It was like the adage about being careful with coworkers because they might end up being in charge one day.

"Maybe. Maybe not. It doesn't really matter. Not to anyone here." Mack hesitated one last time. He then sighed and let it come out. "I committed suicide after my wife died. I couldn't bear to live without her. And this is what I got for it. To spend the rest of eternity, or whatever the hell you call this, without her. You're wrong. I deserve it."

Mack let a quiet, gut wrenching sob escape his throat as he thought about her and what he'd done one more time. It was so hard. Hindsight.

Byron was taken aback. He'd never considered that. Not even thought about someone being here for that reason. "I'm envious of you, Mack."

Mack stopped and turned to face him. He could not see his face, but he couldn't believe what he had heard. "What? How can you be envious of me?" Mack was getting angry. He'd made a mistake telling Byron. Shit. Two mistakes. One got him put here, and the other spilled his guts.

"Don't get angry, Mack. I mean no disrespect. I'm envious of the life you had and the memories of the wife you had. I don't have any of that."

Mack's anger left as quickly as it had come. That was the right thing to say. That kind of thing he could handle.

"My turn, Mack. I torched the barn where my dad was sleeping. He'd gotten drunk again and beat my mother and sister. I couldn't handle it anymore. The beatings. When he passed out that night, I tied him down and set the place on fire. Never got caught and thought I got away with it. Pushed the memory far away. I always meant to repent. Never did. Then I figured I didn't have to because I became a cop. Starting doing good and figured it would cancel itself out as even."

"You never think about the future, or really think about the hereafter, if this is what we can call this shit. If I had any idea, I wouldn't have done what I did," Mack said as he turned around and started to move. "I would be on the surface waiting for my time and I could have looked forward to seeing my Melody again. Just to see her…"

"I should've been man enough to get my family away from him some other way. I just didn't realize it until I landed here. I should be here. You're entirely different than me."

"It doesn't matter. I mean really. Does it? We're both in the same place and the same situation. The means delivered us to the same ends."

"True," Byron agreed.

Mack stopped suddenly. Something had changed. Some little, tiny change. Like someone moving a picture on a desk in his office and Mack noticing when he came back to the office. It was small, and very subtle, but something changed.

Mack put his arm on the center of Byron's chest and pushed slightly against him. Byron had been a cop for many years. He knew immediately that Mack was telling him to stand still and not move. Not to make a sound.

Mack turned his head and strained his ears. He closed his eyes and focused his entire being on using the only sense he could in this complete stillness. If there was something, anything, then his ears had to tell him about it.

There it was again.

He heard it distinctly this time.

It was a low, barely audible sound. He strained his ears and turned his head in the direction he thought the sound came from. He had to be sure.

Byron hadn't moved an inch. He stood stock straight and still. He held his breath and listened. All the talking they were doing, if there was anything else in this blackness with them, had made them easy targets. Very easy.

The sound came again. This time louder. It was low and desperate. And Mack knew one other thing.

It was a growl.

Byron clutched at Mack's shirt. "Did you hear that?"

"I heard it. Whatever it is doesn't sound like it's in a good mood."

"I don't mind the mood. I hope like hell it's not hungry. I don't care if it's mad."

"We have to move," Mack whispered into the dark. He grabbed Byron's hand and moved quicker. As fast as he could reasonably go. There was no right direction. No signs or scrolls to help this time. He would have to guess and hope. Neither of the traits that he enjoyed using.

The growl got louder and Mack sensed it was closing in on them. Marking them by their smell or the sound of their feet across the floor. However, it was tracking them didn't matter. He had the uncanny feeling that it could see them. An unbelievable advantage.

Byron felt something soft and callous brush against his leg. He immediately drew in a quick gasp, and then kicked out at whatever just touched him. His foot struck something on the floor that felt large, judging from the sound of the "thud" when his foot collided with it. His foot impacted the object and then, with little resistance, went farther into the thing. His leg got wet as his foot sunk itself inside. Byron heard a soft "plop" and then a "whoosh" when he tried to pull his foot backwards.

It was stuck.

Byron let out a small yelp and tried to yank his foot back, but whatever had it would not let go. The more he pulled it backwards, the wetter the feeling got. Byron felt his testicles shrink from the intense cold of the wetness, like he just stepped into a pond in the Antarctic. The harder he pulled, the farther the wet thing crawled up his leg. He struggled to get free and tried to kick harder and harder against it.

Mack had no idea what happened to Byron, but he could feel him struggling and pulling his shirt violently. He put out his other hand and tried to steady Byron as he felt him fell to the ground. Whatever was happening to him, he was losing his balance quickly.

"Some fucking thing has my foot!" Byron screamed into the darkness.

Mack couldn't feel anything below him but the floor. He turned to help Byron, and at that moment felt a presence standing directly in front of his face. In the pitch black room, he couldn't see anything at all, but he knew there was something standing less than three inches from his face.

And he could feel its breath.

Mack was hit with an overwhelming smell of long dead breath, like a coffin was opened after centuries of being locked under a sea of moss and silt. Simultaneously, he felt the heat of the thing, as if it had just finished a meal and was breathing straight into his nostrils. The smell made him involuntarily jerk his head backwards, and he stumbled to the floor.

Byron screamed again, and Mack reached out in the darkness to locate him. He was momentarily disoriented and couldn't be sure exactly which side the scream came from, his left or his right. He felt something struggling. Mack rolled over and felt a pair of hands pushing him back down to the floor. The pressure was strong and controlled. It collapsed to the middle of his chest and he felt the weight bearing him downward. He fought back against the hands, but they were stronger and better leveraged, and he fell back to the floor.

The weight centered itself on this chest, and as he tried to sit up, the pressure intensified. He was being forced to the ground like he was under a pile of rocks, and the rocks were getting heavier with each passing second. Like someone was piling them on top of him one at a time. He felt his chest constricting.

Byron's screams turned to a muffled yell, like he was inside a paper bag and it was closed on one end. Mack could hear him in the darkness, but not tell where he was exactly. The struggling and yelling turned to quiet mode, and Mack figured Byron lost the battle the same as he.

He lay in the darkness with an immoveable weight on his chest restricting his movement when something ripped his shirt and then crawled up across his back. It wasn't a set of fingers or arms or even tiny feet that were climbing his back, but felt more like a wave of cockroaches moving all at once. The wave started in the center of his spine and spread upwards and down his buttocks and legs at the same time. As he tried to control his emotions and figure a way out of this, the wave moved steadily across his body.

It was like a thick jelly wave of semen advancing across his body from head to toe. It had texture and substance, and Mack knew it also had *purpose*. It covered his back now and pressed small pinpricks against his skin like a thousand little needles. They didn't penetrate his skin so much as simply to probe him from all sides at once, like it was looking for a way in. The wave advanced further and, in a matter of minutes, had reached his neck and was squirming up the back of his head until it centered on his scalp and then moved down across his face. He jerked his head and tried to knock the wave off of by pounding against the floor, but it kept consuming until his face succumbed and was completely covered by the mass.

Mack felt the jelly wave enter his nose and mouth and he choked as his breathing was cut off. He retched and vomited up nothing because his throat was completely covered by the scum. It wormed its way down until he felt his esophagus tighten and try to stop it to no avail.

Byron had stopped fighting and languished in the darkness, rolled up in a fetal position. The wave had covered every inch of his skin until it found an opening to let it come quickly into his body for as long as it wanted. The wave stopped its advancement when Byron stopped breathing and rested in a place where it had total dominance over him. He could feel the wave constrict like a python in the jungle curled up around its prey. It was going to squeeze him until it crushed every bone in his body.

Mack lurched up with a whimper of a scream and then collapsed into his own misery as the wave of scum choked him into unconsciousness. He could feel it hardening, like modeling clay up and down his back. The sounds of cracking and creaking as the wave hardened were deafening inside his cocoon. Like I'm being buried alive by semen, he thought. He was tied tightly underneath the cracking encasement.

Mack had one try left. He gathered his strength and then, forcing all of his concentration to one central point, he threw his weight against whatever was pining him to the floor and against the hardening wave at the same time.

Gritting his teeth and fighting to stay conscious, he jerked as hard as he could against the pressure.

For just an instant, there was a surprised reaction, Mack could tell. He'd caught it off guard. The wave seemed to understand that if it could make him pass out, it would win. Mack would be at its pleasure.

Again, he lunged forward and thrust upward and this time he also tried to twist to his immediate right. As he came back to the floor, he hit his head on the floor as hard as he could. There was a sharp crack and Mack felt a piece of the scum fall off his head. He jumped and jerked again and slammed his head down as many times as he could and each time another piece of the mold fell away until he could actually feel his face opening to the air in the darkness.

Mack rolled one more time and gasped, a desperate chest full of air into his aching lungs. When he bumped into something struggling against his leg and fighting in the dark, Mack rolled to it and thrust hard against it as best he could. The wave was falling off in chunks and more and more of his body was breaking free.

When his arms could move, Mack grabbed the wave of scum and ripped it off from anywhere he could grab. With another lunge and a tumble, Mack rolled into the cocoon that was struggling next to him and then, in the darkness, both of them plunged over the side of a crevice and fell.

Like water over a fall, he plummeted down into the darkness. Mack turned and flipped over and over as he fell. The cocoon was gone and he could swing his arms and legs, but to no avail because he couldn't find anything to grab onto or touch. He felt something was falling beside him and he could hear the air rushing past them as he fell faster and faster. He plunged into the darkness with no idea of what lay at the bottom.

When he hit the ground, he yelled out from the pain and in the next instant, something fell on top of him. It stunned him momentarily, but he wasn't hurt badly and he regained his composure quickly. He kicked out and rolled over and could hear Byron coughing, as his cocoon must have broken up when it hit the bottom of the pit. Reaching out, Mack knocked a couple of chunks away and then grabbed Byron by the shoulder and helped him to his feet.

Looking up, Mack saw a sliver of light ahead. Without saying a word, he pulled Byron by the arm and ran to the only thing he could see.

CHAPTER-THIRTY SIX

Annicka entered the council chamber in a dark mood. One of the council members had deliberately tried to deceive her patrons. Her patrons. They'd gone behind her back, which was an accepted and expected practice. But the manner in which this was acted out, in which this deceit was played out on her minions, had infuriated her.

It didn't bother her that the other council member, whoever it was, acted to deceive her. It didn't bother her that someone stepped in and altered the path that her patrons were following. She almost expected that as they got her closer to the prize. None of that was a problem.

What was a problem is that fact that whoever on the council had changed the maze ending knew of the scroll. There could be no other explanation.

How could anyone know?

She'd lost her advantage. If one council member knew of the scroll, then the others would quickly learn of it. And try to take it away from her in some manner. Not directly because that would have caused Stapleton, the council lower, to come down on them. The council members weren't permitted to steal items of worth from each other. It was, however, permitted to employ whatever means they could to gain an edge against another council member. Open theft wasn't tolerated, but brazen cunning was encouraged. She knew that whoever had turned the maze around had been trying to stall her patrons long enough to figure out what the scroll meant. More than likely, whoever handled the deception already visited the Professor and knew the truth. It was the only way to find out the power of the Rose. What purpose it served to the holder.

But that still left the question of how the council members figured out she possessed the scroll. She knew none of her minions would reveal it, and she was sure of the silence of her daughters. It would be an act of treason punishable by promotion for her daughters to even consider divulging her trust. Annicka may have been their mother, but in the City, it was more important they feared what she could do to them rather than what they meant to her. Maternal instincts be damned.

Stapleton materialized from an unseen door in the chamber's side. He stood quietly, contemplating Annicka. She could be an imposing character, if he let her, but Stapleton knew his position as a lower member and the holder of the last chair kept her at bay. It mattered not what her physical presence represented to others. To him, she was a higher and therefore beneath him. She would have to speak first. She asked for the meeting.

Annicka gauged Stapleton from where she hovered just above the ground. He was never the same being in form as he presented the last time. Stapleton could change his outward appearance at will, to morph, and he used it to unsettle those around him. She might have been expecting to see a half decomposed animal and instead he appeared as a female child of twelve years. Or he might appear as a bull with a set of testicles that dragged on the ground and had to be moved by human arms. He had appeared as a minotaur, a mosquito with a human face, a dragon with its innards exposed, or any of several other things. He was always unexpected.

For this meeting, Stapleton appeared as a butler in all the regalia. He wore a neatly pressed black suit with a blue striped tie, a perfect walking cane at his side. Where his head should have been was an enormous scab-like thing that had no eyes or ears that Annicka could discern. There were flies buzzing around his head nonstop, and the smell of feces permeated the room.

She hovered an appropriate amount of time without speaking. Stapleton made sure she knew he was the lower being in the room. Decorum was all he owned.

"I have requested this meeting," Annicka stated. Her eyes turned to a deep blackness that belied her fury. There were depths in those eyes where no one dared venture.

His voice seemed not to come from the scab-head, but rather to come from a voice box located directly behind her. It was tinny and deeply saturated with malice and sarcasm. Every word that reverberated from the voice was filled with hatred.

"Continue," was all he said. Stapleton had never minced words. He didn't get to be the lowest on the council by playing nice with the other kids in the school yard.

"One of the council members has broken an immortal law."

Stapleton hesitated for a moment. It was a bold charge. Annicka wouldn't have called him here or made such a statement lightly. "You may continue."

"As you know, the immortal laws are the only rules in the City. They must be obeyed without question."

"Of course." Stapleton's head was expanding slightly. It was billowing up by small increments and with every small push, the smell of feces increased.

"Every council member knows the laws. To break one is expulsion from the council."

"Continue." At any time, Stapleton could dismiss her and the meeting would be over. She had to structure her presentation to keep him interested. If he left suddenly, or didn't believe her, she'd pay dearly for the mistrust. Her seat on the council could be at stake.

Annicka decided she'd waited long enough. "A council member has stolen something from me. Something directly. That is forbidden." She let this sink in on Stapleton. His head had grown to twice the size as when he materialized earlier. Annicka could see several round orbs of swelling horse turds. Crawling throughout and up and over the scab-head were thousands of maggots. Small white worms snaked their way across his head with abandon. On a mission each, like ants, but undefined as to purpose.

"What was taken?"

"A path was altered. Two of my patrons were robbed of their chance to succeed. They were ordered by me to proceed on this path. One of the council members altered that path and stole from me the right to succeed."

Stapleton followed this line of logic, but didn't wish to engage in a debate with a higher council member. On the surface, he was a lawyer of some merit, but that was no longer his style.

"That is a stretch at best of the immortal law of stealing. What were your patrons attempting to do? At what were they trying to succeed?" he asked. His voice added smell to the sound so that now Annicka had the smell of feces and garlic to contend with. She had faced much worse.

Annicka's eyes flared to emerald green as she realized Stapleton did not know of her quest. He did not know of the secret. He should've known, but

Annicka knew instinctively that he did not. Whoever on the council had fucked with her, had kept him in the dark.

"I am sure this is deeper now than I originally envisioned. Since now, I believe you should be concerned. The traitor among the council members, the *thief*, is attempting to overthrow you. To take your rightful place at the last seat." She deflected his question without answering it. An expert politician on an important issue. No answer was frequently the best answer.

Stapleton was much more interested now than he was previously. His seat wasn't something he took lightly. He was always guarding against being usurped by another member. They were the only ones who were a threat to him.

"Continue," he said.

"My minions are working to secure a package. Something that I will use to strengthen my seat on the council and you could also use to strengthen your seat."

"I do not need your help, Annicka." It was the first time he'd used her name directly. She definitely had his attention. "What is in the package?"

Annicka floated away from him and turned her shoulders suggestively to him at the same time. She would use whatever she could to gain an advantage. She shook her long locks of red hair, deliberately letting some of the hair fall across her face. She was being as demure as she could, with a mass of horse turds and maggots staring at her. Not to mention the overwhelming smell.

Stapleton noticed her look. He'd sealed many deals with sex and he was considering doing the same now. He felt himself getting excited.

"I do not know what is in the package. One of my highers has discovered a trail and is looking for the package. I planned on sharing it with you to seal my seat," Annicka finished her lie.

Stapleton was no fool. He hadn't gotten to this position by believing what council member or other highers told him. He had to see and bear witness for himself.

"If it is true that an immortal law has been broken by a council member, I will have to take action immediately. A council seat could be at stake."

"Agreed," Annicka said as she took the claws of her cat out of her shoulder and sat the immobile creature on the ground. It hadn't hissed since entering the chamber. Annicka then slipped the gown off of her shoulder, revealing her breasts. They were yellowy and wrinkled, with gray nipples on the ends that pointed straight ahead.

"I will deal with this personally. Do you know who the council member is who displayed the failing?" he asked as saliva appeared at the corners of a slab of dung.

"I do not know," Annicka replied.

"Then I will have to find out. Come to me, my child."

Annicka dropped the rest of her gown onto the floor and floated into his outstretched arms. He climaxed while inside her, his scab-head exploded into an orgasm of dung.

CHAPTER THIRTY-SEVEN

She was black. Her skin was a startling display of pure femininity and elegance, held together with a touch of grace. She stood in the silent room, waiting patiently for the two of them. Mack and Byron had entered and were facing her. Mack saw her as they ran closer to the pinprick of light. She didn't look threatening at all, but stood quietly off to the side of the light, as if an eagle was eyeing its prey from a high loft on a mountainside.

She came out of the shadows and angled towards them. Neither one of them moved as she approached. Her strides were long and cat-like smooth. Her posture was straight and poised. She came to them knowing she was in charge and they had no say in the matter.

Mack waited for her to speak. As she got closer, he could make out her features. Small, aquiline and perfectly appointed nose under coal-black eyes; a supple mouth with ruby red lips surrounding it; and blonde hair, not platinum blonde that was repulsive, but a soft, peaceful color like a flowing field of golden wheat. Combined with her jet black skin, she left a striking memory and an indelible lust with any man that came into contact with her. She was short, maybe five feet two or three, with firm breasts and curvy hips. Long legs.

And she was completely mesmerizing.

Both Mack and Byron stood riveted to the spot where they'd stopped running after seeing her. Mack was so taken aback by the beauty of this woman in such a cruel place like the City that he was holding his breath and didn't realize it. Here was a woman that nations would go to war over.

"I am Simone," was all she said. Neither of them felt equal talking to her.

Byron tore his one good eye away from this vision and cast it to the floor. He reached into his jeans pocket and fondled his other eyeball. He was getting tenser by the moment. He could handle the pain, but the woman in front of him was so unsettling that he didn't think he could handle even looking at her.

"I'm Mack. This is Byron."

"I am aware."

"Why have you come?"

Simone turned and appraised Mack directly. She was so comfortable in her own skin, so forthright and intense that he was having trouble keeping his eyes clear enough to look at her. He thought he might fade under her scrutiny. Wilt under the heat. He could easily fall into uncontrollable love with this woman. A love he knew every other man who met her felt.

She tilted her head and squinted the coal-black eyes. Her lips parted, and she spoke to him as if he were a child. "You have been deceived."

Mack snapped out of his reverie at this proclamation and Byron immediately looked up from the ground.

"By whom?" Mack asked.

"It does not matter. My mother wishes to even the playing field for you."

"Your mother?"

"Annicka is my mother."

Mack remembered Randi sitting in his office telling him she had a twin. Surely this was not her. Perhaps Randi had other siblings. It was certainly possible. "Randi is your sister?"

At the mention of the name "Randi," Simone stood a little taller and let her gaze and attention rest entirely on Mack. "Yes. She is my twin."

Byron had seen some strange shit before, but he distinctly remembered Randi being white, while Simone was obviously black. He spoke up at last, "Fraternal, would be my guess?"

Simone shook her shoulders in a shrugging motion and never let her eyes leave the face of Mack. She'd taken an interest in him. "Words that do not make sense on the surface have less than no meaning here in the City. Your definitions matter not to me. Or to my family."

Byron dropped it immediately. This was one for the record books.

"You will follow me," she said simply.

She took her eyes away from Mack and turned to lead them. Mack couldn't take his eyes off of her for even a second. She was like a good elixir and he was drinking it in.

As he followed her, Mack looked around at the area. It was simply a barren wasteland and reminded him of when he was a child and had driven across the western part of Wyoming with his parents. There was nothing but sand and tumbleweeds in any direction. This was exactly like that. He felt an oppressive heat bearing down as they got closer and closer to the light. One moment in total blackness and now they were moving to a white-scorching sun. The temperature was climbing quickly and must've already been in the high nineties. He was sweating immediately after they started walking. It was uncomfortable but not unbearable.

His interest picked up as he looked ahead and saw nothing but sand in the distance. It was swirling around like in a desert. There was nothing else to even look at.

"Do you know who deceived us, Simone?" Mack asked.

"I do," was all she said.

"Why doesn't it matter?"

"It doesn't matter to you."

Mack stared at her shapely legs and her backside as she led them through sand pile after sand pile. There were no roads or markings. He looked back at Byron and saw he was keeping up with little trouble.

"Is the heat a problem for you, Mack?" Byron asked.

"Not really. This is a desert of some kind. Nothing on top of nothing. I don't see any doors ahead, do you?"

"No," Byron answered as he looked ahead of them as far as he could. He noticed that although both Mack and he were sweating profusely, Simone didn't seem to even notice the temperature.

"How would we have gotten out of here?" Mack asked.

"You would not have gotten out of here."

"I suppose that was the purpose of the deception?"

"Yes. You would be delayed in your journey."

Mack had not been a stupid detective. Neither had Byron been a stupid cop. They both saw the meaning immediately. Byron asked, "We're not the only ones looking for the Rose, are we?"

At this, Simone stopped in her tracks and turned to face a sweating Byron. "No. You are not alone in your journey."

Mack noticed that twice she had called it a journey. Not a quest or a search. Perhaps that meant something? He got an idea. "Simone?"

She resumed her walking as they followed her. "Yes." It was a statement, not a question, as if she was acknowledging the fact that he got her name correct rather than responding to him.

"May I ask you a few questions while we walk? It would help me in our journey."

"Yes." Another statement. Simple and to the point. She didn't waste words. Whether it was because she was a lower being and didn't wish to converse with the two of them or something else, he couldn't be sure. But here was a chance to get some answers, and he figured he'd better take advantage of it.

"You call this a journey. Not a quest. We're looking for a specific object. Why call it a journey?"

Simone paused for just a moment before answering. Mack didn't think she was the kind of woman who would hedge her answers or pull any punches. It made little sense anyway, and she was apparently connected.

She answered him in her no frills voice. "You are on a journey to locate a prize within the City. Many have looked for the Rose over the eons. It has been well hidden by those who wish to keep it hidden. The City does not give up its secrets easily. You are on a journey that will lead you to your demise."

Mack continued without hesitating. He expected almost that exact answer or something very similar. If the thing had been easy to find, then it would've been found a long time ago.

"Yet you bailed us out when we got deceived? Strange, don't you think? That Annicka would want to help us?" Byron asked. He picked up on the demise part and didn't like that at all. "Why not just send another couple of highers after the Rose if we failed?"

Simone didn't hesitate this time. "Because you have gotten farther than was anticipated." Another simple statement proving they'd actually been on the right track.

"The last room. The John Wayne Room. The arrows were pointed in the wrong direction. We read it right, but somebody turned the arrows. Didn't they?" Mack said. It came to him a while ago. It was the only way they could have been wrong. All the other clues were on the scroll itself.

Byron looked at Mack. He was right. It had to be. Byron knew it as well.

"Yes," Simone said.

"What will happen when we find this prize?" Mack asked.

"That is not your concern. The fact that my mother wants it is all you must know."

"What will happen to us if we fail?"

Simone stopped and pointed just ahead of her into the distance. Mack could see a small door-like opening imbedded into a sand bank. It was nearly impossible to see and was color blended perfectly. There were no signs or markings at all, and this sand bank looked like all the others. It would have been virtually impossible to find without a guide. They could have wondered around for centuries and never found it.

"Your demise."

Mack figured as much. What else would there be? Annicka would have just left them alone in a place like this and the two of them would have been forgotten for all time. On a tread wheel of sand running nowhere.

Suddenly, Mack noticed something he hadn't heard before. It was a low rumbling sound. A steady sound that was increasing in pitch and strength the closer they go to the opening in the sand. It was clearly the rumbling of a machine. Or more precisely, many machines.

"They are not moving towards you, Mr. Teacher," Simone said. She had read his thoughts. "You are moving towards them." She pointed again at the door. "You said so yourself in the maze. The machines are coming."

Mack looked back at Byron. The next stanza of the scroll had mentioned legs of steel. Simone was leading them back to the machine room. To the place where all the rejects in the factory were disposed of but not turned off.

With a wistful look back at them, Simone turned her sultry shoulders and walked in the opposite direction from where the door was located. She was leaving them to their own vices.

Mack grabbed the handle of another door, this one vibrating with the sounds of the machines behind it, and opened it for them to enter.

The door to the antechamber opened, and although there was little sound, there was movement. Whoever entered the cavern crept and lurched, unsure of their steps, but sure of the destination. The shuffling sounded hesitant and muffled, but still with a sense of purpose.

Pulling some rocks aside and gingerly locating the crevice she was looking for, the woman peered inside at the beauty she found some time ago. No one ever came back here anymore, and she made sure that if they stumbled upon this room by accident, this object was hidden. She jealously guarded her secret.

Looking into the blackness as best she could, she held her breath and stared in unconcealed awe at the object in the rocks.

In the crevice of the cavern, staring back at her, was a Black Rose standing straight up with its petals unfurled.

It had grown since she saw it last and was in full bloom again.

CHAPTER THIRTY-EIGHT

Victor and David ran as far as they could in the scaly rain that was falling constantly down upon them. It was like trying to run through a thick forest. The shit never let up and seemed to fall harder the faster the two of them ran. David figured this kind of stuff happened here all the time. Rain that didn't refresh or cleanse anything but added weight and texture to the objects it fell on. Nothing more.

"I can't run much farther," David gasped as he slowed down. They'd left the Leech Blender so far back that the sound of the machine had all but disappeared.

Victor slowed to a steady walk as well. He was tired of running. The more he thought about it, the more he wished he was just back at the operating table, hacking up the innards of a pain baby. Making someone else's welcome to the City fucking miserable. "I'll slow a little, ass wipe, but if you don't keep up, I'll leave your sorry ass here in this miserable place," he answered without turning around.

David nodded, although Victor didn't see it. He was mostly ignored and did his best just to keep pace. He was fairly sure that Victor was going to leave him in the jaws of that blender thing, but Victor had helped him. David thought it was a good sign that he wanted him around longer. At least for a little while.

The Doctor pulled up and stopped. He was still on an asphalt highway, but there appeared to be a doorway up in front of him, just a little farther down the road. He took off at a slow trot in that direction. He really didn't worry about what waited on the other side of those doors. The rooms on this level were above him, mostly. Unless one machine came after him like just happened, he could use his status to get out of trouble. He could avoid the machines, and if he had to, he could feed David to them while he made his escape. At some point, he would find the Rose and then be able to get back to his level. And finish the cocktail.

He looked over his shoulder at David. His head was still scarred and blackened in certain places from the bout with Eikken, but the pain had mostly rescinded. At least he could think clearly now.

"Come on, ass wipe. I want to find this last ingredient and get back to my lab." He turned completely around and grabbed David by the throat. He squeezed his fingers tightly around David's windpipe and cut off the air, at the same time lifting the little man off the ground. He brought him to where he was, only a couple of inches from his face. "Tell me you didn't lose the package we got from the drugstore? Tell me that or I'll snap your neck like a twig and leave you here for that blender thing to find you."

"I didn't! I didn't! I swear. Look, Victor. It's right here." David lifted the small envelope up so the Doctor could see he still had it. "I kept them the whole time. Put them in my pants. In my underwear. To protect them."

Victor set him down and dismissed him. As long as he had the drugs and could make the cocktail up for him, then he was useful. To a certain degree, anyway.

Victor opened the door he stopped at and stepped inside with David close behind.

David threw one last glance over his shoulder in the direction they'd left. He wanted to make sure nothing else followed them out of this place and into the next. Grateful that they were on their own and not being followed by something he didn't like, he pulled the door shut.

David heard it before he saw it. Victor was standing directly in front of him and had quit moving. Like he walked into a wall of solid steel. He stood right where he was, and David had just enough room to squeeze up against him. He didn't know why the Doctor wasn't moving, but his first thought was it had something to do with the sound he heard.

It was a rasping, breathing sound, and although Victor was completely blocking his view, it sounded big. Really big. The noise was so overwhelming that David couldn't think of anything else. He shoved the envelope containing the drugs back into this underwear without a conscious thought. Here we go again.

The breathing was closely followed by a stench that filled the air and was so thick David thought he could actually feel the weight of the bad breath more than smell it. He'd gotten an education on terrible smells since he arrived, but this was so strong, so overpowering, that he thought he might actually pass out. It wasn't a smell so disgusting as to cause him to gag or vomit, but felt like it was forcing itself down his throat and into his lungs of its own accord. Like nothing he could do would stop this poison from entering his lungs and then running through his bloodstream with a mind all its own. Taking over his blood one cell at a time.

Victor hadn't moved. He stood frozen to the spot where he was, less than five feet from the door. Just enough room to feel David pressing up against him and pushing him forward. Victor's eyes went dark, and he concentrated on the thing that was turned away from him at the moment. Any second now, he knew the thing would turn around and be facing him.

He quickly scanned the room, motionless from the neck down. He didn't want to make a sound and attract the attention of this thing. No attention would be good. He looked for an exit. He would just bypass this entire area if he could and look in the next room. He'd made a mistake coming here for this piece of the cocktail. Maybe they could use something else. He would not find what he needed here, because he would not stay here long enough to ask questions.

There weren't any doors he could see, and he knew the thing was blocking the door with its giant body. He knew the rooms had at least two doors, one in and one out, and he'd come through the entrance. The exit was on the other side.

Behind the thing.

"Have you met my pet, gentlemen?" The question was easily asked, like whoever raised it was interested in the weather and wondered if it was going to be sunny today.

"She truly is a magnificent specimen. Would you like some details?" The voice came from his right side and emerged from a darkened corner. The Doctor hadn't seen the owner of the voice before this moment and as she came out to show herself, Victor could only stare. Here was someone he'd not heard about.

"I am Catherine Flanagan, of British ancestry. On my mother's side. She named me after a very famous aunt who was a nurse in the One Hundred Years War." She extended her hand to be kissed. The first person to do that in a long time.

David worked his way around to the side of Victor where he could see. He stopped when he saw Catherine with her hand out.

She was about five and a half feet tall, with a chunky build and broad shoulders for a woman. She appeared to be in her early or late fifties. That's where the normal ended. There wasn't anything else that a reasonable person would add to the description, David thought.

David tried to look away from Catherine but found himself compelled to stare. She was real enough, not see through or ghost-like in any way, but there were other things. Her head was completely covered, neck to hair without a single inch of skin visible anywhere, with some sort of spider. There were enormous spiders and little spiders. Tarantulas and wolf spiders. Black widows and trap-door spiders. Daddy long legs and brown recluses. They scurried all over her head in constant motion. Each one of them alive and in transition. Moving from one side of Catherine's head to the next. Her eyes, nose and mouth were covered, as was every visible part from the collar of her shirt up. Spiders moved up and down, back and front, side to side over her head and then would alternately crawl down the shirt and disappear. David could see little humps of movement under the shirt and pants. They were everywhere.

David looked down and saw the outstretched hand was covered as well and then on down to where they were crawling out of her pants legs and onto the floor. He followed the movement of a large black spider as it ran away from Catherine and towards the middle of the room. Looking up, he saw what had stopped Victor in his tracks.

Catherine continued on unabated by the stares of her guests. "We don't get many visitors here, especially a celebrity like the Doctor. Oh, my sister will absolutely adore this moment. Oh, well. It's my personal pleasure to welcome you to my web anyway," she said.

Victor's hand came out and grabbed Catherine's, preferring to shake it instead of kiss it. From the second their hands touched, Victor could feel the spiders' bite him on the palm. They were smart, short, pointed bites, and the fangs dug in deep to deposit a small amount of poison each time. Victor tried to pull his hand back, but she held on for just a second longer to allow several more bites. Her way of welcoming them.

David completely forgot about Catherine as he stared open mouthed at the giant spider in front of them. The spider had its back turned towards them and was obviously feasting on something on the other side of the room. David could hear slurping sounds and crunching sounds as the spider ate. He had been terrified of spiders since he was a small child. This was like somebody reached into his head and pulled out his worst imaginable fear.

Catherine continued, "This is Margaret Higgins, my sister. I raised her from when she was just a tiny Black Widow, just the size of your hand, to the size she is now. Isn't she magnificent?"

"Your sister?" Victor asked.

Just then, there was a sound like someone sneezed and coughed, and a large, yellow pus filled web shot out of the back of the black widow and covered both Victor and David. Victor was thrown back by the force of the shot, and David tried frantically to dislodge himself from the sticky substance. The aim had been off slightly to the right and both of them were able to pull the web away from their faces and off most of their bodies.

Catherine clapped and laughed a small quick laugh. "My precious! My precious Margaret. These are our guests. We cannot feed on them. Please control yourself." She clapped her hands together twice rapidly, and Victor saw several spiders on her hands crushed to death. There were many more. Thousands.

The giant black widow moved awkwardly as she turned around to face them. David shrunk back in sheer terror.

"As I was saying, it's a pleasure to welcome you to our web. Mine and Margaret's. It's not much, but we try to make the most of it."

Catherine stepped forward and placed herself between Margaret and Victor. With a nod of her spider infested head, the giant black widow turned her attention elsewhere momentarily. And David breathed for the first time in what seemed like an hour. She was no longer interested in them. He scanned the room and didn't like what he saw.

The room was circular in structure. All the walls and ceiling appeared to be moving in unison with each other. One continuous motion of bodies. At several locations around the room were wooden poles stuck into the floor and to each pole was tied a person. It looked like there were probably ten or twelve different poles with pain babies attached to them. All the patrons were awake and tied securely to their respective poles. Their hands were tied behind their backs and across the poles, and afforded them little movement. The ropes were just loose enough to allow them to move away a little every time the giant spider turned in their direction.

As David watched, Margaret tuned from the pain baby on the other side of the room and took a slow, steady step towards another woman. She drank and the woman on the pole couldn't move. It was the same principle as being caught in a web, except this web was man made. Or spider-woman made, in this case.

"I see you noticed that my Margaret has turned her attention to another one of our patrons. Since she has six, she can move between them all simultaneously or independently. That way, while she's drinking the blood of one of my customers, she can watch the others."

"I can't. I can't. I can't...."

WHACK!

"I can't stand spiders, Victor. Can we leave?" David asked.

"Shut up ass wipe." Victor turned back to Catherine. "Tell me about your pet." Victor smiled his best. He had an idea.

Catherine grinned, her largest smile possible. Her mouth was filled with small brown and white spiders. They were quick to scuttle back and forth between the cracks in her teeth. David had no idea what species of spiders these were, but he'd seen them many times in his mother's house when he was a kid. He knew they posed no threat. Physical threat at least, but mental threat was another matter altogether.

"Margaret Higgins is a South American red and black widow spider, usually found in the jungles and certain parts of the rain forests. Her bite, though not usually lethal on the surface, has evolved to be ever so lethal here in the City. I have personally crossbred her with the most vicious species of tarantula that I could find. Black Widow Spiders, as I'm sure an intelligent man like yourself is quite aware, are world renowned for their deadly bite and the pain of the bite. It is extremely painful, and the poison attacks both the central nervous system of the victim and the cell structure. The poison breaks down the cells and renders the poor victim immobile within seconds. Then my pet may feed." She was moving towards the giant spider as she spoke. Victor walked closely behind him with David pressed up against his back, whimpering softly.

"How big is your pet? She's a most beautiful combination of colors, I think. Did you take care of that yourself? It's looks to me like very selective breeding." The Doctor turned on his enormous charm on this spider woman.

Catherine swelled with pride. "Yes! I'm so glad you noticed. It took me many tries to get this deep a red color and the venom to perform like it does on the victim. I am most proud of her. And Margaret is always hungry."

"Most impressive." Victor admired his pet from behind him. "Why did you name her Margaret Higgins?"

David gingerly stepped over and around the spiders. As he carefully walked, he looked at the floor that was completely covered with scurrying bodies and legs. They came in every size and shape from miniscule to twelve inches. Every part of the floor was alive. They were running around like this was a giant ant hill and they all were playing a part in the construction. He didn't want to crush any of them, but every step brought the familiar crunch of bones and cartilage. And then the innards would squirt out from underneath the soles of his shoes. The spiders were everywhere.

"Margaret Higgins was my sister's name on the surface. Alas, they hanged both of us for crimes we didn't commit and I haven't been able to locate her here in the City. So I named my pet after her as a kind of tribute. They called us the Black Widows of Liverpool. I never understood that until recently. This is so appropriate, don't you think?" Catherine shook her head and a couple of spiders flew off. She changed directions. "I've tried to get her to diet, but the smell of blood affects her. Especially blood she hasn't tried before. Like yours, for example."

David looked over at her as she said this to see who she was referencing, Victor or him. He hoped she'd forgotten all about him. It looked like she was staring at Victor, but since she had no actual eyes, the spiders continued crawling in and out of her eye sockets. He couldn't really be sure where she was looking. He couldn't figure out how she could see.

"We've come for a sample. I was hoping you and your pet might be able to help us." Victor ignored the last comment.

"What may I help you with, dear Doctor?" Catherine was happy to oblige. She knew how it worked in the City. Tit for tat. She'd get something in return.

The Doctor continued, oblivious to either the spiders crawling up his legs or the giant one feeding directly in front of him. "I'm in the middle of a delicate amount of research for a council member. I need an enzyme to complete my work. If I'm right, then the digestive juices of Margaret are enzymes. Ones that break down carbohydrates? You're the expert on the subject. Correct?"

"How truly observant you are, my doctor. That's her trademark. All black widows produce enzymes during the digestive part of their feeding. They break down the innards of their prey bit by bit until just a shell of the carcass is left. Carbohydrates and anything else. Same thing as muriatic acid."

"May I get a specimen?" Victor asked.

Catherine turned her spider face to Victor. "Can you get close enough?"

"Possibly. I was thinking of a trade. You said she particularly likes new blood? Margaret could feed from my assistant for a moment or two while I extract the enzyme."

David had followed this entire line without saying a word, but this was too much. "Victor. Anything but this. Not me. Maybe we can try something else?" He was hopeful, but didn't think he had a chance of getting out of this. He resorted to begging. "What if she kills me, Victor? Drains all my blood or something? Then I can't make the cocktail for you." David was shaking like a leaf on a tree and sweating so much, his shirt stained yellow under his arms. He hated spiders. And that big one was scaring him so bad he thought he might just shit his pants standing there.

"Perfectly acceptable. I'm sure Margaret would enjoy it and also the patrons would get a breather for a moment or two. I think we have a deal." The spider-woman must have been grinning.

Victor nodded, turned around, and grabbed David by the throat again. Slapping him across his face, he put him down on the ground. He looked up to see where the spider-woman went while dragging David among the spiders on the floor.

David struggled and screamed as he was pulled to a post next to where the spider-woman was standing. As Victor hauled him up to his feet, he cried like a baby. The spider-woman motioned to the floor and several thousand spiders converged onto the shoes and up the legs of David. He shrieked in horror as they entered his pants and covered his testicles and swarmed his chest. As he cried out, a million small legs shuffled up and down his body, covering every square inch of skin. They left nothing untouched and entered his mouth, nose, and ears, until he couldn't scream anymore and choked on the little bodies running down his esophagus. Within seconds, David

Masters stopped crying and was violently twisting back and forth against the webbing that the spiders were spinning around him for Margaret's feeding. He could no longer do anything but writhe against the webbing binding him to the metal post.

Nodding at the spider-woman, Victor took up a position against the wall while the spider-woman emitted a high-pitched squeal that was more screech than vocal. The giant spider responded to the noise by halting her feeding on the other side of the room and tuning to face the metal post that held David upright. The black widow stalked slowly towards him and then stopped directly in front of her new prize.

All the tiny spiders on David suddenly pulled backward and left his head uncovered. He sputtered and spit out a mouthful of spiders onto the pavement, and then, shaking his head, he squirmed violently against the webbing. He opened his eyes as soon as he realized they were free from the spiders and as Victor watched with an amused grin on his face, David's eyes widened in pure terror. Less than six inches away in front of his face were the eight jet-black eyes of a thirty foot tall black widow. And they were admiring David.

He screamed as loud as he could as all eight eyes bore down on him. He could see a mirrored reflection in the shining eyes of the spider, and the terror that David felt was unlike anything that he'd ever experienced. He promptly defecated in his pants and his bladder released before passing out from the mind numbing shock of having those eight eyes tasting him for their next meal.

The spider-woman allowed none of that and made another sound, and a thousand little spiders descended the throat and nose of David to choke him into consciousness. With a start, David's head snapped up as he spit the spiders out, and then he screamed again in stark terror.

The black widow unfolded its long pincers in a downward motion and then let them drift up to where her prey could see them clearly. Until now, David had been focused on the eyes, but when he saw the pincers flexing as they approached, his body started shaking and convulsing in a pure panic. His muscles took over and destructively pitched against the webbing that held them. His brain finally shut down when it realized he was about to be a meal.

He slumped into unconsciousness again and his head lolled from side to side. His eyes rolled upwards and his tongue fell out of his mouth and swelled like he was having an epileptic seizure.

Victor slunk quietly around behind Margaret when she moved in closer to feed. With her attention squarely away from him, he positioned himself behind her abdomen. Acting in haste, he pulled a scalpel out of his shirt pocket and sliced through the outer layer of the thick skin of the spider's skeletal coating.

He then punched a small hole for drainage and, holding up his vial, he let the fluids from the abdomen run into the glass. Satisfied that he had enough, he receded from the black widow and pushed back against the wall for protection.

He could hear distinctive slurping noises coming from the spider.

He was about to go back and get David when he noticed a woman near him, tied to a post. She was small and looked like she'd actually *collapsed* in on herself. Obviously, she'd been drained by the giant spider. David's fate if he didn't get back to him quickly.

"Did you get what you needed, Doctor?" the spider-woman asked when Victor reappeared at his side. She was still facing David and appeared to be watching her pet closely to make sure she didn't drain all the blood from him.

Margaret had inserted her pinchers into two spots directly behind David's ears and then pushed the pincers until the ends were buried into his skull. It looked to Victor liked the ends of the pinchers were probably touching each other inside David's brain. Most painful, he thought. He would have to give some consideration to using that technique in the operating room soon.

"I did, thanks to you and your beautiful pet," Victor said.

Catherine was obviously pleased. "Thank you. She is most impressive. A true marvel." She turned back to the giant spider and made another high sound from her throat and Margaret pulled her pinchers out of David's head with a sucking sound and then clapped them together several times like she was applauding a performance at the opera. Blood and grey matter were flung across the floor with each clap. "Would you like to leave him here with Margaret and me?"

Victor shook his head. "I still need him, I think. I'd better take him with me. We need to be going. I do have a question, though," he said as he remembered Eikken's charge.

"Yes?"

"Do you know anything about a Black Rose? Somewhere in the City? I'm looking for it. At a council member's request, of course."

"Possibly." The little spiders on her head where her eyebrows should have been furrowed themselves together like he was in deep thought. "I'd try the Carnage Room. One of the women there might know something about it."

"Excellent. I was heading there for another purpose. This just fits."

"A pity that your assistant can't remain with us. Truly. But I'm glad to have shown you my little web. If you think of it, I would always appreciate a kind word to a lower about demotion."

"I won't forget you or Margaret anytime soon," Victor said.

David fell down as all the thousands of spiders running up and down his body cut through their webbing. He was free. He opened his eyes and searched for Victor.

"Come ass wipe. We're leaving."

David sobbed again and stood up on wobbly legs. He felt two gaping holes in the sides of his head, and he was weak from the loss of blood. He did not know how much she had taken, but he felt like he couldn't stand up for long.

"If you don't keep up ass wipe, I'll leave you here to Margaret," Victor said as he walked towards the door on the other side of the room.

Giving the black widow a wide berth, David wobbled over behind Victor. He could not bear to be left here.

CHAPTER THIRTY-NINE

The raucous was a combination of metal gears rubbing against chains and squeaky ball bearings spinning in hollow casings. Too often left without proper maintenance, the soiled and complaining gears announced their assault to anyone within listening distance. The decibel level was too high to be recorded and Mack's ears throbbed in tempo to the beating of a drum he couldn't see. The noise was deafening.

They had wandered into an arena. A stadium that was set up for a classic Christians versus Lions battle. Except there weren't any Christians present and the part of the lions was played by man-machines of the darkest concoctions that Mack could've imagined. The field was full of them. Wherever he looked were different machines whose only purpose was the dispensation of pain. And it looked like some of them were very good at delivering on their designs.

On his left was a stadium style bleacher section, complete with rows of both people and morebats. The patrons were flayed upon the bleachers like discarded bits of meat in a closed butcher shop. Many were cut and bleeding; others had a distraught, distant look in their eyes like they could no longer comprehend the horrors they were forced to endure.

To his right were several morebats dressed as cheerleaders. Some of them had on tight fitting and short grass skirts that let their elongated phalluses pop out every time they danced or performed for the crowd. On their sweaters were various slogans proclaiming their loyalties: "ESPN: Entertained by Shredding Patrons Network"; "Tell Someone You Love Them With a Chain Saw"; "Dismemberment is a choice, not a right!" and "Testicles Bounce - Try It!" Some morebats were acting out dance routines, spinning and yelling encouragement to their favorite man-machine. Others were stroking their phalluses and looking for anything to mate with as the other cheerleaders egged them on in an orgy of lust.

In the bleachers were hotdog vendors hawking their products, although Mack seriously doubted the quality of the meat. It could've been anything.

He could hear the roar of the crowd swell and then subside to a relative calm as the action on the field slowed. Most of the noise came from the groans of the patrons and the cheering of the morebats.

On the field were the man-machines. There was a game in progress, and the man-machines were the stars. Mack heard scraping and grinding, honking and squealing in every direction. The people on the field added their screams and yells of panic to the din of the crowd. The noise was so overpowering he could feel it thumping in his chest like the rhythm of a beating heart.

Simone led them here before she disappeared. Conglomerations of man and machines were welded together in the factory and transported to the arena for use by the room mother. As he scanned the room, Mack counted the number of active man-machines. There were two currently in operation, running at full speed. In one corner of the stadium sat several older forms of torture that must have fallen out of favor somehow. Discarded and just idling, they sat like a runner-up in a beauty contest, ready to step in if the pageant winner couldn't fulfill her obligations. As he squinted across the room, he saw a busy morebats oiling one of the unused machines. Just to be ready if needed. The room mother didn't want the punishment to be broken. Not even for a minute.

"What the fuck kind of organ music is that?" Byron asked as he pointed to the center of the arena.

On top of one of the man-machines sat a magnificent pipe organ. The organ would bellow and screech with each push on the keys by the organist, who was very dramatic as he swayed and moved to the sounds issuing forth from the long pipes that sat on top of the music maker.

But it wasn't music that came out of the pipes. On top of the organ itself were several people deliberately stationed at specific locations. On the right of the organ were two men; on the left were two women; and in the center of the organ were both men and women. They sat like stone gargoyle statues entranced in their positions with their knees drawn up under their chins and arms crossed over their chests. A look of pure pain on their faces belied how uncomfortable it must have been. Many of the human organ attachments were simmering like they were just doused with a bucket of water.

Mack couldn't see exactly what was going on with the organist, but every time he played a certain series of keys, the people on top of the organ would scream out in pain. The organist, who was dressed in a flowing black gown with crimson fringes and a long tail that hung over his bench, was playing a hard movement by the appearance. He would swing his arms and legs in a flowing motion over the keys and then pounce on a section of the keyboard and the patrons would wail out in pain.

"My guess is that they're all sitting on some kind of probe. Probably electric by the look from their burned hair and missing eyebrows. Every time that bastard at the keyboard hits the right keys, the people on the probes get a couple of thousand volts of electricity shoved up their asses," Mack said. "He put the men, the altos, on one end, and the sopranos, on the other. In the middle, it's a mix. The sick bastard is trying to get the sound of the screams to match the music."

A bullhorn suddenly sounded behind them. Mack turned to the sound of the metallic voice talking through it to anyone in earshot. "Visitors! We have visitors! Welcome to the Garbage Disposal!" The voice was attached to a man in a yellow sports jacket wearing a dark pair of sunglasses that threw a glint of reflection off of them from a nonexistent sun. He stood atop a tower at the end of the field of play and wore a fedora hat. The coach.

The crowd broke into a roar to welcome the visitors. "Enjoy the game, but make sure you get your hotdogs early because they go fast. It's the secret ingredients that make them so tasty," the coach crowed through the bullhorn. He was far enough away that neither Mack nor Byron could see his face clearly.

The morebats cheerleaders jumped up in haste and cheered for the hotdogs. They couldn't spell the word hotdogs, so they just shouted out various letters and syllables. "Gimme a H. Gimme a Z. Go kill the motherfuckers!!!" the man-machines responded with more honking and a revving of their engines. The organist took up a new song for the visitors. Between the screaming of the crowd, the roar of the man-machines, and the organ people screaming from the electric shocks, the noise was overwhelming.

"On bloody legs of steel?" Byron asked.

"Yeah. We're in the right place. The man-machines have the metal legs." Mack took the scroll out of his pocket and unrolled it. He was going to resist viewing the carnage taking place in front of him if he could.

A buzzer sounded loudly throughout the arena and a couple of the machines moved into their positions on either side of the field, facing each other. A ramp descended on one end of the arena and several more people came running out of a tunnel. They were being propelled forward by the same skin ripper machine Mack had seen in the tunnel leading to the lazy river when he first left his office. Only this time, it was after the runners and didn't have any people chained to the front of it. The claws clanged and dinged against the pavement of the tunnel.

Mack looked down as he read from the scroll again. He would have to memorize this passage because he didn't want to look away from the man-machines for long in case they came after him.

The coach's bullhorn rang out. "Ladies and gentlemen. Patrons of all. Welcome to the Garbage Disposal. And let's have a hand for our honored guest, Mr. Mack Teacher!" A round of polite applause reached Mack's ears as the machines came to a temporary rest at midfield and went quiet for a moment. He wasn't too fond of the idea that they'd been announced prior to their arrival. They were expected. He ignored the show and went back to studying the scroll.

The bullhorn blared again from the man in the tower with the fedora. "Today's match is between two of our all-time favorite teams here at the disposal. On my left, facing huge odds of winning, sits Stiletto. On my right is Cut Throat. Everyone to your places. And remember to visit the refreshment center and tip your waitresses. Remember folks, they work for tips!"

> *A key to the hunter*
> *On bloody wheels of steel*
> *Rides a corpse without an eye*
> *Who becomes the meal.*

Mack looked up at the machines that were quietly humming. There were similarities but also a uniqueness about each of them. Foremost, every one of them fit the bloody wheels of steel stanza because all of the tires that Mack could see on either side were covered in blood and mucus of some sort. The colors ranged from dark red to light brown and flowed freely down the sides of the machines and onto the dirt and rock floor of the arena. It was clearly fresh blood and cartilage from whomever the unlucky patron was that got trampled and mashed.

Of the two man-machines squared off, Cut Throat was pointed at both ends with a fine razor-like machete that protruded out of the front and back grills. The machete swung back and forth through the grills, effectively slicing anything in its path into two pieces. Stiletto looked to be the more violent of the two man-machines. It had a mouth full of barbed wire teeth interspersed with six inches spikes. The teeth opened and closed on a hinged lever that acted like a jawbone. Chewed to bits.

Both of the machines were adorned with previous victims, either nailed or stapled to their rectangular body. Over both sides of the man-machines ran parts of people, rats, dogs, cats, and computers used as wallpaper. All the individual body parts were alive and squirming or screaming out in protest and indignation.

"Look at the crows on the people," Byron pointed.

"I see. Stanza number three."

Rides a corpse without an eye

Some people stapled to Stiletto were whole and had several crows perched on their shoulders. The crows would alternately squawk loudly and then pick at their faces. They would grab a section of eyeball or skin and rip it clear of the face or out of the socket as the patron screamed. The crows flipped their heads back and the meat would fly up a couple of feet and then the crow would catch it as easily as a dog catches a Frisbee. Cackling for the other crows to hear, he would eat his treat while the patron's face bled harder.

"None of them have their eyes leftover. That guy over there still has one eye left. Maybe that's the one we want, Mack." Byron was looking at one of the people on the front of the Stiletto man-machine.

"They're all missing their eyes. What better way to let the mind work on your pain than not be able to see when the machine will work on you?"

"Which one?"

Mack read the line again. He looked back at the body parts tied to their man-machines. Heads screamed in pain. Bodies gyrated in agony. Feet flopped. Arms twitched. One set of breasts quivered and shook whenever the man-machine revved; another had two legs welded on the sides that galloped along in tandem.

A shot ran out like a starting pistol and the machines came to life immediately. Each of them charged forward and as the people ran from them, the man-machines systematically hunted them down. Those people that could run the fastest or could trample the others got away first. Several fell to the ground as the throng of people moved as a mass. The man-machines headed for the weakest ones on the ground first.

As Mack watched, Cut Throat's blade flipped to vertical from horizontal and neatly sliced through the neck of a woman who was desperately trying to get up. Her head lopped off and rolled away from the man-machines path, only to be kicked forward by another runner. Her body flopped and spasmed on the pavement and then struggled to stand and look for its head, which had disappeared into the crowd. One morebat saw an opportunity and grabbed the rolling head and, with a swift drop kick, sent the head into the stadium bleachers. Like a helium filled beach ball, the head was bounced from section to section and kept aloft so that it never touched the ground. Part of the fun of the game.

"Look at that move by Cut Throat!" the coach blared. "He's truly learning the meaning of 'team play.' Only a true professional would give up the glory of individual achievement for the sake of his team like that! He could have easily sliced that customer into a thousand pieces, but he understands the game."

Mack scanned the two man-machines. They were moving across the field in both directions, stopping and starting and running in circles as needed to trap the people. Stiletto was devouring and shredding them into bits through the barbed wire teeth and Cut Throat was slicing everything in its way. Both man-machines would trample anything in their paths if they couldn't cut or chew the patrons. Blood and body parts were smashed and strewn over the entire arena.

The morebats cheerleaders broke off into groups of two and gave up attempting to cheer in favor of mating. Many of them fell to the ground and were humping a torso or skull with abandon to get relief.

The organ player was holding down the electric shock keys of all the people and the entire group of them were screaming at once, adding to the chaos that reigned.

"Stiletto has somebody who still is in one piece, more or less. One of his eyes is completely gone. The fucking crow just ripped it out of his head and is eating it. Look there, Teacher."

Mack looked up from the scroll to see who Byron meant. A small man was stapled in an upright position to the front grill and his one eye was completely gone. He appeared to be unconscious, or possibly dead, but Mack knew better.

Stiletto had cornered three people and come to a stop as it debated about which to chew first. The runners were huddled together in fear and stood in a close-knit group to await their fate.

"That has to be the guy. He's got something around his neck. He's the only one I see that fits the stanza."

"It's a key, Mack. I can see it. Around his neck. A key to one of the doors on the other side of the arena, I'd bet. The first line of the stanza." Byron pointed.

"That's got to be it. Okay. Now how are we going to get it off his neck without getting eaten by that fucking machine?"

Byron reached into his pocket and fingered his eyeball again. "He's not going to help. Jeffrey Dahmer never helped anyone in his entire life."

"You know him?"

"Know of him. Another famous asshole. He deserves to be here."

"Whatever you say, Byron."

"Look Mack. I'm younger and faster than you. I'll get the machine's attention and let it corner me. Once it comes to a stop, you come from the other side and grab the key. We'll see what it opens."

"The key isn't a mistake. It was put there on purpose. We're supposed to find it."

"I figure."

"This isn't a good plan."

"Do you have a better one?"

Mack shook his head. "No."

"Didn't think so."

"Be careful, Byron. That fucking thing will make mincemeat out of you literally."

"I know. Let's go."

Cut Throat stopped moving and before Mack could run out into the arena, a small box opened on top of the man-machine. An arm extended itself from inside the doors and stretched out to its full length. It held what looked like a dark red wine bottle in gnarled fingers. The arm shook the bottle from side to side and then targeted the people scattering in front. With a perfect throw, the arm whipped the bottle at the woman.

She let out a desperate scream of agony and rolled over several times in a frenzy of pain. Smoke billowed up from where the liquid touched her skin. She stood up and frantically tried to wipe it off her arm as her skin dissolved and melted away and her screams turned horrific.

Acid, Mack thought. Pure acid.

As she writhed and struggled to protect her skin by wiping her arms off on her clothes, Cut Throat crawled slowly up behind her. She momentarily forgot the man-machine while her skin fell off in hunks of molten puss onto the surface of the arena.

With what was clearly a grin, the man-machine raised a pair of pruning shears and then snapped them closed twice for effect. The women heard the snapping and turning her face reflected absolute terror as the shears closed evenly across her neck. With a smooth acceleration, Cut Throat lopped her head off as easily as slicing through a banana.

The crowd roared its approval as Cut Throat promptly rolled over the head and then turned to the woman's torso, which jumped and smoldered from the acid. Grinding ahead, the man-machine rolled over the torso and crushed it into bits of flesh and bone.

Byron took the noise from the crowd as a distraction and ran straight at Stiletto. He came up behind it and kicked the side of the man-machine. With a slap of leather hitting metal, Byron let it know he was there. He dodged and moved out to the front to make sure it saw him.

"Whoa! Look at that guy! What a move. That's the kind of thing we need here for a great game. You can bet your morebats ass Stiletto won't stand still for that!" the coach bellowed.

The man-machine whirled to locate the patron who had the audacity to tempt its wrath. With a snort of blood out of its stack, it surged ahead and barreled straight for Byron. It was solely intent on destruction.

Byron screamed and ran away from it as quickly as he could. He headed for a corner of the arena close to where Mack was crouching. When he neared the corner, Byron turned and taunted the man-machine.

"Come on, fuck head. Let's see how stupid you really are."

Stiletto ran directly at Byron, who was now up against a wall. With a quick movement and a feint to his right, Byron jumped to his left, and Stiletto slid the other direction. It was grinding its wheels over body parts and carcasses, kicking up smoke and dust. Bile and teeth, skin and hair and blood flew in all directions as the man-machine revved its engines and narrowed all of its attention to the patron with the big mouth. It was going to crush him to bits.

Mack ran up from the side, just out of reach of the man-machine. He kept Byron in his field of view and motioned to him to take the man-machine over against the bleachers. Byron nodded and whipped around in a sudden turn of ninety degrees. The crowd howled and yelled approval of the move as Stiletto was momentarily confused, but regained its bearings quickly and cornered Byron near the bleacher section.

Stiletto stopped coming forward as Byron put his back up against the wall. He was trapped. The machine murmured softly as it waited for Byron's terror to kick in. The patron was trapped with no chance of escape.

Mack took the standoff as his chance and jumped onto the side of the machine. With a reach and pull, he tried to grab the key from the neck of Dahmer. There was no movement or recognition that anything happened from Dahmer, but Stiletto sensed a change and turned in the direction where Mack was perched. His hand missed grasping the key by inches when he was temporarily jarred by the turn.

"Hey, dumb ass! Did you forget about me or are you too stupid to do two things at once?" Byron yelled when the Stiletto turned.

The man-machine honked its horn once and then lunged forward, throwing Mack off. He fell to the ground and rolled over on top of a discarded pair of legs that were still twitching. He jumped up and ran back directly behind the man-machine.

Stiletto's sudden surge forward surprised Byron, and before he knew what happened, his leg was caught under the front grill. Stiletto slowed its movement to barely a crawl. It knew when the prey was caught and couldn't escape. The more Byron struggled, the more the grill closed around his leg like quick sand.

Byron couldn't see behind the grill, but he screamed and struggled as best he could while trying to get his leg free. Many patrons had found themselves in the same grasp, and Stiletto was not going to let this one go.

Mack climbed up to the top of the machine and then raced past the organist, who was playing a diabolical version of "chopsticks" with screams. The organist turned to see Mack run past him to help Byron, and revealed a hideously disfigured face of what at one time must have been a man, but the years and the acid had eaten his face away to nothing more than pock marks and pit holes.

Mack never slowed but threw his arm out and brush the organist hard enough to knock him off his stool. The patrons strapped to the electrical probes let out a chorus of screams of appreciation and then laughter as the organist fell completely off the side of the machine and was crushed under the wheels as Stiletto focused on consuming Byron Michaels.

Byron screamed out again as his leg was dragged into the waiting mouth of Stiletto. The grill revealed thousands of miniature chomping teeth that were perfectly positioned to cut and tear into his legs, but not tear through the bone enough to release him. It was systematically eating him alive. While he screamed, the man-machine grabbed his other leg and pulled.

Mack ran over the top and stopped just as Byron's chest was disappearing into the grill and teeth of the man-machine. He stopped and stared at the closest thing to a friend he had in the City of Hell.

Byron knew he had no chance of escaping. He stopped screaming for a moment as he looked up and saw the key around the neck of Dahmer hanging directly in front of him. Reaching up in a last disparate attempt, Byron yanked the key free from his neck.

Mack looked down at Byron and saw he now held the key, but couldn't keep his hands closed much longer because he was almost engulfed.

> *Rides a corpse without an eye*
> *Who becomes the meal.*

Byron only had one eye. It hit Mack like an ice pick in his throat. The fucking scroll was referring to Byron.

Mack reached down and took the hand of Byron and pulled the key from him. With a last squeeze of his hand, Byron looked into the eyes of Mack Teacher and then disappeared forever inside the man-machine.

Stiletto belched and smoked and the crowd roared. Mack wavered like he was drunk for a moment as he watched tiny bits and pieces of Byron come spitting out of the back of the man-machine. He recognized pieces of clothing and samples of hair that weren't crushed. When the pieces hit the ground, they would roll over twice and then shiver nonstop.

"That was truly epic! The crowd loved it," the coach crowed. "We need more visitors with that guy's guts. Wait. If you stop and think for a second, we can pick up his guts to give to the next visitor. Shit. They're lying on the fucking floor!"

Mack had no time for remorse. He jumped down from the side of the man-machine while it relished its latest meal. Running at full speed, he went straight at the doors under the bleachers.

He tried to read the markings on the key as he ran, but they were scratched off a long time ago. The key had to fit one door. Stumbling up to a stop, he read the writing on the five doors facing him.

Each of the doors had a Roman numeral in the center. They were numbered from left to right *I*, *III*, *V*, *VII*, and *X*.

"What the fuck?" Mack said to no one. He turned the key over several times, scanning it. He could hear the roar of the crowd behind him as the man-machines gobbled up or sliced another patron. He knew the clock was running out until they came after him.

"How the hell do I figure this one out?"

He knew he didn't have time to try all the doors. That would've been too easy. Whichever asshole came up with this kind of shit would have let the key open all the doors, so he could go through the wrong one.

He wiped his hand across his mouth to get rid of some old saliva. "Whoever numbered these doors couldn't fucking count. Where's nine?" No one answered his question.

Mack suddenly knew the crowd had grown quiet. It was a strange quiet after the noise of the arena. Without looking back over his shoulder, he knew immediately what had happened.

Lifting his head slowly and turning around slightly, Mack could feel the man-machine behind him. It was almost breathing on his shoulder. The

286

gears were quietly thrashing behind him. The thing wanted him to turn and see it before it sliced him into little pieces.

Mack looked down at the key in his hand. He read the numbers and the words of the scroll came back to him as he waited for the shears to slice through his neck and chop his head off. Cut Throat or Stiletto, whichever one was behind him, wouldn't wait very long.

Rides a corpse without an eye

Byron had been shredded for that line. Mack shook his head. So close. He was so close. He closed his eyes and gripped the key tighter.

Without an eye

Mack snapped his eyes open and scanned the numbers on the door again. He saw it immediately. The Roman numeral for nine, which should have been the next door in the numbered sequence, was *IX*, but the puzzle maker had dropped the *I* to make it look like a ten. An *X*. A number without an *I*. The door was number nine, without an *I*.

He turned his head and ducked instantly as a sickle looking thing swished through the air next to his head, just missing him but nicking the top of his scalp. A small amount of blood seeped out as Mack rolled over to the front of door number *X*. With a thrust, he put the key in and turned the lock as the man-machine honked behind him and closed the gap.

He jumped through the open door and slammed it closed just as the sickle thing struck metal on metal against the door. Tumbling and falling, he dropped into a chute with rock sides, rolling and cursing as he fell. Grasping for anything to stop his fall, he plunged into the slimy chute, utterly alone.

CHAPTER FORTY

"Are you sure you can make the cocktail if we get this? Are you sure it's the last fucking thing you'll need, ass wipe? I'm getting pretty tired of hauling your skinny ass all over the City so you can make me this one simple drug," Victor chewed on David as they entered the Women's Room of Carnage. It wasn't a place he liked to go near, but they required something that could only be delivered here.

"Yes, Victor. It's the last thing I need. As soon as we get a concentration of female hormones, I can finish the cocktail. You'll be happy with the results." David had returned to his mouse-like state after the session with the giant spider. He still trembled inside and stopped to wipe his pants out from all the feces he deposited when the spider attacked him. He didn't smell good to himself. And his head hurt like hell.

"If you fall behind again, ass wipe, I'll leave you here with the women. You won't like that either." Victor chuckled at the thought of David surrounded by all the women.

The door slammed with the familiar clink of metal on metal and the ring of finality as the lock merged with the bolt. They were here to stay until someone else released them. There was no mistaking the intent.

The room was a cave with slime covered walls of gray and green and several low wattage bulbs hung from decades old chandeliers. The lights cast off shadows along the walls as all the chandeliers swung back and forth from a persistent wind. The room was chilly and Victor could see his breath come out with every exhale. Icicles hung from both the lights and the walls. Dirty ice, like it'd been run through a meat grinder of blood before freezing in position.

The women surged forward towards Victor and David as if they were one.

Hundreds of women. All circling them quickly and closing in from every side. Victor backed up at the mass of humanity coming at him. The circle closed around him like a noose around his neck.

They were all shapes and sizes. Wearing tattered clothing and pristine gowns and business suits. Some dressed up like witches from a Halloween dance that went wrong. Big hair and little wisps of balding. Some wore makeup applied at random and in the wrong places. Eye liner too thick and clumpy, that covered their eyes and ran down their cheeks. Mascara that ran in circles like whoever put it on did so without the aid of a mirror. Ear rings hanging from holes in their cheeks.

And lipstick.

Every woman he saw had dark red lipstick applied heavily over their mouths. Covering their teeth.

"Men!!!" several of the women shouted in unison and salivated while licking their lips and smearing the lipstick even further.

Victor pushed David in front of him to face the advancing women. The safety in numbers mantra was echoing in his head. If he couldn't get them to leave him alone, then he could divert their attention to David while he made his getaway. David stood quaking in his shoes at the sudden screaming from all sides. He didn't know what to make of the noise.

"Men!!!" The sound wasn't a happy greeting. It was more of a blood curdling lust. As they screamed out, the woman's voices were fever pitched and devoid of empathy for their prey. The voices rose in pitch and volume with the one syllable word that stretched out for a full five seconds. They weren't glad the men were here.

"Control yourselves. Ladies, control yourselves." It was the voice of reason in the middle of chaos. Insanity ruled this room, and Victor thought maybe he didn't really need this part of the cocktail to make it work. He was regretting coming into this room.

"Gentlemen. Visitors. Welcome to my humble abode. I am Madame Maria Catherina Swanenburg. This is my room." She was walking to them at a pace consistent with total control. She was the hunter, and they were caught in her trap. The only escape might be to chew off their legs and bleed to death. To run from her or try to get out of the room would be certain to cause her to unleash the masses on them. "To what do we owe this magnificent moment? Why have you come? Would you like a drink from my fountain?"

David put a hand on Victor's arm. "She poisoned all of her victims. At least thirty of them. I wouldn't drink from her fountain." He thought about not telling Victor for a moment and letting him drink, but then he might not get out of here.

Madam Swanenburg cackled. "You know of me? How divine!"

"I'm in need of something for my laboratory experiments. For a council member." Victor tried the subtle approach.

"I've seen some of your more famous experiments, Doctor," the Madame replied.

"We can be gone as quickly as we came."

"Impossible," she moved her hair to the side. It was hanging across her face in little strands and hadn't been combed or washed in longer than Victor could have guessed. The hair was a pure white and had been a wig at one point. She must've gotten from someone else along the line. "You cannot leave until we are both through with each other."

"What would you require of us, Madame? How can we assist you?"

Madame Swanenburg ignored him and resumed her praise of the women. "Each of my girls has two things in common, Doctor. One, they hate men; and two, they're in the first day of their periods."

Victor didn't know about the hating men part, but it made sense when he thought about it. On the first day of their periods and stuck in the City of Hell? Someone, probably a male someone, was going to pay for that.

"I need a vial of blood from anyone of them."

"Why don't you try and get it?"

The women moved like a pack of dogs closer and closer in on David, who was whelping like a mouse in a snare trap. They weren't giving up their blood without a fight. They were going to tear him apart bit by bit. Lipstick had turned to dripping blood.

As the circle tightened around David, a noise to the right of the pack caused a momentary stop of the impending rage. There was a stumbling noise and then a hacking sound, and the pack of women stood momentarily confused.

Mack Teacher tumbled into the room from a chute in a corner.

CHAPTER FORTY-ONE

In the instant the pack of rabid women hesitated, David took the reprieve to make his escape. Their focus turned to the man who dropped from a box cut out of the wall, and for the moment, he was forgotten. He dropped to the floor and crawled through the legs of the women encircling him. The ones who noticed him dismissed him as they focused on the new prey.

Mack stood up on wobbly legs. He hurt from head to toe and was pretty sure one of his ribs was broken. He was shaking the dust off and righting himself as the women closed in on him. The pack had split and moved in like they practiced this maneuver all the time. Wolves on a prize piece of meat.

"My goodness!" Madame Swanenburg exclaimed. "Three men at the same time! It's like a buffet!"

Mack had no idea what she was talking about, but he rapidly sized up the menacing looks of the women coming straight for him. They meant to hurt him. Now.

He held his palms up in a gesture of surrender. His right arm hurt like hell, but he needed it to work. "Easy. Easy ladies. I didn't come here to fight. I mean no harm and don't want any trouble. I got dropped here."

The women ignored the plea and descended on him. Mack was grabbed and pulled from all directions at once. He struggled and tried to fight them off, but there were too many of them to even slow down. He punched several and threw a couple off, but the sheer numbers and the intensity of their rage couldn't be controlled. They were all over him.

Someone grabbed the leg of David and pulled him back before pitching him into the center of the vicious women. Victor was set upon at the same time as David and together they fell to the ground as the weight of the women pinned them to the floor. Biting and pulling and grasping the men, both men screamed as they were literally being eaten alive by the women.

"Ladies! Ladies!" Madame Swanenburg screamed at the throng. "Take your time and savor this moment. Do we need some hot sauce?" She giggled with delight.

All three of the men were fighting and screaming from the pain of the bites. Mack curled into a fetal position and did not know that the women were even attacking anyone else. They were biting his head, legs and torso all at once and the pain was shocking. He drew himself in tighter to protect himself as best he could. The room shimmered and swirled as Mack faded in and out of consciousness.

Bright lights and rainbow colors were thrown against the shining walls. Streamers fell from the ceiling and party trinkets crashed off each other as Madame Swanenburg reached repeatedly inside a knapsack and threw handfuls of beads into the air over the feasting women. It was Mardi Gras in the Carnage.

The cave was suddenly plunged into darkness and for a second; the women stopped biting and ripping at the men. Confused by the darkness and sudden stop of carnage, the women reacted as one and held fast, as all was still for a moment. The instant metamorphosis from intense screams and yelling to total blackness stunned Mack, and he used the time to recover.

The blackness gave way to an intense heat, and then a drafting of wind swept through the room. Mack stood up, bleeding and in pain, and watched as a whirlwind of colors emanated from the far side of the room. All the women were deathly still as Annicka materialized through the light.

"Enough! Madame, call off your whores," Annicka ordered the room mother as she stepped into the center of the cave.

Madame Swanenburg hissed at the interruption of what she considered to be her prizes. She yelled a single word, and the women stopped as if they were puppets and she held the strings. They backed away from Annicka in fear. A council member had come to their space, and they were terrified by the very thought.

Victor was battered and bruised, with bite marks from head to toe. He was bleeding and several chunks of his skin were gone. A couple of the bites were deep enough to rip through his muscle. He looked up as he gathered his strength and saw a small redheaded woman still chewing as the end of his finger protruded from her mouth. She was rolling the finger in and out between her cheeks and savoring the succulence. He would get even with that bitch.

David couldn't stop crying. He bled from everywhere, and several patches of hair had been ripped from his scalp. He sobbed quietly in the corner and patted his hands against the open wounds.

"These men are mine. By rights. They came into my room and that makes them mine, Mistress," Madame Swanenburg pleaded her case.

Annicka rested a little above the floor. Her gown huddled against her form like it was cold and could get warmer by winding itself around her. Her hair was flowing in ribbons of red and black behind her and light was thrown out in all directions. Her presence encompassed and controlled all in the room. Her feral cat was screaming and spitting from her shoulder.

"I know the rules, Madame. Remember your place, or I will address your insolence."

Madame Swaneneburg hissed again and stepped a little farther away from Annicka as she moved closer to the center of the cave. The women shrunk back into the shadows and were whispering among themselves in deference to Annicka's status.

Annicka glided towards Mack. He was standing on wobbly knees and felt like he would pass out at any moment. She moved to him and touched her hand to his forehead. Mack blinked and felt like a mule kicked him in the chest. He recoiled from the touch and fell back. He shook his head as his grogginess disappeared and his mind cleared. He could feel his strength returning and he no longer hurt from the bites.

Annicka glided away from him and back to the center of this stage. It was hers to command. "I need your mind clear, Mr. Teacher. I have been monitoring your progress through the City. You have done well to this point. I released your pain for the moment, but I will summon it back if you fail." She turned slowly around in a circle so she could view the cowering women. "This man is my higher being and is not to be touched while he is in your room." The threat was not veiled in the slightest.

Madame Swaneneburg knew an opening when she saw it. "What of these two?" She motioned to Victor and David. "Can I have them?"

Annicka completed her turning and focused her attention on the two. Victor had his head down, and David had got his legs to hold him upright for a moment. "I know the Doctor. Why are you here? Why now?" Annicka was no fool. This could not be a coincidence. The timing was never a mistake. "Answer me."

Victor looked up. "I was sent to recover the Black Rose. I was led here by a lower being." He wasn't ready to tell her about the cocktail. She could take it from him and he wouldn't have anything in return. This wasn't the time.

Mack's ears perked up. He figured a long time ago that he wasn't the only one on this quest. He also knew that all of his assumptions to this point were correct. He was in the right place. But a thought occurred to him. Why did he have to unravel a scroll and the other guy was led here? That meant someone, one of the lowers, knew where the Rose was the whole time. It was all a ruse of some kind. A plot that got Byron dismembered. But whom and why?

Annicka's eyes flared from green to black and she threw her head back and let out a primordial scream of rage. Another lower was on the same trail. She had to hasten. She refocused her attention on Victor. "Do you know where the Rose is?"

Victor shook his head. "No."

"Is it in this room?"

"I don't know, Mistress."

Annicka turned back to Mack. "You have followed the trail to this room. Is the Rose here?"

Mack took the scroll back out. "I believe it is. The clues in the scroll have led me to this place. It must be here somewhere."

Victor looked across at Mack for the first time. He did not know who this man was, but he held a parchment that Victor had never seen before. Did not know it even existed. Victor calculated the odds. The scroll meant that this man had an advantage.

Annicka called to the room mother. "Madame Swanenburg. Is there a Rose, a Black Rose, hidden within the walls of this cave?"

"I have never seen such a thing. If it was here, I would have seen it. I know every crack and crevice of this place. It doesn't exist. Your man is mistaken."

The small redhead that was chewing on Victor's finger spit it out. She saw this as a chance. She spoke up from behind the mass of women. "I know of such a Rose, Mistress." She spoke timidly, afraid but unwilling to let this opportunity pass.

"Shut up, bitch. You forget you place. I am the room mother fucker here and you will not open your mouth again," Madame Swanenburg screamed at her. She couldn't afford to lose control with a council member in attendance.

"Enough, Madame. I will deal with this. Come here and speak to me, woman," Annicka said.

The redhead walked forward as the women opened a path for her. They were mindful of the significance of this moment. If this girl could produce the Rose, the room mother's position would be in jeopardy.

"State your name," Annicka's eyes had gone green again as she viewed the woman standing in deference before her.

"I no longer remember my name, but at one time I was called Mary on the surface, I think." She was mousy looking and maintained a slight build. Her voice was weak and hard to hear. If it went wrong for her, she would be punished and she knew it.

"Tell me about the Rose. I seek it."

"There is a chamber in the far corner of this place. Across the aisle from where we have remained for so long. It resides in the shadows of the cavern. I can show you." She pointed to the wall next to Annicka and into the darkness behind the women.

Annicka turned to follow her finger. She could see nothing, but quickly she glided towards the spot where Mary pointed. The throng of women shrunk back and scrambled to get out of her way. Madame Swanenburg was seething and casting piercing looks at Mary. She would personally feed Mary to her hungry women once the council member left her side.

Annicka moved into the far reaches of the darkness. She glided rapidly and the light that shimmered with her beamed ahead of her. Her hair was flowing in straight lines behind her and changing colors as she moved along. She hesitated only long enough for Mary to keep up.

"Where? Where is it? Show me now. Quickly." Annicka felt the weight of time pressing on her. The other council member would be here at any minute and she must possess the Rose before he arrived.

Mary ran up behind her and pointed to a far corner. There were a couple of stalactites in the way, but she motioned to the wall behind them. In a small crevice just to the right of the last piece of hanging rock sat a narrow chamber. As Annicka hovered up to get a better look, she saw a stunning Black Rose standing in the crevice, hidden from passers.

It was encased in a clear glass box and looked to be about a foot and half tall. It stood straight up on its own stem, which was growing out of a small pile of dark, fertile soil. The Rose was crisp and shining a high gloss black set against a red satin back ground. It stood out as a thing of incredible beauty in this place of pure evil. Annicka was momentarily aghast as she took in the raw beauty of the Rose.

At the bottom of the glass case was a simple combination lock. It was pure gold and contained slots for sequenced numbers to be dialed into their places. To open the case and allow the Black Rose to be held.

The Rose was well hidden and only someone looking in the crevice itself could have ever seen it. She turned to Mary, who was standing quietly behind her with a look of triumph on her face. She could tell from Annicka's reaction that this was the Rose she sought. "How did you discover this, Rose? It is hidden well in this place."

Mary nodded. "I have spent many hours in hunger and looking for blood, Mistress. In my searching, I found this, and then hid it from others by placing rocks in front so they would not discover it."

Annicka turned to Madame Swanenburg. She threw her head back and closed her eyes for a moment and then opened her eyes again. They were now pitch black. "You have failed me. Whores, you may have this Madame for your meal."

Swanenburg screamed "No!" as the women set upon her as one. They tore her limb from limb and scrambled in a panic to eat her. Every one of them wanted a taste. She fell under the mass of bodies and screamed over and over as she was devoured by the hungry women.

Annicka turned back to the glass encased Rose. "I assume that I cannot just reach in and grab the Rose. Mr. Teacher. You will open this glass box for me so that I may retrieve my prize."

Mack cocked his head and moved around to the front of the crevice, which contained the glass box. He looked around the sides of the case and then up and down the walls of the cavern. The numbers to the combination lock were not hidden anywhere that he could see.

"Quickly, Mr. Teacher. Before I lose my patience with you and give you to these hungry whores," Annicka stated behind his back.

Victor crept up to the rear of the little group, hoping that Annicka forgot about him. He wanted to be in a position to play his trump card when the time presented itself. David retreated to a far corner and was trying to make himself invisible in the shadows of the light that Annicka cast off. He stared dumbfounded at the women as they dined on their Madame. They paid him no mind, temporarily sated.

Mack didn't even know any numbers to try. The combination required four numbers, and simple math said the combinations were limitless. He rubbed the back of his arm across his brow, where several wet drops of perspiration had formed. He was cornered, without an answer.

Unrolling the scroll from his back pocket, Mack silently wished for the answer to appear before she lost her patience again. Summoning all his strength, Mack glanced down at the scroll one more time, looking for numbers that weren't there.

> *To touch the petals*
> *Of a Rose made of sin*
> *The answers increase*
> *Under folds of human skin*

The stanza held no numbers. Nothing that even a demented play on words could be construed to mean numbers. This was the only stanza that had to do with touching the Rose at all. It had to be here.

Mack closed his eyes and let his mind escape the bounds of the City of Hell. It wondered freely across the meadows of his home. He was no longer a prisoner confined to be tortured for eternity.

He saw her then, standing by his side one more time. On the shores of San Francisco, returning from a morning run along the bay with sweat pouring down the front of her shirt and golden hair tied up in a ponytail, she was as beautiful as the day he met her in the library. Melody was with him again, if only for a moment. His hand wondered unconsciously up to the third finger on his left hand and he rubbed the place where his wedding ring used to live. She was all he ever needed. She was his salvation in this cruel existence.

He opened his eyes again and with the courage only she could give him, looked for an answer that had to be there.

> *The answers increase*

Under folds of human skin

Mack crinkled the scroll. It was centuries old papyrus and felt like it had withered under the sun for many years. It protested his maneuver and made a wax paper noise. Like it'd been sunbathing on a beach for too long and got an unbearable sun burn. A burn that turned to dark red and then peeled off. Like skin. Like peeled skin.

Mack crinkled the scroll again. It wasn't paper. It was skin. Human skin.

He lifted the scroll up and then turned it over. It wasn't that simple, he knew, but it was there. He was on the path. She was leading him to it. Moving his arms and controlling his thoughts. The memory of her was all he still owned. He looked up at Annicka, who was staring intently at him with green eyes.

Scanning the stanzas again, he glanced up at the top of the page when he turned it back over. There wasn't anything written on the back of the scroll that he could see. His eyes drifted away from the words and landed on the picture at the top of the scroll. He hadn't really looked at it before, but now Melody moved and controlled his very eyes. They came to rest of their own desire, staring directly at the picture of the two roses facing each other.

The answers increase

Mack grasped the edges of the scroll and, moving like he was in a trance, folded the human skin one time over on top of itself. Talking to no one in particular, he said, "It doesn't mean the chances for the answers increase. It means the answers are in the *crease*. In the crease of the skin. Once I fold it back and make a crease and put the two roses on top of each other, I can see under the folds of human skin. And this is what I get." He turned the picture around for Annicka to see.

Even Victor and David strained forward to see the picture Mack was holding up. As he squinted through the light cast off from Annicka's image, David could just make out the piece of paper he was showing her. Clear in the picture as the roses came together were four numbers: 1, 3, 5, and 7.

Annicka made a sound like a cat cornering a mouse. It was a satisfying exhale of pent up breath, and then she shuddered. The conquest of the Rose was within her grasp.

"Out of my way, higher being. I am through with you for the moment." She pushed Mack aside roughly as she rushed to dial in the combination. With the sound of a lock's tumblers being rotated, Mack waited patiently in the shadows. His show was over. He'd done the job.

Victor didn't know what connection the scroll keeper had to this council member, but he saw Mack as a threat to his demotion. He was lying in wait for a chance to make his move. He sensed it was close.

Annicka dialed in the four numbers in sequence and then screamed when the glass partition didn't move and release the Rose. She quickly dialed the numbers in reverse order and when that didn't work, she turned back to Mack. "It seems I need you one more time, Mr. Teacher," she said as she regained her composure. She was so close to the prize. She couldn't quit now. "Open this for me."

Mack almost smiled, but didn't want to incur her wrath if she thought he was laughing at her. As soon as he saw the four numbers, he knew what order would work. As surely as he knew, this was almost over.

He reached around Annicka and dialed in the numbers that were so familiar to him. Numbers he used so many times while he was a prisoner here. Spinning the combination locks around, Mack dialed in 5 3 1 7, and then stepped back. It was always about the L I E S.

There was a whirring sound and then a clasp unlocked, and the glass rolled smoothly upwards. The Rose flashed a blackness of its own glory as Annicka reached in and grasped it with both hands. Holding the Rose with infinite care, she pulled it free from the soil and pressed it to her breast like she was fondling a new born.

The power of the Black Rose belonged to her.

CHAPTER FORTY-TWO

"You didn't think I was going to just let you take the Black Rose from me, now did you Annicka, my sweetheart?" Eikken asked as he descended from his perch in the shadows of the ceiling. He could have been there from the beginning, just sitting and calculating like an alligator waiting for its prey to make a mistake so he could pounce.

Mack took an involuntary step backward and shuddered. He didn't want to be anywhere near these two council members. He could smell trouble. They both wanted the same thing, and anyone close to the two of them could get dragged into it.

Victor reacted and stepped back as well. He wasn't surprised to see Eikken here, but he knew instinctively that it wasn't Eikken who led him to this room. Something else brought him here.

"Eikken. My suspicions were correct. I smelled your stench behind this ruse. The Doctor is of your doing?" Annicka said. Her hands were crossed over themselves in front of her chest, protecting the Rose.

"Of course, Annicka, my pretty. The Doctor has always been mine, whether he knew it or not. He belongs to me. As does that Rose. Now hand it over." Eikken's tentacles were expanding and contracting back and forth like he was stretching his muscles before a fight. The eight legs seemed to be everywhere at once. His bulbous head turned a crimson shade and his attention was entirely on Annicka and what she held against her chest.

"If you led the Doctor here, then you knew where the Rose sat the whole time, Eikken. Why the production of the scroll? What was the purpose?" Annicka was slowly raising herself farther and farther off the ground as she prepared for the fight she knew was coming. Her hair was streaming colors like a broken rainbow. Blue, red, green, yellow, and purple fought themselves for dominance as her eyes turned a coal black. The ever present cat on her shoulder stood up on its hind legs, claws out. Eikken would prove a formidable foe, but she was convinced that she could overcome him.

Annicka felt a lurch against her chest and then a scrape, and pulling the Rose from its place against her chest, she lifted the Rose up in front of her face. There was a reaction in the room, and as near as Mack could tell, something subtly changed. More like a shadow shifting in the dark. There was something there that wasn't there a moment ago when the Rose was up against her chest.

Mack heard a popping sound and then watched as in the center of the room, a light shot out, and then with a blue and black reflection as a background, an oval hole twisted once and then appeared directly between where Annicka and Eikken floated. A hole standing straight up and down, about six feet tall, with a sucking sound like water rushing over falls emanating from its center.

A portal. Mack knew he was witnessing the birth of a portal.

"The Doctor was working for me. I didn't lead him here." There was a slight undertone of confusion in Eikken's voice. He was looking into the portal in awe. Was it possible that the legend was true?

Annicka lunged forward immediately. She was going into the portal. If the legend was true, the portal led up to the surface, and she would be released from the City of Hell. It was an escape.

Eikken was faster than she was and as she jumped forward, Eikken grabbed her with all eight of his tentacles. He wrapped the arms around her and tried to drag her back to him as she fought against the binds. Quickly he pulled his tentacles up against his body, and Annicka with them, preventing her from escaping.

Annicka screamed and clutched the Rose to her chest as Eikken tightened his grip around her. The tentacles twisted and writhed, moving nonstop and aggressively clutching their prey. He would smother her if he could.

As she pressed backward, Annicka lifted her form off the ground and away from the portal. She gouged upwards with her right arm, still holding the Rose with her left. Grasping the folds of his eye, and sticking her fingers deep inside his left eye socket, Annicka commanded her fingernails to grow, and the nails turned to hardened steel and pierced themselves as deeply into the eye of Eikken as they could get. In a matter of seconds, the finger nails wormed themselves deep into his brain and then pushed out the other side of his soft, pliable head.

Eikken yelled and reacted like he grabbed a hot iron. His eye socket and brains were pouring gray matter out onto the floor as Annicka probed deeper. She grabbed as much of his brain as her hand would hold and ripped outward. Eikken screamed again, and he shoved one of his tentacles under the dress of Annicka, seeking to pierce her vagina.

Crossing her legs, and raising them even further off the floor, Annicka crushed Eikken up against the roof of the cavern, impaling him on one of the stalactites. Working his tentacles furiously in all directions, Eikken lashed out at Annicka by running the suction cups on the ends of the tentacles all across her bare skin. He would grab a portion of her skin and rip it off in little three inch sections.

Victor dove for cover when the fight started. As they hovered and rotated farther above the ground, Victor hid behind a pile of rocks. He looked around for the redhead that had bitten off his finger. Spying her crouched in a corner, he crawled towards her. He was going to finish her once and for all. As soon as he cut her into little pieces, he would get the guy that held the scroll.

"I can't. I can't. I can't..." David sputtered behind Victor as he crawled across the floor. Everyone was staring wide eyed up at the ceiling as the fighting raged. The two council members were locked in an embrace of arms and tentacles, moving and probing for strangle holds.

Mack stood riveted to his spot, watching the violence of the battle. Every time he thought one of them had the advantage, there would be a grunt and a clipped scream and then the two of them would pirouette across the ceiling, and the fighting would continue.

Eikken at last pushed a tentacle up through the encrusted vagina of Annicka. He shoved his arm as far as he could up through her, ripping apart her insides piece by piece until he finally grabbed her heart and, with a deft squeeze, clutched it. Annicka reacted like she was having a mammoth heart attack. She clutched her chest with both hands, dropping the Rose. Her face contorted into a vision of pure pain, and she lost her ability to hover. Collapsing against the tentacles of Eikken, she fell to the cavern floor.

Victor crawled up behind Mary and, grabbing a fist full of hair, pinned her to the floor. He rolled himself on top of her and straddled her, using his weight to hold her on the ground. He pulled a scalpel from his jacket pocket and held it up for her to see. He was going to cut her into little tiny pieces.

"The bitch is finished," Eikken declared, unwrapping himself from Annicka's form. She lay unmoving on the floor.

Glancing once around the room, Eikken chuckled to himself and then flew into the portal. There was a sound like the splash of a boulder dropping into a puddle of water, and then with a flash around the edges of the portal, and a twinkle of the blue and black lights behind it, Eikken was gone.

CHAPTER FORTY-THREE

"It appears we have a vacant seat on the council. One that will have to be filled, I think. What do you think, Annicka?" Stapleton asked as he walked into the cavern. He was dressed as though he just finished a ride on his horse during a fox hunt. He wore an open collared white shirt, covered by a green vest and tan pants. A brown leather beret and a short riding crop he struck against his thighs emphasized his presence. The only thing missing was his face. He had no visible features. His eyes, nose, and ears were removed from a hairless face. Only a mouth and teeth could be seen.

Victor stopped and glanced down at Mary under him. He only made one cut across her cheek, and it wasn't deep. Yet. Quickly, he drew a vial of her blood to get her hormones for the cocktail. Her pain would have to wait.

"Pity. Really. The portal is closing too fast," Stapleton said, like he was missing an old friend.

Annicka was struggling to sit up. Her chest hurt, and she wasn't sure she had the strength to stand. She could feel the blood flowing freely down her legs.

"I think I can help with that, your Eminence," Victor said as he dropped the scalpel and walked to where Stapleton stood.

"I have healed you, Annicka. You may rise now." Stapleton waved his hand at her and with a sudden flash of energy, she stood up. Looking down to where she laid on the floor, Annicka saw the Black Rose crushed from the fall. She landed on top of it when she hit the ground and it crumbled into several pieces. So small and vulnerable. No longer the beauty it once was. No more magic.

"Do not worry about the Rose itself. What were you saying, Doctor?"

Victor pointed at the portal. "I can extend it, if you wish."

Stapleton was taken aback. "Extend it how?"

"I have developed a cocktail that will keep the portal open for an extra six minutes longer. If you would like, I can keep it open for you. My assistant has the cocktail."

"This is an important piece of work. I will present it to The Lowest, who will no doubt bestow a seat on the council for such a discovery. You have my attention, Doctor. Proceed." Stapleton instantly calculated how he could use the knowledge of the cocktail for his own gain.

Annicka's eyes had gone to bright green. She saw a chance to get out of here once and for all. Mack was standing quietly in the shadows. This doesn't make much sense, he thought.

David turned, lowered his head, and ran into the wall. With a thud, he rammed his head against the wall, and then, with one shake of his body, stood straight up. His eyes were alight. He walked over to Victor.

"Give me the cocktail, ass wipe. I will show the council members of my discovery." Victor grabbed the syringe from the outstretched hand of David. He quickly mixed in the blood of Mary and turned to the portal, which was now getting smaller with each passing moment. A fleeting thought crossed his mind: When did David learn to correct his stuttering by himself? With a shrug of his shoulders, Victor leaned into the portal and administered the cocktail the same as he did in the portal cage. He quickly injected the contents of the syringe into whatever was inside the hole.

He reappeared after only a moment. This was his time. He would finally get the attention he deserved. Finally, get the council seat that should have been his eons ago. He looked to his right at Stapleton and saw that his featureless face was smiling. Annicka was staring passionately at the portal.

"It doesn't work, *Doctor*. Never did," David said nonchalantly as he picked a piece of lint off his shirt. He smiled at Victor.

"The fuck it doesn't. I saw it work." Victor wasn't sure what the ass wipe thought he was doing, but he concentrated on the portal once again.

"Nope. Never did."

With a wink and a corresponding pop of exit, the portal collapsed like a book being closed and the blue and black light vanished, leaving behind only a wisp of smoke that they all watched float upwards and leave through the ceiling.

"Arghh!! You asshole. I saw it work! In the portal room. It worked. You must have changed the formula. I'll tear you apart with my bare hands for this."

David took this moment to laugh openly in the face of Victor. "It never worked. The cocktail was worthless from the beginning. I bribed the morebats in the portal room and told him to let the puller extend the time. Made it stop for just a second. I knew that with your impatience, you wouldn't wait around long enough to verify the results. I only had to get a couple of extra seconds. You bought the cocktail without knowing that it worked. Who's the ass wipe now, *Doctor*?"

"So you lied to me openly, Doctor?" Stapleton's grin disappeared when the portal closed and he now centered his full attention on Victor. Annicka moved forward. She took out her vengeance on the Doctor for starters.

"No! It wasn't a lie. He tricked me!" Victor pointed at David, who had a smug grin on his face. He'd been waiting a long time for this moment.

"As soon as you taught me how to correct myself, I planned on getting even with you. Every time you hit me on the head with that fucking shovel of yours, I waited. And I planned. Now it's my turn."

Victor cowered backwards as Stapleton moved towards him. "Would you like the first strike, Annicka?" he offered.

Mack's attention was drawn to the women still huddled across from him. They were gathered in a semi-circle and were whispering furiously back and forth between themselves while the drama unfolded in front of them. He moved a little to his side until he could hear what they were saying.

Mary, the new room mother, was staring with insanely furious eyes at the Doctor as both Stapleton and Annicka closed in on him. "Its gotta be him. I recognized him when 'e was on top of me. I swear, ladies, that's the bloke." She spoke with a British accent Mack hadn't noticed before. It was short and clipped, but still there. She hadn't lost it in her years in the City.

Another girl, dressed in torn and dirty clothing, agreed. "That's 'im. I'm sure of it." Another Brit.

Mary nodded. "We owe 'im. Ladies," she motioned, and they moved forward with her in the lead.

"Your Eminence," Mary shouted. "Might we 'ave a go at 'im?"

Stapleton stopped and addressed them. "Why?"

"Several of us recognize 'im. From the surface. He put us here, he did."

Stapleton regarded Victor again. "Who is he?"

"They called him 'Jack' on the surface."

"Jack who?"

"Jack the Ripper."

"Indeed? I didn't know that about you, Doctor. Jack the Ripper? You were a celebrity and hid it from us the entire time. A pity, really. We would have treated you worse had we known, but I think you knew that, didn't you?"

Victor snorted and turned to run. He hadn't gone by that name in many years. Had actually forgotten it. Before he could move one step, Stapleton waved his arm and froze him in his spot. Victor tried to move his arms and legs, but they were stuck like he was wrapped in gauze. He couldn't lift his arms or move his legs. He was helpless.

"He's all yours, Ladies."

Victor screamed out in agony, and pain as the women set upon him with a possessed aggression. It the moment's insanity, they swept down upon him. Ripping his arms from the sockets and his testicles from their sack, and then furiously biting every square inch of his body, they devoured Victor Stevens, bit by bit, until there was nothing left to eat. Several of the women sat on the ground and ripped sections of his flesh apart and stuffed it into their mouths. Some would pull pieces off and hand it around to the others in the group; some would whack the bones on the ground and then gnaw through to the marrow. In a matter of minutes, there was nothing left but bile and blood on the floor.

Stapleton watched the havoc, immensely amused by the whole thing. He hadn't seen a grown man eaten in quite some time and forgot how it looked. "Looks like we need a new doctor, too. Mr. Masters? Would you like the position of Hell's Doctor?"

David nodded. "I'll make sure you are happy with my work, your Eminence," he said as he cast his eyes down to the floor.

"You did all this, didn't you?" Annicka said.

"Of course, my dear. Remember at the council meeting, I told you one of you had gotten a little too bold and was moving to take over the last chair on the council? My chair? I don't think so."

"Why the elaborate scheme? Eikken won. He's gone, but the portal is closed and we can't use it again." She looked at the crushed Rose on the floor. Its sheen had vanished and as she watched, it turned to dust and was gone.

"Mr. Teacher. You've proven to be quite intelligent. Can you answer that?"

Mack came out of the shadows. "My guess would be that you needed Eikken to go into the portal of his own accord. You couldn't get him there without his help. He probably needed to believe the Black Rose story also."

He slapped the riding crop against his thigh. "Bravo, Mr. Teacher. Everything they said about you was correct." He turned to Annicka. "I planted the Rose. I nurtured the story about the Rose being able to reverse the portal. I had the Professor write the scroll and let you find it. Eikken had to believe it was all real or he wouldn't have fought you to get to the portal. Remember, no one can change the free will of a council member. He had to go into the portal on his own."

Mack understood. He looked to where the portal was a moment before. "It doesn't lead up, does it? The portal? It just reverses the direction." He now understood completely. Byron had been sacrificed. For nothing.

"Bravo again, Mr. Teacher." Stapleton was obviously happy with someone figuring out his genius. "Perhaps you would like to explain?" The riding crop was slapping against his thigh in a furious rhythm.

"The portal normally leads to the City. If the Rose reversed the direction of the portal, then it would lead *away* from the City. Not necessarily up."

"Excellent! Excellent! Everyone assumed that the Rose allowed the portal to lead up. But in fact, it just leads away from the City. I figure Eikken is not very happy with his predicament. He is going away from the City. But to where?" At this, he laughed openly.

Mack blinked his eyes. He was missing something. It was right there in front of him again. But what was it? He stroked his chin absentmindedly while he thought.

"The legend of the Rose was a complete myth. I let it grow. Eikken is no longer a threat, is he?"

Mack snapped his fingers. How could he be so stupid?

Stapleton stopped gloating for a moment. He didn't like the look on Teacher's face. "What? I demand you tell me what you're thinking!"

Mack reached for the scroll again. "What about the last stanza of the scroll? The fifth one about the becoming?"

CHAPTER FORTY-FOUR

"What?" Stapleton screamed. "What fifth stanza? The scroll only has four stanzas. I watched the Professor write it." He was confused, and no longer seemed supremely confident.

Mack showed the scroll to him.

When the Rose becomes one
And the black burns bright
Havoc is foretold
And change destroys the night.

"What is the meaning of this? Who wrote this? I demand to know!" Stapleton looked around the room at all the eyes of the women staring at him.

"You're wrong about the myth of the Rose, Stapleton, among other things." Annicka said with a soothing voice, like talking to a child who got into trouble for stealing cookies from the jar. "Come out, my darlings," Annicka said as both Simone and Randi emerged from behind her.

"What is this? Annicka? What have you done?" Stapleton was cowering just slightly. Something was very wrong. The leader of the council felt a tremor of fear course its way down his spine.

"Mr. Teacher. Can you solve the riddle of the Rose for our dear Stapleton?"

Mack looked at the two daughters standing at the sides of their mother. Simone on her left and Randi on her right. He shook his head. He didn't need the scroll for this. "Simone," he said as he looked at her, "What's your last name?"

"I was named for my father."

"Who was that?"

"Eikken. My father is Eikken." Her black skin was mesmerizing.

Mack nodded. Right in front of him the entire time. "Mr. Stapleton. May I present Randi Owen and Simone Eikken? R-O-S-E. The true Black Rose of the City."

Stapleton let out a howl as Simone wordlessly reached across and grasped Randi's hand. The two of them trembled for just a second and then, as Mack watched, they melded before his eyes. They seemed to consume each other. Like an opening of a doorway, Simone widened and engulfed Randi. There was a slippage of sound and a burst of orange light, followed by a sucking noise with a trace of smoke as the two forged themselves into one being. Simone shook violently for just a second and Randi's blond hair finally disappeared inside Simone along with the rest of her. Where two of them had been now stood only one person. Each of their traits could be seen in her face.

"Now, my darlings," Annicka said.

Stapleton screamed and dropped the riding crop to the ground. He waved his hands toward Randi/Simone, but it had no effect. Annicka's hair raced out from behind her body and entangled the arms and legs of Stapleton to keep him from running. Like weeds growing uncontrolled, the hair wrapped itself around Stapleton and held him securely. He twisted and turned and fought as hard as he could, but the power of the Black Rose welded him to the spot. With a sudden yank and a grunt, Annicka pulled Stapleton into a thousand little pieces that flew across the ground and landed at the feet of the women. With no encouragement, they scooped them up and popped the loose parts into their mouths.

"You were the one who was trying to take over the last seat on the council, weren't you, Mistress?" Mack asked Annicka as her daughters returned to their separate beings. "You lured him here."

"Yes. It was me all along. Now I am in charge. I knew that the power of twins born in Hell would surpass Stapleton's. He had no idea of the power of my Rose."

Mack cast his eyes down. His work was finished.

"I believe there are some vacant seats on the council to be filled. Mr. Teacher, by rights you've earned one of those seats. Do you wish me to grant it to you?" She was actually smiling at him when he looked into her eyes. The cat sat hissing softly on her shoulders, content with the blood it helped spill for this night. Mack would be a valuable ally sitting on the council and owing his appointment to her.

He thought for less than a second. "I'll have to pass on that offer, Mistress. Not my style."

"I understand. I thought as much. I will repay you, though. Randi, we owe Mr. Teacher. I believe you are holding something for him."

Randi reached under her shirt and wrapped her hand around a small trinket in an unseen pocket. With a flip of her wrist, she threw it to Mack.

He reached up and snagged it out of the air with a one-handed catch. Opening his hand, his eyes grew wide in wonder at the circle of gold.

He was holding the wedding ring Melody gave him.

He put his face in his hands and started crying.

"You may return to your office, Mr. Teacher. I will protect you from now on as gratitude. No one may punish you."

Mack nodded and as he watched, Annicka's light shimmered and withdrew and she and her daughters were gone from the cavern.

Glancing back across the floor to where the Annicka had held the only thing of beauty in the City of Hell, Mack noticed a single black petal of the Rose was lying in the dust and blood. He walked silently over to it and, reaching down, scooped the petal up. He held it close to his face and felt a strange sensation of warmth, if only for a second. Breathing in deeply, he inhaled the most intoxicating scent he had ever smelled. With a shudder from the power of the beauty he held in his hands, he put the petal into his jeans pocket.

Turning, he started towards the door. His work was finished, and he was going back to his office.

He put the ring on his finger and then dropped the scroll to the ground.

CHAPTER FORTY-FIVE

With a jerk of his unsteady hand, the Professor put the quill pen back inside the ink well. He looked down at what he wrote and a self-satisfying smile crossed his lips. He recorded the events of the Black Rose for all time in his journal and would need to file it before his task here was finished.

He closed the book with a thud and watched as the dust flew up. It was so seldom that he got to record anything of merit anymore. It was the last little thing he liked to do at the end of an incident.

Turning to his bookshelf, he placed the book back on the shelf in the empty spot. It had all gone well, really. Stapleton was gone, and now Annicka was in charge. Just like he envisioned so long ago.

He turned back to his podium and reached up to straighten his broken glasses. He would have to remember to be a little more subtle next time. Almost fell in on him. They almost turned the tables against him. That would not have been good. He never wanted that to happen.

With a little chuckle, he knew there would most certainly be a next time.

All in all, it was just too much fun.

And he was The Architect of the whole thing.

Note from the Author

Word-of-mouth is crucial for any author to succeed. If you enjoyed *Hell's Doctor*, please leave a review online—anywhere you are able. Even if it's just a sentence or two. It would make all the difference and would be very much appreciated.

Thanks!
Lee F. Jordan